PARADISE

Also by Simone Elkeles

Perfect Chemistry
The Rules of Attraction
Chain Reaction

PARADISE

SIMONE ELKELES

SIMON AND SCHUSTER

First published in Great Britain in 2013 by Simon & Schuster UK Ltd
A CBS COMPANY

These titles were originally published individually
as ebook originals in Great Britain

First published in the USA by Flux, an imprint of
Llewellyn Publications, 2007 and 2010

1 3 5 7 9 10 8 6 4 2

Simon & Schuster UK Ltd
1st Floor
222 Gray's Inn Road
London
WC1X 8HB

Simon & Schuster Australia, Sydney
Simon & Schuster India, New Delhi

A CIP catalogue copy for this book is available from the British Library.

ISBN: 978-1-4711-1903-3

Printed and bound by CPI Group (UK) Ltd, Croydon, CR0 4YY

www.simonandschuster.co.uk
www.simonandschuster.com.au

LEAVING PARADISE

For Brett
who brightens my day just by looking at him

ONE
Caleb

I've been waiting a year for this moment. It's not every day you get a chance to get out of jail. Sure, in the game of Monopoly you just have to roll the dice three times and wait for a double, or pay the fine and be free. But there are no games here at the Illinois Department of Corrections– Juvenile complex; or the DOC as we inmates call it.

Oh, it's not as rough as it sounds. The all male juvenile division is tough, but it's not like the adult DOC. You might ask why I've been locked up for the past year. I was convicted of hitting a girl with my car while driving drunk. It was a hit-and-run accident, too, which actually made the judge in my case royally pissed off. He tacked on an extra three months for that.

"You ready, Caleb?" Jerry, the cell guard, asks.

"Yes, sir." I've been waiting three hundred and ten days for this. Hell, yeah, I'm ready.

I take a deep breath and follow Jerry to the room where the review committee will evaluate me. I've been prepped by the other guys in my cell block. *Sit up straight, look full of remorse, act polite,* and all that stuff. But, to tell you the truth, how much can you trust guys who haven't gotten out themselves?

As Jerry opens the door to the evaluation room, my muscles start to twitch and I'm getting all sweaty beneath my state-issued coveralls, state-issued socks, and yep, even my state-issued briefs. Maybe I'm not so ready for this after all.

"Please sit down, Caleb," orders a woman wearing glasses and a stern look on her face.

I swear the scene is out of a bad movie. Seven people sitting behind six-foot-long tables in front of one lone metal chair.

I sit on the cold, hard metal.

"As you know, we're here to evaluate your ability to leave here and begin your life as a free citizen."

"Yes, ma'am," I say. "I'm ready to leave."

A big guy, who I can tell is going to play "bad cop," puts his hand up. "Whoa, slow down. We have a few questions to ask before we make our decision."

Oh, man. "Sorry."

Big Guy checks my file, flipping page after page. "Tell me about the night of the accident."

The one night in my life I want to erase from history. Taking a deep breath, I say, "I was drinking at a party. I drove home, but lost control of the car. When I realized I hit someone, I freaked and drove back to the party."

"You knew the girl you hit?"

Memories assault me. "Yes, sir. Maggie Armstrong . . . my neighbor." I don't add she was my twin sister's best friend.

"And you didn't get out of the car to see if your neighbor was hurt?"

I shift in my chair. "I guess I wasn't thinking straight."

"You *guess?*" another committee member asks.

"If I could turn back time, I swear I would. I'd change everything."

They question me for another half hour and I spurt out answers. Why I was drinking while underage, why I'd get into a car drunk, why I left the scene of the accident. I don't know if I'm saying the wrong thing or right thing, which puts me on edge. I'm just being me . . . seventeen-year-old Caleb Becker. If they believe me, I stand a chance of getting released early. If they don't . . . well, I'll be eating crappy food for another six months and continue rooming with convicts.

Big Guy looks right at me. "How do we know you won't go on another drinking binge?"

I sit up straight in my chair and direct my attention to each and every one of the committee members. "No offense, but I never want to come back here again. I made a huge mistake, one that's haunted me day and night since I've been here. Just . . . let me go home." For the first time in my life, I'm tempted to grovel.

Instead, I sit back and wait for another question.

"Caleb, please wait outside while we make our decision," the woman with the glasses says.

And it's over. Just like that.

I wait out in the hall. I'm usually not a guy who breaks under pressure, and the past year in jail has definitely given me an invisible piece of armor I wear around me. But waiting for a group of strangers to decide your fate is majorly nerve-wracking. I wipe beads of perspiration off my forehead.

"Don't worry," guard Jerry says. "If you didn't win them over, you might get another chance in a few months."

"Great," I mumble back, not consoled in the least.

Jerry chuckles, the shiny silver handcuffs hanging off his belt clinking with each movement. The dude likes his job too much.

We wait a half hour for someone to come out of the room and give me a sign of what's next. Freedom or more jail time?

I'm tired of being locked in my cell at night.

I'm tired of sleeping on a bunk bed with springs pushing into my back.

And I'm tired of being watched twenty-four hours a day by guards, personnel, cameras, and other inmates.

The lady with the glasses opens the door. "Caleb, we're ready for you."

She isn't smiling. Is that a bad sign? I'm bracing myself

for bad news. I stand up and Jerry pats me on the back. A pity pat? Does he know something I don't? The suspense is freaking me out.

I sit back on the metal chair. All eyes are on me. Big Guy folds his hands on the table and says, "We all agree that your actions last year concerning the accident were reprehensible."

I know that. I *really* know that.

"But we believe that was an isolated incident never to be repeated. You've demonstrated positive leadership qualities with other inmates and worked hard on your jobs here. The review committee has decided to release you and have you finish out your sentence with one hundred and fifty hours of community service."

Does that mean what I think it means? "Release? As in I can leave here?" I ask the Big Guy.

"You'll be meeting with your transition coach tomorrow morning. He'll arrange your community service duties and report your progress to us."

Another member of the committee points a manicured finger at me. "If you screw up, your transition counselor can petition the judge to bring you back here to serve out the rest of your sentence. Do you understand?"

"Yes, sir."

"We don't give breaks to repeaters. Go back home, be a model citizen, finish your community service requirements, and have a good, clean life."

I *get it*. "I will," I say.

When I get back to my cell, the only one here is the new kid. He's twelve and still cries all the time. Maybe he should've thought twice before he buried a knife into the back of the girl who refused to go to the school dance with him.

"You ever gonna stop crying?" I ask the kid.

He's got his face in his pillow; I don't think he hears me. But then I hear a muffled, "I hate this place. I want to go home."

I change into my work boots because I get the pleasure of having to clean the dumpsters today. "Yeah, me too," I say. "But you're stuck here so you might as well suck it up and get with the program."

The kid sits up, sniffles, and wipes his nose with the back of his hand. "How long have you been here?"

"Almost a year."

That sets the kid plunging back into his pillow for more wailing. "I don't want to be locked up for a year," he cries.

Julio, another cell mate, walks into the room. "Seriously, Caleb, if that kid doesn't shut up, I'm gonna kill him. I haven't slept for three nights because of that crybaby."

The wails stop, but then the sniffles start. Which are actually worse than the wailing.

"Julio, give the kid a break," I say.

"You're too soft, Caleb. Gotta toughen these kids up."

"So they can be like you? No offense, man, but you'd scare a serial killer," I say.

One look at Julio and you know he's a tough guy. Tattoos all over his neck, back, and arms. Shaved head. When my mom comes for visits, she acts like his tattoos are contagious.

"So?" Julio says. "They gonna let you outta here?"

I sit on my bed. "Yeah. Tomorrow."

"Lucky sonofabitch. You goin' back to that small town with a funny name? Wha's it called again?"

"Paradise."

"So I'll be stuck here alone with crybaby while you're in Paradise? Ain't that a bitch." He gives the kid a wide-eyed stare. If I didn't know Julio better, I'd be afraid, too.

This sets the kid off again.

Julio chuckles, then says "Well, I'll give you the number to my cousin Rio in Chicago. If you need to hightail it out of Paradise, Rio will hook you up."

"Thanks, man," I say.

Julio shakes his head at the crying kid, says "Later, *amigo*," and leaves the open cell.

I tap the kid on his shoulder. He jerks away, scared.

"I'm not gonna hurt you," I tell him.

He turns to me. "That's what they all say. I heard about what goes on in jails." He scoots his butt towards the wall.

"Don't flatter yourself, kid. You're not my type. I like chicks."

"What about the guy with the tattoos?"

I fight the urge to laugh. "He's hetero, too. Dude, you're in a juvenile facility."

"He said he'll *kill* me."

"He says that because he likes you," I assure him. Julio has a sick sense of humor. "Now get off the bed, stop the crying, and go to group."

Group is group therapy. Where all the inmates sit around and discuss personal shit about their lives.

Tomorrow I'm getting the hell out of this place. No more group. No more cellmates. No more crappy food. No more cleaning dumpsters.

Tomorrow I'm going home.

TWO

Maggie

I think physical therapists like their job a little too much. I mean, why do they always look so happy and smiley as they make you sweat and wince from pain?

Sure enough, Robert, my physical therapist, is waiting for me with a big white-toothed smile in the lobby of the outpatient area of the hospital.

"Hi, Maggie. You ready to work that leg of yours?"

Not really. "I guess so," I say, looking down at the floor.

I know it's Robert's job to try and make me walk better. But there's no use in helping me walk normal because my leg is all messed up inside. The last surgery I had to fix my tibial plateau fracture lasted over seven hours. My orthopedic surgeon jokes with me and calls it a bionic leg.

All I know is that I have more nails and plastic inside me than the average tool box.

When I go to Spain next semester the screeners at the airport are going to have a field day with me. They'll probably ask me to climb inside the x-ray machine to make sure I'm not concealing a weapon inside my knee.

Robert escorts me into the physical therapy room. I have to come here twice a week. Twice a week for almost a year and still people stare at me when I walk.

"Maggie, lie down and put your foot on my shoulder," Robert instructs, getting down to business-as-usual.

Sighing, I lay down on the mat and put my foot on Robert's shoulder. He holds my foot in place and leans forward. "Put pressure on it."

After the accident, all I can do is a little baby push.

"Come on, Maggie. You can do better than that. I hardly feel it."

I put my forearm over my eyes. "It's never going to get better than this."

"Sure it will. Look, you never believed you'd be able to walk again and here you are."

I put more pressure on my foot.

"Thatta girl. Rate your pain level right now from one to ten, ten being excruciating."

"Eight."

"An eight?"

It might even be a nine.

"If you work hard now, the payoff will show later," he says.

I don't answer, but keep the increased pressure on my foot. He leans back and lowers my foot. Phew, that's over.

"Great. Now keep your legs straight and alternate bending them one at a time."

I start with my right leg. The accident didn't mess it up too much and the scars have healed. For the most part.

But when I have to bend my left leg, it feels like a weight is attached to it. I bend it an inch at a time. Just lifting my leg makes me sweat like a long-distance runner. The word *pathetic* pretty much sums up my seventeen-year-old life.

"A little more," Robert says just as I'm about to lower it. "What's your pain level from one to ten?"

Before I can answer a nine, his cell phone rings. And rings. And rings. "Aren't you going to answer it?" I ask.

"Not while I have a client. Keep bending those legs, Maggie."

"Maybe it's important," I say with hope in my voice.

"If it is, they'll leave a message. Dr. Gerrard tells me you'll be leaving us in January," he says as I alternate legs.

"Yep," I say between clenched teeth. "I got a scholarship to go to Spain for a semester. I had to petition for an extension because of the infection."

Robert whistles appreciatively. "Spain, huh? You're a lucky lady."

Lucky? I am *not* lucky. Lucky people don't get hit

by cars and have to go through painful physical therapy. Lucky people don't have divorced parents and a dad they see once a year. Lucky people have friends. Now that I think about it, I'm probably the unluckiest person in the entire universe.

I endure leg torture for another twenty minutes. I'm so ready to leave, but I know it's not over. The last thing Robert does in physical therapy is massage my leg muscles. I pull down my workout pants and sit on the metal table in my shorts.

"Is the redness fading?" Robert asks as he rubs medicated cream on my leg with gloved hands.

"I don't know," I say. "I don't like to look at it." In fact, I'd look anywhere except my scarred left leg. It's ugly, as if a two-year-old drew red lines with a crayon up and down my calf and thigh. But the marks aren't from a crayon. They're from my various surgeries after Caleb Becker hit me while driving drunk.

I try to forget about Caleb, but I can't. He's embedded into my brain like cancer. My nightmares of the accident have stopped, though, thank God. Those lasted for over six months. I hate Caleb. I hate what he did to me and I'm glad he's far away. I try not to think about where he's gone. If I think about it too hard, I'll probably feel guilty. So I don't think about it and trudge through my life ignoring the parts that'll pull me under so far I won't be able to get up.

As Robert studiously massages my leg muscles, I wince.

"It shouldn't hurt when I do this," he says.

"It doesn't." It's just . . . I don't like people touching my scars. I can't even stomach touching them.

Robert examines my leg. "The deep redness will fade eventually. Give it a few more months."

Robert finally announces he's finished. As I put my workout pants back on, he writes something down in my file. His pen moves faster than I can talk.

"What are you writing?" I ask warily.

"Just evaluating your progress. I'm requesting Dr. Gerrard come visit during your therapy next week."

Don't panic, Maggie, I tell myself. "Why?"

"I'd like to switch up your program."

"I don't like the sound of that."

Robert pats me on the back. "Don't worry, Maggie. We just need to come up with a physical therapy plan you can do in Spain without me."

Physical therapy in Spain? Not exactly what I imagined myself doing while overseas. I don't tell this to Robert. Instead, I give him a weak smile.

After my appointment, I head to Auntie Mae's Diner where my mom works. I know it's not glamorous, but she had to get a job when my dad left two years ago. Her boss, Mr. Reynolds, is pretty nice and gave her time off a lot when I was in the hospital. We're not rich, but we have a roof over our heads and Auntie Mae's Diner food in our stomachs.

I sit down at a table and my mom goes in the kitchen

to get dinner for me. I'm about to read a book when I look up and see Danielle, Brianne, and my cousin Sabrina enter the restaurant. God, they look so . . . perfect.

I used to be friends with Danielle and Brianne. Leah Becker and I used to hang out with them all the time. The four of us were on the high school tennis team and inseparable since our first tennis lesson at the Paradise Community Center when we were nine years old. Sabrina was the outsider, the non-athlete. I remember Mom making me ask Sabrina to tag along with my friends when we went out.

The accident turned Paradise upside down. When Caleb hit me, he not only destroyed my leg, he also destroyed my friendship with his twin sister, Leah, and Mom's friendship with Mrs. Becker. There's an invisible fence now between our house and the Beckers' house where there once was an open-door policy.

At first I didn't have time to miss Leah; in the hospital my phone rang constantly. My mom kept busy answering calls and urging me to cut my conversations short so I could concentrate on healing. But as the months passed, the calls dwindled, then finally stopped altogether. Everyone else got on with their life while I recovered at home.

Sabrina used to come over and give me updates on school gossip. Now my cousin is close friends with Brianne and Danielle, which is totally strange because before the accident they didn't give her the time of day.

I've never asked Sabrina about Leah . . . and Sabrina never offers any information. Leah's brother went to jail because of me. I was sure she hated me because of it. We'd literally gone from best friends to strangers overnight.

Every time I think of going back to school on Monday, my stomach starts to do flips. I've been home-schooled by public tutors assigned by the school district almost my entire junior year because of the infection in my leg after my first surgery. Now I'm a senior. I don't know which will be worse; getting out of the house or going to school and facing all the kids there. What if I run into Leah? What should I say?

My cousin and old friends are standing at the hostess stand, waiting to be seated. Okay, so it's times like these I wish Mom didn't work as a waitress. Knowing she wears a pink polyester uniform with buttons that read *ASK ME ABOUT MY DOUBLE DECKERS* doesn't usually bother me. But that, on top of having her serve my former friends, makes me want to hide under the table.

Mom walks out from the back kitchen with my dinner. I watch in agony as she spots Danielle, Brianne, and Sabrina. Her eyes light up. "Hi, girls!" She waves at me to get my attention. "Look Maggie, it's your friends and cousin!"

Brianne and the others give my mom fake smiles. Mom is oblivious.

I give a little half wave and look down at a tiny chip in the corner of the table, hoping my mom will get the hint.

"Why don't you sit with Maggie? She's all alone," I hear Mom say.

Why doesn't she just tell them I'm a loser now, too? Maybe I should get a big "L" for "loser" button and pin it to the front of my shirt.

The girls, including my cousin, just look at each other and shrug. "Sure."

Why pretend to be friends and be all fakey? It's not worth it.

"Hi," I say when Mom leads them to my table and places my favorite dinner in front of me: a French dip, split pea soup, and a side of fries with gravy.

"Mrs. Armstrong, what's your double deckers?" Brianne asks.

The rest of the girls snicker while I sink deeper into my chair.

Mom doesn't flinch and goes right into her spiel. "We have a new selection of double decker sandwiches with turkey and bacon layered with lettuce, tomato, mayonnaise, and our special sauce. We also have new roast beef and cheese double deckers. They all come with two layers of bread in between."

Danielle looks like she's going to be sick. "My arteries are clogging up just hearing about all that cholesterol."

"Forget the cholesterol," Sabrina says. "Two layers of bread? Carb city."

Since when did my cousin become concerned about carbs? I look down at my plate. Carbs and more carbs, cholesterol and more cholesterol.

"I'll have a Diet Coke and a side salad, Mrs. Armstrong," Brianne says.

"Me, too," Sabrina says.

"And me," Danielle chimes in.

"We have thousand island, blue cheese, ranch, low-fat Italian . . ."

"Thousand island for me," Sabrina says. "On the side."

Danielle furrows her waxed brows, thinking it over. "I guess I'll take the low-fat Italian. On the side."

Brianne cocks her head to the side and says, "No dressing."

No dressing? What happened to pigging out on chips and pizza? I've only been away a year and I'm totally lost.

Mom leaves to enter the orders, and I'm left with my salad-eating cousin, ex-friends . . . and my French dip, pea soup, fries and gravy. I was seriously hungry before, but now I can't eat.

Brianne fumbles through her purse and pulls out a small mirror.

"Give me that when you're done," Sabrina says. When my cousin has the mirror, she attempts to check out the back of her head. Which she really can't do with one mirror, but I'm not going to break that news to her.

"What are you doing, Sabrina?" Danielle asks.

"I think I need to get my hair cut before tomorrow."

Danielle laughs. "Girls, stop freaking out. It's a party, not a presidential ball."

"What party?" I ask, then want to die for asking.

Obviously I wasn't invited. I don't want to go, anyway. But now it *looks* like I want to go.

The girls eye each other. They don't want to tell me about the party. Ugh, why did I even ask?

"A back-to-school party," Danielle finally says. "At Brian Newcomb's house."

Wouldn't you know, Mom comes with their Diet Cokes and an extra large piece of pie for me at that exact same moment. "Oh, a party! When? Maggie would LOVE to go to a party, wouldn't you honey?"

Instead of answering, I bite off a huge chunk of the French dip. It saves me from having to answer, but now I feel like I'm going to gag on the gargantuan piece of beef in my mouth.

Brianne looks like she's gonna puke just watching me.

"Uh, you can come if you *want*, Maggie," my cousin says.

It was definitely a pity invite, anyone but a waitress at Auntie Mae's Diner would realize that. I'm not going to the party. I just don't know how I'm going to break it to Mom and let my ex-friends off the hook at the same time.

I take my time chewing.

Before the accident I was a sophomore on the varsity tennis team. But now as a senior I wouldn't even make the freshman squad. Not that I would want to, because then I'd have to wear those short tennis skirts. I'm never wearing a tennis skirt again because I'm never showing anyone my ugly leg scars. Besides, you can't play tennis when you can't even walk straight.

As I swallow the last of the wad of beef, I realize they're all waiting for an answer.

Umm . . .

The hopeful look on my mom's face makes me realize she feels sorry for me. As if I care that I'm not friends with them anymore. Mom cares. She's got to deal with paying for half of the medical bills that the insurance didn't cover. My parents are divorced and I hate feeling like I'm adding to her stress. Guilt, like a big wad of roast beef, settles in my French dip-filled gut.

I want to wince when I hear myself say, "Sure, sounds like fun."

Mom lets out a breath while the girls suck in theirs.

"Can you pick her up?" Mom asks my cousin.

"Sure, Aunt Linda," Sabrina says.

Seriously, I feel like a little kid having my mommy make a playdate for me. Especially when I hear my mom ask, "What time?"

"I guess around eight."

"Grrreat!" Mom says like that tiger in the cereal commercial.

How am I going to get out of this without my mom finding out? There's no way I'm going to a party and have people stare and gawk at me. It's bad enough I'll have to deal with the ridicule in school on Monday.

After Mom brings their side salads and leaves us alone

for two minutes, Brianne flashes me a sly smile. "Do you know the big news?"

News? Um, I haven't exactly been in the gossip loop lately. "That Mr. Meyer wears a toupee?" I heard that about our school principal a while ago.

Brianne laughs. "No, that's totally old news. I'm talking about Caleb Becker being released tomorrow."

What?

Danielle dips her fork in her dressing and stabs a piece of lettuce. "Mrs. Becker called my mom today and told her. Early release. I wonder if they'll let him back in school."

Early release? He was supposed to be away for at least six more months. I had the perfect plan—to leave for Spain before he got back. A deep, sharp pain in my chest jabs me when I take a breath, and my fingers are shaking. I'm having a mini-panic attack, but trying not to let everyone else know.

"Maggie, are you okay?" Sabrina asks as I push the pie away from me.

No. I'm definitely not okay.

THREE
Caleb

As if having my dad stare at me throughout the entire drive from St. Charles to Paradise wasn't torture enough, my mom has been wringing her hands together since I was discharged from the DOC this afternoon. I don't even think she's looked in my direction once.

What the hell am I supposed to say? *Stop being nervous, Ma.* Yeah, I'm sure that'll go over well. Her son is a convicted felon. I just wish she would stop constantly reminding me of it.

Okay, so it'll take some time. She never excelled at being the doting mother to begin with.

When we turn down Masey Avenue, Paradise Park is in front of us. I got my front two teeth knocked out at the

Paradise Park playground when I was five and had my first fist fight on the basketball court there when I was nine. Those were the good old days. I can't believe I'm seventeen and thinking about the good old days.

A block later we reach the familiar two-story brick house with four white pillars flanking the front door. I step out of the car and take a deep breath.

I'm home.

"Well . . ." Dad says as he opens the door. "Welcome to Paradise."

I nod instead of laughing at the most common greeting to visitors in this town. I lurk in the foyer. The decorating hasn't changed in the past year—I can see that right off the bat.

Strangely enough, it doesn't feel like home.

It smells familiar, though. Like apple spice. I haven't smelled this sweet, tangy scent in what seems like forever.

"I'll, uh, be in my room," I tell them, although I say it like I'm asking permission. Why, I have no clue. It used to be my room, it still is my room. So why am I acting like this place is just a pit stop?

I step up the familiar staircase, but this feeling of claustrophobia overcomes me and I start to sweat. I venture farther up the stairs and scan the hallway. My eyes rest on a black vision leaning against the door frame of my sister's room.

Wait.

That black vision is my twin sister, Leah. She's not just

a silhouette of my sister, that's her in the flesh. And she's wearing nothing but black.

Black hair, black makeup. Damn, she even has black painted nails. Goth to the core. A shiver runs up my spine. It's hard to believe this is my sister. She resembles a corpse.

Before I let out another breath, Leah throws herself into my arms. Then these huge sobbing noises come out of her mouth and nose, reminding me of my cellmate.

Even when Judge Farkus eyed me with disgust and told me I was going to be locked up for almost a year for my gross negligence and stupidity for driving drunk, I didn't let out a peep. Man, when they made me strip and did a full cavity search, I was humiliated beyond comprehension. And when Dino Alvarez, a gang member from the south side of Chicago, came up to me during exercise hour and cornered me my second day in the DOC I almost shit my pants. But I never once in all that time cried.

I pat my sister's head, not knowing what else to do. I've hardly had any physical contact in the past year, and craved it when I sat in my cell for over three hundred days and nights. But now, when I'm getting some from my own sister, it feels like the walls are closing in on me.

"I need to lie down for a while," I say, then gently push her away. What I really need is a break from this old/new barrage of family in my life.

As I walk into my room, the dark wood floor beneath my feet creaks, the sound reverberating in my ears.

It's a kid's room, I think to myself. Sports trophies and my Star Wars Anakin Skywalker lightsaber are still on my bookshelf where I left them, and a Paradise High School pennant is nailed above my bed. Hell, even the picture of Kendra in her cheerleading uniform is taped to my headboard as if we're still a couple.

I cut all ties with her when I got arrested. Kendra is a girl used to being pampered by her parents and would be grossed out by the people I've been living with for the past year. I could just imagine her snubbing Dino Alvarez's girlfriend during weekly visiting hours. The last thing I needed in the DOC was other inmates kicking my ass because I have a girlfriend who wears designer clothes and carries a two-hundred-dollar purse.

Visiting day for me consisted of Mom wringing her hands nervously and staring at me like I was someone else's kid, and Dad rambling on about weather and nothing in particular just to fill in the silence.

Walking to my bedroom closet, I finger all the new clothes Mom must have bought for me. What was she thinking? My t-shirts and jerseys are gone. In their place are geeky, button-down plaid shirts hanging like soldiers. On the shelves, all folded up like in a Gap store, are different shades of pleated pants.

I pick up a pair and hold them in front of me. They're way too small. When should I break the news to her I'm not the skinny kid who used to live here? I worked out every day for the past year to blow off steam and fend off guys like Alvarez. Muscles don't just weigh more, they change the entire structure of your body.

Sitting at my desk, I look out the window and glance at the Armstrongs' house. My window faces Maggie's bedroom.

Maggie Armstrong.

The girl I was convicted of maiming.

Okay, I know it's unfair. But it's hard not to want to blame her. If it wasn't for her I wouldn't have been locked up. I've thought about Maggie and the events leading up to the accident more times in the past year than I want to admit.

"Caleb, you there?" Dad asks, then knocks.

Gotta love it when people knock. I haven't heard a knock in a year. I open the door and gesture for him to come inside.

My dad walks in and I close the door behind him. He's still got a full head of dark hair and a tailored mustache. He's okay as a dad, but a total wimp when it comes to standing up to my mom.

"Your mom's invited a few of her friends over after dinner." He hesitates, then adds, "For, um, a homecoming party."

A knot on the back of my neck starts to form. I rub it. A homecoming party for a guy who just got out of the slammer? Unbelievable. "Cancel it," I say.

The veins in his neck tense up and start turning a strange shade of purple. "Listen, it's what your mother wants. She's been through a lot this year with you in jail.

Just . . . do what she wants and put on a show for her friends. It'll be easier for everyone if you play along."

"A show?"

"Yeah, plaster a smile on your face and humor the women in her social club. I do it all the time," he says, then leaves the room as quickly as he entered.

It takes a second to register what he just said. Smile? Show? I feel like I've been transported to some Hollywood movie set. But it's not a movie, it's my life.

Taking the lightsaber in my hand, I turn it on. Laser sounds fill the room when I wave the saber like a great Jedi warrior. God, how I used to spend hours dueling imaginary demons with this thing when I was a kid.

Now I've got new demons to fight.

Ones I can't make disappear with a wave of a toy.

FOUR
Maggie

"Maggie, look at what I bought for you." My mom stands at my bedroom door in the evening, holding up a pair of pink velour pants and a zippered jacket. "The saleswoman said all the teenagers are wearing these. They're very, very hip."

"Nobody says *hip* anymore."

"Cool?"

I take the outfit from her. It's a Juicy Couture set, totally soft and nothing like my Wal-Mart clothes. "Mom, this must have cost over a hundred dollars. It's very *cool*, but we can't afford it."

"Don't worry about the money," she says, waving my concern away. "I put in some overtime at the diner and have a little extra this month. Besides, school starts Monday and I wanted you to have something hip, cool, whatever. Try it on." Mom does a little excited dance as she waits.

I wanted her to leave for work so I could call Sabrina and tell her I'm not going to the party. "Mom, it's seven thirty. Don't you think Mr. Reynolds will be upset if you're a half hour late?"

She smiles, her excitement hasn't waned. "Sweetie, I'm waiting for Sabrina to pick you up."

My stomach sinks to my knees. "Why?"

"Because it'll make me *so* happy to finally see you go out and have fun."

I feel the pressure building up and entering my lungs.

I dress in the velour outfit, and as soon as my mom sees me she's beaming. "Oh, sweetheart, you look *gorgeous*. Pink goes so well with your olive complexion."

I have to admit, the outfit is gorgeous. But I'm not. Although the pants hide my hideous scars, no amount of money can make an outfit hide the awkward tilt in my stride. After Mom watches me brush my stringy, dull brown hair and lends me makeup to wear, I find myself standing at the door waiting for Sabrina.

"Now, if you have any problems, I wrote down some emergency numbers for you." She hands me her cell and a piece of paper. "The first one is the number to the diner, the second is Aunt Pam's, the third is Dr. Gerrard's emergency line, and the fourth is 911."

Images of Spain race across my mind. She treats me

like my head is as messed up as my knee. "Come on, Mom, 911? It's been ingrained in my head since preschool."

"People forget numbers all the time when they're under stress, Maggie."

I open my Wal-Mart purse and shove the paper inside. "I'll be fine," I assure her, although I'm not so sure myself.

"I know. I just want you to be happy. And safe. But if your leg hurts or you want to come home early, I'll leave work and come get you."

Suddenly it hits me. Why she's giving me the attention she'd give to a newborn baby. "You know Caleb is coming back today, don't you?"

Her deer-in-headlights look doesn't go unnoticed. "Someone *might* have mentioned it at the diner yesterday."

I moan and groan, "Moommm."

"Sweetie, don't think about it. Just look the other way and pretend the Beckers don't exist."

I guess now wouldn't be the best time to talk about how much I miss my ex-best friend who also happens to be "one of those Beckers." A car horn beeps outside. It's Sabrina.

"Go," Mom says. "And call when you get there so I know you're safe, even if you think I'm being overprotective or *uncool*."

I walk out the door, trying to count the days in my head until I leave for Spain. I think it's a hundred and eighteen days, obviously not soon enough. When I get in the front seat of my cousin's car, she says, "Nice outfit."

Sabrina knows well enough that we struggle financially

and my clothes are an extravagant expense we can't afford. Two years ago my dad left on a business trip to Texas. It was supposed to be for four weeks, he was trying to convince a group of investors to move their digital-chip manufacturing facility to Paradise. They rejected his proposal, but they offered him a job traveling around the country as their consultant.

In two years my dad has been back to Paradise three times. Once to ask my mom for a divorce, once to announce he's getting remarried, and the last time was after the accident. He came for one week, then left. He says he's happy, that he wants me to come visit his new home, but he never makes any commitments or sets up any dates. I wasn't even at his second wedding.

"Thanks." I run my fingers over the soft pants one more time.

And that's our entire conversation until Sabrina parks on the street and we walk toward Brian Newcomb's house.

"What's wrong?" Sabrina asks. "You're limping worse than usual. I thought your leg was better."

"It was . . . it is." But a spasm reared its ugly head today.

I hear rock music blaring out of the windows of Brian's house and take a deep breath. There's going to be dancing. Dancing involves moving around and bumping into people. What if I fall? Worse, what if I can't get up and people start laughing?

At the front of the house, I'm ready to hightail it back home and hide out in my bedroom until I leave for Spain. But Sabrina eagerly opens the door before I can retreat.

As we enter the foyer, I'm hypersensitive and aware all eyes are focused on me. A chill runs down my spine. Could it be I have a zit the size of an avocado pit growing on my nose? Is my limp *that* bad? Or is it gossip they crave? Either way, I don't like the attention. I'd just about do anything to remain lost in the background forever.

"Hey, guys, it's Maggie Armstrong back from the dead!" yells a guy on the football team.

"I heard Caleb Becker is back, too," a guy named Ty calls out.

"That's what I hear," I say glibly, not feeling at all glib. I can't hide. Do they know I want to? "It's no biggie." I'm surprised that I'm able to get the words out; my throat is threatening to close up.

"But he almost *killed* you," someone else says. I don't even know who said it; the crowd has become one big blur. I don't even think I could take a deep breath now if I wanted to.

"It was a year ago. I'm over it." Gulp. Being brave is not as easy as it looks. Especially when your heart is racing faster than the beat of the music, which has now faded into the background. Lucky music.

"How can you be? Weren't you in a wheelchair for, like, four months?"

One hundred and twenty-three days to be exact, but who's counting? "I guess."

"People, give her room to breathe." I turn to the voice. It's Kendra. Caleb's old girlfriend. We used to hang in the same circles, but we were never close. She reminds me of a fake, plastic doll. To my surprise she grabs my arm and pulls me out on the back patio. With my limp it's hard to keep up with her without tripping over my own feet, but she doesn't seem to notice. Or care.

"Have you seen him?" she asks in a whisper.

For a second I'm confused. Kendra is popular, someone nobody can ignore. But I'm not really here, am I? Sure, my body is. But my serenity is back at home, in my room where I can hide from the past and reminders of the accident.

Kendra shakes me, and I'm back at the party.

"Did you see him?" she asks. The way she looks at me you'd think her eyes were darts.

"Who?"

She's annoyed, her curly blonde hair bouncing with each movement of her head, emphasizing her mood like exclamation points. "Caleb."

"No."

"But he lives right next door to you," she says almost desperately, those darts narrowing into little slits.

"So?" Okay, so I never did particularly click with Kendra. She knows it, I know it. Not many others know it; we'd been very good at pretending we were on the same page. It feels like a standoff, her challenging me for information she wants and thinks I have. But I don't have it, so I don't even have the satisfaction of holding back information from her.

Brian peeks his head out the screen door. "Kendra, what're you doing out here? Come in and save me from having to play spin-the-bottle."

Kendra looks from me to Brian, then back. "I'm coming," she says, tossing her hair once again with a flick of her head, before entering the house. I'm left alone. Outside.

I'm fine with alone. I'm used to alone. Alone is comfortable for me, it's quiet and doesn't demand I be happy or satisfied or . . . asked any questions. I try not to think about what it was like when I wasn't alone, when I was an integral part of the social scene. When Kendra and I weren't enemies or friends, but hung with the same people. And even if we weren't socially equal, then at least we were on the same social playing field.

Get-togethers wouldn't have been the same without me.

Now it's not the same with me.

I sit on a lounge chair by the pool. A few minutes later the party has multiplied and people start congregating and dancing on the patio. I am still alone, but within the crowd.

Brianne is hanging onto Drew Wentworth, Paradise High's varsity quarterback. His hands are all over her as they dance close to a slow song blaring from the second-story window.

Danielle and Sabrina are huddled in a corner, gossiping

and giggling. After a while some guys pull them onto the patio and start dancing with them. The scene reminds me of those California teen reality shows. I stick out like a sore thumb wearing a pink Juicy Couture outfit. I open my purse, glance at the emergency numbers my mom gave me just to make sure they're still there, then close my purse back up. Surely becoming an outcast when you were previously popular isn't considered an emergency, is it?

Kendra and Brian start putting on their own public dance show right on the diving board after changing into bathing suits. Everyone gathers around, chanting for the couple to jump in. Kendra loves the attention, she's used to it. Her family has owned the biggest parcel of land in Paradise for the past two hundred years. Her dad has been the mayor for the past ten years, and her grandfather was the mayor before that. Some girls are born to have it all.

Soon a bunch of other seniors come out of the house wearing bathing suits. Danielle walks over to me. "Did you bring a suit? Sabrina and I are going to change in Brian's room."

If I came out wearing a bathing suit showing all my scars, I'd probably clear the place out. "My doctor says I can't swim yet," I lie.

"Oh, sorry. I didn't know."

"No problem," I say, pulling out the cell.

While Danielle and Sabrina run up the stairs, I hobble out the door and dial the number to my mom's work.

"Auntie Mae's Diner. Can I help you?"

"Hey, Mom, it's me."

"Are you okay?" she asks.

"I'm fine. Having a blast," I say as I limp away from Brian's house and start walking down the street. I don't know where I'm going. Someplace private . . . quiet . . . where I don't have to think about what I'm missing. A place I can close my eyes and focus on my future.

A future without Paradise.

I can imagine the smile on my mom's face as she says, "See . . . and you were worried you wouldn't fit in. Don't you feel silly now?"

"Absolutely." The truth? I feel absolutely silly that I have to lie to my mom.

FIVE
Caleb

I'm keeping a permanent smile on my face at my mom's welcome-home party for me, just like my dad ordered. It's a fake smile, but my mom's friends seem to be buying it.

I think.

My mom has been all over me, laughing and hugging me in public as I play the reformed son. I wonder how long I can keep up this farce before I can't take it anymore. Forget me, how long can *she* keep it up? Dad doesn't even seem to notice her Jekyll and Hyde transformation. Why do appearances matter so much to my parents?

"Caleb has become religious while he's been away," Mom tells Mrs. Gutterman as she grabs my elbow and makes me face the reverend's wife. "Isn't that right, Caleb?" she says.

"I prayed every day," I say, not missing a beat, and knowing it's not only Mrs. Gutterman who's listening. The truth? I prayed every day that I'd survive the juvenile system, come back to Paradise, and make things right again. Mom's declaration that I've become religious is hollow, because we've never discussed what I did while I was in jail. She's never asked, and I've never told her.

Besides, she doesn't want to know the truth. If pretending will heal this family, I'm okay with it. I think it's bullshit, but I'm okay with it.

Mrs. Gutterman is whisked away by someone else, leaving my mom and me standing together.

She leans closer to me. "Button that shirt up more," she whispers.

I look down at my shirt. I only have two buttons unbuttoned. I'm not willing to argue with my mom today. It's not worth it. There's so many things I need to fix, fighting about a damn button would be laughable.

As I'm buttoning up my shirt, I glance at the Goth Girl leaning against the side of the house. I pour a glass of root beer and walk over to my sister. I've tried holding a smile for as long as I can, but my face is starting to hurt from the effort. "Here," I say, handing the drink to her, "your favorite."

She shakes her jet-black hair. "Not anymore."

So now I'm standing here with the drink nobody wants

in my hand. I take a sip. Yuck. "Tastes like licorice. I don't know why you ever liked the stuff in the first place."

"Now I drink water. Plain, old water."

This, coming from the girl who used to spike her lemonade with root beer and refused to eat chicken without smothering it with her own concoction of barbeque sauce, ketchup, mustard, and parmesan cheese. Plain water doesn't fit Leah, whether my little sister wants to admit it or not.

I stand beside her and take in the setting. Paradise isn't a large town, but the word "party" brings people out in droves. "Quite a crowd here tonight."

"Yep. Mom went all out," she says.

"Dad didn't try to stop her."

Leah shrugs, then says, "Why would he? She'd still do it her way in the end." A few minutes pass before I hear Leah's voice again. "Did they make you cut your hair like that?"

I run my hand over the prickly buzz cut. "No."

"It makes you look tough."

Should I tell her what her dyed black hair looks like? I briefly consider it, but quickly realize her blackness goes deeper than her hair. Broaching that subject at a party wouldn't be the best course of action.

Leah shuffles her feet. "Brian is having a party tonight at his house."

"Two parties in Paradise in one night? Boy, things sure have changed."

"More than you realize, Caleb. You gonna make an appearance at Brian's?"

"No way." It's shitty enough I have to be gawked at by a bunch of adults. "Why? You going?"

Leah raises her eyebrows and looks right at me. I get it. She's not going either.

"You should probably keep an eye on Mom," Leah says, biting on one of her black-painted nails.

"Why?"

"Because she just picked up a microphone."

As if on cue, a loud, buzzing sound comes from the porch, then our mom's voice bellows through the yard. "Thank you all for coming," she announces with a flair that would make the Queen of England proud. "And for welcoming my son Caleb back with open arms."

Open arms? My own mother won't lay a hand on me unless it's in a public forum. I can't stomach another word. More than I dread that upcoming meeting with my transition counselor, I dread getting up and speaking into that microphone.

Because what I'm itching to say won't be fake or phony.

I duck out the side gate. As I head down to Paradise Park, I untuck the geeky shirt from my too-tight trousers and unbutton each button until the entire shirt is open.

This is the first time I've felt any freedom since I've been home.

I can go where I want and unbutton my shirt as much as I want. I don't have anybody watching me or looking at me or talking to me or gawking at me. How I wish I could rewind the past year and start over. Life doesn't let you do that. You can't erase the past, but I'm going to try and make other people forget it.

I reach the park and gaze at the familiar, old oak tree I climbed when I was a kid. Drew and I once had a contest who could climb the highest. I won, right before the branch I was on snapped and I fell to the ground. I had a cast on my arm for six weeks after that fall, but I didn't care. I'd won.

I look up, trying to locate that broken branch. Is it still here, evidence of that day long ago? Or has the tree gone through enough seasons to erase the past?

An intake of breath takes me by surprise as I circle the tree. Right in front of me, sitting leaning against the trunk of the old oak, is Maggie Armstrong.

SIX

Maggie

I notice movement beside me and realize I'm not alone.

I snap my head up. There's a guy standing in front of me, one I recognize from my nightmares. He isn't a figment of my imagination, either. It's really him—Caleb Becker in the flesh, looking up as if searching for something important. A big gasping sound automatically escapes from my mouth.

He hears me and quickly focuses on me. He doesn't move, not even when his icy blue eyes connect with mine.

He's grown in the past year. He acted tough back then, but now Caleb has a menacing look about him. His hair is cut short, his shirt is unbuttoned, showing off his muscled chest. That, combined with the tight-fitting pants he's wearing, screams *danger*.

I can't breathe. I'm paralyzed. With anger. With anxiety. With fear.

We're at an impasse, neither of us speaking. Just staring. I don't even think I'm able to blink. I'm frozen in time.

I've been face to face with him many times, but now everything has changed. He doesn't even look like himself, except for his straight nose and confident stance that has been, and I suppose always will be, Caleb Becker.

"This is awkward," he says, breaking the long silence. His voice is deeper and darker than I remember.

This is not just seeing him out of my bedroom window.

We're alone.

And it's dark.

And it's oh, so different.

Needing to go back to the safety of my bedroom, I try to stand. A hot, shooting pain races down the side of my leg and I wince.

I watch in horror and shock as he steps forward and grabs my elbow.

Oh. My. God. I automatically jerk away from his grip. Memories of being stuck in a hospital bed unable to move crash through my mind as I straighten.

"Don't touch me," I say.

He holds his hands up as if I just said "Stick 'em up." "You don't have to be afraid of me, Maggie."

"Yes . . . yes I do," I say, panicking.

I hear him let out a breath, then he steps back. But he doesn't leave, he just stares at me strangely. "We used to be friends."

"That was a long time ago," I say. "Before you hit me."

"It was an accident. And I paid my debt to society for it."

It's a totally surreal moment, and one I don't want to last longer than it has to. While my insides shake from nervousness, I say, "You may have paid your debt to society, but what about your debt to me?"

After the words leave my lips, I can't believe I've said them. I turn away and limp back home without a backward glance. I don't stop until I open the front door of my house.

When I reach my room, I sit inside my closet and close the door like I used to do when I wanted to block out my parents' fights. All I had to do was close my eyes and put my hands over my ears . . . and hum.

I close my eyes. The image of Caleb, standing in front of me with those intense blue eyes of his, is branded in my brain. Even though he's nowhere near, I can still hear his dark voice. The night of the accident, the pain I've suffered, my whole life changing, it all races back to haunt me.

I start to hum.

SEVEN
Caleb

I'm being tested. Jail. Mom. Leah. Dad. And now Maggie. When I left Mom's ridiculous party, the last thing I needed was to come face to face with Maggie. She looked at me as if I'd run over her again, given half a chance. I only talked to her because . . . because maybe I wanted to prove to her that I'm not the evil monster she obviously thinks I am.

I'm still standing in the park like an idiot. Wind makes the leaves of the trees rustle as if they're talking to each other. I look up at the old oak. In a few months those talking leaves will fall to the ground and die, only to be replaced by new leaves and new gossip.

Right now I feel like an old leaf. I went away, and

deep inside a part of me has died. I vowed I'd come back to Paradise and get that life back, that old life where everything was easy.

I lean against the oak, its trunk so thick nothing but a bulldozer could destroy it. If I could be like the tree instead of an insignificant leaf. I would talk to my mom, to Maggie, to Leah . . . I'd be strong enough to convince them to stop acting like the accident had to change everything.

It was an accident, for heaven's sake.

The kid in jail who stabbed the girl . . . that was no accident. Julio dealing drugs for money . . . that was no accident. I'm not saying driving drunk isn't a crime—it is. And when I pled guilty to the charges, I was ready to take whatever punishment the judge ordered—without regrets.

I was accused of the crime, I did the time. It's over.

There's one glitch: Maggie Armstrong doesn't want to forgive me.

She said I haven't paid my debt to her.

Is there any end to this punishment I've put upon myself?

I won't let Maggie, or my family, make me unfocused. If being stuck in the DOC didn't screw me up, the people in Paradise can't. My sister is going to have to figure out why she thinks being a fuckin' weirdo outcast is better than going back to the way things were before I left. And my mom is going to, somehow, get real and stop acting like she's in a movie. My dad . . . my dad's gonna have to grow some balls one of these days. And Maggie . . .

Maggie's going to have to realize that the accident was just that . . . an accident.

No matter what happens, I'm not leaving Paradise. She might as well get used to me.

They all better get used to me.

EIGHT

Maggie

"How was the party?" Mom asks as she irons her uniform for work the next morning.

"Great."

"Is your leg okay?"

"It's fine." I haven't even thought about my leg this morning; it's the least of my worries. I'm obsessing about Spain. Last night, seeing Caleb reinforced my determination to leave this town. "Did we get the packet from the International Student Exchange Program yet?" The website said the packets would arrive a week ago.

Mom continues ironing. "I haven't seen it. I hope it includes information about wheelchair accessibility. If your leg starts giving you problems, you'll have to get one."

"Mom, please. Do we always have to discuss the *what ifs?*" I head to the refrigerator walking as straight as I can.

"It doesn't hurt to be prepared, Maggie. I won't be there to push you along or help you once you're there."

"I'll be fine, Mom. Stop worrying."

It's sad. One minute Mom is pushing me to go out and do things with my friends like before. In the next breath she's being overprotective, overconcerned and smothering. She contradicts herself all the time. I think it's because she's trying to act as a take-charge father and protective mother all at once. She's getting all confused in the process. She's confusing me, too.

She puts the iron down and gives me a big hug. "I want you to go to Spain. You've been looking forward to it for so long. But I also need to know you're taken care of. It's only because I love you so much, you know that."

"I know," I squeak out. I don't add that her love, like her hugs, can smother a person to death.

NINE
Caleb

I'm playing a one-man game of pool in the basement while my transition coach is yakking to my parents upstairs in the living room. If the situation weren't so invasive, I would find it frickin' hilarious.

My transition coach is Damon Manning, a guy who went through the juvenile justice system just as I did. He's assigned to check up on me and supervise my community service. Lucky me. I have a parole officer with a fancy title.

It's bullshit, but Damon's report will go directly to a judge assigned to my case and the review committee, so I have to play nice. It won't be easy. I've been on edge since I've been home.

I met Damon right before I left the DOC. The guy is a big black man who doesn't take shit from anyone.

My dad sticks his head into the basement as I accidentally sink the eight ball. "Caleb," he calls out. "Mr. Manning is ready for you."

I enter the living room and watch my mom.

"Can I get you anything?" she asks Damon nervously. She's not used to big, black ex-cons in her house, but she's still playing the consummate hostess.

"No, thanks. I'll just be having a little chat with your son, then be on my way."

I sit down in one of the silk-cushioned chairs, but Damon immediately stands.

"Let's go for a walk," Damon says. It's not a suggestion.

I shrug. "Sure. Whatever."

Damon holds onto a manila folder while we walk down Masey Avenue toward the park and end up sitting on a picnic bench.

"How's it goin'?" Damon asks. The guy opens his folder and clicks his pen. Click. Click.

"Fine," I lie.

"Be more specific." Damon makes it sound like an order. Everything the guy says sounds like an order. It just winds my nerves that much tighter.

"About what?"

Click. Click. "Tell me about your family. Seems like you've got a pretty nice home life."

Seems being the operative word. "Listen, my mom is a

robot, my dad's a wimp, and my sister is a fuckin' zombie. I'd say that pretty much sums it up."

I watch Damon close his folder then look straight at me. "Nobody said it would be easy."

"Yeah, well nobody said it was gonna be this fuckin' hard, either."

"Does it make you feel like a big guy to cuss in every sentence that comes out of your mouth?"

"Lay off, man."

"It's my job to stay on you, Caleb. But I can't help if you won't share with me."

I look up at the sky and shake my head. "I don't need your help. My parents and sister . . . they need help more than me. Why don't you treat them like the guinea pig?"

"You've been away for almost a year. Give 'em a break. You act as though they should be apologizing to you instead of the other way around. What did they do wrong, huh? Maybe you should blame yourself once in a while, Caleb. The experience might be eye opening."

"The *truth* would be eye opening," I say back.

Click. Click. "What?"

I shake my head. "Nothing. Just forget it."

Damon opens his folder again. That folder probably tells Damon everything about my life before, during, and after my arrest. I wonder if the time I tee-peed Joe Sanders' house is in there. Or the time I beat up a guy from Fremont High for teasing my sister about her perm gone wrong. I used to be looked up to, the cool rebel. Now I'm a convict. Not cool.

He hands me a few sheets of paper. "You live in a small town, Caleb. Not much in choices for community service jobs, but on your questionnaire you said you had experience in construction and small home improvements."

"I worked construction during summers for my uncle," I tell him.

"Okay, then. You'll be required to check in at The Trusty Nail hardware store on Monday after school at three forty-five sharp. Don't be late. They'll assign you a job site and drop off all supply materials needed. When you're done with a job, get a completion sheet signed. Easy enough?"

"Sure."

"I just have a few more questions. Then you don't have to see my ugly mug for another week." When Damon looks up at me he asks, "Any physical contact?"

"As in sex?"

Damon shrugs. "I don't know, you tell me. Was the old girlfriend waiting on your front stoop when you got home yesterday?"

The urge to laugh gets caught in my throat. "Hardly. My sister hugged me, my dad shook my hand, and I got a few pats on the back from my mom's random friends last night."

"Did you initiate it?"

"No. You're creeping me out, man."

"Caleb, some guys have attachment problems when

they get home. They have a hard time understanding what physical contact is appropriate and what—"

"I touched a girl," I say, interrupting.

Click. "Tell me about it."

I think back to last night, when Maggie tried to stand. The fierce pain she felt was emphasized by her clenched teeth, balled fists, and furrowed eyebrows. Since I've been home, Maggie has been the only person *I've* actually reached out to touch. It hadn't gone well.

"A girl needed help getting up, so I tried to steady her. End of story." Well, sort of.

"Did she thank you?"

I hesitate, then pick up a rock and chuck it all the way to the baseball field on the other side of the park. "She yanked herself out of my grasp. Isn't that what you want to hear?"

"If it's the truth."

I turn and give him a look. He knows I'm not fuckin' with him.

"Maybe you were too rough."

"I was *not* too rough," I say harshly.

"Who was she?"

I reach around and massage the persistent knot on the back of my neck. If I don't answer, Damon'll probably show up tomorrow and every day until I spill the beans. What's the big deal anyway? I glance at the old oak, half expecting to spot Maggie sitting there, her expression wary and angry.

I look over to Damon who's still waiting for an answer.

Then I finally say it. "I touched the girl who I went to jail for maiming."

Click.

TEN
Maggie

"Are you okay?" Sabrina asks.

I'm sitting on the floor in front of my locker at school, figuring out which books I need to bring with me to first period. First days of school are always hard to adjust to after a summer off. I've had a whole year off. I look up at her and say, "Yeah, except I'm dreading Mrs. Glassman's trig class."

"So you're not freaking out?"

"I hear she's tough, but I can—"

"I'm not talking about Glassman, Maggie. I'm talking about Caleb being in school today. Duh!"

I lose the grip on the book I'm holding. "What?"

"He's in Meyer's office."

Wait. One. Minute. "I heard he wasn't coming back to school." Mom told me this morning; she heard it at the diner.

"You obviously heard wrong, 'cause Danielle saw him." I peek down J Hall.

"I thought you said seeing him was no biggie."

Um . . .

Brianne runs down the hall, heading in my direction. "Did you hear?" she says when she catches her breath.

"She heard," Sabrina says, her hand on her hip. "But she says it's no big deal. The girl has serious denial issues."

Forgetting my locker, I shove the mass of books inside. I'm still sitting on the hard tile floor, but don't trust myself to stand without making a bigger scene.

To make matters worse, now Danielle is walking down the hall with five people flanking her. She's deep in conversation, probably relaying the story of the year.

And it's only the first day of school.

Too bad I didn't get the packets for Spain in the mail yet. I need something positive to focus on today. Because seeing Caleb—again—is a big deal. The biggest. And I can do nothing but sit here and play the unaffected girl. The affected doesn't do so great playing the unaffected. At least when it's me.

"There she is!" Danielle's excitement makes everyone crowd around me. I wish I could snap my fingers and make them all disappear. Or make me disappear. I liked it better when I was invisible.

"So, what's the scoop?" Sabrina asks Danielle.

"Well . . ." Danielle says, pausing on purpose to make sure she has everyone's attention. "My mom is on the school board and I overheard they made Caleb a deal. He has to take junior final exams in all his classes and then he can officially be a senior. If he fails, he'll be held back a year."

"He's a dumb wrestling jock," Brynn Healey chimes in. "He'll never pass."

He's not dumb; I know he's smarter than people think. When we were in elementary school, Caleb got a ribbon for getting the highest GPA in sixth grade one semester. He was proud; you should have seen the huge grin on his face as they handed the ribbon to him.

Caleb got teased by his friends for proudly displaying it on his sports trophy shelf. They started calling him names and accused him of having a secret affair with our three-hundred-pound English teacher, Ms. Bolinsky. After that, Leah told me he gave her the ribbon. Caleb's grades dropped and he never got another ribbon. The relief on his face each time they presented it to someone else was so obvious. Well, obvious to me.

The bell rings and, luckily, the mob starts to disperse.

I just pray Caleb ignores me if we ever come face to face again.

I grab my locker to steady myself and stand. Closing the door, I head toward my first-period class. I'm late, but assume my limp excuse will work.

I catch sight of Leah coming out of the bathroom.

My old best friend walks toward me, not paying attention because she's looking down.

If things were different, I'd ask her why she wears all black clothes. If things were different, I'd ask her how it feels having her brother back.

When she finally does look up and notices I'm in her path, she makes an about-face and scurries away.

ELEVEN
Caleb

The school principal is standing over my desk. The desk has been placed in the man's office so I can take the dreaded exams.

I should never have come back to school. I'd gone to classes in the DOC; it was part of the juvenile inmate program. The tests aren't the problem, either. It's the way Meyer is staring at me like he's never seen an ex-con before. The unnecessary attention is driving me insane.

I focus on the second final exam placed in front of me this morning. It isn't as if I'm acing the tests so far, but I haven't flunked them either.

"You done?" Meyer asks.

I have one more algebra question left, but with the guy

standing over me it's close to impossible to concentrate. Not wanting to fuck it up, I'm doing my best to answer the question correctly.

It takes me five minutes longer than it should, but I'm finally ready for the next exam.

"Go have lunch, Becker," Meyer orders after collecting the test.

Lunch? In the cafeteria with half the student body? No way, man. "I'm not hungry."

"You gotta eat. Feed that brain of yours."

What did he mean by that? *Stop being paranoid*, I tell myself. That's one of the side effects of being jailed. You always analyze people's words and expressions as if they're playing with you. A joke on the ex-con, ha ha.

I stand. Beyond the principal's door are over four hundred students waiting for a glimpse of the guy who went to jail. I rub the knot that just reappeared on the back of my neck.

"Go on," Meyer urges. "You have three more exams so move those feet. Be back here in twenty-five minutes."

I put my sweaty palm on the door handle, twist, and take a deep breath.

Out in the hallway, I don't waste any time and head for the cafeteria. Once inside, I ignore all of the stares. Coffee. I need strong, black coffee. That'll ease my nerves and keep me awake the rest of the afternoon. Scanning the room, I remember there's no coffee available for students. I bet they have a coffee pot in the teachers' lounge, though.

Would they notice if I steal one cup? Or will they call the police and claim I'm a thief in addition to the other labels already tattooed on my back.

I spot my sister sitting alone. She used to sit by Maggie and their other friends, giggling and flirting with my friends.

That's what sucked about having a twin of the opposite sex. It was bad enough when my sister had crushes on my friends and would bug us when they'd hang at my house. She'd slap on the makeup and act all giggly and flirty . . . I still cringe thinking about it. What's worse is when I realized the tide changed and my friends actually wanted to get into my sister's pants. That changed it into a whole new ball game. I spent a lot of time last summer threatening to cut my own friends' balls off. I've always made sure my sister was protected, her reputation as well as her social status.

A year has gone by.

Boy, how things have changed. Nobody even looks in Leah's direction now.

"Hey, sis," I say, straddling the cafeteria bench opposite her.

Leah twirls spaghetti around her fork, the hot lunch special of the day. "I heard about the exams," she says.

I let out a short, cynical laugh. "My brain is already fried and I still got three more to go."

"You think you passed?"

I shrug. "Don't know."

"Rumor has it Morehouse made up a social studies exam you couldn't possibly pass."

Didn't I already pay my debt to society? "Really?"

"Yeah. Caleb, what if you flunk?"

I don't want to think about it, so I ignore her question. When I happen to glance at the entrance to the cafeteria, in walks Kendra. Is she my ex, or did we just take a leave of absence from each other? The answer lies in her reaction to me. She hasn't spotted me yet. Good. I'm not ready to talk to her in front of the whole frickin' school. "I gotta go."

I bolt out the side door of the cafeteria, the one leading to the small gymnasium.

Man, Kendra looked hot. Her hair is cut different than I remember, her shirt a little tighter. How will she react when she sees me? Will she throw herself into my arms or will she play it cool?

I miss her.

I gaze at the wrestling mats piled in the corner of the gym. Kendra used to cheer me on during matches. I remember the last wrestling tournament I competed in. I jumped two weight classes to wrestle the big guy. It was a 1-1 tie before I made my move. His legs were as dense as a python, but I was quicker. I'll never forget his name . . . Vic Medonia.

I wasn't intimidated, although I probably should've been. Vic was last year's state champion. But I won the match. The guy had one word to say to me after the match. *Later*.

I was arrested a week later.

"You're back." Coach Wenner is standing at the door to the gym, eyeing me.

I shove my hands into my jean pockets. "That's what they tell me."

"You gonna wrestle for me this season?"

"No."

"My team could sure use a good one-sixty-five."

"I'm one-eighty now."

The coach whistles in awe. "You sure? You look leaner than I remember."

"I've worked out a lot. Muscle weight."

"Don't tease me like that, Becker."

I laugh. "I'll come to some matches. To watch."

Coach Wenner slaps the wrestling mats. "We'll see. Maybe when the season starts you won't be able to resist."

I check my watch. I better get back and finish those exams. "I gotta get back to Meyer's office."

"If you change your mind about joining the team, you know where to find me."

"Yeah," I say, then walk down the hall.

Back in the office, Meyer plops the next test in front of me.

Damn. I forgot to eat. Now the words on the page are blurred, the knot on the back of my neck is throbbing, and Meyer is staring at me from his desk.

The guy sits there, his eyebrows raised like little French accents over his eyes. "Something wrong?"

I shake my head. "No, sir."

"Then get to work."

Easy for him to say. He doesn't have to take a social studies test the president of the United States wouldn't have a chance in hell of passing.

I should purposely flunk it; that'll show 'em. Then I can skip my last year of high school. There's no way my ma will let me be a junior again. Or will she?

I fill out answers until my pencil wears down and my ass is numb from sitting on the hard metal chair. It's a fifty-fifty chance I've passed Morehouse's stupid test. Only two more of the things to go before I can leave for the day.

Two hours later, I answer the final question on the last test. I almost smile. Almost. My brain is too tired to use any facial muscles. So when Meyer dismisses me, I practically run from his office.

I have to take a bus to the hardware store. Bus number 204 from Hampton will stop a block away from school at three twenty-nine.

My watch says three twenty-seven.

That gives me two minutes to run to the bus. I'm ready to book as fast as I can to catch the thing, because if I don't, Damon'll know I was late.

As soon as the bus is in sight, Brian Newcomb steps in front of me, holding his hand to my chest and stopping me.

"Caleb, buddy, I've been looking all over for you."

Brian and I had been best friends since kindergarten.

We haven't talked for almost a year. I told him not to visit me in jail, so I don't know if we're still buds. But right now isn't the time to find out. Community service sucks, but I have to do it. My freedom depends on it.

"Wha's up, Brian?" I say quickly, then look behind him as the bus pulls away from the stop. Shit.

"You know. Nothing . . . and everything. What up with you?"

"Oh, you know. Getting used to living without bars in my bedroom."

There's one of those really long pauses, where Brian looks like he doesn't know how to respond, before finally saying, "That was a joke, right?"

"Right." Not really.

Brian laughs, but there's something else behind it. Nervousness? What reason does he have to be nervous? The guy knows me better than my own mother.

I narrow my eyes at my friend who'd been my confidante since kindergarten. "Are we cool?" I ask.

There's a slight, almost unnoticeable hesitation. But I see it, and, more importantly, feel it. "Yeah, we're cool," Brian says.

The bus turns the corner. "I gotta go."

"You need a ride? My dad got a new Yukon and gave me his," Brian says, jangling the keys to the car in front of my face.

I'd settle for an old, rusted junker at this point. I murmur a "No, thanks," because I learned in jail not to have expectations or rely on others.

"Listen, I'm sorry I never wrote. There were crazy things going on and you told me not to visit . . ."

"Don't sweat it. It's over, man."

Brian shifts his feet. "I'd still like to talk about it."

"I said it's over. I really got to go," I say, then start walking toward The Trusty Nail.

The last thing I need is my best friend acting stranger than my mom. I have enough to deal with right now, like how Damon is going to spit fire when he hears I was late for my first day of community service.

TWELVE
Maggie

I borrowed a Frommer's book about Spain at the library today. Looking in the mailbox after school, I say a little prayer, hoping the information packet arrived.

There's a letter from the program, not a packet. I rip the envelope open, getting a paper cut as I slide my finger between the folds. I don't care. This is my ticket out, my chance to get away from Caleb and Paradise. Time to forget the accident and get psyched about independence and anonymity.

I unfold the letter quickly, as if it's the Golden Ticket in *Willy Wonka and the Chocolate Factory*. I have a huge smile on my face as I read the letter.

To: Miss Margaret Armstrong
From: International Exchange Student (IES) Program

Dear Miss Armstrong:

It has come to the attention of our IES committee that the scholarship for which you originally applied was an athletic scholarship. Since your records indicate you have not been active on a high school athletic team for the past twelve months, I'm sorry to inform you that your scholarship has been revoked. We are under legal limitations to distribute the athletic scholarships solely to current high school athletes.

You are still welcome to participate in the IES program provided you arrange your own transportation and pay tuition costs which include discounted room and board on the University of Barcelona campus. The cost of tuition for one semester of high school in the IES program is $4,625.

Please remit payment by December 15th to the IES office in order to hold your place in the program. If you have any questions, please don't hesitate to contact me.

Sincerely,
Helena Cortez, President

International Exchange Student program,
University of Barcelona, Spain

When my brain comprehends the words *scholarship revoked*, my smile instantly fades.

"I can't go," I whisper. Mom had to work overtime just to get me a Juicy Couture outfit that cost a hundred dollars. There's no way we can afford over four thousand dollars. I squeeze my eyes shut. *This isn't happening.* Not now. My hands start to shake again. I feel them shivering as I cover my eyes with my palms.

When my mom gets home from work in the evening, I hold the letter out to her.

"Okay, don't panic," she says after reading it. "There must be some way we can manage."

"Mom, it's useless to even think about. We don't have that kind of money."

"My boss might let me work enough overtime. Let's see . . ." She grabs a piece of paper and starts scribbling numbers down.

"Mom, forget it."

"Wait. Sixty hours a week minimum, sometimes seventy . . . and if I work on Thanksgiving and add in my Christmas bonus—"

"Mom!"

She stops writing and looks up at me. "What?"

"Stop writing, stop compensating . . . just stop."

I'm depressed enough as it is without watching her attempt to kill herself to make me happy. I'll figure this out. But it's my problem, not hers.

The phone rings. It's Mr. Reynolds telling my mom

she forgot her paycheck at work. Now she's got to go back and get it. "Come with me, Maggie."

"I don't want to."

"Oh, come on. I saw Irina baking some new pies this afternoon. Pie always cheers you up."

Irina is one of the chefs at the diner. She likes having me try her new pie creations before she offers them on the menu. Irina's pies are one of the reasons I've gained weight this past year.

At the mention of pie, I give in. If there was any time I need pie to cheer me up, this is it.

"The place is crowded tonight," Mom says to Mr. Reynolds when he hands her the forgotten paycheck.

Mr. Reynolds, usually so calm and in control, seems panicked. "It's the men's bowling league," he explains. "They just came in and Yolanda went home sick ten minutes ago."

There's about thirty hungry men milling around the tables, and I only see Tony, a new waiter, looking more frazzled than Mr. Reynolds.

Mom taps her boss on the shoulder. "If you need help, I'm sure Maggie won't mind if I stay for a bit."

Mr. Reynolds smiles. "Really? That would be great."

"No problem."

"You're the best, Linda. I owe you one."

My mom rolls her eyes playfully as she heads behind the counter to wrap an apron around her waist. "You owe me more than one, Lou, but we can discuss it later."

"You got it," he says, then rushes to greet new customers who've just walked in the door.

Mom scurries to the group to help Tony take orders while I follow behind her with a pitcher, filling water glasses.

After I pour the water, Mom tells me to sit down at a booth. I pull out the Frommer's book on Spain from my purse and stare at it longingly. If only we were as rich as Kendra's parents, I'd be able to go to Spain. Even if we were as rich as Caleb and Leah's parents, we'd probably be able to afford it without thinking twice. Their dad is an oral surgeon and has just about every southwest Illinois resident as a patient.

It's times like these I wish my dad and mom never got divorced. I can pretend to forget about the fights, the screaming, the anger lurking around every corner of the house. Mom said they just grew apart while he traveled for work and she stayed home. When he came home on weekends, he wanted to relax while my mom wanted to go out. Eventually Dad stopped coming home on weekends. And Mom stopped caring if he was home.

I'm not sure where Judy (his new wife) fits into the divorce equation. I miss my dad, but he never asks me to come to Texas and visit. I don't want to ask him why he doesn't invite me because, to be completely honest, I don't want to hear he doesn't want me as a part of his new life.

As I'm waiting for my mom, Irina comes out of the

kitchen. "Moggie, Moggie!" she says excitedly in her heavy Russian accent, "I hove a new pie for you."

"Is it with carrots?" I ask, worried. The last time Irina made a carrot pie using an old family recipe of hers, there were chunks of carrots in the middle. I'm happy to say it didn't end up on the menu.

"I promise no weggies. It's a vhite pie viz chocolate cheeps and graham cracker crumbs laced viz caramel. Sounds delicious, no?"

My stomach growls, ready for the rush of sugar. "Bring it out. I need something to cheer me up," I say. "There's a problem with my trip to Spain."

Irina gasps. "Oy, vat hoppened?"

I shrug. "It's a long story."

"I come bring cake right now, da?" Irina says before disappearing into the kitchen. She comes back a few minutes later with a huge slab of pie. I can tell before I taste it this is going to be a best-selling dessert at Auntie Mae's Diner next week.

Before I take the first bite, I say "You're the best, Irina," and dig my fork into the white moistness speckled with graham cracker, caramel, and chocolate chips. She always waits next to me until I swallow the first bite and give her my analysis.

"It's awesome," I say, savoring the moistness of the creamy part and the soft crunch of the chips blended with the smooth caramel and crumbly texture of the graham crackers. "One of your best."

Irina whisks herself back into the kitchen with a flutter.

"I see Irina found you," Mom says as she holds a tray full of double-decker platters. "By the time you finish the pie, I'll be done here and we can go home."

I watch as my mom places the platters expertly in front of the hungry bowlers.

When I take my second forkful, another customer walks in. It's an old lady with grey hair, white pants, and a turquoise jacket. Mr. Reynolds greets her with a kiss on her cheek. "Mom, why didn't you tell me you were coming?" he asks the lady. "Wait, where's Gladys?"

"I fired her yesterday," the lady says. "She was a pain in the you-know-what. Besides, I don't need a caretaker. I made it here without one, didn't I?"

Mr. Reynolds looks worried. "Mom, why can't you get along with anyone I hire to help you? I swear you just fire them to spite me."

The old lady stands up straight with her chin in the air like a three-year-old. "I don't need any help."

"You have a heart condition," Mr. Reynolds says.

She waves her hand in the air, dismissing his concern. "Who says?"

"Your doctor."

"What do doctors know, anyway? They call it practicing medicine because that's all they ever do. Practice. If you'd visit me once in a while, you'd know I'm doing fine."

"I just saw you on Saturday." He huffs, then says, "Are you hungry?"

"What do you have on special this week?"

"Irina will make you anything you want, Mom. Name it."

She narrows her eyes at him. "Corn and a big, juicy steak."

Mr. Reynolds shakes his head and chuckles. "Mom, you have diverticulosis and a heart condition. Try again."

"You're no fun, Lou."

"And you're a barrel of laughs. Just sit down at a table. Wait . . . follow me and you can meet Linda's daughter. You've never met her before."

I look down at the pie, trying not to give away the fact I've been eavesdropping on their conversation.

"Maggie, this is my mother," Mr. Reynolds announces. "Mom, this is Linda's daughter Margaret. Everyone calls her Maggie."

I smile and hold out my hand. "Nice to meet you, Mrs. Reynolds. Are you *the* Auntie Mae?"

The old lady takes my hand and shakes it. "Dearie, Mae was the name of my son's first dog."

No way! I look to Mr. Reynolds for confirmation. He's smiling sheepishly.

"It's true," he whispers. "Shh, it's a secret. If the town finds out I named my restaurant after a dog, this place will be deserted within a week."

I highly doubt that. Auntie Mae's is crowded almost

every night. Besides, there's not another diner within a ten-mile radius.

"I didn't know Linda had a daughter. How old are you, Margaret?" she asks, ignoring the fact that her son told me everyone calls me Maggie.

"Seventeen."

"She just started her senior year of high school, Mom," Mr. Reynolds announces loudly, as if his mother is hard of hearing. "And she's going to Spain in January for school. Why don't you sit with her while she tells you all about it. I'll go in the back and have Irina fix you something to eat."

"Tell her not to make it too healthy," Mrs. Reynolds orders before sitting down on the opposite bench from me. She eyes my plate. "Lou, tell Irina to cut me a generous slice of that pie, too."

I don't think Mr. Reynolds was listening to her last request, or maybe he wanted to let her *think* he wasn't listening.

The old woman places her purse beside her in the booth, then looks at me. She doesn't smile, she doesn't frown. She tilts her head, as if trying to figure out what's inside my thoughts. "Why do you want to leave Paradise so badly?" she asks, almost as if she really can read my mind.

"I just do," I say, hoping she'll leave it at that.

She makes a tsking noise with her tongue. "If you don't want to talk about it, just say so. No sense in beating around the bush."

I had been busy chipping the nail polish off my fingers,

but I stop and look at Mrs. Reynolds. "I don't want to talk about it."

The old lady claps her hands together. "Fine. If you don't want to talk about it, we won't talk about it."

The only thing standing between me and this woman is the pie I have and she wants. And awkward silence. It's not that I'm trying to be rude, I just don't want to put into words how my life has become one disappointment after another. It's almost as if misery is following me and I've been cursed. If I only knew how to break that curse . . .

"I'm sure you have your reasons for not wanting to talk about it. I can't imagine what those reasons are, but you're probably better off being silent and brooding about it rather than talking it out with someone who has nothing better to do than listen."

I shove another forkful of pie in my mouth and focus on the salt shaker at the end of the table.

"You want the salt?" Mrs. Reynolds asks, knowing full well I don't have salt on my mind.

"They revoked my scholarship," I blurt out, then look at the old lady sitting across from me.

She doesn't have a look of pity on her face like I expected. She looks kind of . . . well, angry. "Well, why would they go and do a thing like that?"

I take my time chewing and swallowing, then look up. Mrs. Reynolds has her little hands folded on the top of the table and she's looking intently at me, waiting for my answer.

"I applied for an athletic scholarship, but I'm not on a team anymore so it's been revoked. I can go, but now I'll have to pay tuition we can't afford."

She nods her head, lets out a long breath, then leans back in the booth. "I see. Well, dearie, maybe one day your luck will change."

Yeah, right. All I need is a little magic dust and a fairy godmother. I'm not holding my breath for either of those.

THIRTEEN
Caleb

"Caleb, I hope you passed the tests," my mom calls out from the kitchen.

I'm washing my hands for the third time tonight. I've got paint up to my elbows, compliments of my community service job. The old couple from the senior center signed up to have their kitchen painted a bright pink to match their fake pink roses on their kitchen table. "I tried my best," I say.

"Let's hope your best was good enough."

I dry my hands on a towel, wondering when she'll stop treating me like a stranger. One day I'm going to cut through her plastic exterior. One day soon.

The phone rings. My mom answers, then hands it to me. "It's for you. It's Damon."

I take the phone. "Hey."

"The manager from The Trusty Nail said you were late."

Oh, shit. "I had to stay after school because—"

"I've heard it all, don't waste your breath," he barks out, cutting me off. "Zero tolerance. You sign in for community service on time. Period. You got it?"

"I got it."

"This goes on your record, Caleb. I can petition a judge to have you sent back to the DOC. Keep screwing up and I'll do it . . ."

He's still babbling, but I'm too pissed off to listen.

". . . I told you to be a model citizen and be on time for your job. You let me down. *Don't* let it happen again."

"It wasn't my fault," I argue.

"If I had a dime for every time I heard those words, I'd be a millionaire."

Hardass. "I get it, Damon. Loud and clear."

"Good. I'll check in with you tomorrow," he says, then hangs up.

When I put the phone down, I realize Mom's been listening to my half of the conversation. She's staring at me, but there's an emptiness in her eyes—like she's not all there. "Is everything okay?"

"Yep," I say. Just peachy.

"Good." She grabs her purse off the couch. "I'm off

to the grocery store. I'm going to bake my Spaghetti Spectacular for the Fall Festival Saturday night."

Mom is always volunteering for shit. She loves the attention, I guess. Her Spaghetti Spectacular dish has won the Ladies' Auxiliary best recipe award every year. She's even got the awards neatly stacked on top of the mantle in the living room.

Mom flies out the door in her usual flurry of chaos.

"She's nuts, you know," Leah says from the kitchen doorway.

Today my sister is wearing black jeans with chains dripping from them. The end of one chain is attached to one of her pant legs and the other end is attached to the other pant leg. How can she walk like that?

I watch Mom drive down the driveway as I look out the living room window. "Tell me about it."

"Do you think things will ever get back to normal?" Leah asks, hope filling her voice.

"They'd better." I'm going to spend my days trying, starting right now with my sister. She's about to walk back into the kitchen, but I blurt out, "Do you ever talk to, you know, Maggie?"

She freezes, then shakes her head slowly.

"Not once since the accident?"

She shakes her head again. "I don't want to talk about it, Caleb. Please don't make me talk about it. Not now."

"When, then?" She doesn't answer. "One day we're going to discuss it, Leah. You can't avoid the conversation forever." I put my jacket on, grab a basketball from the garage, and head outside. I avoid even looking at the Armstrong's house as I head for the park in the opposite direction. I need to shoot some baskets to clear my mind.

My screwed-up sister is the one who needs group therapy. I'm the one who was locked up and everyone who stayed home is a frickin' nutcase. Oh, the comic irony.

————

The next day I'm sitting in the principal's office. Mom and Dad had to come with me to hear whether or not I've passed the tests. God this sucks.

Meyer opens a folder and stares at it. Folders suck, too. Especially ones that have anything having to do with me.

The defense lawyer assigned to my case after the accident had a folder outlining the accident, my arrest, and the history of my life. The warden in the DOC had a folder much the same. It's like I wasn't a guy anymore. I'd been reduced to words written by others about me. Even Damon relies on a damn folder. I could tell them a hell of a lot more than any folder could say.

"While Caleb did surprisingly well in almost all of the exams," Meyer directs his attention to my dad, "he hasn't passed the requirements for social studies."

Gee, that's no surprise considering what Leah said.

Mom's smile loses its brightness for a second. "I'm sure it's a mistake."

I look over at my dad. He glances at me before saying,

"Caleb went through the academic program at the, uh, Department of Corrections."

Meyer puts a hand up. "That may be, Dr. Becker. But he didn't pass social studies or rack up enough credits to be a senior."

I'm going to say what I've been wanting to say all along, to hell with the consequences. "I could just drop out."

Mom frowns. "Caleb, no." Yeah, a real live public reaction!

Dad's eyebrows furrow. "Son, you're not dropping out. I'm sure Mr. Meyer can work something out. Right?"

The guy takes a deep breath and pulls out yet another folder, which seriously makes me want to laugh. He studies the contents while we all wait in silence. "Well, I could put him into a junior level social studies but keep all of his other subjects at the senior level."

"Oh, that's a wonderful idea," Mom shrieks.

Dad nods.

"He'll have to take summer school and graduate late. It's not ideal but—"

"That's fine, isn't it, Caleb?"

Oh, man. Summer school? Why don't they just stick bamboo under my fingernails instead? "Whatever it takes, Dad."

I stare out the window at the cars driving past the school and birds flying to who knows where.

"Caleb, why don't you get a class schedule from my

secretary," the principal says, then checks his watch. "You can catch the last half of third period if you hurry."

Dad and Mom are silent as we exit Meyer's office.

The secretary hands me a piece of paper. "Here's your class schedule."

I walk to senior English. Leave it to old Meyer to make me enter the classroom smack in the middle of class. I wince as I open the door.

I can almost hear an announcer's voice in my head. *Yes, ladies and gentleman, the main attraction . . . straight from juvenile jail . . . Caleb Becker!* I feel sixty eyes on me, burning into my skull as I walk up to the teacher, Mr. Edelsen. "Can I help you?" he asks.

"I'm in this class."

Silence.

Eyes.

Muscles tightening.

"Well, have a seat then."

I walk to the back of the class and pick a seat next to Drew Rudolph. We used to hang out. You know . . . before.

After class I have lunch. I pay for an apple and Coke from money my parents gave me this morning. As I walk through the lunchroom, I hold my head high. Let them talk about the ex-con all they want. Facing these kids is nothing compared to the guys at the DOC.

When I turn the corner, I bump into Kendra. It's the first time we've been this close since my arrest.

"Hi, Caleb," she says with a teasing lilt to her voice. "Drew told me he saw you in English class."

I nod.

"Remember when we had English together?"

Boy, do I. We used to take bathroom breaks at the same time and meet in some deserted hallway to make out and feel each other up. "I remember."

She smiles at me with her bright teeth and killer full lips. I could have kissed those lips forever. I still can.

"Well, I guess I'll catch you later," she says.

"Later," I say, watching her butt sway as she walks away.

————

After school, for community service, I fixed an old lady's fence and hung up her light fixture.

Before I got convicted I'd come home to find at least ten messages from Kendra, begging me to call. But this time I got home and the answering machine only had one message . . . from Damon.

I called him back. Our conversation went like this.

"Caleb?"

"Yeah?"

"Good job today. On time and everything."

"Thanks."

"Keep it up. I'll call in two days."

Woo hoo! He'll leave me alone for a whopping two days.

My dad is working late tonight so it's only me, my mom, and Leah. Leah is pushing her food around on her plate, not really eating. Mom is too busy yakking to her friends on the phone. I don't think she even realizes Leah and I are sitting at the table with her. I'm thankful when everyone in my house is sleeping. It's the only time it resembles the old days.

At night I'm lying in my bed, staring at the clock like I've been doing for the past two hours. Three o'clock in the morning. I can't sleep. Too many thoughts running through my useless head. Maybe I need an uncomfortable and overly used mattress like I had in the DOC in order to get a full night of sleep.

Throwing the covers back, I stand up and pace my bedroom. The picture of Kendra on my headboard is staring back at me, her smile a secret promise between the two of us. I snatch the cordless phone from the living room and take it back to my bedroom.

I dial Kendra's number, her private line that only rings in her bedroom, but I hang up before it rings. What if she's dating someone else and doesn't want to talk to me? I sure as hell don't want to be running after her if she's hanging with another guy.

I look out the window, gauging how long it'll be until the sun comes creeping up. In the DOC, there were always guys who couldn't sleep. You could see them across the way sitting in their bunks, or you could hear them tossing and turning. The new guys and youngest kids had the hardest time. They'd be crying silently, the only indication being a random sniffle or shoulders slumped over and shaking. Even though some of them were just twelve or thirteen, they tried to act like men.

But they were, in the end, just boys.

I notice a light turn on in Maggie's bedroom, the glow outlining the curtains covering her window. I have computer class with her, but usually I sit in the back while she takes a seat in the front row. I keep my head down because the kids in class are analyzing my every move. When the bell rings, Maggie is the first one out . . . sometimes I think she's out of there before the bell even rings. Does she think she's the only one affected by the accident?

FOURTEEN
Maggie

I can't sleep after my nightmares and have to turn my light on to stay awake. At least this time I didn't wake Mom up screaming.

This nightmare was different. Kendra Greene drove the car, not Caleb. In all my other nightmares, it's Caleb at the wheel of the car that hit me.

I guess it's because I saw Kendra talking to Caleb in the cafeteria yesterday. He didn't see me because I sit right next to the doors so I can leave as soon as I've finished eating.

The cafeteria is a strange place. The populars can be spotted right away. They're loud and laugh a lot. The regular people sit in their own cliques, totally separate from the popular lunch tables.

I used to be a popular. Most athletes in Paradise are populars. But now I'm a loner who doesn't even mingle with the regulars, not even the lowest ones.

Loners sit by themselves, scattered throughout the lunchroom. They eat alone, then make their hasty exits.

I never knew where the loners went to, they just disappeared during lunch hour. But now that I am a loner I know that secret place.

The school library. It's the mysterious place you can go to and not be seen.

Caleb isn't afraid of attention. He walked right into the cafeteria yesterday, his head held high as if he was Mr. Meyer himself. Then he went right up to Kendra Greene and said something to make her smile. I swear everyone in the room was silent, watching them reunite. Does he know Brian and Kendra are a couple? The way Caleb stared at her butt when she walked away from him makes me think he's oblivious to what's been going on since he was in jail. Some things haven't changed.

I pull back my window curtains and stare out at Caleb's window. It's a little past three a.m. He's probably sleeping like a baby without a care in the world.

But he's not. His light is on and I see his silhouette pacing his room.

I let the curtains fall back to cover the window, turn the light off, and hurry back to bed. I can't fall into old habits, not now after everything that's happened.

The reality is I had a crush on Caleb since first grade.

He used to tease Leah and me as we played with our Barbie dolls and dressed up in costumes. But when we needed a boy to play a part in one of our shows, we could always coerce him into acting the part. And if we made up a ballet show, we could count on him to be an audience member as we jeté'd and plié'd our hearts out in front of him.

But the time I fell head over heels in love with Caleb Becker was in sixth grade, when he took the blame after I broke his mom's ceramic statue of an owl that had been given to her great-great-grandmother from some former U.S. president.

Leah was upstairs getting ready and I was waiting for her in their living room. We were going to play tennis at the park. Caleb surprised me by flying down the stairs with a Star Wars lightsaber in his hand, waving it around. I laughed and put up my racquet as a weapon, challenging him. He came at me with the saber, and I swung my racquet to ward off his attack. I counted on whacking his saber, not the ceramic owl on his mom's credenza.

His mother heard the crash and came running. Caleb said it was his fault, that he was playing around with the saber. He never named me as the one who broke the statue; he didn't even name me as an accomplice. I was too scared at the time to tell the truth, even when I knew he got grounded for a whole month. Without even realizing it, he became my hero.

After that, I used to watch Caleb through my window when he played catch with his friends or had Boy Scout meetings in his backyard. When we were in seventh grade he started mowing the lawn while listening to music. I could hardly concentrate on my homework while I watched him weave back and forth across the lawn with the mower, his muscles bunching through his t-shirt as he gathered grass clippings and shoved them into garbage bags.

Sometimes he'd catch me looking at him and wave. Sometimes I tentatively waved back, but then I'd close my curtains and keep them closed for a week so he'd never know how I really felt about him. Other times I'd pretend I didn't see him, although I suppose he knew I'd been spying.

Caleb never let on that he liked me more than a friend. That was okay by me. I just kept up hope that one day he'd see me as a girl and not his twin sister's pesky friend.

He had girlfriends over the years, but was never serious about any of them.

Until Kendra.

They started dating in the beginning of our freshman year. Kendra hung out at his house every day after school; they were inseparable from the start. Every time I happened to glance out my window and spot them in an intimate embrace, my hopeful heart crumbled little by little.

That was also about the time my dad left. So here I was, desperately waiting for my dad and Caleb to love me as much as I loved them.

What could I do to make the ones I loved love me back? The only thing I was good at was tennis. So I practiced and played and challenged myself every day during the summer between our freshman and sophomore year. Surely, once Caleb saw I was the only sophomore on the varsity squad, he'd notice me.

And I sent my dad articles from the local paper about my success, never forgetting to add the tennis coach's prediction that I'd make it to the Illinois state championship in October.

That season my dad never saw me play.

That season was also when Caleb lost his virginity to Kendra.

Once, just once, I saw them having sex one night under a blanket in his backyard. I never told anyone, although I could have sworn Caleb looked up at my window and knew I'd been watching.

He never said anything to me about it. And I never told Leah. She'd be grossed out anyway. In fact, after that I felt so embarrassed I stopped watching Caleb.

I keep going over the night of the accident in my head. The conversation I had with Caleb before the accident and the stories I heard about afterward.

He was obviously drunk; the policemen who arrested him gave him an alcohol test immediately after he admitted to hitting me with his car. But was he so drunk he didn't know what he was doing?

So what if he hated what I told him that night, it was the truth. His girlfriend was cheating on him.

"You're lying," he'd said that night.

I was determined not to let him get away from me before

I told him. *"I'm not, Caleb. I swear I saw her with another guy."* I didn't add that the other guy was his best friend.

He grabbed my shoulders so hard I winced. Caleb had never laid a hand on me before. His rough touch made tears roll down my face.

"I love you," I'd told him. *"I've always loved you."* I'd let my fear of the truth and my love for Caleb all come out that night. *"Open your eyes, Caleb. Kendra is playing you for a fool."*

He took his hands off me like I was on fire and he was getting burned. Then he said something I'll never forget. *"You don't get it, Maggie, do you? You and me will never happen. Now stop spreading lies about my girlfriend before you get hurt."*

That warning has echoed in my head from that day until now. The logical part of me knows it was an accident. Of course he didn't mean to lose control of his car. But in the dark recesses of my mind there's this little nagging doubt that creeps up every once in a while.

I finally fall asleep, but it's not a restful slumber because my dreams are haunted by the fact that I won't be able to escape Paradise and go somewhere far away— where the past can't catch up with me.

The next day after school I get off the bus and come home to a message on our answering machine from Mrs. Reynolds—the old lady I met yesterday. She left her number and told me to call her as soon as I got home. When

I call her back, she says she wants to interview me for an after-school job . . . as her companion.

"Are you sure?" I ask.

"I can strike a deal with you so you can go to Spain," she says, totally tempting me. "Can you come to my house in Hampton so we can talk?"

As fast as my limpy legs can carry me I'm on a bus heading to Hampton. It's not far, just a fifteen minute bus ride from Paradise. The whole time I'm thinking of the deal Mrs. Reynolds wants to offer me. What does a companion do? Play checkers and listen to her talk about the old days?

It can't be that hard. I can do it, even with a bad leg. Visions of making the old lady tea sandwiches and lemonade while we sit and talk float in my head.

Leah and I used to talk—for hours on end about nothing and everything. I know talking with an old lady won't be the same as talking to an old best friend, but I think it could be cool.

I ring the doorbell to Mrs. Reynolds' house and she greets me with a smile. "Come in, Margaret."

I sit primly on her expensive, cream-colored sofa, trying to make a good impression. *Maggie, forget about the past and focus on the future,* I tell myself.

Mrs. Reynolds has bright, alert, green eyes that defy her old age, and an attitude that rivals the senior girls on the pompom squad. "Would you mind working for a crabby old lady like me, Margaret, if at the end you'd be able to take that trip to Spain?"

"Besides needing the money for studying abroad next semester," I say, holding my hands in my lap and trying not to fidget, "I believe one can learn a lot from people with life experience."

Did I just hear Mrs. Reynolds snort? "Don't you mean 'old people'?" she retorts.

I bite the inside of my mouth. "Um, what I meant was, um . . ."

"Take it from someone with *life experience*. Don't pussyfoot around, it only wastes time. Can you cook?"

Does macaroni and cheese count as cooking? "Yes."

"Play gin?"

"Yes."

"Do you talk too much?"

Her question throws me off guard. "Excuse me?"

"You know, do you just talk to hear your voice, or do you keep quiet until you have something interesting to say?"

"The latter," I answer.

"Good. I don't like senseless chatter."

"Me, either."

So much for not *pussyfooting* around.

"I'll expect you here from three thirty to seven o'clock on weekdays, a few hours on weekends. I can give you an hour break so you can do homework."

"Does that mean I'm hired?" I ask.

"It seems so. I'll give you fifteen hundred dollars a month, enough to pay for that tuition you need. You can start after school on Monday."

Wow. Way more than I'd make if I worked anywhere else. "It's too much," I admit. "You could probably get someone for a lot less money."

"Probably. But you want to go to Spain, don't you?"

"Of course, but . . ."

"No buts. Buts can be categorized as senseless chatter."

I want to kiss and hug the woman and thank her a hundred times. But I don't think she's the kissing and hugging type. And if I thank her a hundred times, I think she'd have an aneurysm from the amount of senseless chatter.

Mrs. Reynolds stands, using her cane to steady herself. Which reminds me to add, "I have a limp."

Instead of asking me about it, the woman just says, "So do I. So do most of my friends. At least the ones who aren't dead. As long as you don't complain about yours, I won't complain about mine."

And that, if you can believe it, is the end of my interview.

FIFTEEN
Caleb

"Yo, Caleb, come sit with us," Brian yells from the middle of the cafeteria.

I had planned on grabbing a sandwich and sitting next to my sister. Today she's wearing jet-black lipstick to match her black, faded jeans. Mom didn't even flinch when Leah walked down the stairs this morning. I shuddered at the sight. Whoever made up that black lip stuff has got some serious issues.

I'm standing next to her, contemplating what to do. She doesn't look up from reading a book and says, "Go sit with Brian. I don't care."

"Leah, come with me."

She looks up, black lipstick and all. "Do I look like I want to sit with them?"

That's it, I can't stand it anymore. I lean my hands on the cafeteria lunch table and say, "You might want to freak me out with all this black crap, but I'm not buying it. Now why don't you wipe that shit off your lips and cut the death act already. It's wearing thin on my nerves."

Instead of being grateful I'm being brutally honest, she abruptly picks up her books and runs out of the cafeteria.

What the hell am I supposed to do now?

Brian is still waving me over, but I hesitate.

It's not that I don't want to sit with my old friends; I just don't feel like being bombarded with questions about jail. Because these guys wouldn't last one day in the DOC and they'd probably think I was lying if I told them what really goes down in there.

Don't think for one minute that anyone is immune to being convicted. Man, there's so many guys of all different races and religions and colors and sizes. Jews and Christians, Muslims and Catholics. Rich kids who thought they were above the law and dirt-poor kids who didn't know any better.

It's a whole different ball game when you're on the inside, with an unspoken inmate hierarchy and rules. Some stuff you can figure out right off the bat and some things you have to learn the hard way.

Accidents happen at the DOC, and some of them are intentional. Gangs are rampant, even in the juvenile jail.

When there's an altercation between two rivals, you better get the hell out of the way.

Warden Miller has this thing about greeting a new inmate on their first day at the DOC. He thinks it eases the new kid's mind knowing his expectations, but all it does is scare the crap out of them. Unless, of course, they're repeaters. Miller is on a first-name basis with a lot of repeaters. They get a very different version of the welcome speech.

His first-timer speech goes something like this: *"My name is Scott Miller. Welcome to my house. You'll get up at five forty-five every morning and go to the showers. You get five minutes, no more, to wash up. You'll get three squares a day and you'll attend classes for eight hours. We'll get along just fine as long as you respect the rules in my house. If you don't . . . well, then you and I will have ourselves a problem. Ask anyone around, they'll tell you that you don't want a problem with me. My problems get twenty-three hours straight cell time. Any questions?"*

Warden Miller doesn't explain the absence of toilet paper in the cells; that's one of those things you have to find out the hard way. It's when you're sitting on the can and need to wipe. The call button to borrow a roll is on the other side of the cell, nowhere near the seat you're crapping in.

I head over to Brian and the guys, ready to distract them from talk about jail. "Wha's up, guys? Where are all the girls?" I ask.

Drew is sitting across from me and rolls his eyes.

"Practicing for cheerleader tryouts. Don't get me wrong, I love when the chicks jump up and down for me. I just don't know how it could be all that difficult that they'd need to practice for three weeks straight."

"Brianne and Danielle are going out for cheerleading instead of tennis?" I ask. Brianne and Danielle were die-hard tennis fanatics.

"It's because of Sabrina," Tristan says. "She doesn't have enough hand-eye coordination to be a tennis player, so she's convinced Brianne and Danielle to try out for the Pantherettes."

Maybe I've been gone too long. Or maybe I didn't hear correctly. "What's a Pantherette?"

"Caleb, you got to get up to speed, man." Brian is trying to control his amusement as he says, "Pantherettes are the cheerleaders for the wrestling team. Get it . . . Paradise Panthers . . . Panther*ettes*."

Huh? "Wrestling cheerleaders?"

Drew nods. "Pantherettes, dude. Gotta love 'em. Lots of schools have wrestling cheerleaders, so last year we got 'em, too."

"You wrestling this year, Becker?" Tristan chimes in. "It might be Wenner's last year coachin'. He's got a kid due in the summer, and I think he wants to keep his Saturdays open to stay home with the brat."

"I can't," I say. "I've got to work after school." I intentionally leave out the part that work is actually community service and if I ditch it, I may have to go back to jail.

Brian takes a bite of his sandwich and says with a full mouth, "We need you, or we'll suck like last year."

Tristan and Drew nod their heads, agreeing with Brian. Nothing like peer pressure to make one give in. But the truth is I missed these guys. "Okay, listen," I say. "If there's a match I can make, I'll compete."

Brian holds up a hand for me to give him a high-five. "That's what I'm talkin' 'bout."

I slap his hand. "You're seriously pathetic if you think I can single-handedly make a difference."

Drew shakes his curly-haired head. "You pinned *Vic Medonia*, Caleb. The guy is huge and a legend. Remember when you kicked his ass, getting that five point throwdown ten seconds before the round ended?"

"Drew, please," Tristan says. "Don't disrespect CB here. It was four minutes when he did the throw-down."

"Whatever, Tristan," Drew says, "I forgot you know everything."

Tristan crosses his arms in front of his chest. "Damn straight."

I take a bite of my sandwich while Tristan and Drew are at each other's throats. It's just like old times, except Kendra's not here . . . and my sister refuses to join the land of the living.

Before that thought leaves my head, the girls minus my sister strut into the cafeteria. Sabrina, Danielle, and Brianne come in first, followed by Kendra and her best friend Hannah.

"How'd practice go?" Tristan asks Brianne.

Brianne reaches out and touches his shoulder. "That is so sweet that you care," she says.

Drew coughs. "Why don't you guys do a cheer for us?"

"Right here in the cafeteria?"

"Why not?"

Kendra winks privately at me, then says, "Sure, let's do it, girls."

Kendra stands up front while Brianne, Sabrina, Danielle, and Hannah settle into a pattern behind her. Kendra gets her hands up as if she's about to clap and says, "Ready?"

The other girls respond, "O-kay," then they all start clapping and jumping and chanting:

> *Takedown, tilt 'em,*
> *Or go for the pin!*
> *Stay off the bottom,*
> *And get that win!*
> *You gotta ride 'em, roll 'em, get that pin!*
> *Come on Panthers, leeeeettt's win!*

The girls end their overly energetic cheer on a jump/kick combination.

Drew stands up and claps. "That was *in*-credible! Can you do that end part again where you bounce up and down and talk about riding them?"

"Shut up, Drew," Kendra says.

He holds up his hands and shrugs. "What? I was just admiring the cheer."

"Please," Danielle says as she sits down next to Brian and gives Drew a disgusted look. "You were admiring something, all right. Our chests."

"That, too," Drew admits. "I'm a teenage guy with raging hormones, what do you expect? I bet Caleb admired them, too, 'cause he hasn't seen any in almost a year. Isn't that right, CB?"

I should have known it was just a matter of time before my jail time got thrown in my face. Great, now everyone is looking at me, waiting to hear the ex-con's response. Including Kendra. I stand up and walk out of the cafeteria. I don't want to deal with this crap right now.

"I was just kidding, Caleb. Come back here!" Drew yells.

Every week in the DOC we had rage-intervention classes. They stressed avoiding confrontation, teaching us instead to release anger in other, non-violent ways. Since punching Drew in his mouth that runs like diarrhea isn't an option, I head to the school workout room.

I walk right up to the punching bag and whack it until there's a permanent dent in the side. I don't even care that my knuckles are bleeding.

"Caleb, take it easy on that thing."

It's Coach Wenner, standing near the free weights with a cup of coffee in his hand. He's wearing a golf shirt with *Panther Wrestling* embroidered on the front.

I stop punching the bag and stuff my hands in my pockets to hide my bleeding knuckles. "They tell me this is your last year coaching."

"Yep. I'll be teaching drivers' ed as well as gym classes come next fall."

I shake my head in disbelief. "Drivers' ed?" The guy lives and breathes wrestling.

"The wife doesn't want me to be away on the weekends after the baby is born. Above all else, you got to do what you think is best for your family. Right?"

"I guess."

Wenner takes a sip of the drink and leans against the wall. "You know, what happened last year shocked the hell out of me. I would have bet my right arm a kid like you wouldn't leave the scene of an accident."

"Lucky for you, you didn't make that bet," I counter.

"Uh huh," Wenner says, then adds, "go to the nurse and get those knuckles wrapped," and casually walks out of the room.

SIXTEEN
Maggie

It took Caleb a week to slide right back into his life without a hitch. I left the cafeteria this afternoon when the popular girls did a cheer right in front of him. I could have sworn he thought the cheer was just for him.

As if that wasn't bad enough, I heard Tristan Norris say in earth science that Caleb is going out for wrestling this year.

Not only did I lose Leah as a friend and everyone else thinks I'm a walking freak, I have no hope of joining the tennis team or playing sports ever again.

I'm chastising myself for comparing myself to Caleb as I ride the bus to Hampton for my first day working for Mrs. Reynolds. I just wish it was easier for me . . . or less easy for him. I realize I'm bitter, but I can't help it. I've been through such pain and agony the past year, and going back to school has only emphasized what an outcast I've become.

I reach Mrs. Reynolds' house and ring the doorbell. She doesn't answer. I keep ringing, hoping nothing bad has happened to her. Just my luck she decided to fire me before I even started the job.

Placing my book bag on the ground, I head to the back of the house.

Mrs. Reynolds is sitting on the porch swing. Her head is slumped over, but her chest is rising and falling with each breath. Okay, the woman is sleeping. Phew. Balancing in her hand is a glass of lemonade.

This job is going to be a piece of cake. I feel ashamed for taking so much money from Mrs. Reynolds for doing nothing.

I tiptoe toward the swing. I have to take the glass out of Mrs. Reynolds' hand before it spills all over or, worse yet, shatters when her grip loosens and the glass hits the ground.

Slowly, silently, I reach out and slip the glass out of her hand.

"What do you think you're doing?"

The old lady's voice startles me and I jump back. Mrs. Reynolds has one eye open like that guy from the cartoon monster movie. "I, uh, thought you were napping."

"Do I look like I'm napping?"

"Right now you don't."

Mrs. Reynolds sits up straight, her grey hair perfectly styled on top of her head. "Enough chatter. We have lots of work to do today."

"Do you want me to refill your lemonade? Make you a snack?" *Fluff your pillows?*

"Nope. You see those bags over there?" Mrs. Reynolds says, her crooked finger pointing to the side of the yard.

About ten huge paper bags are lined up in the grass. They're all labeled with strange names: Apricot Whirl, Chromacolor, Decoy, Drift, Yellow Trumpet, Lemon Drops, Rosy Cloud. "What are they for?"

"We're going to plant them. They're daffodils. Well, they don't exactly look like daffodils right now. They're only bulbs."

Plant? I peer inside the bag marked "Drift." There must be more than thirty bulbs in it. I limp over to the next bag, "Lemon Drops," and there's more in this one than the first.

"Don't look so startled, Margaret," Mrs. Reynolds says. "It doesn't suit your face."

I grab a few bulbs from the next bag, the one marked "Audubon." Behind me Mrs. Reynolds says, "Don't even bother picking them up right away. You need a plan first."

"A plan?"

"Of course. Have you ever planted before?"

"Just some herbs in preschool. But that was in a little planter we took home for Mother's Day."

"No bulbs?"

I shake my head.

Mrs. Reynolds looks worried. "Let me tell you something about daffodils, Margaret. They're fragrant, beautiful, and hardy."

I scan the eight bags lined up. "These are *all* daffodils?"

"Oh, yes. But they each have their own unique scent and personality."

Wow. I don't know much about flowers in general, let alone details. My favorites were dandelions, because when we were younger, Leah and I used to search and pull all the dandelions from our neighbors' lawns, sing *Mama had a baby and her head popped off,* and flick the tops of the flowers off of the stems as we sang the word *popped*. Although, to be technical, dandelions aren't flowers. They're weeds.

"You'll need a shovel to start with," my employer says, interrupting my daydream. "I think there's one in the garage."

I place the bulbs back in their respective bags, then head for the detached garage in the back of the yard. It's a large, two-story structure. Yellow paint, though cracking and peeling from years of neglect, indicates this had once been a place of pride. There are stairs on the side, leading to the second level. Dirty, dusty windows outline the upstairs room. Is it an office of some sort? A private room?

The garage door is closed, so I have to lift it using my own strength, which isn't easy. With a loud creak of protest, the door finally lifts to reveal a large, black Cadillac parked inside. The place is dark and full of spider webs. Which means the place is full of spiders.

I'm not fond of either.

Maggie, you can do this. As I venture farther into the darkness, my eyes do the spider-scan. My mom used to make fun of me that I had peripheral vision specially designed to detect eight-legged creatures.

A shovel hangs on the wall, not far from the entrance. Good. I slowly inch forward, reaching out to grab the handle. Once I hold it, I let out a breath I didn't even know I'd been holding. I scurry out of the garage and head back to Mrs. Reynolds, sure at least a few webs have managed to stick to me.

"I got it," I say, holding out the shovel like a prized trophy.

The woman doesn't look impressed. "First, we'll have to prepare the soil."

I walk over to the empty flower beds and start poking the shovel into the dirt to loosen it. I do this for a few minutes. It's not so bad.

Mrs. Reynolds sneaks up behind me. "Wait."

I turn around. The woman is holding out a long, pink and green flower-print robe.

"What is *that*?" I ask.

"My muumuu. Put it on. It'll keep your clothes clean."

"Mrs. Reynolds, I can't wear that."

"Why not?"

Mrs. Reynolds clutches the muumuu, a big, ugly

housedress. I'm self-conscious enough as it is without wearing something my great-aunt Henrietta probably has in her closet.

"It's . . . it's not my size," I say lamely.

"Don't be a ninny, muumuus fit everyone. One size fits all. Put it on."

Reluctantly, I take the muumuu and slide the material over my head. The dress hangs on me like a tent.

Mrs. Reynolds steps back and surveys me. "Perfect."

I smile weakly at her.

"Okay, let's get to work."

For the next forty minutes Mrs. Reynolds directs me on how big to dig the holes, how to measure the extra soil needed in the bottom of the holes to create a pillow for the bulbs, and the best way to plant the bulbs—not in rows but scattered five inches apart.

I'm sweating now, and I fear Mrs. Reynolds is just getting started. But I'll do anything to keep this job. If it means creating pillows for her precious bulbs for the next few weeks until colder weather bears down on us, that's just fine. I can handle anything if the end result is earning the money to get away.

Sitting back, I wipe the dirt from my face with the sleeve of the muumuu. "What's over there?" I ask, pointing to a pile of lumber.

"The gazebo that never happened."

"I was in a gazebo at the Botanic Gardens last year," I say, imagining a huge gazebo in the middle of the yard.

"It reminded me of that scene in *The Sound of Music* where Liesl's boyfriend sings 'Sixteen Going on Seventeen' to her."

Mrs. Reynolds looks longingly at the pile. "Yes, well, I'm afraid the wood will probably be sitting there long after I'm dead and buried."

"You should totally get someone to build it," I tell her excitedly. "I can imagine it, with a pointed roof and all."

"Let's take a break," she says. "No more talk about gazebos that will never be."

Oh, yeah, I forgot. No senseless chatter for Mrs. Reynolds.

Since the accident, trying to stand hasn't been easy. Being covered in a muumuu makes it that much harder. Especially when I have to extend my leg in front of me to get up.

"What're you doing?"

"Getting up."

Mrs. Reynolds waves her hands around as if her limbs can talk. "Usually people bend their legs when they do that."

"I can't bend my leg."

"Who says?"

I turn and look straight at Mrs. Reynolds. Is she kidding? Obviously I'm crippled. Okay, so not crippled. But I got hit by a car. I'll never be the same again.

"You bend your leg when you walk. Don't know why you can't bend it when you stand, that's all," she says.

I finally stand, then take a deep breath. I'm itching to say something, but can't. Mrs. Reynolds is the first person in over a year that treats me as though nothing is wrong with me. It's refreshing and frustrating at the same time.

SEVENTEEN
Caleb

Mom knocks on my door on Saturday night before she leaves for the annual Fall Festival.

"Are you sure you don't want to go, Caleb? It'll be fun."

Yeah, right. "I'm sure."

"Leah's coming, too."

How the hell did Mom manage that? Leah lives in her room as if she's a bear in perpetual hibernation. I think I've seen her more in the halls at school than I have at home. "I'm gonna stay home and hang out," I say. There's no way I want to go to the fair and be one of the main attractions.

Mom opens the door and peeks her head inside. "Your father and I would like you to make an appearance. Dr. and Mrs. Tremont are going to be there. Your dad relies on his referrals. Put on one of the new outfits I bought and show off the clean-cut person you are."

I don't feel like dressing up in clothes that make me choke, and putting on another fake "happy" show. "Is that what you really want?"

She nods. "I do."

"Fine, I'll meet you there later," I say curtly. This bullshit is wearing me down fast.

"Thanks, Caleb. I appreciate it," she says, as if she's talking to a colleague.

Who is this lady who I used to call Mom? I need to make her realize I'm the same person as before. She can love the old Caleb Becker without trying to create a new and improved one.

After my parents and Leah leave, I head outside and make myself some chicken on the grill. I'm gonna eat here in my comfortable, ripped jeans and t-shirt before I dress up like a banker and head to the fairgrounds.

I'm sitting at the patio table when I hear a familiar voice.

"I thought I might find you out here."

I turn to my ex-girlfriend. Kendra looks great, dressed in a tight, pink shirt and short, white skirt. No trace of conservativeness in her attire, that's for sure.

"You're not going to the fair?" I ask.

She comes up real close to me and bends down. "I went, but you weren't there," she says in a sexy whisper.

"Did you want me to be?"

"No, because I want you all to myself. You're a legend in Paradise. Everybody's clamoring for a glimpse of the mysterious and dangerous Caleb Becker."

"Is that what they think, that I'm dangerous?"

"I'm just reporting the rumor. You *were* in jail, you know. I heard a lot of things happened to you when you were there to make you change."

"And what do you think?" I ask, confused by her motives for coming here. "Do you think I'm dangerous?"

"Absolutely." She's looking straight at me, but I sense she's thinking about something else. "Was it really as tough as they say?"

"Sometimes."

She twirls her blond curls around her finger. "Did you think about me?"

"Just about every day," I admit. "What about you?"

She smiles. "I missed you. But I couldn't handle what happened."

"Don't sweat it, Kend. That night was totally fucked up."

"You're telling me."

I look at her sideways. I've been dying to know the answer to this question. "Do you remember what happened?"

She blinks twice before answering. "Not much. I was almost as plastered as you were and ran when the cops came. My dad *is* the mayor, you know. His daughter couldn't be caught in the middle of that whole messy scene."

"Uh huh."

"I didn't expect you'd go to jail, Caleb. I just . . . it freaked me out."

"Freaked me out, too. But I'm back now."

"You sure are."

My ego needs me to ask this next question. It's strange, but this discussion is our way of figuring out where each of us stand in thie relationship. "Have you been with anyone else?"

"Not anyone that matters."

What the hell does that mean? I'm not jealous. Okay, I am. *But she's here with you now,* a voice inside my head tells me.

And I missed her so much. Too much. I've dreamt about kissing her again, those full lips on mine, rubbing against her until I think I'll die from the sheer pleasure of it.

"Come here," I say, moving my chair out so she can sit on my lap. My libido kicks into gear, ready for this immediately. "It's been a long time, Kend, but I'm game if you are."

She settles herself on my thighs and wraps her arms around my neck. I watch her lips with interest as she smiles at me. Wet, shiny lips from whatever she put on them before she came over.

Whoever made *that* glossy lip shit up is a genius.

I take the curled ends of her golden hair between my fingers and twist them between my thumb and forefinger. Her hair feels different than I remember. It used to be softer. I always loved playing with it. "You changed the color," I say.

"It's lighter. Do you like it?"

What can I say, that it feels more like straw than silk? "I need time to get used to it."

I know I should have kissed her by now, but I'm hesitating. I've kissed Kendra a thousand times before. She's an awesome kisser, and those lips are begging to be messed with. So what's my problem?

She feels the top of my buzz cut with her palm. "I hope you'll grow out your hair. I can't grab onto it now."

"We'll see."

"So noncommittal, aren't you." She laughs, then says, "I missed you, CB."

If she missed me so much, why do I have this strange feeling she's holding something back? Shit, I've got to stop playing mind games with myself and overanalyzing stuff. I know what'll make me stop thinking.

I put my hand on the back of Kendra's head and guide her mouth toward mine. As my lips touch hers, the scent of cherries from the glossy stuff is overpowering.

In a bad way.

My lips and tongue slide against hers, but all I can think about is that I hate cherries. I hate cherry pie, I hate cherries in my fruit cocktail or on top of a hot fudge sundae. I even hate Cherry Coke.

Kendra moans while our mouths are still meshed. Her tongue is working overtime and she twists her body so she's straddling me.

I open my eyes while we're kissing. My gaze focuses on Maggie Armstrong's room. Now not only do I have cherry lips attached to mine, I'm hoping Maggie Armstrong doesn't see me lip-locked and tongue-tied with Kendra.

Don't even ask me why I care.

I pull back and say, "Let's go inside."

Kendra slides off my lap, and we hold hands as I lead her to my bedroom. I wipe off my lips with the back of my hand, hoping the cherry flavor will disappear.

Kendra lies on my bed when we reach my room, not even hesitating or questioning why we're moving so fast after not being together for a year. "It's just like old times," she says.

Except somehow it doesn't feel as exciting or daring as it used to. Maybe it's because we're older now.

I take my shirt off, then slip into bed next to her. She starts kissing my chest. "Jeez, Caleb. Your pecs are huge."

With my forefinger I lightly wiggle her new, shiny bellybutton ring. "I guess we both changed, huh?"

"Let me investigate how much." She kisses her way down, past my chest and stops at the waistband of my jeans.

When she starts unbuttoning them, I put my hand over hers to stop her.

She looks up at me, confused. I don't blame her. I'm all screwed up in the head and need to take everything slower than before. I swear, a year ago I'd be jumping her bones before we even reached my room.

"What's wrong?" she says.

I shake my head, rub my hand over my hair, and take a deep breath. Fuck. I'm screwing everything up.

She rests her head on my shoulder and places her arm across my stomach. It feels real good and I'm glad she doesn't make me talk about it. Maybe she gets it, maybe she understands I can't verbalize my fucked-up thoughts. But then she starts getting restless after a few minutes and sits up. "I should probably go back to the festival before my parents find out where I've gone."

In the end she doesn't understand. Just like everyone else.

With a flip of her hair over her shoulders, she slips her shoes back on and stands up.

I convince myself things will get back to normal soon enough. I'm back home, I have my girl again. Okay, I'll admit things are strange between us. Her hair is fake, her lips taste different, and her kisses are frantic instead of sexy.

"I saw you talking to Samantha Hunter in the hall yesterday," she says, turning back and looking at me.

I sit up and lean against my headboard, still shirtless. "Yeah, she wanted to know if I'll wrestle this year."

Kendra blows out an annoyed breath. "You don't think she's cute, do you?"

I shrug. "She's all right, I guess."

"Because girls like that are totally manipulative."

"I'm not lookin' at other girls, Kend, if that's what you're worried about."

"That's good." The corners of her mouth turn up, but then she bites down on her lower lip. "I'm glad you're back, but . . ."

"But what?" I ask.

"Can we keep this thing between us a secret, Caleb? The kids at school are expecting a big show between you and me, and I don't want it to get weird. Besides, my dad is up for election in November and he's already forbidden me to have any contact with you. It'll be best if nobody knows about this right now."

Her comments shouldn't surprise me, but they do. I just say, "That's cool," because, well, what else can I say?

Following Kendra out to her car, I wonder what our lives would have been like if I hadn't been locked up. I wouldn't have to keep our relationship a damn secret, that's for sure.

When we're in the front yard, Kendra climbs into her car. Then she opens her purse and pulls out a tube of lip gloss. Twisting the rearview mirror, she carefully glides on more cherry gloss, essentially erasing away our power make-out session. When her lips are as glossy as when she came here, she drives off.

Shaking my head, I head back inside. I spot the picture of Kendra when I get to my room. Removing it from my headboard, I stare at it.

It's hard keeping everything the same when the same things look and feel so different.

EIGHTEEN
Maggie

I'm wearing a long print dress that touches the ground and a powder blue sweater over it. Mom bought me the dress because she knows how I feel about exposing any part of my left leg. Deep down I know she also hopes boys will see me as Maggie Armstrong and not as *the girl who got hit by Caleb Becker*. Guess what, it's not going to happen.

I didn't have the heart to tell her a pretty dress can't erase the ugly scars hiding underneath.

We head over to the Paradise County Fairgrounds. They've transformed the fairgrounds into an amusement park, complete with a Ferris wheel and dunking booth.

The Ladies' Auxiliary sponsors the festival each year. Usually the entire town attends.

The food pavilion is covered in twinkling lights, reminding me of Christmas.

Mom puts down the brownies she made on the pot-luck table, then scans the crowd. "Look, there's Lou," she says, pointing.

Sitting next to him is his mother, *my* boss. "Should we go say hi?" I ask.

Mom shrugs. "It would be nice."

When we reach the table, Mr. Reynolds stands up and smiles. "Linda, glad you made it. Hi, Maggie."

"Hi, Mr. Reynolds. Hi, Mrs. Reynolds."

Mr. Reynolds leans close and whispers in my ear, "We're not at the diner. You can call me Lou."

"That'd be weird," I say. Calling Mom's boss by his first name is just too . . . I don't know . . . familiar.

"Okay, well, when you don't feel weird about it give it a try."

Mom sits next to her boss and I walk around the table and plop down next to Mrs. Reynolds.

"Mrs. Reynolds, it was so generous of you to give my daughter a job," Mom says. "As I told you on the phone, I'm very grateful."

"I'm the grateful one," Mrs. Reynolds says. "We've had a productive first week. Haven't we, Margaret?"

My fingernails still have dirt under them that I haven't

been able to scrape out. "Mrs. Reynolds is an expert on daffodils, Mom."

"When you get back from Spain they'll be up and blooming," Mrs. Reynolds says.

I smile, thinking about leaving for Spain. It's about the only thing making me smile lately.

Mrs. Reynolds looks longingly at the buffet table. "I'm famished," she says. "How about we take a gander at the food and see if there's anything worthwhile."

"Mom, don't stuff yourself," Mr. Reynolds says over the loud dance music the band just started to play on the makeshift stage in front of the Fun House.

Mrs. Reynolds rolls her eyes. "My son thinks I'm a child."

"Mom, you know what the—" Mr. Reynolds' gruff voice chimes in.

Mrs. Reynolds silences her son with a single stare. Mom looks kind of nervous and I feel the same way. I don't want to get involved in this. It's clearly out of my jurisdiction as companion.

Mr. Reynolds turns to my mom. "Linda, how about showing the teens some old dance moves?"

Wow, that came out of left field. Mom never dances. She and my dad would come to the festival year after year and I never once saw them sway to the music, let alone dance.

"I'd love to," Mom says. "Maggie, you don't mind, do you?"

When I shake my head, she takes Mr. Reynolds' outstretched hand and he leads her away from the food pavilion.

I'm sitting here with my eyes wide open. What just happened? Did my mom accept a dance with her boss?

Isn't that illegal?

I can see the dance floor from where I'm sitting. Right away, Mom is wiggling her body and moving around like a teenager. I scan the fairgrounds to see if anyone else is paying attention. Sure enough, a group of kids from school are watching her.

I want to die.

Why would Mom want to dance in the first place? She's making a spectacle of herself, jumping around as if she doesn't care people are staring. Isn't it bad enough people stare at me?

"Margaret, I'm ready to load up my plate now that my son who thinks he's a doctor is out of my hair. Will you help me?"

I tear my gaze away from the dancing queen. "Uh, yeah, sure."

Mrs. Reynolds leans on her cane as we head to the food line. I hold her plate and pile food on as she points to various dishes. The old lady is totally oblivious to the scene on the dance floor.

"What do you keep staring at?" Mrs. Reynolds asks.

"Nothing."

"That nothing's getting a lot of attention."

I make a harrumph and move down the line. But when I get to Mrs. Becker's famous Spaghetti Spectacular, I freeze and wonder if Leah and Caleb are here.

"This one looks good," Mrs. Reynolds says, referring to the spaghetti dish.

"It tastes good, too," I admit. "But can you eat it? Mr. Reynolds said—"

"Margaret, I'm an old lady who enjoys her food. If I can't eat what I want, you might as well bury me six feet under right here and now."

"Okaay," I say warily. "If you insist." I place a small spoonful on Mrs. Reynolds' plate, but she raises her eyebrows and urges me to heap on another spoonful. When we get to the end of the buffet line, I'm afraid to take another glance at the dance floor.

It's like a car wreck. You know what you're going to see is bad, but you can't help it. I wonder if that's how people felt when they saw me lying on the ground after the accident.

Okay, so I'm just like everyone else. I check out the dance floor and, thankfully, my mom is nowhere to be found. But I do see Kendra Greene. She's slow dancing with Brian Newcomb as if he were the love of her life.

My dream is to find a guy who'll love me despite my flaws and won't turn away from me when a perfect girl walks by. Maybe a boy like that doesn't even exist.

I'm sitting at the table watching Mrs. Reynolds eat. I have no clue how she packs it all in for such a small woman. She takes a small bite of the Spaghetti Spectacular and gives me a nod. "It's like a burst of flavor and different textures making it taste . . ."

"Spectacular?" I say.

"Quite," she agrees, and we both laugh.

Mom comes sidling over to the table. Was that a shimmy I just saw her do as she sat down?

"What's so funny?" Mom asks.

"The spaghetti dish," Mrs. Reynolds says. "It *is* spectacular."

There's silence now, because Mom immediately knows we're talking about Mrs. Becker's award-winning specialty.

Mr. Reynolds is sweating and takes a sip of water. "Is something wrong?"

Mom shakes her head.

The band guy is yelling for the over-twenty-one crowd to get on the dance floor. Parents flock to the middle of the floor, ready to show off their moves.

I watch the other kids in my grade running around and enjoying themselves. Brian and Kendra enter the Fun House. Drew Rudolph is trying to coax Brianne onto the Tilt-A-Whirl. My cousin Sabrina is sitting next to her sister on the Ferris wheel.

"Go on," Mrs. Reynolds says. "Join your friends."

"I don't have friends," I admit. "I'm what you call a loser. Or a loner. Take your pick."

"Pshaw."

"Huh?"

"Pshaw. Hogwash. You're a smart, pretty young lady. Girls like you are not losers. Or loners."

"I'm not pretty, that's for sure. And I limp."

She looks me up and down. "You may lack fashion

sense, but you have fine features when you're not pouting or looking startled. And the limp . . . as long as it doesn't bother you, it shouldn't matter what people think."

I believe I have that startled look on my face right now.

"And what's this nonsense about you not having any friends? Everyone should have at least one friend."

I glance around and spot Leah Becker, sitting alone at one of the tables. Her parents are in a deep conversation with another couple a few feet away. I would walk up to her, but she'd probably ignore me.

Mrs. Reynolds puts her hand on mine. "Is she a friend?"

"Used to be."

"Go talk to her."

"I wouldn't even know what to say."

Mrs. Reynolds lets out a frustrated breath. "Suit yourself, child. But when you're an old bird like me you'll be wishing you had more friends in your life. Being alone isn't fun, is it?"

"No. Being alone isn't fun."

I look over at my mom, who is now line dancing. She doesn't look alone. In fact, she hasn't looked this happy for a long time. Mom smiles at Mr. Reynolds and he smiles back.

Mr. Reynolds. Lou. My mom's boss. My boss' son. Well, whatever his name is, it's clear to me he has the hots for my mom.

I don't know if I should be embarrassed, angry, or happy for her.

NINETEEN

Caleb

My pants are too fucking tight and this shirt has so much starch in it I feel like a mannequin. But I'm here, at the Fall Festival. Once I'm done acting like the model son, I'm outta here.

I spot my parents by the food pavilion, talking with another couple. Nothing has changed since I've been back. My sister is still a zombie, but it's worse now, because since she ran out of the lunchroom Monday, she's ignored me. My parents haven't brought up the accident since I've been back. I tried to talk about it, but I've been shut down.

When I walk up to my parents, my mom smiles. "We were waiting for you, Caleb."

"Well, I'm here," I say unenthusiastically, not in the least ready to put on this show.

My dad looks tired; there are circles under his eyes and he's not walking as tall and straight as I remember. "Caleb, do you remember Dr. and Mrs. Tremont? Dr. Tremont owns a dental practice in Denton, and just opened one up in Paradise now that Dr. Kryzanowich retired."

"Really?"

Dr. Tremont points to the east. "Over by Central and Carriagedale Roads. You know, the new building next to the Paradise cinemas."

I shake my head. "I haven't seen it yet."

"Where have you been hiding out?" Dr. Tremont says, laughing. "It's the building with the big tooth out front."

My dad is turning red under his collar. "I'm starving," he says before I tell Dr. Tremont that I haven't seen his big toothed building because I've been locked up in jail for the past year. "Why don't you taste some of my wife's dish while Caleb *finds his friends.*"

Mom does a really good job of directing the Tremonts to the buffet table and away from me. Do you think Mom realizes it wasn't the best idea to try and pretend like I'm a perfect son? My sister joins them, totally ignoring me.

The Fall Festival is a zoo. It's hard to believe Paradise is a small town when there are so many people around. Brian and the guys are hanging out near the parking lot.

"Wow, Caleb, who dressed you?" Brian quips, shaking his head in disbelief.

I grimace. "Would you believe it if I told you my mother did?"

Brian nods. "Yeah. Paradise wasn't the same without you, man. But those clothes have *got* to go."

Drew chuckles while he lights a cigarette. "You're right, Brian. Paradise isn't the same. I saw Mrs. Armstrong dancing with that guy from the diner. They looked pretty tight. Do you think they're . . . you, know? God knows Maggie's not gettin' any. That girl needs a bunch more surgeries before she'll attract any dude. Maybe she could get a prom date over the internet."

Nobody laughs, because Drew is not funny. He's been a jerk ever since I came back, trying his best to piss me off on purpose.

Tristan throws a football in the air. "We're heading over to the field to play ball. Let's go before our moms try to make us dance with them."

I take off the ridiculous shirt while I play, but my balls are being strangled by the pants I'm wearing. After forty-five minutes, we head back. But when Tristan and Brian are ahead of us, I grab Drew by the shoulder and push him back into a tree. I take him completely off guard. He has no clue I'm tempted to kick his ass. One thing I learned at the DOC from the inmates . . . take them when they least expect it.

"Here's the deal," I say low and harsh as I grab his shirt and twist it up close to his throat. "You stop bringing up Maggie or jail or the accident. Got it? If you want to keep running your mouth off, that's fine, but next time you do it you'll find my fist in it. Guaranteed."

"I was just kidding," Drew chokes out, a faint thread of hysteria in his voice. "Jeez, Caleb, lighten up."

I let go of his shirt, but give him one last warning. "Up until two weeks ago I was living with a bunch of gang members. Don't tell me to lighten up."

———

It's Thursday night, five days after the festival. I'm in Kendra's bedroom while her parents are at some dinner function. We're supposed to study; we've both got tests tomorrow.

Unfortunately, I realized about a half hour ago she's not interested in studying. Kendra is strutting in front of me, modeling different outfits she bought at the mall yesterday. "Well . . ." she says, showing off a designer dress. "What do you think?"

I'm busy reading about the *Magna Carta*. "I can't flunk this test, Kend."

She puts her hands on her hips and pouts. "I swear you pay more attention to the girls at school than you do to me."

I look up from my book. "Are you kidding me?"

"No. Samantha Hunter is, like, lusting after you during gym class and you're falling for it. And I heard you and Emily Steinway were having a pretty intense conversation in biology."

"I haven't said two words to Samantha, Kend. And Emily and I are bio partners. What are you doing, spying on me? I'd be glad to tell everyone we're back together. You're the one who wants to keep our relationship a damn secret."

This week we've met at the forest preserve, under the high school bleachers, and now I had to enter her house through the back door so none of her neighbors would see me coming in. I'm sick of sneaking around.

"I told you my father is up for election in November, Caleb. His daughter can't be seen dating an ex-con."

She says it so easily. There's not a speck of apology or hesitation in her voice as she spurts out the word "ex-con." "I gotta go," I say, then close my history book.

She comes toward me, placing her hand on my chest. "Don't go. I'll make it worth your while."

"What are you talking about?"

She slowly pulls the spaghetti straps off her shoulder, revealing bare skin. A few seconds later she's stripped her dress off and is standing in front of me wearing only a black lace bra and matching thong.

My gaze travels over her creamy white skin. Hell, yeah, I want this. But she's not acting like a girlfriend. She doesn't have to strip to keep me here. She doesn't have to use her body to lure me. This is so fucked up. "Kendra . . ."

She steps toward me, putting her finger on my lips to stop me from talking. "Shh, I hear my parents in the hall-way," she whispers.

Shit.

Sure enough there's a knock on her bedroom door a

second later. "Kendra, you home?" her mom says through the door.

"Uh, yeah," Kendra says loudly as she picks up her discarded dress. "Caleb, get in the closet," she whispers.

This is seriously not happening. "I'm not getting in the closet," I say. There's no way I'm going to get locked up again, even in my girlfriend's closet instead of a cell.

"Shh, they're going to hear you."

Her mom knocks again and says, "Who are you talking to? Kendra, open the door."

Kendra scurries to get her dress back on. "Nobody, Mom, I just have the radio on. I'm getting dressed. I'll be out in a minute, okay?"

"Hurry up. Senator Boyle came all the way back here to meet you," her mom says, then I hear footsteps moving away from the door.

"When are you going to tell them we're together?" I ask Kendra. "After the election?"

"Can we talk about that later?" she whispers as she quickly checks out her appearance in her mirror. I watch as she rolls massive amounts of lip gloss on her lips. Cherry flavor wafts to my nostrils and I wonder how long I can be stuck in this cherry-scented room before I pass out.

I open the window.

"Caleb, what are you doing?"

I throw my history book to the ground below, praying it'll still be intact when I retrieve it. Then I heave one foot over the ledge. "Leaving."

"It's a two-story house. You'll kill yourself."

I'm not about to hide in her room like a prisoner. Besides, if I jump hard enough and high enough, I just might be able to catch a branch on the tree a few feet away from the window.

She runs toward me. "Don't, CB."

I stare right into her blue eyes. *Why, not? Because you love me, because you don't want me to get hurt . . . because you want to take me downstairs and announce to your parents and their friends that no matter what happened in the past, we're together and nobody can separate us?*

"I'll get into trouble if they see you," she announces.

"See you on the other side," I say to Kendra before standing on the window ledge, saying a quick prayer, and taking a leap.

TWENTY

Maggie

Mrs. Reynolds is waiting for me on the back swing with the muumuu in hand when I get to her house, just like she's done since my first day on the job. I tried protesting the offending garment with no success. So now I put it on and look like a complete dork as I'm working.

It's not like I need to worry about looking good, anyway. Caleb and his friends said the only way I'd even get a date for prom was to advertise on the internet. I heard them at the Fall Festival talking about me. I cried that night because I can't turn back the clock and erase what happened. Caleb stood there with the guys as if he had nothing to do with making me this way. His non-reaction hurt more than Drew's words.

"Today we're going to clean the attic," Mrs. Reynolds announces. "Here, take this broom. I'll bring the dustpan and pail."

"What about planting bulbs?" I ask.

"I'm sick of looking at bulbs. We can continue planting tomorrow."

She leads me up the stairway to the attic. "Don't close the door, it'll lock us in."

"That's dangerous," I say. And scary, like something out of a horror movie. There's a door stopper that she puts in place before we enter. It's a small, dark place filled with boxes and pictures and . . . spider webs. "Mrs. Reynolds?"

"Yes, Margaret."

"I'm afraid of spiders."

"Why?"

"Because they have eight creepy legs, they bite, and they have sticky string that comes out of their butts to capture bugs before they suck their blood."

I think Mrs. Reynolds is going to laugh at me. But she doesn't. Instead she says, "Spiders control the insect population. They're a necessity and that's all there is to it."

While that might be true, I still don't like them. But that doesn't stop Mrs. Reynolds from leading me farther into the attic—pail, dustpan and all. I'm ready to go into a rendition of "It's a Hard Knock Life." I look around. This attic is definitely creepy—large trunks in one corner and moving boxes in the other.

Mrs. Reynolds finds an old chair and sits in it. "You can start by dusting the trunks first."

Thank God those are in the middle of the floor, untouched by webs. The old lady is totally prepared. She pulls a rag and a can of Endust out of the pail. I spray the top of a wooden trunk, cleaning it until it shines.

"Open it," Mrs. Reynolds says.

I look at her, unsure.

"Go on."

I unhook the latch, lift the top, and peer inside.

The first thing I see is a framed picture of a man and woman. "Is this you?"

"Yes, with my late husband, Albert, may he rest in peace."

In the picture a much younger Mrs. Reynolds is wearing a knee-length tailored dress and satin gloves that go up over her elbows. Mr. Reynolds isn't even looking into the camera, he's gazing at Mrs. Reynolds as if she were a rare diamond. "Did you get married young?"

"I was twenty and he was twenty-four. We were very much in love."

I hand the picture to her. "I wish my parents loved each other. They're divorced."

"Yes, well, life does keep going on, doesn't it?"

"Yep." Even after the accident, when I knew I'd never

be able to walk normally again or play tennis anymore, life kept rolling on.

Whether I wanted it to or not.

Mrs. Reynolds leans over and studies more pictures. "I've spent a little time with your mother at Auntie Mae's," she says while studying a picture of a little boy. "She's a lovely lady."

"Thanks," I say, proud of Mom. She's cool, for a mom. I just wish my dad thought she was *lovely* enough to want to stay married to her.

Mrs. Reynolds hands me the picture of the little boy. "That's my son."

I almost laugh at the picture. Who thought this little boy would grow up and one day be my mom's boss?

"He was married once. She died of ovarian cancer five years later." She sighs.

"They didn't have any kids?" I ask.

She shakes her head. "Okay, enough dawdling. I have a bunch of boxes that need to be tossed. Why don't we pile them in a corner so they can easily be spotted and taken to the trash. Somewhere around here are boxes labeled 'taxes'." She points to one of the corners of the attic. "I think they're over there."

I walk over to the boxes and do the spider-scan. Eek. Webs line the ceiling corners, just waiting for an unsuspecting insect to fly by. I don't even see the spiders. It's like they're undercover spies until their prey struggles, hopelessly stuck in the web.

I shudder just thinking about it. Thank God I'm not an insect.

"Margaret?"

"Yes."

"I'm getting older every second, you know."

I put my hands in the sleeves of the muumuu and shove boxes aside with muumuu-covered fists. I'm trying not to think about my leg and how I'm going to maneuver around the boxes with spiders staring down at me from the ceiling.

I've made a path and head behind the stack of boxes. I check out an orange, plastic container made to look like a picnic basket. "What kind of boxes are they? Bankers boxes or moving boxes?" I ask.

"I don't remember, but I'm pretty certain they're labeled."

Okay. I start turning boxes around, hoping to find the words TAXES on the front.

I shriek when I hear something behind me.

Spinning around, I see it's only Mrs. Reynolds.

"Oh, calm yourself," she chides. "Did you find any?"

"I think so." I pick up a box marked *TAXES, 1968.* "Is this one?"

She claps her hands, like a teacher would do if a student gets an answer correct. "Yes. Put it by the door. There's so many to toss, I think this may take a few days."

As soon as I place the first box in the "toss" pile, the

doorbell rings. Mrs. Reynolds doesn't hear it. "Someone's ringing the doorbell," I say.

She furrows her brows and tilts her head to listen for it. "I don't hear it, but then again these ears are about as good as my eyes. Be a doll and answer it, would you?"

"Sure." I head down the stairs. The doorbell rings two more times before I can get to the door. I open it quickly, then stumble backwards. Because the last person I expected to see standing in front of me is Caleb Becker.

And, for the second time since he's been back, he reaches out to touch me.

TWENTY-ONE
Caleb

I swear, *my* leg almost just gave out on me. Because the last person I expected to answer the door to Mrs. Reynolds' house was Maggie Armstrong wearing a ridiculous, oversized dress with pink and green flowers plastered all over it.

I try and grab her arm when she loses her balance, but I'm too late. Once on the floor, she refuses my outstretched hand.

"Wh . . . What are you doing here?"

"What are *you* doing here?" I ask.

"I work here after school," she says while trying to pretend she's content to stay sprawled on the floor.

I quickly shove my Justice Department ID in my back

pocket. I double-check the address again before saying, "I'm here to see a Mrs. Reynolds. This *is* her house, isn't it?" Maggie's hatred is evident in her stare. "Listen, seeing you here is a surprise to me, too," I say. "The manager at The Trusty Nail sent me. This lady's house is the next job site on the list."

I watch as Maggie pulls herself up. It's painful, I can tell just by watching her fingers curl into a tight fist.

God, watching her struggle is making me sick to my stomach. Because I indirectly did this to her. "I'm sorry," I say.

"Tell it to the judge," she mumbles.

"I did," I respond truthfully. Not that it mattered to Judge Farkus. The guy wanted to make me an example for all delinquents who drank then got behind the wheel of a car. "What do you want from me, Maggie?"

"I want you to leave."

"I can't," I tell her.

An old lady appears from the back of the house and shuffles to the door. "You must be from the community service program," she says.

"Yes, ma'am." I introduce myself and hand her my community service ID for inspection. It's a requirement to show it before entering a house.

Mrs. Reynolds scans my ID, then hands it back. "Well, come on in. This here's Margaret, my companion. Margaret this is . . . what did you say your name was again?"

"Caleb."

Mrs. Reynolds tells Maggie, "Caleb is going to help us. Show him to the attic and explain our project while I check on some cookies I have baking in the oven."

I set my backpack on the ground after Mrs. Reynolds is out of sight. "Another awkward situation, huh?"

Maggie is as still as a statue.

"I wish you never came back," she says quietly, hugging herself.

I'm tempted to leave and face Damon's wrath for ditching community service, but I won't. I'm stuck here with her.

"I'm not going anywhere until I finish this job for the lady."

Maggie's eyes widen. Her mouth opens and closes, but no words come out. She turns around and walks farther into the house.

I silently follow her up a narrow staircase on the second floor to the attic.

Maggie points to a box. "That needs to be thrown out. I'll put boxes there and you can dispose of them."

I nod.

We work in silence. Maggie places the boxes in the discard pile and I carry them down the stairs. Mrs. Reynolds has me stuff the boxes in huge garbage bags and then lug them to the recycle bin at the end of the driveway.

Mrs. Reynolds comes out of the kitchen and hands me a plate of cookies. "Here, bring these up to the attic. You and Maggie can share them while you work."

I enter the attic for what seems like the hundredth time today with the cookies in hand. Maggie throws a box in my direction, but I move out of the way to avoid it. It was intentional, no doubt about it. "Watch it, will ya?" I drop the plate on a trunk in the middle of the attic.

She turns her back to me and ignores the plate.

Maggie thinks she's the only victim in this whole mess. But I have to keep my cool. No matter what happens, I can't let her get under my skin and let the truth come out.

"Listen, Maggie, it was an accident. If I could take back that day, I would. If I could turn back time, I would."

She turns to me now, her head tilted to the side. "Tell me, Caleb. Why does your apology sound so hollow to me?"

I stand, speechless, as she takes the plate of cookies and leaves the attic. Why can't this be easy? I pick up the next box and don't look up until all the boxes are trashed.

Maggie leaves Mrs. Reynolds' house first, but I stay behind. The old lady is in the backyard when I hand her the completion sheet and pen. "Thanks for letting me work here," I say.

"My husband, Albert, may he rest in peace, felt it important to help out the less fortunate. Don't get me started on the juvenile justice system or we'll be here for weeks. You did a good job today."

I flash her a smile of appreciation.

She starts to sign the form, but stops herself. "It says here you have experience in construction. You know . . . I may have another job for you. That is, if you're up to it."

"What kind of job?"

"How good are you with your hands?"

"Better than most," I say, then chuckle.

The old lady points to a tall pile of lumber stacked in the corner of the backyard. "Okay, Mr. Better-Than-Most. You think you could build me a gazebo out of this pile of old wood? You *do* know what a gazebo is, don't you?"

Yeah, I know what one is. Building a gazebo will take at least a couple of weeks, probably even fill up enough time to finish my community service.

What am I thinking? I can't work with Maggie. No way. It would never work.

Although it's not like I'd actually be working *with* her. I'll be on my own, building the gazebo. The way Mrs. Reynolds is looking at me with confidence strengthens my bruised ego. I'm not thinking about Maggie. I'm not thinking about what's right or wrong. I blurt out, "I can do it." I should be honest with the lady and tell her about why I was convicted. And, more importantly, who I was convicted of hitting. "Mrs. Reynolds, I have to be honest with you . . ."

As if on cue, the phone rings. The old lady takes her cane and hurries into the house. "Just come back tomorrow and we'll finish our conversation then."

So now I run to catch the bus because I'm late. When I get on, Maggie is sitting up front so I head for the rear.

The fifteen-minute bus ride seems like an hour. At our

stop, we're the only two left on the bus. We get off and I let her lead the way while I follow behind.

My sister is outside. The expression on her face when she sees Maggie and me walking up the street together is priceless.

"Did you just come home with Maggie?" Leah asks, following me into the house.

"We were on the same bus. Don't get all hyped up about it."

"Don't get all hyped up about what?" my mom says, coming into the room in the middle of a conversation I don't want her to know anything about.

"It's nothing," I tell Mom, then narrow my eyes at my sister and say through clenched teeth so only she can hear, "so stop making a big deal about it."

Leah runs up to her room and slams her door shut. My mom goes back into the kitchen, totally oblivious.

The Beckers are a picture-perfect family. A picture-perfect, royally-fucked-up family.

TWENTY-TWO

Maggie

On Monday I head for the bus after school. As I step into the aisle, I catch sight of Caleb already sitting in the back. It was bad enough working side by side in that small attic last week. If I have to work with him again I'll quit.

But then I won't be going to Spain.

And if I don't go to Spain, I won't be leaving Paradise next semester.

And if I don't leave Paradise next semester, Caleb and his friends will be laughing all the way to prom while I sit home and prove them right.

Maybe he's not going to Mrs. Reynolds' house today and I'm going off on unnecessary tangents for no reason.

Maybe he's working somewhere else doing odd jobs. But as he follows me into Mrs. Reynolds' backyard, my fears are realized.

"Now come inside, both of you. Irina brought over some pie." Mrs. Reynolds walks into the house, not realizing that neither me nor Caleb has followed her.

"Took you long enough," Mrs. Reynolds says when I enter the kitchen. "Here, I cut some pie for both of you."

I sit down at the kitchen table and stare at the pie. Normally I'd dig right in, but I can't. Caleb walks in and sits across from me. I focus my attention in the opposite direction, as if the painting of the fruit bowl on the wall is the most interesting object I've ever laid eyes on.

"Margaret, remember you told me I should have that gazebo built?"

"Yeah," I answer cautiously.

Mrs. Reynolds holds her chin up. "Well, Caleb is going to help make that a reality. It may take a few weeks, but—"

A few weeks? "If he stays, I quit," I blurt out. A few *weeks?*

I hear the clink of Caleb's fork hitting the plate, then he stands and storms out of the room.

Mrs. Reynolds puts her hands on either side of her face and says, "Margaret, what is all this nonsense about you quitting? Why?"

"I can't work with him, Mrs. Reynolds. He did this to me," I cry.

"Did what, child?"

"I went to jail for hitting Maggie with my car while I was drunk," Caleb says, reappearing in the doorway.

Mrs. Reynolds makes some tsking noises, then says, "My, my, we are in a pickle, aren't we?"

I look up at Mrs. Reynolds with pleading eyes. "Just make him leave."

I can tell she's going to do it, she's going to tell Caleb to get out.

Mrs. Reynolds walks up to Caleb and says, "You have to understand that my first priority is Margaret. I'll call the senior center and have them contact your community service officer."

"Please, Mrs. Reynolds," Caleb tells her, his voice pleading. "I just want to finish the job and just . . . be free again."

Mrs. Reynolds looks back at me, her wise eyes telling me more than words could say. *Forgive.*

I can't forgive. I've tried. If he'd innocently lost control of the car and hit me, it would have been forgivable. I don't know how innocent the accident was. God, I can't believe in my heart of hearts he deliberately hit me with the car. But too many questions have gone unanswered.

Questions I want to remain unanswered.

They said he left me lying in the street as if I were an animal. *That* is unforgivable. I don't know if I can ever get over it.

Because it reminds me too much of what my father

did. He left me without looking back. And worse, Caleb destroyed the one chance I had to impress my dad. I push my way past Caleb and head to the attic, a place that's dark, secluded, and private. I'm not even thinking about black widow spiders as I open the attic door and hobble inside.

Gosh, I used to worship the ground Caleb walked on. He was tall, handsome . . . clearly one of the populars, where Leah's and my status teetered on the edge. As if that wasn't enough, nothing ever bothered the guy. Maybe it's because guys like him always get what they want, they never have to work hard for anything. Maybe, deep down, I'm glad he's having a hard time. And deep down I know it's selfish for me to think this way. I shouldn't thrive on someone else's unhappiness.

But as the saying goes, misery likes company. And I feel miserable, inside and out. Isn't it fair that the person who's miserable with me is the guy who made me this way?

Mrs. Reynolds followed me, I can tell by the powdery scent that travels with her.

"This is a mighty interesting place to hide out. I thought you were afraid of spiders."

"I am, but in the dark I can't see them. Is he gone?" I ask hopefully.

She shakes her head. "We need to talk."

"Do I have to?"

"Let's just put it this way. You're not leaving the attic until you hear me out."

Defeated, I sit on one of the trunks. "I'm listening."

"Good." She takes a seat on the chair, still left here from the other day. "I had one sibling," she says. "A sister named Lottie. She was younger than me, smarter than me, prettier than me, with long, slender legs and thick, black hair."

Mrs. Reynolds looks up at me and continues. "You see, I was the fat kid with bright red hair, the kid you look at and have to stop yourself from cringing. During summer break from college one year, I brought a boy to my parents' summer home. I'd lost weight, I wasn't in my sister's shadow anymore, and I finally started feeling like I was worth more than I ever thought I deserved."

I can picture it in my mind. "So you overcame your fears and fell in love?"

"I fell in love, all right, head over heels. His name was Fred." Mrs. Reynolds pauses, then sighs. "He treated me as though I was the most amazing girl he'd ever seen. Well, he did until my sister came to the summer house for a surprise visit." She looks directly at me and shrugs. "I found him kissing her by the docks the morning after she arrived."

"Oh my God."

"I hated her, blamed her for stealing my boyfriend. So I packed up, left, and never talked to either one of them again."

"You never talked to your sister again?" I ask. "Ever?"

"I didn't even attend their wedding two years later."

My mouth drops open. "She married Fred?"

"You got it. Had four kids, too."

"Where are they now?"

"I got a call from one of their kids that Lottie died a few years ago. Fred's in a nursing home with Alzheimer's. You know what the worst part is?"

I'm riveted by her story. "What?"

Mrs. Reynolds stands, then pats me on my knee. "That, my dear, is what you're going to have to figure out all by yourself."

"You think Caleb should stay and build the gazebo, don't you?" I ask when she starts walking to the door.

"I'll leave that decision up to you. He won't go back to jail if it doesn't work out, I would never let that happen. I just figure he's a boy who wants to right his wrongs, Margaret. He's waiting downstairs for your answer."

She walks out of the attic. I hear her orthopedic shoes shuffling as she takes each stair. Can I just stay here forever, living with the spiders and cobwebs and antique trunks filled with an old lady's memories?

I know the answer, even as I stand and head down the stairs to face the one person I've been dying to avoid.

He's sitting on the couch in the living room, leaning forward with his elbows resting on his knees. When he hears me enter the room, he looks up. "Well?"

I can tell he's not happy I have the control. Caleb used to always have the cards and knew which ones to play to get his way. Not this time. I'd love to tell him to leave. That's his punishment for not loving me back. But I know that would be idiotic, childish, and stupid. Besides, I don't love Caleb anymore. I don't even like him. I'm convinced he can't hurt me anymore, physically or emotionally. "You can stay."

He nods and starts to stand.

"Wait. I have two conditions."

His eyebrows raise up.

"One, you don't tell anyone about us working together. Two, you don't talk to me . . . I ignore you and you ignore me."

I think he's going to argue because his lip curls up and his eyebrows furrow as if he thinks I'm an idiot.

But then he says, "Fine. Done deal," and heads to the backyard.

I find Mrs. Reynolds in the kitchen, sitting at the table drinking tea.

"I told him he could stay," I inform her.

Mrs. Reynolds gives me a small smile. "I'm proud of you."

"I'm not."

"You'll get over it," she says. "You ready to plant more bulbs today?"

I pull old, worn overalls out of my backpack so I can spare myself from having to wear the muumuu.

Caleb's back is to me when I walk outside. Good. I take a bag of bulbs and slowly, carefully sit on the grass. With a small shovel in hand, I start digging.

"Don't forget, Margaret. Six inches deep," Mrs. Reynolds says from behind, leaning over me to inspect my work.

"Got it, six inches."

"And make sure you place the bulbs right-side up."

"Okay," I say.

"And scatter them. Don't place them in a pattern or else it looks funny."

The old lady takes a lawn chair and places it right next to me so she can oversee my work.

"Why don't you supervise him?" I ask, pointing to where Caleb has taken panels of wood and seems to be attempting to put them in some kind of order.

"He's doing just fine. Besides, I don't know the first thing about building a gazebo."

I dig three holes, carefully make soft soil pillows for them, then place the bulbs into the holes and scoot myself down to plant more. After a while Mrs. Reynolds falls asleep in the chair. She usually does this at least once a day, and when I tell her she dozed off for an hour, she totally denies it. I'm surprised she can sleep with all the hammering Caleb's doing, but the lady hears, as she more often than not admits, like the dead.

I glance up at Caleb. He's a fast worker, already starting to nail planks together as if he builds gazebos every day. His shirt is soaking wet from sweat in his armpits, chest, and back. And it obviously doesn't bother him that one of my conditions is that we ignore each other. He does an incredible job of ignoring me. I don't think he's even glanced in my direction once.

But now he stops hammering, his back still to me when he yells, "Would you stop staring at me?"

TWENTY-THREE
Caleb

You ignore me, and I'll ignore you. Maggie, like every other girl in my life, is trying to control me. I'm sick of the games, I'm sick of feeling like a jerk. And most of all I'm sick of people gawking at me because I went to jail.

I know she's staring at me, I can feel her eyes on me like little pin pricks poking into my back. Out of frustration, I pound the next nail into the two-by-four harder than I normally would and whack my forefinger with the hammer.

I glare at Maggie.

The girl is sitting on the ground wearing torn and stained overalls. "I . . . I wasn't staring at you," she stutters.

"The hell you weren't," I bark back. I hold my arms

out wide. "You want to gawk at the ex-con, you got it. Just answer one thing for me, will ya? You like it when people stare at *you* when you limp around like you're gonna topple over any second?"

Maggie sucks in a breath, then covers her nose and mouth with her hand as she hobbles inside the house.

Oh crap.

My finger is throbbing, my head is pounding, and I insulted a crippled girl—a girl I'm responsible for crippling. I should just go to hell right now because the deal with the devil is probably signed anyway.

Mrs. Reynolds has no clue what's happening, her head is slumped in the chair and she's snoring.

I throw down the hammer and go into the house to find Maggie. I hear sniffling sounds coming from the kitchen. Maggie is standing at the counter, taking vegetables out of the refrigerator. She pulls out a cutting board and starts cutting them with a huge butcher knife.

"I'm sorry," I say. "I shouldn't have said that."

"It's fine."

"Obviously it's not or you wouldn't be crying."

"I'm not crying."

I lean my hip against the counter. "There's tears running down your face." Plain as day I can see 'em.

She picks up an onion and holds it out to me. "My eyes tear when I cut onions."

My fists clench together, because I can't shake her and

make her yell at me. This time I deserve to be yelled at. "Say something."

Instead of responding, she chops the onion in two. I imagine she's pretending that onion is my head . . . or some other part of my body.

"Fine, have it your way," I say, then leave her. If she wants to live in silence, that's her choice.

I clench my teeth so much they hurt, and the rest of the afternoon I work outside on the gazebo. It feels good to create something useful, something to finally make someone proud of me for a change. Because the rest of my life I've totally fucked up.

Maggie abandoned her post in the yard. She hasn't been outside since I went off on her.

At seven I inform a waking Mrs. Reynolds I'm leaving for the day and head for the bus stop. Maggie's not far behind.

I'm standing on the corner of Jarvis and Lake Streets, backpack flung over my shoulder, when a car screeches beside me.

"What are you doing slumming on this side of town, rich boy?"

Oh, man. It's Vic Medonia. And some other guys on the Fremont High wrestling team.

"None of your fucking business," I say.

Vic laughs, bitterness dripping off the cackling sound. "Your friends in jail taught you how to stand on the street corner and pimp yourself? How much you charging for that used booty of yours, anyway?"

The other guys in the car laugh, then Vic gets out. He looks to my right and says, "Is this your new girlfriend?"

I turn to see Maggie not far away, limping toward us as she heads for the bus stop.

"Maggie, go back to the house," I warn her. I've seen enough fights to know that Vic is looking for one. Hoping to redirect Vic, I say, "This is between you and me, man. Leave her out of it."

Vic laughs, the high pitched sound making my skin crawl. "Check her out, guys. Jeez, Becker, you really are scraping the bottom of the barrel. Does it turn you on when she struts around like a retard like that?"

I drop my backpack and charge him. We both land on the ground, but one of his friends grabs me from behind and pins my hands back. Before I can free my arms, Vic clocks me right on the jaw and the ribs.

Before I know what's happening, Maggie is in the middle of us, swinging her book bag and hitting Vic. The chick has more in her than she lets on.

Through all the commotion, I break free and push the prick who'd been holding me, then I grab Maggie and act as her shield before she gets herself killed. "Run," I order her as I tackle one of the guys.

I'm punching and grasping at shirt collars as much as I can in a three-against-one fight. Odds are against me and it's not a pretty sight. All mayhem freezes when I hear a siren, attached to a cruiser with red and blue lights flashing. An officer flies out of the car and has us kneel on the ground with our hands over our heads. "What's going on here, boys?"

I don't see Maggie.

"Nothing," Vic says. "We were just playing around. Right, Becker?"

I stare straight at Vic and say, "Right."

"Doesn't look like nothing to me." The cop holds his hand out to me, palm up. "Let me see some ID."

Since my driver's license was revoked, I only have my community service ID tag from the DOC. I'm not about to pull it out and have him call Damon. I'll be locked up again before you can say "hit-and-run."

"I don't have any," I say.

"What are you doing in Hampton?"

"Visiting a friend."

The guy does a great cop stance from the movies, with his feet apart and his hands on his hips positioned right above his gun belt. "Let me give you a piece of advice. We don't take kindly to strangers coming into our town and causing trouble." He turns to Vic. "I suggest you meet your friend on his turf or I'll have to get your parents involved. Got it?"

This should be about the time I tell the cop the truth: that I'm in Hampton by the order of the Illinois Juvenile Department of Corrections. But I won't.

"Got it," Vic says.

The officer gets back in his squad car and orders Vic

and his friends to move on. He follows Vic's car. I watch until both cars are out of sight.

When I look around for my backpack, I quickly realize it's gone. One of Vic's friends probably snatched it. But that's the least of my worries.

My jaw is starting to protest Vic's punch, and I put my hand up to my face to feel if it's bleeding. When I do, Maggie reveals herself.

Our eyes lock.

The bus to Paradise comes rumbling down the street and we both get on it. I sit at my usual spot in back and she follows, sitting right next to me. I'm surprised until I notice her fingers shaking.

She's scared.

It's demented and strange after all that's happened, but she feels safe with me right now. I don't dare touch her, 'cause that would mean this is something more than it is. And I know this . . . this feeling of friendship is a fleeting, temporary thing. What scares me to fucking death is that some part of my brain has decided this insignificant act of Maggie sitting next to me is the first step in fixing all that's gone wrong in my life.

Which makes it all the more significant.

TWENTY-FOUR

Maggie

I saw Caleb today at school. Rumors are running rampant about the bruises on his face.

None of the rumors are true.

After school I get on the bus to go to Mrs. Reynolds' house. I walk down the aisle to where Caleb is sitting. He doesn't look up. I take the seat next to him like I did yesterday.

This time he doesn't walk behind me after we're dropped off at the bus stop by Mrs. Reynolds' house. We walk side by side, as if there's an unspoken understanding between the two of us. I'm the only one (besides Vic and his thug friends) who knows how Caleb got his bruises. The fight yesterday scared me. Did Caleb get caught up in the fight because Vic insulted me? Whatever the reasons were, it was us against them. Caleb and I were on the same team and we didn't have a chance of winning.

That's why I ran behind a tree and called 911 from my cell, to protect him/us, because he would never be able to fight off three guys by himself, and God knows my cheap book bag couldn't take much more. I've never been able to stomach a fight anyway. The fight is over, but its aftereffects have lingered.

So now it's another day at Mrs. Reynolds' house working together, but not.

Caleb still follows my conditions: he doesn't talk to me as he works on the gazebo and I plant more daffodils.

I hum songs as I work. Sometimes Mrs. Reynolds hums along with me, until she starts belting out words to the songs so loud that I stop working and blink my eyes at this old lady who doesn't care what people think about her. It's really mind-boggling.

When Mrs. Reynolds starts nodding off, I walk inside the house and pour myself a glass of water. Before I leave the kitchen, I pour one for Caleb too. Quietly, I set it down on one of the wooden planks beside him.

Heading back inside to prepare a small snack, I remember I forgot to bring the cookie plate down from the attic last week. I go up the two flights of stairs to the attic and pick up the plate.

The door closes and I shriek. Caleb is standing in the attic with me, the glass of water in his hand. "Oh my God!"

"I'm not going to hurt you, Maggie. I just wanted to say thanks for the water and . . . well, and I know it's not easy working together, but I do appreciate you not kicking me out."

"You can't leave," I say.

"Why not?"

"Because that door locks automatically."

Caleb eyes the door stopper he just kicked out of the way. "You're joking, right?"

I shake my head slowly. I'm trying not to panic at the reality of being stuck with Caleb Becker in an attic. *Breathe, Maggie.* In. Out. In. Out.

Caleb tries turning the knob, then tries a turn-door-knob-while-pushing-on-door action. "Shit." He turns to me. "You and me. In the same room. This is *not* supposed to happen."

"I know," I say.

"We could yell for Mrs. Reynolds. She's sleeping outside, but—"

"She'll never hear us all the way out there. Her hearing is marginal if you're ten feet away. When she wakes up we'll hear her and then yell our heads off."

"So you're saying we're stuck here?"

I nod again.

"Shit."

"You already said that," I inform him.

Caleb starts pacing while running his hands over his buzz cut. "Yeah, well, this sucks. Being locked up is getting to be the theme of my life," he mumbles. "How long before she usually wakes up?"

I shrug. "It could be a half hour, but sometimes she sleeps for an hour or more, like yesterday."

Taking a deep breath, he sits in the middle of the floor and leans against Mrs. Reynolds' trunk. "You might as well take a seat," he says.

"I'm kind of afraid of spiders."

"Still?"

"You remember that about me?"

"How could I forget? You and Leah used to make me your personal spider killer," he says.

I look at him strangely.

"Sit," he orders. "I'm giving the old lady two hours to free us and then I'm breaking that door down."

Neither of us say anything for a long time. The only sound is our breathing and the eerie bangs and creaks of the old house.

"Was it scary in jail?" I ask, breaking the silence.

"Sometimes."

"Like when? What did they do to you?"

I turn and look at him. His expression is wary. "You know, you're the first one who's asked for details."

"I'll admit I've heard the rumors. I suspect most of them aren't true."

"What'd you hear?"

I curl my lip, nervous to be the one to tell him. "Let's see . . . you had a boyfriend in jail . . . you joined a gang . . . you attempted to escape and got solitary confinement . . . you beat up a guy who afterward needed to be hospitalized . . . should I continue?"

"You believe any of it?"

"No. Why? Are they true?"

He leans his head back against the trunk and lets out a long breath. "I was in a fight and got thrown in solitary for it." He puts his palms over his eyes. "I was in solitary for thirty-six hours. God, I can't believe I'm talking to you, of all people, about this."

"Did they give you food and water?"

He laughs. "Yeah, you still get meals. But you're sleeping on a slab of cement and a one-inch foam mattress on top of that. A stainless steel toilet is your only companion."

"At least you were alone," I say. "I had to wait for someone to bring a plastic bowl for me to go to the bathroom while I was in the hospital. Then I had to lay there while they wiped me. It was so degrading."

"Do the doctors say you'll ever walk without a limp?"

"They don't know. I have to go to physical therapy twice a week until I go to Spain."

"Spain?"

I explain why I'm working at Mrs. Reynolds' house every day and about my dream of leaving Paradise so I can get away from the past.

"I couldn't wait to get back home," he admits. "Coming back here meant I was free of being locked up."

"That's because you're Caleb Becker. People will always

accept you. The only thing that kept me from being a loser before was tennis and Leah. Now that I've lost both, I have nothing except humiliating stares and comments people say but don't think I hear."

Caleb stands and paces the attic again. "Coming home has sucked. But leaving Paradise would be a copout."

"To me," I tell him, "leaving Paradise means freedom. I feel locked up just living in this town where everybody reminds me what a loser I am now."

Caleb crouches down, his face right in front of mine. "You are *not* a loser. Hell, Maggie, you always knew what you wanted and went for it."

I tell him the honest truth. "Not anymore. When you hit me, a part of me died."

TWENTY-FIVE

Caleb

"Caleb, phone!" Mom yells from the kitchen. I've been in my room, trying to figure out these mixed-up thoughts I've been having since Tuesday, when Maggie and I got locked in the attic. We sat there for maybe forty minutes. In that short amount of time I probably shared more with her than I have with Kendra. Ever.

I'm in serious trouble here.

I pick up the cordless and head to my room. "Hello?"

"Hey, CB. It's Brian."

"What's up?"

"It's Sunday," Brian says in a way-too-cheery tone.

"And?" I say.

"Come on, dude, don't tell me you forgot our ritual. You, me, Drew, and Tristan . . ."

I remember. Sunday afternoons watching football—me, Brian, Tristan, and Drew. *No chicks allowed* was our motto.

"I'm leaving for Tristan's in ten. Be ready," Brian says, then the line goes dead.

I'm in my briefs. I'd sworn to myself I'd sleep all day. But if I want to get back into a normal routine, Sunday football can't be ignored.

I take a quick shower—believe me I'm used to them. And when I'm pulling on some old sweats and a t-shirt, I hear Mom downstairs fawning over Brian.

I'm so glad you called Caleb. You're such a good friend. Here's some leftover Chinese food from last night. I swear she's like an out-of-control machine.

When I get downstairs, Brian says to me, "Your mom rocks, CB. Check out all the stuff she packed for us."

I glance into the large grocery bag. Mom must have put half of the food from our refrigerator in it. I'm about to hug her, but she picks up a dish rag and starts wiping off the kitchen table when I come close. "Go on," she says, "and have a good time."

At Tristan's house we have to wait for the game to come on. It's the Packers against the Bears. Before I got arrested, I could have told you every date of every game and every Bears' opponent playing in those games.

I park myself on the couch in his basement and lean

back. I can hardly wait to watch. The other guys have no clue how much I missed this.

Hell, I didn't even realize how much I missed this.

I got Kendra back, I got my friends back. I've got to forget about Maggie. I'm sure I'm just thinking about her so much because we're working together. I came back to Paradise with a mission to get my life back to normal. Sitting back and watching the game makes me realize that the status quo isn't all that bad.

Until Tristan starts tossing cans of Michelob to each of us.

"Where'd you get the brew?" Drew asks.

"From the Fourth of July. I snatched a case from my parents' party and hid it. My mom didn't even know it was missing."

"Way to go, man," Brian says. "Toss one of those puppies over here."

Brian and Drew catch theirs and open them right away. I catch the one thrown to me. Tristan holds his can up. "To a new season of Bears ball."

"To a quarterback who can actually throw the ball," Brian says.

"And a running back that can actually run the ball," Drew offers.

They all turn to me, waiting for my dumb football wisdom.

I'm holding the can, the coldness against my palm sending a chill up my arm. "And a punter who could kick the ball," I add, wondering if they realize I haven't flipped the top and opened it yet.

They all take a swig. Except me. I may have jeopardized going back to jail when I got in a fight with Vic when he insulted Maggie, but that was worth the risk. I haven't even been near alcohol since the night of the accident. I'm not about to jeopardize going back for a stupid can of beer.

"What do you think you're doing?" an adult voice from the staircase calls out.

Shit, it's Tristan's mom.

I would try to hide the beer, but that'd be pointless. We've already been busted.

She storms down the stairs and rips the Michelob out of Tristan's hand. "Not in my house, you won't," she says, then points her finger at me. "You may think you can just come back here and suck everyone into your lifestyle, Caleb, but I won't let that happen."

Tristan steps forward. "Ma, stop."

"Don't protect him, Tristan." She looks down at the beer can in my hand, then shakes her head in disgust. "Caleb, please leave my house."

I put the unopened can down on the table. Mrs. Norris doesn't even look at the can. She's too busy staring at me and sneering. "Stay away from my son," she orders as I head out.

There's no use even defending myself. Mrs. Norris already has her mind made up about me. Verdict: Guilty.

Besides, if I explain the truth she won't believe me. The way she glared at me says more than words ever will.

"That was a buzz kill," Brian says when we're back in his car. "Where are we gonna watch the game now? It's probably close to halftime."

"We can go back to my place," I offer.

Ten minutes later we settle ourselves in my basement and watch the game. The Bears are up by three, but the Packers have the ball and it's the fourth quarter.

I'm totally into the game when Brian says, "I need to tell you something."

"Shoot," I say, taking a handful of potato chips and shoving them into my mouth. My attention is still on the game, but I chance a small glance at my friend.

Brian is leaning forward, the expression on his face totally serious. "She'll kill me for telling you."

I glance back at the TV. The Packers just fumbled and it's the Bears' ball. This could clinch a victory for them. "Who?" I say, only partially listening to Brian.

"Kendra."

Kendra was recently in my arms and a willing partner in my bed. It wasn't the most romantic reunion; I guess I expected it to be like old times. It's been anything but.

"Did you see that?" I ask Brian, getting totally riled about the Bears game. You can't blame me for being excited when I'd been restricted from watching football for the past year. I missed a whole season. "They just sacked Edmonton!"

"We're together, CB. I just thought you should know."

I look at him, confused. "What the hell are you talking about?"

"Me . . . and Kendra."

It hits me like a brick smacked into my head at lightning speed. "*You* and Kendra?"

"Yeah."

Jeez. The word comes out of my mouth faster than my brain can comprehend it. "When?"

"You don't want to know."

That means it was before I was arrested. Maggie wasn't lying to me that night I freaked out on her.

Maggie had told me the truth while Kendra looked me right in the eye, feeding me lies. Kendra was the manipulative one and I fell for it.

But it all makes sense now, why Kendra is desperate to keep our relationship a secret. Perfect time to fuck with my head once again.

Brian is watching me, gauging my reaction. There's no way in hell I'm going to tell him I've been messing around with Kendra.

In a matter of seconds, I lose my demented perception of reality. There is no getting back together with Kendra, there is no hanging out with the guys like before. My life now has no resemblance to before. How could I ever have thought it had?

I have to ask. "Are you guys, you know . . ."

"Yeah."

I close my eyes and lean back into the cushions of the couch. Wow. My girlfriend was screwing both of us and I was oblivious. But Maggie knew and tried to warn me. As a thank-you, I insulted her and then the night spun out of control, ending up with Maggie in the hospital.

The Bears game forgotten, I shake my head and stare at the ceiling.

"At first it was just a hook-up, a mistake," Brian continues. "We both didn't mean for it to happen."

I wish Brian would just shut up. Now I know what Damon means about taking the blame. "You were probably so stoked I was convicted, you could finally have my girlfriend all to yourself," I say.

"It's not like that." Brian pauses. "I love her, Caleb. Jesus, I'd marry her right now if I could."

"Damn," I mumble. I wonder who's going to be there when Brian comes back from la-la land and falls flat on his face. Kendra told me there were no guys that mattered. Or was that all bullshit, too?

"She made me promise not to tell you about us. But I think it's cool if we're all up front about it, don't you? Then we can be a couple at school again, instead of pretending we're not together."

I stand, needing some distance. This is my best friend from when I was in kindergarten. I remember when Drew took a crayon away from Brian in first grade and I pinched Drew on the arm in retaliation.

And when I had chicken pox in sixth grade and had

to stay home for over a week from school, Brian secretly came over and played Dungeons & Dragons with me. And we never told our parents, even when Brian got stuck with the pox two weeks later.

I'd never thought Brian would betray our friendship.

"You're a prick," I blurt out.

Brian stands and grabs his car keys. "I knew you wouldn't understand. That's why I didn't tell you."

"Dude, you were screwing my girl behind my back. How'd you think I'd react?" A shiver just ran up and down my spine when I actually put the truth into words.

"I thought you'd listen. And try to understand without wanting to rip my head off. This is real, Caleb."

I give a cynical laugh. "I'll tell you what's real. Real is that I was in jail for the past year, rooming with drug dealers and eating crap food your dog wouldn't touch. Real is not being able to wear your own frickin' underwear and showering with twenty-five other dicks every day while guards watch. Real is my next-door neighbor who walks like she's balancing on stilts because her leg is so fucked up from the accident. Brian, your perception of reality is totally off."

Brian heads for the stairs, his back stiff. He stops when he's halfway up. "When you want to forgive me and move on, you know where I am."

My fists are clenched so tight they're getting numb.

That's when Mom walks down the stairs. She smiles wide and says in a cheery voice, "Did you have fun with your friends?"

TWENTY-SIX
Maggie

I wish my mom didn't insist on going to my physical therapy appointment.

"You can just drop me off," I say. "Just come back and get me in an hour."

Mom shakes her head. "Dr. Gerrard wants to talk with both of us."

Oh, no. "Mom, I'm fine. Robert expects his patients to do the impossible, that's all."

"I know it's not easy, Maggie," she says. "Don't worry, you don't have to do what feels uncomfortable. Just do your best."

When we enter the hospital, sure enough Robert is waiting for us. "Hi, Maggie, how we doing today?"

We? "Fine."

"Been doing those strengthening exercises I taught you?"

Uh . . . "Yeah. Well, sometimes."

Robert shakes my mom's hand. "Nice to see you again, Mrs. Armstrong."

"You too," she responds, then takes a seat while Robert leads me to the workout mat.

"Let's start with stretching," Robert says. "And warm up those muscles to help them work hard. Put your legs in a V."

I do, but my legs resemble an "I" more than a "V" because my left leg doesn't want to warm up right now. It's not me, it's the leg.

"That's the best you can do?"

"I think so."

Robert kneels beside me and says, "Touch your left foot with your left hand."

I try, but I only get as far as my knee.

"Come on, Maggie. A couple more inches."

I reach about another half inch, which doesn't impress my physical therapist.

"She can't," my mom interjects. "Can't you see she's in pain?"

"Mrs. Armstrong," Robert says. "Maggie has to push herself in order to retrain those muscles."

Mom is about to respond when Dr. Gerrard walks in. "Hello ladies. Robert."

My mom stands and hugs my surgeon. After the accident,

he was the one who always gave us hope and had the hands to reconstruct the inside of my leg. I remember the first time I met him in the hospital. He came in with a big white coat, a big smile, and big fingers that were going to cut my leg open and fix it.

Dr. Gerrard kneels next to me. "How's it going, Maggie? Run any marathons lately?"

I raise my eyebrows.

"I'm just kidding," he admits. "Bad surgeon joke."

"Dr. Gerrard, you need new material," I mumble.

"That's what my interns say, too." Dr. Gerrard has me sit on the examining table and inspects my scars. "Looks good," he says, then looks up. "Robert tells me you're a little timid in physical therapy."

Robert stands there with his clipboard in his hands, the traitor.

I shrug. "I can't put a lot of pressure on my foot."

"It hurts her," Mom chimes in.

My doctor steps back and takes a deep breath. "Okay, walk to the door and back for me, Maggie."

He helps me off the table while I limp to the door.

"Can you put more pressure on your left foot?"

"Not really."

"Okay, come back and sit down."

I limp back to the table and sit on it. Mom comes up to me and rubs my back.

"I'm going to give it to you straight," Dr. Gerrard says.

"You've got to start pushing yourself and stop favoring your left side."

"I'm doing my best," I say.

Dr. Gerrard doesn't accuse me of lying, but I can tell he's not convinced by the way he's pursing his lips together.

"Maybe we should let up on the physical therapy," my mom says.

Dr. Gerrard sucks air into his clenched teeth, the hissing sound clearly a no-go to Mom's suggestion. "I'd hate to see her stop physical therapy."

"I have a suggestion," Robert pipes in. "What if Maggie starts playing tennis again?"

My heart pumps faster, the beats within my body thumping in my chest like an Indian tribal dance.

"Are you okay?" Mom asks.

I can't answer. My esophagus feels like it's constricting.

"I need to get some air," I say, then get off the table.

Robert comes up to me. "Maggie, we're just trying to help you."

"I know. But I can't do this anymore. I just can't." I pull on my sweats, limp past my mom, and head for the exit. I'm passing people in wheelchairs, doctors, and nurses. Do they think I'm as crazy as I feel?

When the doors open I suck in fresh air and try to breathe deeply.

Breathe. In. Out. In. Out.

Isn't breathing supposed to be something you do unconsciously? Right now I'm hyperconscious about it. So conscious, in fact, that I think if I stop concentrating, I might just forget to do it. I close my eyes.

Breathe. In. Out. In. Out.

I felt this way the day my dad left the last time, when I realized it might be his last visit. I wasn't strong then, either.

I blink back tears as I try hard to forget. Because it hurts too much knowing his love for me wasn't strong enough to make him stay. I wasn't worth being loved enough.

Tennis was my saving grace, but even that didn't work. I deserved to be admired on the court, because I was worth something when I played. Not only was I part of the team, I was the one my teammates looked up to.

The more that other dads showed up to matches, the harder I would play. It was as if I wanted those dads to regret I wasn't their kid. No matter if my dad loved me or not, there would be other dads that would do anything to have me be their daughter. Having other dads congratulate me was worth more to me than the varsity trophy I earned my sophomore year. I might not be worthy of my dad's love, but I was worthy of that trophy.

A pain in my leg shoots up into my spine, a mocking reminder that I'll never be a champion again.

"Maggie?"

I turn toward my mom, who's now officially freaked out.

"I can't play tennis," I tell her.

"Dr. Gerrard wants you to try. You will try, won't you?"

But I won't be good, and then my dad won't have any-

thing to be proud of me for. He'll never want me to be part of his new family. "Can we go home? I want to go home."

Mom sighs. I hate feeling like I'm disappointing her. I know she tries so hard to support us emotionally, physically, and financially. She's like the little cheerleader of our family.

When we get in the car, I calm down. I look at my mom, driving the car with a sad look on her face. "Mom, what do you want out of life?"

She gives a little laugh. "Right now, money."

"Besides money."

She cocks her head to the side, thinking. When we reach a red light, she turns to me. "I guess I'd like a partner to share my life with."

"Do you miss Dad?"

"Sometimes. I miss the companionship, I miss going out as a couple. I don't miss the fights."

The light turns green and we accelerate, our car passing a woman and man holding hands with their daughter. "Will he ever want me to visit him?"

"One day," she says, but I can tell she's not so sure.

"Do you want to date Mr. Reynolds?" I ask.

Her eyes go wide. "Why would you ask such a thing?"

"Because you were dancing with him at the Fall Festival. He doesn't have kids. I think he came to be with you."

Mom laughs, this big laugh that fills the car, and the people in the next car could probably hear her, too.

"Auntie Mae's Diner was a sponsor of the event, Maggie. That's why Lou was there."

"Well," I say defensively, "you two were looking pretty chummy."

"He was just being nice."

I shake my head. "I don't think so."

"Hmm . . ."

"What does that mean?"

"Nothing. Just go back to being a kid, will ya?"

We sit in silence the rest of the way home. When we walk inside the house, I ignore the lump in my throat as I say, "For the record . . . if you want to invite Mr. Reynolds over for dinner one night, I wouldn't mind," and head upstairs to my room.

In my room, I want to take my words back. I only said them because I know how miserable Mom has been lately.

But the truth is I miss my dad every day, too. More than anything. And I know he has another wife and another life. What if Mom and Mr. Reynolds start dating or, even worse, get married. Will they want to start a new life without me, too?

I lock my door and open my closet. In the back, in the darkest shadows, is my racquet. I know it's there although it's hidden behind clothes. I feel its presence when I'm in my room, kind of like kryptonite for Superman. Desperation washes over me.

I reach out and grab the handle, the weight of the racquet foreign but, at the same time, familiar.

"Maggie, open the door."

Panic. "Just a second."

I toss the racquet in the closet and unlock my door. Mom is staring at me strangely.

I brush the hair from my face, hoping she can't see right through me and realize I've always known where my lost racquet is. "Mom, what's up?"

"I was thinking. About Lou, my boss. Were you serious when you said I should invite him for dinner?"

TWENTY-SEVEN
Caleb

I asked Brian to meet me at the park for some one-on-one. I'm practicing free throws when he drives up in his Yukon.

"You look like a middle-aged man in that thing," I say.

He gives a fake-insulted huff. "It's better than the car you drive."

"I don't drive one."

"Exactly."

We stand facing each other. I say what needs to be said. "Listen, about you and Kendra. How about we call a truce."

"Fair enough."

I pass him the ball. He dribbles the ball too far away from his body, so I knock it and grab it away from him.

"B-ball's still not your game, is it?" I say as I dribble down the court.

Brian's shuffling backwards, following my every move. When I stop, his hands are up and ready to block my shot. "Get me on a wrestling mat and I'll kick your ass."

I take a shot. It bounces off the rim and Brian gets the rebound.

Brian is an anxious player. He runs down the court and shoots too quickly, missing the basket by a mile. The ball lands in the grass. I take the ball inbounds. "You're a light-weight, Bri," I say. "I'd pin you in less than ten seconds."

"Put your money where your mouth is, big guy, tomorrow after school."

I move around Brian and make an easy lay-up. "I have to work."

He holds the ball. "You say that, but you never say where. Rumor has it you're a homo and meet up with your lover after school. Is he the one who gave you the bruise on your face?"

My muscles start to tense up. "Don't give me shit."

Brian starts dribbling down the court, his eye on the basket. "Why? You gonna threaten me like you threatened Drew?"

Brian shoots and the ball goes right in.

This time I hold the ball under my arm, stopping the game. "He was trying to piss me off and you know it."

My old friend crosses his arms on his chest. "You've

changed, Caleb. I don't even know you anymore. And this has nothing to do with Kendra."

"Bullshit. I'm the same person."

He laughs. "You've got a chip on your shoulder. Everybody knows it but you. That's the scary part."

No, the scary part is that people don't realize how much *they've* changed. "So everyone else is the same except me?"

"No, dude. *Everybody's* changed, nobody is the same. You're the only one who can't accept it. You're not a sophomore anymore, you're not dating Kendra, you're not the wrestling stud. You're a bad-ass, brooding ex-con."

I'll show him a brooding ex-con. I dribble the ball down the court, and when Brian gets in my face I push him down before I take the shot.

"Foul!" Brian calls out.

"You said to accept my bad-ass ex-con self. I'm only taking your suggestion."

I hold out a hand. He looks at me suspiciously, then grabs my wrist as I pull him up. I get three more baskets and recover two of Brian's rebounds.

"You know what you need?" Brian says as he wipes sweat from his brow.

"A new best friend?" I suggest.

"No. You need a girlfriend. Name a chick you think is hot. Just throw out a name."

"Maggie Armstrong."

"No, seriously. Name a chick."

"I am serious."

"Dude, that's sick. You went to jail because of her."

"I'm well aware of that."

"You're telling me you have the hots for *the* Maggie Armstrong? Your next-door neighbor? The girl who walks weird because you ran over her leg with your car?"

"Brian, you're starting to act like Drew."

Brian looks confused as he's trying to comprehend what I just admitted to him. Then he bursts out laughing. He can't stop and falls to the ground in hysterics, holding his stomach. "That's . . . *hilarious!*" he yells when he can catch his breath. "Oh my God, it *can't* be true . . ." he says, then goes back to laughing hysterically again.

I'm seriously considering kicking his ass right now. But this isn't Vic or Drew, this is Brian. I take the ball and head back home, but not before telling Brian to go to hell.

Nobody is home; I have the house all to myself. I want to yell at the top of my lungs, but just as I'm about to do it the doorbell rings. Brian is an idiot if he's stupid enough to come here to laugh in my face again. Maybe, after all, I will use his head as my punching bag.

But I open the door and my ex-best friend isn't standing in front of me. It's Kendra, my ex-girlfriend. Shiny lips and all. "Hi," she says.

"Hi."

"Are your parents home?"

"Nope." She already knew they weren't.

"Can I come in?"

I open the door wider. She heads straight upstairs to my room. I watch her back and my eyes focus on her thong underwear sticking out of the top of her shorts before I follow.

Closing my door like I always do when we're about to fool around, I lean back against the door and watch her. But this time we're not going to fool around. I know it. She doesn't, obviously, I can tell by what she's wearing. A ridiculously low-cut shirt, I swear her nipples are millimeters below the ruffled collar. And her shorts reveal way more than I'd ever want any girlfriend of mine to reveal. But she's not my girlfriend, she's Brian's.

Kendra wanders around my bedroom, fingering my desk, my dresser, and my bookshelves. When she picks up my lightsaber and turns it on, I'm tempted to tell her not to touch it.

"When are you going to get rid of these toys?" she asks, waving it in the air.

I don't answer.

Sighing, she says, "I know Brian told you about him and me. But I still love you, you know." She closes the distance between us, close enough that I can smell her cherry lips. She licks them and leans in for a kiss.

I turn my head away. "What? One boyfriend isn't enough for you?"

"I want you both."

"It's over, Kend. Way over."

"It's not and you know it. Because—and I know this

sounds selfish, but it's true—I don't want anyone else to have you."

"Break up with Brian. The guy wants to marry you."

She chuckles. "My parents think he's good for me, so I'm playing along. Besides, I need a boyfriend I can hang with in public. But you can be my private boyfriend, CB."

"Never gonna happen."

"Wanna bet?" She steps back, points the tip of the saber at me, and pushes the blunt tip against my throat. A wicked grin crosses her mouth. "You can be my little secret. You like keeping secrets, don't you Caleb?"

My pulse quickens, and the mood in the room changes instantly. One thought burns in my brain . . . *she knows*.

"What do you want?" I say evenly.

"CB, don't look so sad. I just want you," she says, then lowers the saber and goes in for another kiss.

This time I don't turn away.

TWENTY-EIGHT
Maggie

It took a week for Mom to invite Mr. Reynolds over for dinner. She asked me about twenty more times if it was okay with me. I didn't have the heart to say no.

Mr. Reynolds comes in the house wearing a grey three-piece suit and red tie, as if he's going to court for a traffic violation. In his hands are a dozen purple tulips for my mom and a box of Frango chocolates for me.

"Thanks," I say awkwardly as he hands me the box. Do I open it now, or wait until later . . . or tomorrow?

"Why don't you have a seat and make yourself comfortable, Lou," Mom says nervously, her hands fidgeting with the black, sophisticated dress she decided to wear. "Would you like a drink? Wine . . . brandy . . . soft drink?

Mr. Reynolds smiles, a warm smile that I can tell is sincere. "Surprise me."

Mom laughs, a sweet, soft laugh I haven't heard in years.

When Mom is in the kitchen, Mr. Reynolds turns to me. "How is it back at school after being away for a year?"

I shrug. "It's okay, I guess."

He stares out the window. Where's my mom? The clock on the fireplace mantle is ticking, each second a reminder of how time is passing so slowly.

Tick. Tick. Tick.

Mr. Reynolds rubs his hands together. I can tell he's as eager as I am for my mom to come back.

Tick. Tick. Tick.

I want to excuse myself and hide in my room. I don't think I can handle watching my mom on a date with someone other than my dad.

Just as I'm about to stand up and excuse myself, she comes in with three drinks and a big smile. "Martinis for us, Sprite for Maggie."

Mr. Reynolds takes the glass from my mom. Their hands touch slightly when she hands it to him. I know I encouraged her to invite Mr. Reynolds over, but he's too big, too blonde, and . . . and he's not my dad.

I stand up.

Mom looks at me, her expression wary. "Where are you going, sweetheart?"

"To my room. I forgot to call Danielle."

Mom has this puppy dog look on her face; I think she knows I'm lying.

In my room I open the top drawer of my desk. In an envelope I keep my dad's phone number. My hands are shaking as I dial his number.

It rings three times before he answers. "Jerry Armstrong here."

"Um . . . Dad?"

"Maggie, is that you?"

"Yeah."

"How's my little girl holding up?"

"Fine."

"And your leg? The last time we talked you were having a bit of trouble."

"It's better, I guess."

It feels good to talk to my dad. Hearing his familiar voice takes away the black cloud that always seems to hover over me. I don't want to tell him the truth about my leg because I only want to share good news. If I'm positive, then maybe he won't want to forget I'm his daughter.

"Great. And school?"

I swallow the reality and say as cheerfully as I can, "Perfect. I'm getting all As," I lie.

"Wow."

There's silence, but I don't want him to hang up. I feel desperate. He sounds enthusiastic, but I'm not sure.

"How's your mother doing?" he finally says, breaking the silence.

She's currently having a date with her boss in our living room. "She's fine."

"Glad to hear it. I miss you, sweetheart."

"I miss you, too. When can I see you?"

No matter how many times I promise myself I won't beg him, I fail. It's like something inside me snaps when I think he's going to end the conversation. I want to yell, *Aren't I good enough?* but I don't.

"Sometime soon, when business settles down."

The black cloud returns—I've heard those exact words before. Too many times.

"Maggie, can you do me a favor?"

I'm holding back tears as I say, "What?"

"Tell your mother I sent her a check last week. And to have her lawyer stop calling mine. It's costing me a fortune every time he calls, like a hundred and fifty an hour."

"I'll tell her."

Someone else is talking in the background and I can tell I'm losing his attention. "I have to take another call, sweetheart. I'm sorry, it's important. I'll call you soon."

"Okay. I love you, Dad."

"Love you too, Mags."

Click.

I swallow hard and lean my head back against the wall. As much as I tell myself not to, I'm crying. I'd love to throw myself onto my bed and sob into my pillow, but Mom'll probably hear me.

The phone rings, startling me. I'm still holding the

cordless in my hand. Could it be my dad calling back so soon? He always says he'll call but never does. Maybe he's changed. Maybe he realizes after hearing my voice he misses me so much he can't stand it anymore.

"Hello?" I say excitedly.

There's a hesitation on the line, then a female voice recording says, "This is High Spring Water Company reminding you that there's a special on our five-gallon water bottles for the month of October. If you'd like to order—"

I hang up the phone in the middle of the recording. God, I feel so alone. There's nobody in my life who remotely understands what I've been going through.

Except one person.

My fingers dial the Becker's number automatically before my brain can comprehend what I'm doing.

"Hello."

It's him—Caleb. I don't even know what to say.

"Maggie? I know it's you, we have caller ID."

I forgot about that. "Hi," I mumble.

"What's up?"

Tears come to my eyes. "I just . . . wanted to talk to you."

"Why are you crying? Are you hurt? Did you fall?"

I can't talk because I don't want him to know how weak I am . . . how much I need his friendship right now. God, all those years I thought I would die if he didn't love me as much as I loved him. But now I realize how stupid I was.

"If you don't answer me, I'm coming over whether

your mom's there or not." His voice is hard and commanding, and I know he means it.

"No, don't come over. Can you meet me at Paradise Park in ten minutes?"

"I'll be there," he promises.

I take the sleeve of my shirt and wipe at my eyes. "Caleb?"

"Yeah."

"Thanks."

I splash water on my eyes in the bathroom, tell my mom that I'm going over to Danielle's, and head for the park.

Caleb walks up a minute later wearing jeans and a t-shirt with a plain button-down shirt over it. He slows his stride when he sees me and, without a word, pulls me into an embrace.

Now I'm losing it, right into his shirt. I clutch onto him as the sobs start and don't stop. I let it all out—my mom's date, my dad's conversation, my confusion about it all. Caleb doesn't laugh, he doesn't pull away, he doesn't talk . . . he just lets me be me.

When I settle down, I lean back and witness the mess I've made on his shirt. "I made your shirt all gross," I say between sniffles.

"Forget the shirt. What's going on? I couldn't understand a word you mumbled into my chest."

Now I'm half laughing and half crying. He looks down at my hand. I do, too. He slowly reaches out and takes my fingers in his. God, how I dreamed of us holding hands all those years ago. He'd take my hand in his and we'd walk down the street together. I look up at his eyes. Usually they're dark and brooding, but now I see a warmth there I'd never noticed before. He leads me to the old oak. We both sit down, then he leans back against the tree right next to me and lets go of my hand. "Okay, now talk."

It's easy because I don't have to look at him, I can just spurt out all the stuff that's going wrong in my life. I take a deep breath. I'm going to attempt to say it all without going into hysterics again. "My mom has a date over, her boss and Mrs. Reynolds' son. I think my mom likes him, but I don't know if I'm ready for her to start dating. I know it's selfish, but my dad has practically ignored me ever since the divorce. He's re-married, you know. And I think his wife wants a kid, as if he doesn't already have one. To top it off, my doctor said I should play tennis again, and every time I think about it my throat starts constricting and I have to remember to breathe . . . and then I call you because you're the only one I feel I can talk to. Which is ridiculous because it's *you*."

Caleb plays with a piece of grass he's plucked from the ground. "Do you think your mom would be happy with this boss guy?" he asks.

I think back to the way Mom laughed at the Fall Festival and how nervous she was tonight. "Yeah, I do. But that's the part that scares me. It's like ending a chapter in your life and starting over. A single mom, boyfriends . . . so much has changed."

"You're stressing too much about what might be. Do

something to take your mind off thinking about what might never happen."

"Like what?"

"Pick up a racquet."

"That's not funny," I say, already stressing and wanting to flee.

"I'm not trying to be funny, Maggie." I hear him sigh, a low breath that comes out slow. "Can I see your scars?"

Oh my God. "No." I shake my head feverishly while still staring at the ground. And I'm aware that my breathing just got heavier.

"Please don't freak out on me."

"I'm not."

"You are. I went to jail for doing something to you and I have no clue what it looks like."

I turn my head and I'm staring into his eyes, darker and more intense than I've ever seen them. "Why are you looking at me like that?"

"Do you remember the accident?" he asks, totally focused on my answer.

I shake my head.

"You remember nothing? Our conversation before the accident, me hitting you with the car? *Nothing at all?*"

"No. It's a big blank. I only know what people told me."

He blinks, then looks away. "We fought, you and I."

"About what?"

He gives a short, cynical laugh. "Kendra."

I'm trying to breathe evenly so I don't give him a hint

that I do remember. Every word he spat at me when I told him I loved him. It's the only part of that night that's crystal clear to me. The rest is stuck in a foggy haze. "I don't remember," I lie.

"You said she was cheating on me, that you saw her with some other guy but you wouldn't tell me who. You were right, you know," he says. "She was with Brian before I got put in jail." He's staring at me again, and this time I can't look away. "You also said you loved me."

I swallow, still mesmerized by his eyes. Those eyes that never gave me more than a glance a year ago are burning into mine. "I don't remember," I whisper.

"Maggie—" He takes my hand in his and places my palm against his cheek roughened with a day's worth of stubble. He turns his head and kisses the inner, sensitive part of my palm, his eyes holding my gaze. "I should have done this a year ago."

My heart flips over as he leans in and touches his lips to mine.

TWENTY-NINE
Caleb

I couldn't sleep last night, which is nothing new because every night is filled with restlessness.

But last night it wasn't nightmares of jail keeping me awake, or the night of the accident and what I could have done differently. I was reliving what happened a few hours ago. Kissing Maggie was the stupidest thing I've ever done. But, looking into her sad eyes and vulnerable face made me want her more than I've ever wanted anything in my life.

Last night real emotions were flying. Last night honesty was flying. It felt so raw.

As I'm getting ready for school, I think about our conversation after the kiss. She was nervous, I could tell by the shaking of those lips against mine. She'd closed her eyes and clutched at me as our lips met. I swear I've never been more turned on. When I leaned back, she had a worried look on her face as if I was going to give her a flunking grade on her kissing skills.

I can't believe that happened, she'd said.

I don't even know how I responded. All I remember is this feeling of stupidity washing over me, and wondering what the hell made me kiss a girl I should avoid getting close to at all costs. But being close to her felt so damn right, I couldn't resist her. We've been through so much, our lives are meshed and we're stuck in this web together. The sick thing is, I don't want to get out of it.

Maggie is frustrating, she's confused, she's angry . . . and she hums these ridiculous tunes when she's working at Mrs. Reynolds' house. You'd think I'd go nuts from it. I can't help that I like it when she blows her hair off of her face when she's working, or when she looks at Mrs. Reynolds sideways when she's insisting Maggie's planting her stupid bulbs wrong . . . and when she's not humming, I resist the urge to tell her to continue.

Get a grip, Caleb. After you kissed her she ran home as fast as she could.

Okay, so after I kissed her she left me at the tree wondering how I got myself into this mess. As much as I want Maggie, I can't have her. Maybe I should write a letter and slip it into her locker, apologizing for last night.

I sit down at my desk and pull out a sheet of paper.

Maggie,
   Sorry about last night.
   Caleb

I read it back to myself and it sounds idiotic. I crumple it up and start again.

Maggie,
   If I scared you last night, I'm sorry. It was a harmless kiss that didn't mean anything.
   Caleb

I crumple it up almost as soon as I sign my name. Because it did mean something. Kendra's kisses are more hollow to me than a flute. And, dammit, I'm not sorry I slipped up and got close to Maggie. I wanted to kiss her and I still want to kiss her. Okay, so I'd rather have her say something like *Let's try that again,* but I'd settle for her not running away. Getting a grip, I head to school early and try to forget Maggie and last night.

I trudge through my day until I get to computer class. Maggie is sitting in front, her eyes fixated on the screen in front of her. She doesn't even notice when I walk in. I expected to get some sign from her that everything is cool between us, but I get zilch.

Oh, yeah. I do get something—Kendra. She's been giving me her best seduction smiles all day, promising to fulfill all my fantasies. Little does she know my fantasies are consumed with a girl who refuses to look in my direction.

Lucky for me I manage to ditch Kendra and her overexposed cleavage all day.

I head to the bus after school, trying without much success not to be surprised if Maggie sits up front instead of next to me. I plunk myself down in back and catch sight of her pink t-shirt and faded jeans coming up the aisle. Her long hair covers the side of her face, as if shielding it from my gaze. She passes the front seats and heads to the rear, never looking up at me.

When she slides in beside me and the bus heads away from the school, I let out a breath. Being at school is stressing me out. The teachers stare, the kids stare . . . everybody stares at me except Maggie these days.

I look down at our knees, slightly touching. Jeans against jeans. Does she notice the heat transferring from her body to mine? Does she even realize what she's doing to me? I know, I know, I'm not a virgin and the slightest touch of a girl's knee is driving me insane. I don't even know what I'm feeling for Maggie, I just know that I'm *feeling*. It's something I've tried to avoid and deny until yesterday, when I held her in my arms while her tears spilled onto my shirt.

God, our knees touching isn't enough. I need more.

She's knotting her fingers together on her lap as if she doesn't know what to do with them. I want to touch her, but what if she pulls away like before? I've never been such a wuss with a girl in my life.

I bite my bottom lip as I slide my hand about a millionth of a millimeter closer to her hand.

She doesn't seem fazed so I move it closer. And closer.

When the tips of my fingers touch her wrist, she freezes. But she doesn't jerk her hand away. *God, her skin is so soft,* I think as my fingers trail a path from her wrist to her knuckles to her smooth, manicured nails.

I swear touching her like this is driving me nuts. It's more erotic, more intense than any other time with Kendra. I feel as awkward and inexperienced as a freshman again. I look up. Everyone else is oblivious to the intensity of emotions running rampant in the back of the public bus.

When I look back down at my hand covering hers, I'm grateful she hasn't come to her senses and pulled away. As if she knows my thoughts, we both turn our hands at the same time so our hands are palm against palm . . . finger against finger. Her hand is dwarfed against mine. It makes her seem more delicate and petite than I'd realized. I feel a need to protect her and be her champion should she ever need one.

With a slight shift of my hand, I lace my fingers through hers.

I'm holding hands.

With Maggie Armstrong.

I'm not even going to think about how wrong it is because it feels so right. She's avoided looking right at me, but now she turns her head and our eyes lock. God, how come I never noticed before how long her eyelashes were and how her brown eyes have specks of gold that sparkle when the sun shines on them?

The bus stops suddenly and I look out the window. It's our stop. She must have realized this because she pulls her hand away from mine and stands. I follow behind her, still reeling.

We get to Mrs. Reynolds' house. I can smell the scent of cookies invading us as we walk inside.

"Oh, I'm so glad you both are here," Mrs. Reynolds chants. "Come in the kitchen. I have . . ." The old lady cocks her head to the side, eyeing Maggie and me in her living room. "Is it hot outside?" she asks.

Maggie shakes her head while I say, "Not particularly."

"Then why are you both so flushed?" she asks, raising her eyebrows.

Oh, crap. While Maggie shrugs and heads to the kitchen, I inform the old lady, "I'm a guy. I don't flush."

"Uh huh," she says.

After eating the cookies, which she insists are her own secret Snickerdoodle recipe, I head outside. As I'm working, I steal glances at Maggie as she kneels on the ground and plants the bulbs with Mrs. Reynolds' verbal instructions never far behind.

When the old lady takes her nap, I listen to Maggie hum while I work on the gazebo. It's soothing. Her voice floats through the air as I work. But when the humming stops, I look around and Maggie isn't here. I head into the house.

I find her taking lemons out of the refrigerator. I watch as she cuts and squeezes them into a pitcher.

"Are you following me?" she asks, but doesn't meet my gaze.

"Yeah," I say.

"Why?"

"Honestly?"

She looks at me, her eyebrows raised.

I give her the only honest and true answer I have. "You're where I want to be."

THIRTY

Maggie

"Maggie!" Mrs. Reynolds' voice bellows through the house.

Caleb pulls back and gives me a helpless look. Then he says, "I guess that's my cue to get back to work," and walks out of the kitchen.

I'm standing here, holding a half a lemon in my hand. I'm speechless, I'm excited . . . I'm a wreck. *Caleb wants to be where I am.*

This is not some minor guy. This is CALEB BECKER, the boy who I'd dreamed about for what seems like my entire life. The boy who I used to watch from my window just to tide me over until the next time I'd be in the same room with him.

This is the boy who hit me with his car and left me in the street.

But when I look into his eyes, I can tell he's not the same Caleb Becker I used to know. The old Caleb only cared about himself. I never thought he observed or cared about the world around him. Has my heart started to forgive him?

I ran away last night because our kiss was perfect. Like I'd always dreamed our first kiss would be. Afraid that he wouldn't want to ever kiss me again, or laugh, or . . . something would change it from perfect to something less, I left.

When the bus drops us off on the corner by our houses, I ask Caleb if he wants to come over.

"Is your mom home?" he asks.

"Not for another hour."

He shrugs and says, "Sure."

I lead him into my house and up to my room. "My mom would freak if she knew you were here, in my room . . . alone."

"Yeah, mine too," he says. "You want me to go?"

I smile. "No." It's about making our own choices, not ones our parents have made for us.

He studies the yellow and pink décor of my room, walking around the perimeter. He picks up a pair of red and white boxing gloves I have hanging above my bed. "Yours?"

"I got them when I was in the hospital," I tell him. "You know, to remind me to keep fighting."

He smiles wistfully at the boxing gloves. "I'm tired of fighting. I'm tired of reliving the accident." He says it almost to himself, like it's a private thought he's sharing with me.

I take the gloves from his hand. "Me, too." And for the first time since that fateful night, I mean it. When his eyes bore into mine I ask, "Why are you here? Really."

He shakes his head. "I don't know." He runs his hand over his head, frustrated. "And, God, I know this is crazy and I should stay as far away from you as I can possibly get, but . . . and this part is driving me nuts . . . when I'm close to you I can finally *feel* things again. I laid awake last night thinking about holding you until all the hurt and numbness goes away. Like I need you in order to be sane. I thought it was Kendra, that she'd make me forget. But it's you. *You*. Isn't that fucked up, Maggie? Because maybe if you tell me it's fucked I'll believe it."

"It's not crazy, not by a long shot," I sputter, then go up to him and hug him as tightly as possible.

He puts his arms around me and holds me just as tight. "Could you ever forgive me?" he asks, his voice shaking.

A single tear runs down my cheek. I feel its hot wetness on my skin. I don't know the exact moment it happened, but something has changed. I've changed. And I think it's because I've finally let go of the past. I'm ready to live my life again. "I already have forgiven you, Caleb." I tell him.

We stay that way for a long time. I don't know how much time has passed. It's as if I'm taking away his pain and he's taking away mine. Before, I was confused . . . how I feel about him, how I feel about the accident. But when he's holding me, I let go of the feelings of betrayal I've held onto for the past year. When he pulls back, I hear him sniff, and watch as he wipes his eyes with the back of his hand. "I got something in my eye."

"It's okay to cry, Caleb. I won't tell anybody." I look at my closet, where my racquet is hiding. "I cry a lot."

"Yeah? Well I'm gonna change that."

He's already changed it.

"My mom is going to be home any minute," I say as I stare into mesmerizing clear blue eyes.

"I better go, then."

I nod. "Okay."

He steps closer, so close I can feel his heart beating against mine. I hold my breath when he leans back and puts his palm on my cheek. He lightly brushes my lips with his thumb, tracing my top lip and bottom lip as he moves his thumb across them.

"You have soft lips," he says.

"You already know I'm, uh, not really experienced with kissing," I say shyly, then look down and break our contact. I can't look at him while I say this. "I mean, I'm not really like Kendra in that department. You're probably used to girls who know what they're doing, and I'm new at this and *really, really* embarrassed that I'm doing it badly or wrong or . . . oh, I'm really making a fool out of myself right now."

"I wasn't going to kiss you."

"You weren't?" I look up at him. *Well, of course he wasn't, stupid. Why would he hook up with me when he can be with someone who actually knew what they were doing, someone who isn't responsible for sending him to jail,* my brain tells me.

"Nope. The next time I kiss you I'm gonna take my time, and you said your mom's coming home any minute."

I check the clock on my nightstand and nod.

He bites his bottom lip, deep in thought. "No, the next time I kiss you it'll last a long, long time. And when we're done you're gonna realize being turned on is not about experience."

While I'm still awestruck, Caleb heads out of the house.

THIRTY-ONE

Caleb

It's Sunday. Football Sunday. I'm hanging at Dusty's Sports Bar & Grill with the guys, since we can sit in the dining area and watch the game from the three large screens plastered throughout the restaurant.

The place is run-down—even the dark, wooden tables and chairs wobble because they're so old. But their TV screens are big and new, which brings guys from the closest three towns on Sunday afternoons.

I wonder what Maggie's doing today. She works for Mrs. Reynolds in the mornings, but she'll probably head home early. Is she home now, sitting in her bedroom? Or is she at physical therapy?

"Did you see that, Becker?" Tristan asks as the crowd in the bar groans.

"Sorry, man, I missed it." *I was thinking about someone I have no right thinking about.*

Shaking his head, Tristan points to the screen. "I swear, Guerrera needs some glue on his hands in order to keep the ball in his grip. That's his third fumble."

"Fourth," Drew corrects him.

I'm not into the game today.

I catch Brian looking at the doorway and signaling over whoever just came into the restaurant. I turn around. It's Kendra. Followed by Hannah, Brianne, Danielle, and Sabrina. I don't think their wrestling cheer will go over too well at this place. But then again, maybe it will.

"What are the girls doing here?" a balking Tristan asks Brian, who obviously invited them.

"Can't we change the rules just this once? Kendra really wanted to come."

"Ugh, I'm gonna be sick," Drew says, then fake gags. "She's got you by the balls, man. When are you gonna see it?"

Drew, the self-proclaimed asshole of our group, for the first time in his life is right on. Just as I'm about to proclaim Drew an insightful genius, the girls reach the table. Kendra is wearing tight jeans and a Bears jersey. Brian's jersey, the same one I remember him wearing every Sunday.

Brian is staring at his trophy girl, and it's making me sick too. Because if that's what I looked like when I was dating her, all grateful that a girl like her chose to gift me with being her boyfriend. Someone shoot me right now.

"Can we join you guys?" Kendra asks, but as the words spew out of her mouth she's already pulling up a chair next to Brian and motioning for the girls to find some chairs, too.

Seriously, this is a huge violation of the "no girls allowed for Sunday ball games" code. I can tell Tristan and Drew are not happy about the invasion of chicks. The reason the rule was created in the first place was that we all agreed girls (at least the ones in our group, a.k.a. the ones sitting down at our table right now) are not interested in watching the game. They're interested in breaking our concentration. It's like a challenge, to see if they can distract us from football.

"Hey, Caleb," Danielle says as she parks her chair next to me. "Whatcha been up to?"

Before I can answer, the waitress comes over to our table to slap down our food and ask the girls what they'd like to order.

"What kind of salads do you have?" Brianne asks.

The waitress stifles a laugh. "No salads. We got burgers, chicken sandwiches, wings, and fries. Take your pick."

Brianne is stunned by the choices. I can tell by the way she looks at the waitress in horror. This place is all about the beer/alcohol for the over-twenty-one crowd. Food is the afterthought. "I'll just have a Diet Coke," she finally says.

All of the girls order Diet Cokes. Nothing else. Tristan rolls his eyes.

"Wait!" Sabrina says, calling the waitress back. "I'll have a burger. No cheese, just plain."

"One plain burger, five Diet Cokes," the waitress repeats before retreating.

"I'll have a burger, too," Danielle says, piping in. "Plain, like hers."

"Two burgers, five Diet Cokes."

Brianne raises her eyebrows.

Danielle shrugs. "What? I didn't have lunch and I'm starving. Besides, I'm off the no-carb thing, Brianne."

Drew stands abruptly and puts his hands up. "Okay, if you girls want to join us, there's got to be a few rules. No talking about salads, and I don't even want to hear the word 'carb.' If you didn't come here to talk about the Bears or football, or to reminisce about the year 1985, be silent. And for God's sake, if you don't know which side to root for, I expect no cheering or comments. Got it?"

Kendra's eyebrows are furrowed. "What happened in 1985? Drew, I hate to tell you but we weren't even born yet."

While Drew slaps his forehead in frustration, an embarrassed Brian covers Kendra's mouth. "That was the last year the Bears won the Super Bowl," Brian informs her.

He removes his hand from Kendra's mouth.

"You do know what the Super Bowl is, don't you?" Drew asks, sitting down at last.

"Of course she does," Brian comments, then pulls Kendra close and keeps his arm draped over her shoulders.

The rest of the quarter is met with silence from the

girls and hoots and hollers from the rest of the people in the restaurant. When I happen to glance at Kendra and Brian during a commercial break, her gaze is directed at me as she whispers something in Brian's ear to make him smile mischievously.

I swear I just caught her licking his lobe, too.

Disgusted, I get up and head to the can. After I pee, I wash my hands and lean over the sink while I check out my reflection in the mirror. I'm a fucking mess, unable to just chill and hang out with my friends. Especially not with the girls here. Especially not with Kendra here. She puts my nerves on edge, reminding me of the past. The accident. Maggie.

The door to the men's room opens and sure enough Kendra walks in. I'm not surprised.

"Your boyfriend'll follow you in here," I tell her.

She saunters close to me, close enough I can smell her strong perfume mixed with cherry lip gloss. Total overkill.

"He won't. He thinks you're upset, so I told him I'd talk to you. He trusts us both."

"He's an idiot."

"He also thinks you're jealous. Are you?"

"Oh, yeah," I tell her. She wants to hear it, so I give her what she wants. It's a game she likes to play. I'm tired of playing games, but it's the only way to deal with her.

"You've been elusive, CB."

"Try busy."

"I thought we had an understanding."

The only relationship I want is the one I already have, with Maggie. It might not be public, but it's genuine.

The nagging thing is, I don't know what Kendra knows. Every time we're together, she hints she knows more about the accident than everyone else. But what if she doesn't, what if she's yanking my chain? We were both so plastered that night, and she's a lightweight. Maybe my ex has been playing me this whole time and I'm a sucker just like Brian.

No matter how much I want to, I can't risk alienating her.

She creeps her fiery-red fingertips up my shirt like a spider, stopping when she gets to my shoulder. Then she leans in. "You're like a drug, Caleb. I can't quit."

She's thriving on the chase. Not me. It probably turns her on that someone can walk in any minute and catch us this close together. It's the risk factor giving her the rush. "So why are you suckin' on another guy's ear?" I don't know why I asked. It's not that I even care. I put my hand on her waist, ready to push her away if she comes closer. I'm so done with being her pawn.

"I just wanted to get a reaction out of you. It worked. For the past couple of weeks you've given me nothing, no emotion or encouragement. Brian thinks you're into Maggie Armstrong. Isn't that ridiculous?"

Just when I'm about to answer, the door opens. Drew comes in, seeing Kendra and me standing close, touching each other in what might look like an embrace. It's not what it seems, but it looks bad.

"I'm not even gonna ask," Drew says, then heads to the urinals. Before he slides his zipper down, he turns his head to Kendra. "Do you mind taking this somewhere else?"

"It's nothing I haven't seen before," Kendra says to Drew as she steps away from me, breaking all contact.

Drew gives a short laugh. "Yeah, well you may have made the rounds with my friends, but you ain't getting your hands on mine."

"From what I've heard, one hand would be enough," Kendra shoots back.

"Enough," I say. "Kendra, go back to Brian. Drew, take a leak already."

Hurt that I haven't defended her, she storms out of the men's bathroom, but not before murmuring, "asshole" to Drew on her way out, to which Drew responds, "slut."

Drew finishes, then as he washes his hands he says, "Caleb, you think hooking up with Kendra is the answer? Listen, let Brian have the bitch and move onto someone else."

"It's a little more complicated than that."

Drew makes a tsking noise, just like Mrs. Reynolds. "You're making it complicated."

Then it hits me.

For the second time today, Drew is right on. I'm letting Kendra manipulate me instead of the other way around. I don't need to appease her. I can just let her keep the chase going without giving her a chance to go in for the kill. Wow, I've been going about this whole situation all wrong,

I can't believe the solution is so simple. I take out my wallet and hand Drew a twenty. "Here, pay my bill. I'm outta here."

"You don't have to leave. I'm not gonna tell Brian what you and Kendra were doing."

"At this point, I don't even care," I say, then leave the men's room and head out the back door.

THIRTY-TWO

Maggie

Caleb comes over in the afternoon, totally unexpected. I open the door to answer it and here he is, standing in front of me with a determined look on his face.

"I wanted to see you," is all the explanation I get. "Is your mom home?"

"No. She just left for work five minutes ago."

Caleb and I are friends. Okay, we're more than friends. It's strange and complicated, but it's the only unstrained friendship I have.

I lead him to my room and have him wait there while I bring up some drinks and chips. We sit on the floor and munch on the chips. We talk about school and wrestling, and laugh about the times when we were kids in preschool and the stupid things we did. Then we play gin with the playing cards my mother got me when I was in the hospital. He doesn't talk about kissing at all. He doesn't even look at me with that hot, wanting look I've seen before. He's got something on his mind. I don't know what it is, but it's distracting him.

After a while he puts down the cards and says, "I want to help you, Maggie."

"With what?"

"Playing tennis again. I always see you looking into the closet like there's a monster in there, so I checked it out while you were in the kitchen. I found your racquet."

I stand up. My heart starts racing as I hobble away from him. "I'm never playing again."

He stands, too. "I'm not trying to hurt you, Maggie. I'm trying to help."

I turn my back to him. "I can't play."

"Just try, Maggie. What'll it hurt?"

"I'm not going to be good."

"Who says you have to be good?"

He doesn't know being good at tennis has always meant more than being good at tennis. It's so much deeper than that.

When I look at Caleb, I want to make him proud of me. He's trying to fix whatever pain he's caused me. I want to help him, too. "Okay, I'll try," I say. "But don't expect much."

"I won't."

Fifteen minutes later, we're behind Paradise High looking out across the tennis courts. It brings back memories of me trying to prove myself. Taking a deep breath, I follow Caleb onto the hard, green surface.

When Caleb retrieved my racquet, I froze. I didn't even want to hold it. So after he fetched his own racquet and some tennis balls from his garage, he carried everything without complaint as we walked to the school.

Now he's holding out my racquet to me.

I hesitate.

Taking my hand in his, he wraps my fingers around the racquet handle

"I'm scared," I admit to him.

"Me, too."

I raise an eyebrow.

"Yeah," he says. "If you beat me. I have to keep up my tough-guy image, you know."

That makes me laugh. "You don't need me to make you look tough, Caleb."

With that, he takes the tennis balls and heads to the opposite side of the court. "Be easy on me," he jokes.

He hits the ball right to me, nice and slow. Instincts take over and I hit it back. It feels good, I have to admit, but it also feels strange. My body moves differently now, like I'm stiff and can't loosen up. My legs, my stance, are both awkward and wrong. I can't balance on the balls of my feet and pivot when the ball comes at me. I can't lean over in the ready position, ready to strike at the ball when it flies by.

When Caleb hits the ball back to me, I don't swing.

He stands up and shakes his head. "You could have gotten that."

"I didn't want to. Can we go now?"

"No. Hit this back to me ten times, then we'll go."

He hits the next ball right at me. I hit it lightly.

"Nine," he says, counting down.

Three more balls come within arms length and I gently hit them, so they easily fly over the net right to him. My feet still haven't moved from this spot.

"Six."

Five more gentle balls fly over the net and bounce right in front of me. I send them flying back slowly.

"One more, Maggie. Then we're out of here."

Great. Only one more and the humiliation can end.

He sails one hard and fast over the net. It bounces five feet away from me. I don't even try to get it. He does it again . . . and again. I put my racquet at my side and stare at him. "Are you trying to humiliate me?"

"Stop acting like a baby and go for the ball already," he says, shaking his head. "*Come on.*"

How dare he!

This time, as the ball shoots over the net, my anger and nothing else drives me as I take three steps and whack the ball back at Caleb with all the pent-up power and frustration inside me.

It hits him squarely on his arm. "Ow!" I don't ask him if he's okay, because he has this arrogant look on his face and the corners of his mouth turn up in victory. "Did that feel as good to you as it did to me?" he asks.

I throw the racquet at him and head off the court.

I won't give him the satisfaction of knowing it felt exhilarating and awesome.

He steps beside me and pulls me to him. "I'm gonna have a bruise, you know," he says. "But watching you whack that thing was damn hot."

I look over at the welt growing on his arm. "It was?"

In a swift motion, he moves forward and pins me against the fence with his body. "I'm going to kiss you."

My stomach does a little flip; I forget about being mad. My nerves take over all emotions. "Here?"

"Oh, yeah. Right here, right now. You gonna run away this time?"

"I don't think so, but I'm not sure."

He smiles, amused at my answer.

I look up into his eyes that give me a glimpse into his private world, then lick my lips in anticipation.

And that is the beginning of our kissing marathon. All I have to say is that I don't feel inexperienced after an hour of lips and tongues and innocent and not-so-innocent caresses on both sides. I don't feel insecure about kissing anymore.

We moved from the courts to the park and back to my bedroom. On my bed. Caleb leans back and moans. "We have to stop this or my body is going to suffer aftershocks for days."

Relaxing, I lay my head on his chest. "That was nice."

"Yeah, too nice."

He's breathing heavily. We both are. I take a deep, slow breath and bask in the moment. I could stay here forever, just like this. Gazing. Feeling wanted. Feeling protected. Feeling normal.

"I should hate you for making me play tennis."

"Yeah. But you can't, can you? Besides, we've had a makeout session you'll be thinking about for weeks."

"You've got an ego problem."

"Only with you." He chuckles, then yawns.

"Do I bore you?" I ask.

"Not at all," he says, stroking my hair. "It's just . . . I don't sleep too well. And I'm so relaxed and content my body is ready to crash."

I lean up on my elbows. "So sleep."

"Here?"

"Sure. My mom won't be home until late." I start to get up, to leave him my whole bed so he could sleep in peace.

"Don't leave me," he says. "Lie next to me." He pulls me down with him. "You're so different," he says almost to himself.

"Don't say that," I tell him, looking away. I want to keep the false fantasy that I'm the same as other girls, at least for a little while.

"Different in a good way." His brows furrow. "A really good way."

Then he pulls me tight against him. We're spooned together as if we've been dating for years. We're even sharing the pillow I've slept on since I was ten. The last thing I remember before waking up is Caleb's slow, rhythmic breathing behind me as he falls into slumber.

But now I hear the front door open and I'm fully awake. "Caleb, wake up. My mom's home."

It takes him a second to get his bearings, we've been sleeping for over five hours.

"Wait here and don't make a sound," I say, then kiss him on his sleepy lips.

Sliding out from beneath his arm pinning me to him, I close my bedroom door and head downstairs. "Hey, Mom," I say, my voice groggy from sleep.

"I didn't mean to wake you, sweetheart. I hate these late Sunday nights, but I'd rather have them and be able to spend the mornings with you. It seems we spend much too little time together lately." She puts down her purse and starts climbing the stairs. I pray she doesn't want to hang out in my room and have one of those mother/daughter talks. Not now. But I guess if she does, the truth will come out. Maybe it would be a blessing in disguise, but I'd rather not chance it.

"It's fine, Mom. You always worry about the small stuff."

She doesn't hear the creak of my bed behind my door. But I do.

Mom's eyebrows furrow. "Why are you sleeping in your clothes?"

Oops. "I was in my room and must have dozed."

"Well, I'm beat, too. Go back to bed. You have school in the morning. And change out of those clothes."

"Okay. Good night." I hope she doesn't realize I'm anticipating with bated breath the moment she closes the door to her room.

When she closes her bedroom door, I hurry back to my room. Caleb is sitting on my bed, startled. "I'm so sorry," he whispers, still looking as dangerous and cool as ever even half-asleep. "I lost track of time."

"Me, too."

He walks over to the window.

"Caleb, what are you doing?" I whisper.

"Finding a way out."

I put my hand on his arm and tug on it. "You're not jumping out my window. Just wait fifteen minutes and I'll lead you to the front door. My mom sleeps like the dead and she falls asleep really fast. Besides, if we get caught we're in this together. Right?"

It takes him a while to respond. It's almost as if he doesn't believe what I just said. "Yeah. Right," he finally murmurs.

THIRTY-THREE
Caleb

I met with Damon this morning, after convincing my parents I stayed out late because I was at Brian's and we lost track of time. They bought it. Damon came for some sort of evaluation for the State of Illinois. He interviewed my family, even Leah, then we hung out in my room while he grilled me with questions.

I told Damon I asked Maggie to see her leg, leaving out the part that we work together every weekday after school, or the fact that she's the only person who makes me forget the past year even happened. God forbid I should tell him I slept with her last night, in the literal sense of the word.

Damon shakes his head. "It's forbidden to confront your victim, Caleb."

"I didn't confront her."

Damon crosses my room and puts his hand to his head as if he has a headache. "You sweet on her?"

"Who?"

"Maggie."

"No. No way," I lie.

"You small town kids are a breed apart. Okay, here's the deal: stay away from her."

"Do I have a choice?"

"No." Damon opens his folder and clicks his pen. "You're almost done with your community-service require-ments. A gazebo for Mrs. Dorothy Reynolds. I see you've been on that job for three weeks."

"If all goes well I should be done by the end of next week."

Damon seems impressed. "Good work, Caleb. You started out rocky, but you're a decent kid. Let's meet again next week and talk about what's going to happen after your release."

I'm feeling energized after Damon's visit, knowing the jail threat is almost behind me. I just have to keep the fact that I'm with Maggie a secret.

I knock on my sister's door. She's in there. Her room is her cave. My sister hibernates except for school and meals.

She doesn't answer, so I knock louder. "Leah, open up."

"What do you want?" she says through the door.

I sigh. This is harder than I thought. "Just open the fucking door."

She opens it a crack. I push it the rest of the way open and walk inside. It's too dark in here so I pull the shade up.

"Keep it down."

"Yeah, well, we have to talk and I can't see a damn thing."

"I don't want to talk."

"Too bad," I say, my hands crossed in front of my chest.

Leah's gripping the handle of the door, like she's ready to flee.

"Are Mom and Dad home?" she asks nervously.

"They're out."

She lets out a small breath.

I don't even know where to start. I just know I'm ready to say it out loud. It's been pent up inside of me for over a year. The demon's got to get loose. Life is not about covering up for crap and living in a fantasy world.

I take a deep breath and tell my sister, "You hit Maggie with the car and I took the fall for it. It sucked, but it's over. I wouldn't have done it if I knew you'd act like a fucking corpse the rest of your life."

Her eyes are wide as if her brain is registering the truth for the first time.

"Talk, Leah," I order. "Say something . . . *anything!*"

"I can't deal with it!" she cries out, then hurls herself onto her bed face-first.

I grab a box of tissues off her nightstand and toss it to her. I stand over her as she cries hysterically.

"I'm sorry, Caleb. I'm *so* sorry," she says between sobs. "I could have killed her, Caleb."

"But you didn't."

"I stood there and watched as they handcuffed you. I let them take you away."

I was so used to being the troublemaker, used to being the one who screwed up. Leah had been the squeaky-clean twin; I was the rebel. Even drunk, I didn't hesitate taking the fall for the accident. Leah wasn't going to be handcuffed, arrested, and convicted. She couldn't handle it. I could.

The cops didn't question it when I confessed right there. Hell, my own parents never questioned my guilt.

To think, it was all because Leah swerved to avoid hitting a fucking squirrel in the road.

"It's over." I tell her.

"No, Caleb, it's not. It'll never be over. I'm going to carry this guilt around with me the rest of my life. I can't even look at Maggie. Hell, Caleb, I can't even look at you. It's so hard for me, you can't imagine what it's like."

She's right, I can't.

Turning to me, she sucks in a frightened breath. "You're not going to tell anyone, are you? Promise me you'll never tell *anyone*."

I look down at my twin, the girl who I shared my

mom's womb with, shared birthdays with, and grew up side by side with. She should know me like I know her, feel my pain as much as I feel hers. She knows this secret is tearing me up inside. I can feel it just as much as I know how twisted her rationale has become. But she ignores me and focuses only on herself. She really is, after all, a stranger to me.

THIRTY-FOUR
Maggie

I'm humming an old song my mom used to sing to me when she put me to bed, back when I was scared of the dark and refused to go to sleep. Life was less complicated back then. My dad lived at home and Mom's only job was, well, to just be a mom.

Now she's working as a waitress and dating. Okay, that last part is my fault. I can't even blame my mom for her date tonight. Thanks to Caleb, I'm finally coming to terms with it.

That first night he kissed me was magical. I was all ready to just be friends with him, cherish our platonic relationship, when it suddenly turned into something more. When I'm with him I don't think about my limp. All I think about is how good it feels to be able to talk and share and kiss.

Am I falling in love with Caleb Becker again? I don't know. I'm so nervous and scared to be hurt again, I'm keeping a wall up so my heart is protected.

Little by little he's been chipping away at that wall.

After work we've been getting off the bus two blocks away so we could steal an extra few minutes together. Unfortunately, today he had a meeting with some counselor from the Department of Corrections. He said it was important, so I hope it goes well.

I've forgiven him for the accident. Two days ago he tried to bring it up, saying he had something important to tell me about it. I cut him off with a kiss and promises of forgiveness.

The wind is blowing, and the leaves are starting to fall. It's the end of summer. The trees and grass and flowers are getting ready for dormancy. As I plant the last of the daffodil bulbs for Mrs. Reynolds, I think of the winter they'll have to survive before thawing and being ready for their first peek of the sun.

I look up from daydreaming about songs and trees and Caleb to find Mrs. Reynolds standing over me. I stop humming.

"You sure are cheery today."

"I only have five more bulbs before I'm all done," I tell her.

"That's a good thing, too," she says, looking up at the

darkening sky. "The weather is changing. I already feel a winter chill in the air."

"Me too." After I finish the last bulb, we sit down and eat dinner.

"I'd like to invite you and your mother over for dinner one night. But only if it's okay with you."

"Why wouldn't it be?"

"Because my son has been on more dates with your mother than he's been on in the past three years. I've been coaching him, you know."

"You have?"

"Did Lou bring you chocolates the first time he came to your house?"

I nod.

"That was my advice. I told him to bring yellow roses to your mom because they're the best way to start—"

"They weren't yellow roses."

She raises an eyebrow. "They weren't?"

"No. Tulips."

"Yellow?"

"Purple."

"Hmm. And the chocolates, they were caramels?"

"Frango mints. Very tasty."

"Tasty, huh? So much for mother's advice."

I laugh.

My boss waves her arms in the air. "Enough lollygagging, Margaret."

When we're putting the dishes away, Mrs. Reynolds sways and holds the edge of the counter for support.

"Are you okay?" I ask, taking the plate from her and leading her to the sofa.

"These new medications are just wreaking havoc with these old bones, that's all. Nothing to worry about."

I do worry. Before I leave her house, I call Auntie Mae's Diner and tell Mr. Reynolds to check on her.

I head to the bus stop after I'm convinced she's okay. A car screeches by me as I walk. I recognize it as the same car with the guys who got in a fight with Caleb.

"Hey, it's Caleb Becker's retarded girlfriend," someone yells out the window.

I bite the inside of my lip and keep walking.

"I think she wants you, Vic. Why don't you show her a good time," someone else says. Then they all laugh.

The car is driving slowly beside me. I just hope they don't step out of the car. If I stop walking, will they get out?

Will they hurt me?

Deep fear, so intense I'm shaking inside, keeps me from stopping.

I can't go back to Mrs. Reynolds' house. It's too far and I can't outrun these guys. There are houses lining the street. I could try ringing a doorbell and ask someone to call the police.

A plan forms in my head. I turn around and head in the opposite direction, the direction I just came from. But in the process I fall down. My hands are stinging and I feel sticky wetness dripping down my knee from the cut I've just gotten from the fall.

"Did you have a nice trip?" one of them yells out the window.

I get up and hobble faster, praying they won't turn the car around and follow me. Because if they do, I don't know how I'm going to handle it. I listen for the sound of the car turning around. I don't dare look back and give them another reason to come after me. But I can hardly hear anything besides the furious panting of my own breath.

Relief sweeps over me as the bus roars down the street. I hurry to the curb and wave the bus down, then glance to see if the car is still there.

"You okay?" the bus driver asks.

"I'm fine," I say, then scurry to the back to sit.

Nothing can cure me, no amount of physical therapy or surgeries. The old Maggie, the tennis star without a debilitating limp, the old Maggie, who could run away from danger, doesn't even exist.

Caleb is outside mowing his lawn as I limp down the street. He stops the motor and rushes over to me as soon as he glances my way.

"What happened? Tell me what happened."

I'm trying to hold back tears. "I'm fine."

He looks around to make sure people aren't looking, then cradles my face in his hands. "You're not fine. Damn it, talk to me."

I gaze at him in despair. "It was that Vic guy."

"I'll kill him if he touched you," he growls, eyeing my ripped pants stained with blood.

"He didn't. He and his friends just scared me, that's all."

"I'll make sure that never happens again, Maggie."

I smile warmly at him. "You're not going to always be able to protect me. What are you going to do when I'm in Spain, fly over and beat up all the bad guys who make fun of me?"

THIRTY-FIVE
Caleb

I said Vic was going to pay, but I didn't know how to do it . . . legally. That is, until I was talking to the guys at lunch yesterday who told me Vic is competing for his school at our wrestling invitational today.

I am officially a Paradise Panther wrestler now. And I only have to beat out four guys until I come face to face on the mat with Medonia. As I suspected, we're still in the same weight class. I think the guy's using steroids to bulk up.

I'm in the locker room with the rest of the team, getting ready for the match.

"Caleb, you look like you're about to kill someone," Brian says as I jump rope to warm up.

"He's in *the zone*," Drew says. "Ain't that right?"

I don't answer. Coach Wenner stops me and pats me on the back. "You haven't been to practice, Becker. You sure you're ready?"

I put my mouth guard in. "Yeah, Coach."

I win my first two matches with a pin within the first minute. The third match took me a little longer. I think I pinned him in ninety seconds.

"CB's on fire!" Tristan yells as he's plugging up a nosebleed from his previous match.

I focus as they call me and Medonia up to the mat. I can't wait to wipe that smirk off his face.

"How's your girlfriend?" he asks.

"Better than yours, any day."

"She's a cripple, Becker."

"You'll be the cripple after this match."

The ref puts his hands between us. "Keep it clean, guys."

When the match starts, I push him with all my might until he falls. Unfortunately, he rolls off the mat and the ref blows his whistle. "Caution, Panthers. Point for Fremont."

The next time we start, Medonia starts low. I move off the mat when the match starts and Medonia flies past me.

The ref blows his whistle.

When the match starts up again, I get one more caution for an illegal hold which ends up with my elbow in Medonia's face.

One more caution and I'll be disqualified.

The whistle blows, and the ref calls out, "We've got a bleeder for Fremont. Two minute break."

Coach Wenner stalks over to me, eyes blazing. "What are you doing? My team doesn't play dirty, Becker. Now either you go out there and try to win that match, or I'm forfeiting it for you. Which is it?"

THIRTY-SIX
Maggie

Mrs. Reynolds is going to be the death of me. She's determined to make me get behind the wheel of her black monstrosity sitting in the garage.

"It's a classic," Mrs. Reynolds says, her chin held high as the garage door opens and reveals the Cadillac.

"I'm . . . I'm really not ready to drive yet," I say. "But you can drive it and I'll ride on the passenger side."

Mrs. Reynolds opens the passenger door and slides into the seat. "Honey, my eyes can hardly see two feet in front of me. Come on, now. Time's a-wastin'."

She hangs her hand out the window, the keys dangling from her fingers. She shakes them, the keys on the ring clinking against each other.

I'm huffing and puffing as I slip the keys from her hand, hoping she'll get the hint. She doesn't. I open the driver's-side door and slide into the front seat. Wow. The white leather is soft, and the back of the seat is as big as an old Lay-Z-Boy recliner. I look out the front window. The hood is wide and has that shiny Cadillac symbol.

I turn to Mrs. Reynolds, who has her small purse neatly clutched in her lap, ready to go. Making the old lady proud of me would be so great. But . . . I'm not ready. I think.

"I can't do this," I explain, hoping she'll understand.

She's having none of it. Just by the stern look on her face, I know. "Margaret, put the key in the ignition."

I do it.

"Now turn the key and start the car."

I turn the key.

"What are you afraid of, dear?"

"Hitting someone. Getting into an accident." I gulp.

"This part of you has to change, you know. Being afraid to take chances is scarier than actually doing things that challenge you."

"I haven't driven since the accident."

"It's about time you did, then."

I shake my head.

"Back up slowly so you don't hit the fence." Mrs. Reynolds faces forward and buckles her seat belt.

I buckle mine, too. I have no clue why the lady can

make me do things I don't want to do. It's like she has this power over me.

I take a deep breath, press my foot on the break, and put the car into reverse. Slowly releasing the break, I turn back and make sure I'm all clear to back out of the driveway.

"Watch out for the mailbox," Mrs. Reynolds advises.

We're safe at the bottom of the driveway and I back out into the street. I'm trying to convince myself not to have a panic attack, but I don't think I'm being too successful. Part of me is excited to drive again and get that fear out of my life, but the other, stronger part of me, wants to put the car in park and limp home. I hear Caleb's voice inside my head, pushing me to do it.

Mrs. Reynolds pats me on the knee. "Well done, Margaret."

With that vote of confidence, I put the car into drive and slowly head down the street.

My feet aren't used to the pedals and I'm stopping too hard and accelerating too fast. "Sorry," I say after we come to a stop sign and Mrs. Reynolds jerks forward.

She clears her throat. "No problem. Let's take it a little easy on the accelerator and brake, shall we?"

"Uh, sure." But when it's my turn to cross the intersection, I take my foot off the brake and gently put pressure on the accelerator. I pump it a bit because I don't want to jerk Mrs. Reynolds forward again.

But now I'm making it worse. Oops. "You'd probably

be a better driver, even with your vision problems," I say seriously.

"I might have to agree with you, dear. Next time we try this, remind me to take some Dramamine."

I give her a sideways glance. "You look like you're going to be sick."

"Just look at the road, not at me," she orders. "My looking sick has nothing to do with your driving."

She directs me to a place called Monique's. It has cute dresses in the window. By the time we get there my nerves have gone from overdrive to idle. I follow Mrs. Reynolds into the store. Dresses in all colors and patterns are positioned on racks throughout the store.

Mrs. Reynolds runs her fingers over a short, light blue silk dress. "Do you know how to spot quality material?"

I take my hand and run the soft cloth through my fingers. "I've never really paid attention to fabrics."

"Every fabric has its own personality, just like my daffodils. For some, the softness and weight matters. For others, it's the way the fabric moves . . . and you can't discount color vibrancy."

"How do you know so much?"

"Honey, when you're as old as I am, you know more than you want to know."

A woman who works at the store comes up to us, wearing a plum pant suit and blonde hair that's neatly combed and curled at the ends. "Can I help you ladies?"

"We're looking for a dress," Mrs. Reynolds says, then points to me. "For this young lady."

"For me?" I say, following behind as the lady leads us through the store.

Mrs. Reynolds stops and turns to me. "You need a little something to spice up your wardrobe, Margaret. All you wear are solids and, to be completely honest, your clothes are a bit too big and casual."

I look down at my black cotton pants and grey t-shirt. "They're comfortable."

"And totally appropriate for lounging around the house. But, we're having dinner tonight and I want you to dress up. Consider it an early Christmas gift."

The saleswoman leads us to a rack of short cocktail dresses. "These just came in from Europe. It's a new silk/washable blend."

Mrs. Reynolds slides the silky, teal-colored dress between her fingers. "Too stiff. She's used to cotton, so I'd like a softer fabric."

"I don't wear short dresses," I tell them.

The lady leads us to another corner of the store. "How about a cotton/wool blend?"

Mrs. Reynolds shakes her head. "Too hot."

"Rayon?"

"Too clingy."

I'd expect the lady to get frustrated, but she just puts her hand to her chin in thought. "I may have something that you'd like in the back. Wait here." She goes to the back of the store and comes out a minute later with a yellow dress hanging off her arm. Holding it out to Mrs. Reynolds, she says, "It's from Sweden. A new supplier sent it to us for evaluation."

Mrs. Reynolds eyes the dress, then rubs the edge of the fabric between her thumb and forefinger. "Love the fabric, but the color is atrocious. She'd look like a sour lemon in this."

"It came in a light plum color, too. I'll go get it."

"It's a beautiful shade," I say when she brings out the plum-colored dress. I try it on in the dressing room. It has spaghetti straps and a scooped neckline. The middle is cinched at the waist before waves of the material flow down and stop just above my ankle. When I walk in front of the mirror you can hardly tell I have a limp.

The sales woman smiles when I model it for them. "I think we have a winner here."

Mrs. Reynolds smacks her lips together. "It's perfect. We'll take it."

"You have a very generous grandmother," the saleswoman says to me.

I look over at Mrs. Reynolds, who is across the store looking at another dress. "I know. I couldn't have picked a better one myself."

When I go back to the dressing room to take the dress off, Mrs. Reynolds stops me. "Keep it on, Margaret. We'll be going to dinner from here and you won't have time to change."

"Which dress are you trying on?"

"Old ladies don't need new dresses. Now stop the chatter and let's move on."

I put my hands on my cinched, plum-covered hips. "I'm not leaving this store until you buy a new dress, too."

Mrs. Reynolds' mouth opens in shock.

"Don't look so startled, *Grandma*," I say, copying her famous saying to me. "It doesn't suit your face."

Her mouth snaps shut. Then she throws her head back and howls with unabashed laughter.

A half hour later we're back in the Cadillac. I might also add that Mrs. Reynolds is wearing a new silk and rayon, powder-blue dress with a matching jacket.

"I want you to deduct money out of my paycheck for the dress. I insist," I say.

Mrs. Reynolds just smiles without responding.

"I'm serious, Mrs. Reynolds."

"I know you are, dear, and I appreciate it. But I'm still buying it with my own funds."

I shake my head in frustration. "Where to now?"

"A pie run."

"Huh?"

"Just head for Auntie Mae's Diner and you'll see."

I steer the car around and drive to the diner.

Mrs. Reynolds ducks down. "Go to the back, where the dumpster is," she whispers. "And don't let anyone see you."

The woman is serious. I slide down in the seat and creep the car toward the back of the restaurant as if we're here to rob the place. I stop near the dumpsters. "What are we doing here?" I whisper, then wonder why I'm whispering. Her son owns the restaurant.

"Keep the car running, just get out and knock on the back door three times. Then you pause for two seconds and then knock another three times." Mrs. Reynolds sinks lower into her seat. "When someone answers, say, *The red hen has flown the coop*."

"I don't get it."

"You will if you follow my directions. Now go!"

This is comical. I almost pee in my dress as I creep up to the back door and knock. Knock, knock, knock. Pause. Knock, knock, knock.

Juan, one of the bus boys, opens the door a crack.

I burst out laughing as I say, "The red bird has flown the coop."

"Don't you mean *hen*?"

"Oh, yeah. Sorry, sorry, sorry. I mean *The red hen has flown the coop*."

I think Juan is laughing as he says, "Wait here," and closes the door. When the door opens, Irina hands me two boxes.

"What's inside?" I say.

"Don't ask me, Moggie. A surprise for you and Mrs. Reynolds."

When she closes the door, I bring the boxes to the car and slide into the driver's seat. "We got the goods."

"Great, now head back to my house."

Mrs. Reynolds is smirking as I drive up to her house. When I pull up to the garage, I finally figure out what this is all about.

The gazebo is finished, and Caleb has hung white lights all around it. White candles are lit inside, making the whole gazebo light up. Caleb is standing beside it, wearing khaki pants and a white dress shirt and tie.

When he winks at me and flashes his smile, I feel another piece of armor chipping away.

THIRTY-SEVEN
Caleb

I hurry to the car and open the door for Mrs. Reynolds. I hold out my hand and help her out of the car. "You look hot," I tell her.

She pats me on the cheek and says, "If I was only sixty years younger, sonny boy."

"Did you do what I said?" I say close to her ear.

She snorts. "I had Margaret saying that ridiculous sentence we came up with."

Mrs. Reynolds and I are partners in crime tonight. The gazebo is finished. My job here is done. I had the old lady make Maggie drive around town until six o'clock. I've been putting this night together in my head for a week already. A perfect night.

When I turn and catch sight of Maggie, I'm doomed. And speechless.

Mrs. Reynolds says, "Don't look so startled, Caleb. It doesn't suit your face."

Maggie walks up to me, the dress showing off curves I only recently dreamed she had.

"The gazebo looks great," she says.

I don't look away from her. Hell, I can't take my eyes off of her. These two unlikely women are my saving grace.

Maggie blushes, then glides away to join Mrs. Reynolds in the gazebo.

I've set a table inside the gazebo, complete with a three-course meal, compliments of my saved-up lawn mowing allowance and Little Italy Restaurant. I added a little spot heater to keep the gazebo warm, and have a portable radio with music playing softly in the background.

After pulling out a chair for Maggie, I hold my hand out to Mrs. Reynolds. "Would you care to dance, milady?"

She laughs, but I take her hand and pull her into a spin and into my arms. She shrieks. "Caleb, please. I'm an old lady. Where's my cane?"

"I thought old ladies like younger men," I tease, and dance slowly until the song is over.

I lead her to her chair and pull it out. "You better watch out for him, Margaret. He's dangerous."

I wince as I bend down to sit.

"What's wrong?" Maggie asks.

"Nothing," I say after everyone has been served. I take a spoonful of the minestrone and look up. Maggie's not buying it. Neither is Mrs. Reynolds. "Okay, okay. I competed in a wrestling invitational today. No big deal."

"I didn't know you joined the team."

"It was a one-time thing. I think."

Mrs. Reynolds finishes her soup and waves the spoon at me. "You might have a broken rib."

"I'm sure it's just bruised," I say, trying to reassure her as much as myself. Right before I pinned Vic in the second round, he knocked me to the ground and took a five-pointer.

I won the match, but the coach still gave me hell for playing dirty the first round.

"I can't wait until the daffodils bloom," Maggie says, her eyes sparkling with the candles shining on them. My hands are clammy from nervousness, I have no clue why. "You're going to have to take a picture for me and send it to Spain."

I still can't believe she's leaving. Just when I fell for her.

"Speaking of Spain . . ." Mrs. Reynolds hands her an envelope. "Enjoy your journey, but always remember where you came from."

Maggie raises a glass with water filled in it. "Who can forget Paradise?"

We clink our glasses together.

After we eat, I open the boxes from Irina, the chef from Auntie Mae's. As I set samples of pies in front of

Maggie and Mrs. Armstrong, you'd swear they were related by the elated expressions on their faces.

We all take a fork and dig in.

"This has been the most magnificent day of my life since Albert died, may he rest in peace. Thank you both. But these weary bones need a rest."

"Are you okay?" Maggie asks, concern lacing her voice. We both get up to help her.

"No, you two sit down and enjoy. I just need to rest a bit."

Regardless to what the old lady is claiming, Maggie helps her upstairs while I clear the dishes. "She okay?" I ask when Maggie comes back outside.

"I think so. She went to the doctor yesterday. He wants to run some tests on her, but she's too stubborn to go."

I watch Maggie. God, anyone who's with her is infected by her humility and honesty. "Care to dance?"

"I can't," she says. "Not with my leg . . ."

I take her hand in mine and lead her back into the gazebo. "Dance with me, Maggie," I urge as I put one arm around her back and pull her close.

We sway to the music. Slowly she relaxes into my arms. "I never imagined it would be like this," she says into my chest.

When her leg starts to hurt, I clear a place on the floor and we lie side by side next to each other.

"What did you ever see in Kendra?" she asks.

Hell, I don't know. "She was popular and pretty. Someone

who all the guys wished they could date. She used to look at me as if I was the only guy who could ever make her happy."

She sits up. "Okay, now you sound like a jerk."

"I was one."

She lies next to me, my arm as her pillow.

We watch the candles burn down one by one. When there's only one candle left, I kiss her soft lips and trace her curves with my hands until she's breathless and weak.

"Let me see your scars," I say when we're both panting and coming up for air from making out. I take the hem of her dress in my fist and slowly slide the material up.

She stills my hand with her own and smoothes the material back down. "No."

"Trust me."

"I . . . I can't," she murmurs. "Not with my scars."

Her words hit me like a cell door slamming closed. Because even if she thinks she forgave me, even if she made promises of forgiveness, even if she kisses me like I'm her hero, I finally realize she can't get over her anger inside. And never will fully trust me.

I lie back, totally frustrated, and lay my arm over my eyes. "This isn't going to work, is it?"

Maggie sits up. "I'm trying," she says, her voice full of regret.

I want to tell Maggie I wasn't responsible for hurting her leg, but I can't. What if Leah was right? I can't let my sister go to jail when I've already paid for her mistake. I'm committed to living with that blame forever.

The night of the accident, I was supposed to drive Leah home. But I was too drunk and enraged from Maggie's accusations. Staying with Kendra and making sure she didn't go home with any other guy was more important than anything else. My fucking ego. I had no idea Leah took my keys until she came back to the party ranting like a lunatic about an accident.

The rest, as they say, is history.

THIRTY-EIGHT
Maggie

I had everything I wanted and I screwed it up. Caleb loved me, all I had to do was show him my scars to prove to him how much I trust and love him back.

But I couldn't. Something was pulling me back into my protective shell.

I told my mom I was too sick to go to school today, so I'm lying in bed. The dress Mrs. Reynolds bought me is hanging in my closet, a cruel reminder of the most romantic evening of my life. I won Caleb and lost him just as quick.

When he took me home and we parted, he gave me a small smile and said we've always been friends, and we'd remain friends.

That's the most important thing. Right?

So why have I been crying the entire morning?

I call Mrs. Reynolds' house to see how she's doing after last night.

Mr. Reynolds answers the phone. "Hello?" he says, his voice shaken.

"Hi, it's Maggie . . . Margaret. Is Mrs. Reynolds there?"

Mr. Reynolds doesn't say anything for a long time, and my throat gets a huge lump in it.

"My mom died this morning, Maggie."

"No," I whisper as my life comes crashing down on me. "It can't be true. We were together. Last night she was dancing and laughing and—"

"She was grateful to have you in her life," he says. "She loved you as a granddaughter. More than that, she loved you as a friend."

"Where is she? Was she alone when she died?"

Mr. Reynolds sniffles. "They just took her away in an ambulance. She died in her sleep, no pain. Her heart has been bad for years, Maggie. It was only a matter of time."

Tears roll down my cheeks as I remember the times we spent in the past few months. She taught me so much about life. "The daffodils . . . she'll never see the daffodils come up," I say, stifling my emotions.

"Mama loved those daffodils, didn't she?"

I don't know what else to say to him. Mrs. Reynolds may have been up in years, but there was so much she still had planned. Having my mom and me over for dinner, watching the daffodils bloom in the spring. Eating Irina's pies.

"I'll miss her."

"I know you will. She never wanted a funeral. She said they're just an excuse for depressed people to make senseless chatter."

I smile wistfully. "That sounds like her." She just accused me of it yesterday, which reminds me . . . "A dress. She bought a dress."

"The blue one slung over the chair in her bedroom?"

"Yeah. If she's going to be buried . . ." I can't even get out the words.

"I'll make sure of it. Listen, if you want to come over and take something from the house before we sell it, you can."

"You can't sell the house." The daffodils, the gazebo . . . everything she cared about in the last two months are for nothing.

In the evening, my mom drives me over to Mrs. Reynolds house for the last time. She's holding my hand as Lou greets us. "Take anything you want, Maggie."

In the laundry room, all clean and folded, is the muumuu.

I pick it up and clutch it to my chest. It was Mrs. Reynolds' way of protecting me, covering my clothes so I wouldn't get dirty. "Can I have this?" I ask.

Mr. Reynolds seems surprised I'd want it, but says, "I was serious when I said *anything*."

There's two more things I want. I head to the kitchen and open cabinets until I find it. My mom is shrugging to Mr. Reynolds, who is as baffled as her. "It's got to be around here somewhere. Aha." I open one of the top drawers and on a piece of old, stained and ripped linen paper is her favorite Snickerdoodle cookie recipe.

"Anything else?"

"One more thing."

Mom and Mr. Reynolds follow me up to the attic. I head for the trunk and open it up. Holding up a picture frame, I say "This is the last thing."

Mr. Reynolds says, "It's yours."

I stare at the picture of two people madly in love on their wedding day.

May they both rest in peace.

THIRTY-NINE
Caleb

Maggie wasn't at school yesterday, and I haven't seen her all morning. Twice today I've passed by her locker, but she's been as elusive as a ghost.

During third period I can't focus. So I take the bathroom pass and head out the door. But I don't head straight to the bathroom. I turn the corner and go down the hall where I know her locker is. I've turned into a stalker.

"Looking for someone, Caleb?" It's Kendra, with a hall pass of her own dangling from her fingers. "Maggie Armstrong, perhaps?"

"Stop playing games with me, Kend."

She flashes a wicked smile. "No, seriously. I just don't get what you see in her."

"Nothing," I say just to get my ex off my back. "I see nothing in Maggie Armstrong. If anything she's been a distraction because I can't have you." The bullshit is flying because I need to protect Maggie and Leah at all costs.

The sound of someone behind me makes me turn around. It's Maggie. She's heard every lying word out of my mouth.

Kendra slinks toward her. "Caleb, did you tell Maggie the truth about the accident?"

"Kendra. Don't," I say in a warning tone. "Or I'll clue Brian in about what's been going on between you and me. Isn't your dad's election next week?"

If Kendra had claws, they'd be out and she'd be murderous.

Maggie hobbles toward me. "What's been going on between you and Kendra, Caleb?"

Kendra puts her hands on her hips, ready for this battle to begin. "Yeah, Caleb. Tell her how many times we've been together since you came back."

What can I say? I want to tell Maggie the truth, I'm going to tell her the truth. About everything. But not here, not in front of Kendra. She's got nothing to do with me and Maggie.

"Say something," Maggie orders, her eyes on fire.

When I don't, she slaps me and limps away.

———

I hate pep rallies. So I find it insane that I'm stuck in the middle of one today, of all days. But here I am, in the center of the crowd of athletes while the cheerleaders lead the rest of the school in pepping the entire student body.

As if a bunch of wrestlers want to be "peppy." But the guys'll take any excuse to ditch class for an hour.

Meyer stands at the podium as if he's the president of the United States instead of principal of a small-town school. "Settle down, everyone. Settle down." The place is still noisy, but it's the best he's going to get and he knows it. "This is a time to celebrate the students who represent the Paradise Panthers in athletics."

The crowd starts getting restless, the gymnasium floor vibrating from the noise.

"Settle down. Settle down. We're going to honor our athletes this afternoon. Each coach is going to come up and announce the members of their teams. Let's start with our largest team . . . football!"

This sets the cheerleaders into a frenzy, kicking and cartwheeling all over the gym.

"Put your hand up when I call your name," the football coach says. "Adam Albers, Nate Atkins, Max Ballinski, Ty Edmonds . . ." The list goes on and on for what seems like forever.

I'm standing next to Brian. "This is torture, man."

"Tell me about it," he says.

But when Coach Wenner gets up to the podium, the guys on the Paradise wrestling team are never ones to take a back seat. A roar goes up behind me. "Wee-ner! Wee-ner! Wee-ner!"

The guys are pronouncing the coach's name wrong on purpose. I bet Wenner is already planning how many extra push-ups he'll make the team do in practice to make up for it.

The rest of the school gets into it, even as the teachers are trying to put a kabash on the latest chant.

"Wee-ner! Wee-ner."

"Okay, ha ha, very funny. You had your laugh, now let's get to it," Coach says. "Andy Abrams, Caleb Becker, Adrian Cho, David Grant . . ."

Even though our school is small, it takes a while to get through all the names.

Finally, after more than an hour stuck in this hot gym, Meyer gets back on the mic and dismisses us to our sixth period classes. Trying to get out is like a mob scene. Everyone is as restless as I am to escape. But I'm hanging back.

I scan the bleachers. My sister is looking down, oblivious to anything except the stairs. Maggie is standing with the rest of the mob pushing through to get out. She looks so fragile standing there, like a bird surrounded by an elephant stampede.

There's some pushing and shoving. Two junior guys are fighting. And it's right where Maggie is. "Maggie, watch out!" I yell, but she can't hear me. She doesn't notice the commotion behind her, but I'm too late and it's too noisy. The guy is pushed into Maggie, who trips over two steps and lands flat on her knee.

"Maggie!" I yell, pushing people out of the way to get

to her. I finally reach her and kneel next to her. "Maggie, you okay?"

She blinks, looks like she's going to be sick, and sits up.

"Mag-ie, Mag-ie, Mag-ie," the crowd starts chanting.

I look up at the crowd and yell, "Shut the fuck up!" but nobody is listening. I grab Maggie's elbow. She tries to pull away but I hang on tight. "Are you okay?" I ask once she's standing. Most of the kids have stopped chanting her name, but a few assholes still have nothing better to do.

Drew grabs my shoulder and pulls me back. "Caleb, what are you helping her for? The bitch was responsible for putting you in jail."

I take my fist and slam it right into Drew's face. He charges me and we're at each other's throats, fists flying, until Wenner and another coach break us up.

"Where's Maggie?" I ask.

Wenner looks at me like I've lost it. "At the nurse."

"I've got to see her."

"The only thing you're seeing is the principal's office, Becker. What's *wrong* with you?"

I'm escorted to Meyer's office. I have no choice since Wenner has my wrists pinned behind my back. "Wait here for Mr. Meyer," the coach orders.

But as soon as he leaves the office, I hop over the front desk and open the nurse's door. Maggie's pants are rolled up just above her knees.

My gaze immediately focuses on her scars.

The angry lines from where the doctors must have

sewed her up are pink and look like her leg has been clawed by a fierce animal.

By her knee, where the biggest sets of marks are, I think is a skin graft, because it's a darker shade and doesn't match the rest of her soft, ivory skin.

Tearing my gaze away from her leg, I look up at her. "I'm so sorry, Maggie," I say.

Her expression is hard, her eyes shuttered. "Go away, Caleb. Or do you want to take a picture so you could show Kendra? Then you'd both have something else to laugh about."

Maggie

aleb doesn't even know Mrs. Reynolds died. When I saw him in the hall this morning, I was going to tell him. But then I caught Caleb and Kendra together. Before our relationship started, I could understand. But I thought he liked me enough not to need someone else. I thought what we had was real. Ugh. I don't want to think about Kendra Greene and her perfect blonde hair and her perfect, perky boobs or the perfect way she walks.

But I can't help it.

Because I'm not perfect.

I'm sitting in the nurse's office to prove it. Ever since Caleb stood there frozen, gawking at the scars on my leg, I've been dying to get out of here. "Can I go back to class now?"

The school nurse is bent over my leg with rubber gloves, examining it. She looks up. "Does it hurt?"

You mean my heart? "No. It's fine," I say. "Really."

"There's a little blood here. I'm concerned there might be internal damage."

"It's just a little scratch," I say as the woman is putting antiseptic on a cotton ball and rubbing blood off my knee. "A big deal was made for nothing."

I know why Caleb came running over to me and acted all concerned. It's because he feels guilty that I overheard details about his relationship with Kendra. Drew was only telling the truth, that I was responsible for putting him in jail. Caleb and I should never have started talking. We should have kept ignoring each other at Mrs. Reynolds' house.

Because if we didn't talk, I wouldn't be so connected to him.

If we didn't talk, I wouldn't have kissed him and wanted more. I wouldn't have let him manipulate me.

Nurse Sandusky doesn't look happy as I get down off of the examining table and carefully lower my pant leg. But I'm not going to sit here and sulk all day. I'm going to get up and stand tall—to Caleb, to Drew, to Kendra . . . and whoever else decides to get in my way.

When I'm dressed, I breathe a sigh of relief. My scars are covered. So why do I feel so exposed? Because Caleb has seen the scars from the injuries he put on my body.

The forever scars that will make me think of him and the accident every day of my life.

Unfortunately I have to pass Meyer's office on my way out. Caleb is sitting in front of the secretary's desk, his head slumped in his hands.

As if he knows I'm watching him, he lifts his head up. His eyes bore into me as if they're seeking warmth or connection. Does he think I'm a fool who wants to be humiliated? I look away, wait for the nurse to write me a pass, and leave the office as fast as I can.

As if the day couldn't get worse, Kendra and Hannah are walking down the hall. They haven't seen me yet. I duck into the girls' bathroom . . . I've had enough for one day.

I look at myself in the bathroom mirror. Dull hazel eyes, hair that hasn't decided if it wants to be dark or light, and a nose that's too big for my face. On top of all those flaws, I have a limp.

How could I ever have thought I could compete with perfect Kendra Greene?

The bathroom door creaks open. I hide in one of the stalls and soon enough I hear Kendra say, "I can't imagine the two of them kissing. Can you?"

"Puh-leaze, Kend, don't gross me out. Caleb is, like, Hollywood tough guy and Maggie is, like, a total dork. She probably kisses with her lips all pursed and her hands at her sides."

"*Exactly*. You should have seen her this morning. I

thought she was going to cry right in the middle of the hall."

The two of them laugh.

I want to die. Forget standing tall, deep down I really am a dork and a coward.

I peek through the door opening. Hannah is putting on her lipstick while Kendra is playing with her big, blonde hair.

"He's always going to love you. You two have a bond that can't be broken," Hannah says.

Kendra stops playing with her hair and leans against one of the sinks. "Caleb told Brian he was interested in Maggie to throw him off."

"Why Maggie? Isn't she the least likely person to snag him? He *did* hit her with his car, you know. And she milks it for all it's worth."

Kendra hesitates.

"What?" Hannah asks.

"Did you check under the stalls?"

Oops. I'm dead meat. Balancing on top of the toilet seat with a bum leg is not an option.

The door to one of the stalls creaks open. Oh, no. I'm trying to peek through the door, but I don't want to stumble or make any sounds to alert them I'm spying.

"You two are so pathetic. You should have looked before you started babbling about your pathetic lives."

It's Sabrina, my cousin.

"What did you hear?" Kendra says.

"What do you think? I heard all of it."

"And you'll keep it to yourself, won't you Sabrina?"

Sabrina puts her hands on her hips. "I don't know. Why don't you stop spreading rumors about my cousin? She may limp, but she's got more to admire than both of you put together."

The other girls stare at Sabrina as if she sprouted wings, totally shocked that the follower finally proved she has a mind of her own.

"Get a grip, Sabrina. Don't forget, you were a loser and Maggie was in your spot a year ago. Just because you're friends with Brianne and Danielle now doesn't mean you're suddenly hot shit."

She's right. I wasn't nice to Sabrina when I was on top and she was struggling to keep friends that didn't hide in the library during lunch. I think Kendra's words are going to bring Sabrina down a notch, but my cousin doesn't miss a beat.

"Kendra, I used to worship the ground you walked on because you were pretty and popular and had a boy-friend the rest of the girls only dreamed they could get. I wanted to be popular, to be like you. Now I just think you're pathetic."

"You'd better watch yourself, Sabrina, or you might just find yourself a loser again so quick your head will spin." Kendra's eyes are wide and wild, and I think if she had superpowers they'd melt Sabrina with that one stare. But she doesn't have superpowers. Hannah is standing behind Kendra with her thumb and forefinger in an "L" on her forehead, directing it toward Sabrina.

While Sabrina is sticking up for me and being threatened, I'm hiding out like a coward. My palms are sweaty. I realize it's my own fear holding me back. I watch my cousin sticking up for me knowing the end result is not going to be pretty. I feel Mrs. Reynolds' spirit giving me courage.

I push the stall door open wide, the loud creak alerting all three to my presence.

Sabrina's face is as shocked as Kendra's and Hannah's.

Kendra gives a nervous laugh, but recovers quickly. "Is this, like, the designated loser bathroom and I never got the memo?"

"You're just like your cousin," Hannah says to me. "One who'll always follow in the footsteps of girls like me and Kendra."

I hobble next to my cousin. "Hannah, you and Kendra have it all. And yet . . . you're *both* empty shells, nothing worthwhile on the inside. I wouldn't follow you even if it meant healing my legs."

"I think the accident damaged your brain." Kendra spits out the words like a dragon would spit fire at its enemy.

Sabrina is watching me in shock. I know I haven't been strong since the accident. I never stick up for myself and I focus on my flaws instead of my assets. Spending time with a strong woman like Mrs. Reynolds must have rubbed off on me. And spending time with Caleb the past few months has made me feel attractive and beautiful. I just . . . deep down I can't believe he was lying to me. Admiration shined through the depths of his eyes. His fingers trembled when he traced my lips or touched my face. A guy like Caleb, who hides his emotions, couldn't fake those intense reactions even if he wanted to.

Kendra shakes her head and sneers at me. "If Caleb gave you any attention, he just felt sorry for you."

I'm sure he did . . . but what we shared went way beyond that. "I wouldn't sneer if I were you," I say to Kendra. "It doesn't suit your face."

My cousin turns to me. "Caleb? No, it can't be true. Can it?"

I nod.

"*The* Caleb Becker? Leah Becker's brother, Caleb Becker?"

I cock my head to the side and nod some more.

Sabrina's mouth drops open and her eyes bug out.

Like a shock wave, I realize Caleb had been right all along. Going to Spain was just a copout, a way to escape people and a way for me to forget the accident for a little while. But the accident happened. There is no way to forget it. And I limp. I have to face the fact I will never be the same as before.

It's okay. I'm okay. Taking a deep breath, I realize something . . .

I feel stronger and more alive than I did before the accident.

The door to the bathroom opens. Mrs. Gibbons walks

into the bathroom. Her eyebrows go up when she witnesses our little confrontation. "Aren't you all supposed to be in class?"

None of us answer. Kendra is staring at me, Hannah keeps looking from Kendra to me and back to Kendra, Sabrina still has her mouth open in shock, and I'm not revealing anything.

"Okay, then. Let's all take a little trip to Mr. Meyer's office so he can get to the bottom of this."

"Fine with me," I say.

"Me, too," Sabrina says, backing me up. I owe a big apology to her for being such a jerk before the accident. Sometimes you have to steer away from the crowd in order to be a better person. It's not always easy, that's for sure. But it's right. And sometimes doing the right thing feels so good. Even if it does end up in a trip to the principal's office.

Kendra's eyes are still spitting fire. "What*ever.*"

"Yeah, what*ever,*" Hannah says, doing an embarrassing imitation of her best friend. I almost feel sorry for her.

We all follow Mrs. Gibbons to the front office. Sabrina is looking at me, wide-eyed. "No way! Caleb Becker?" she mouths silently.

It's not Kendra's fault she's beautiful and pretty. It's not even Caleb's fault for being attracted to her. It doesn't even matter.

What matters is that I'm not carrying around feelings of hatred and betrayal. It's been too exhausting. Mrs. Reynolds was right.

I don't hate Kendra.

I don't hate Leah.

I don't hate Caleb.

I'm feeling stronger than I have in . . . well, I can't even remember when. All I know is that I feel good. No, better than that. I feel strong.

Caleb

Meyer points to me and jabs his finger into the air with each word as he says, "Okay, Becker. In my office."

I follow him into his office, then he closes the door once I'm sitting in the chair opposite his desk. He's pissed off. I can tell by the way his neck muscles twitch and the colors of his face and bald head turn a deep shade of red. He doesn't even sit in his chair. He sits on the edge of his desk right over me. He's trying to be intimidating, to scare me into being a good kid. But he's never roomed with a guy like Julio. And if Julio didn't intimidate me, Meyer doesn't stand a chance.

"Why did you start a fight with Drew Rudolph?"

I can't tell him the truth. If the whole thing comes out,

Leah could be dragged into this, too. And Kendra. And Maggie. Leah has been acting creepy. I don't know what she'll end up saying. Will she blurt out the truth, that she was the one who hit Maggie? "I don't know," I say dumbly.

Meyer's anger deflates while frustration takes its place. "What *am* I going to do with you, Becker? I've had a parent call and say you were responsible for coercing a peer into consuming alcohol. Another complaint was filed by the wrestling coach from Fremont . . . something about you bullying one of his top wrestlers. You're on thin ice here, on the fast track to being a delinquent forever. Don't you understand the only person your behavior ultimately hurts is you? Unless you can explain yourself, I have no choice but to give you a suspension."

Suspension? Oh, shit. I would defend myself, but it's no use. The guy wouldn't believe me, anyway. I stay silent.

"You have nothing to say about these accusations?"

"Nope."

"Caleb, have a seat outside while I figure out how to proceed with this."

So now I'm stuck in another metal chair outside Meyer's office. Closed doors and metal chairs are the recurring themes in my life.

I look up when the door to the front office opens.

Maggie walks in the office, just feet from where I'm sitting. Only able to check her out from the side, I study her face. She has high cheekbones and a straight nose. It's not small; it has a little bump in the middle, almost as if

God wanted to put it there so her nose wouldn't be perfect. She wouldn't be Maggie without that imperfection. She's not in-your-face pretty like Kendra, but there's something about her . . . that mix of insecurity and regal features that don't fit. Every one of her features reflects who she is. Except her scars.

Those I wish I could take away with a touch of my fingers and transfer them to my own body.

Maggie is focused on the counter, reading something intently. Her hair falls like a curtain shielding her face from me. I'm barely aware of Sabrina, Kendra, and Hannah in the room, too. This place is getting crowded.

Mrs. Gibbons, the art teacher, knocks on Meyer's door. She peeks her head inside when he barks for her to enter his sacred domain. "We've had a situation with some of the senior girls."

The girls head single file into his office. Kendra looks defiant, Hannah looks scared, Sabrina looks indifferent, and Maggie is . . . she seems resolved to handle whatever comes flying at her.

The girls come out a few minutes later. Maggie doesn't look at me. She files out of the office with the rest of the girls.

Meyer reappears at the door. "Okay, Becker. Your turn."

I go into his office and am directed to yet another chair. This one is padded. I rest my elbows on my knees and think of what Meyer said: I'm on the fast track for being a delinquent forever. Maggie was probably right: if you disappear, then you don't have to always be reminded of the past wherever you turn.

I did my community service, but haven't gotten my final release papers. Damon is seriously going to kill me when he finds out I got in a fight. What the hell is going to happen when I go back to the DOC? I hope Mom and Leah don't go over the edge.

I hear the clicking of shoes and look up. My mother is standing in the doorway of Meyer's office. Her lips are tight. I can sense she has a loose rein on control because I see her wobbling slightly from side to side.

"Ah, Mrs. Becker," Meyer says. "Thanks for coming so quickly."

Mom nods and holds onto the door frame. "So . . . should I take him home?"

Meyer walks up to my mom and puts his hand on her shoulder to steady her. "The boy whom Caleb assaulted has not filed any charges as yet, but policy forces me to keep him off school grounds until this is resolved. You'll get a call from me after I've consulted the district superintendent to inform you of the length of Caleb's suspension."

Mom nods, then focuses on me. She looks tired. The deep lines under her eyes and at the corners of her mouth look deeper than I've ever seen them. I put those lines there. Without meaning to, I've broken my mother's spirit.

In the car, I've got nothing to say. And when silent tears start dripping out of her tired eyes, all I want to do is escape. Because I can't tell her anything to make her feel better, I can't fight this snowball of bullshit that has become my life.

I sit in my room until darkness falls, when someone knocks on my door. "Caleb, open up," a familiar transition counselor's voice rings out.

Great, now I get to be reamed out by Damon.

"Let me have it," I say dryly as I let him in.

If you've never seen a black guy's face get red with anger, you've never seen Damon Manning pissed off. "What the hell is going on? I got a call from your principal this afternoon telling me you're suspended for two weeks. You want to go back to the DOC?"

"Sure. You got cuffs ready?" I say, holding my arms out in front of me.

Damon gets in my face, real close. "Listen, punk, I have no problem slapping cuffs on you and hauling your ass back to prison. But I don't think you realize your eighteenth birthday is just around the corner. And you know what kind of eighteenth birthday present you get from the State of Illinois? You get transferred to the big boy jail. That's right, the adult place where the inmates rule, and not one day will go by that you won't be threatened or forced to do shit you've only heard about. I don't want you in there, Caleb, because you'll go in a confused smartass boy and come out a hardened bastard. They'll eat you alive there and nobody can save your ass. You hear me? Now tell me why the hell you've been getting into fights."

I'm so used to pleading guilty, I forget sometimes to

tell the truth. I look Damon straight on, no playing around this time. "I was protecting Maggie. Drew insulted her."

Damon takes my desk chair and sits in it. He puts his hand on his forehead and starts rubbing it, kind of like Meyer did this afternoon. "Caleb, what're you doing? She's your *victim*. You hit her with your car."

"I didn't do it."

"What?" he snaps.

"I said I didn't mean to do it."

Damon takes his hand off his forehead and leans forward. "I don't know what you're trying to pull here, but it's not good. If you can't pretend Maggie doesn't exist, then leave town. She called my boss this morning expressing concern about her safety. She said you've been sexual with her, and now that it's over you've harassed her."

"What?"

Damon looks straight at me. "Maggie Armstrong says she's filing a complaint. Oh, don't look so shocked, Caleb. What did you expect? When you don't follow the rules you pay the consequences. It's simple."

Nothing is that simple. I swallow. My throat feels constricted. Maggie hates me enough to send me back to the DOC?

"I need to know," Damon continues. "Did you have a sexual encounter with her?"

I sit on my bed and rest my head in my hands. Jeez, this cannot be happening. "That depends on what you mean by a sexual encounter."

"Don't fuck with me, Becker."

"I *didn't* have sex with her."

"Did you harass her?"

I shake my head. "We had a relationship, a *mutual* relationship. It was no big deal. It's over. Done."

"How did it end?"

"Abruptly."

Damon blows out a breath in frustration, then pulls out a stack of papers from his briefcase. "I got your release papers signed. You finished your community service."

I stare at the papers as if they have angels' wings on them, but my head is still reeling. I thought what Maggie and I shared was . . . well, it was a hell of a lot more than I ever had with Kendra. If Maggie hooked up with me just for revenge . . . oh, hell.

"You're released, but we have a bit of a problem. You can't go back to school. Caleb?"

"Yeah."

"Everybody isn't against you, you know."

I nod. Right now, I can't agree. I was so pumped to fix everything when I returned home. But all I've been doing is fighting instead of fixing. I'm at a loss here.

After Damon leaves, I head to the kitchen. Mom is leaning against the sink. She's shaking as she takes a bunch of pills and swallows them with a gulp of water.

"Mom, what are you doing?"

"Taking medication for tension and stress."

I snatch the bottle of pills off the counter.

"Give me that back," she orders.

Taking a closer look at the drug's name on the bottle. Diazepam. Valium. "How long have you been taking these?"

"Give them back," she says, pulling the bottle from my hand and clutching them as if they hold her sanity.

"You can overdose on that shit, Mom. It's dangerous."

My mom laughs, a throaty laugh so strong it makes her cough.

"Is that why you've been avoiding getting close to me. You've become a closet pill popper?" Damn, why didn't I see this before?

"It's not in the closet anymore, is it?"

"Does Dad know?"

"What do you think? It's the only way I can keep a smile on my face all day. He doesn't like to think about the bad stuff. He's too busy. I've been a failure, haven't I? A terrible wife, a terrible mother . . . it's no wonder I was kicked out of the Ladies' Auxiliary."

"Stop caring what everyone thinks!" I yell. "You're killing the entire family."

"Did you think about *the entire family* when you hit Maggie?" she whispers, then huffs out a disgusted breath.

"This isn't about me, Mom." I don't tell her it never was about me.

She shakes her head. "You don't get it, Caleb, do you? There's four people living in this house and we're all strangers. It *is* about you. It's about all of us."

I don't even know who I am anymore. I thought I did, but with Maggie's betrayal I'm back where I started.

My mom turns to face the sink, her body shaking and wrought with despair. As I walk over and put my arms around her, I want to tell her I'll help her. I need help, too. But she stiffens as soon as I make contact. "Don't touch me."

I take my hands off her and back away. Everything around me is crashing into a million pieces. There's no way I can mend them no matter how hard I try. "Don't wait up," I grind out before leaving the kitchen and taking the stairs two steps at a time. I bang on Leah's bedroom door. "Open up."

"What do you want?" Leah says through the door.

I pound harder. "Leah, open this door or I'll break it down."

She opens it right before I'm about to kick it open. "What?"

"How long has Mom been abusing prescription drugs?"

She shrugs. "After you got sentenced. She stopped for a while, but started up again when you got released."

"How can you just stand there like it's no big deal?"

Leah stares at me and cocks her head to the side, her black makeup in stark contrast to her white skin, making her look like a mime. "When she's numb she doesn't ask questions."

Huh? I stare at my sister as if she's a ghost, a shell of a person I once knew. "Do you even have a conscience anymore?"

Leah shrugs.

I grab her shoulders and yell, "Leah, grow up and finally take responsibility for something . . . anything!"

Tears start streaming down her cheeks. I shouldn't be satisfied that I'm making my sister cry, but I swear any emotion from her pleases me. I feel her emotions, too. But they're so conflicted with mine I can't be close to her. Not now. A part of Leah has always been a part of me. Her misery has become mine, and right now I want nothing to do with it.

She's sobbing while I leave the house and head down the street.

I walk ten houses away before I realize where I'm headed: Mrs. Reynolds' house. The lady is the only one who's tough enough to help. Maybe she'll let me live with her, in that little room above the garage.

Waiting twenty minutes for a bus to come to take me to Hampton seems like forever. When it comes and I take one look at the old lady's house, I feel like I'm home.

I ring the doorbell, hoping she can hear it. Maybe I'll install one of those bulbs that light up every time the doorbell rings, so if her hearing really goes she'll be all set.

The second time I ring, the door opens. But it's not Mrs. Reynolds, it's the guy who owns Auntie Mae's Diner. "Is Mrs. Reynolds home?"

"Aren't you Caleb Becker?"

"Yeah. I—"

"How do you know my mother?" he demands.

I put my hands in my pockets. "I worked for her."

He hesitates, confused, then his mouth goes wide. "*You* built the gazebo?"

"Yeah."

"While Maggie Armstrong worked here? The both of you, together?"

"With Mrs. Reynolds," I assure him.

"Did she know you were the one that hit Maggie? Forget it, from the look on your face I assume my mother knew. She probably tried to patch everything up, didn't she?"

"Yes, sir. I need to talk to Mrs. Reynolds." She's the only one I have left now.

"She passed away yesterday morning."

No. No, this can't happen. A hole forms in my chest and spreads through my veins. "You're lying."

"My mother had a heart attack in her sleep. Now I don't know what's been going on here, but I know Maggie's mother doesn't want you hanging around her daughter. Respect the family and leave her be."

"No problem. No problem at all," I say.

Maggie

Mom told me Mr. Reynolds had a surprise for me. I went to Auntie Mae's Diner after school and Mr. Reynolds gave me the keys to his mom's Cadillac. I protested, but Mom assured me Mrs. Reynolds would want me to have it.

So now Mom is driving me to Mrs. Reynolds' house on her break. She helps me open the garage. I smile when I see the car, remembering the time Mrs. Reynolds helped me get over my fear of driving.

"You sure you're ready to do this?" Mom asks.

"Yeah, I'm sure. Now get back to work. I'll be fine."

"Maggie, you've been so strong lately, but I don't know if you're ready for this."

It's time I tell her how I'm feeling. I've been trying to hold it in so I don't hurt her, when all along I think I'll hurt her more if I don't say anything. "Mom, I need some space," I say, then gauge her reaction. She's looking at me skeptically, but I can tell by the way her lips are together in concentration that she's listening and attempting to understand.

I take a deep breath and say, "I know it's hard for you. It's been unbelievably difficult for me . . . but I'm finally ready to accept my body and my limitations. I'm me . . . the new me. It might not be a perfect me, but I'm okay with that. It's about time I stopped trying to escape my life, don't you think?"

A tear runs down my mom's cheek. She smiles at me, this warm smile that reaches her eyes. "The accident . . . it took a part of you away."

"Only because I let it."

Now we're both crying. I give her a long hug.

After a few minutes she gets in her car and drives away from the house, giving me the space I need. Taking a deep breath, I scan the yard. And swallow hard. The gazebo is standing like a castle in the middle of the grass, outlined by the flower beds. The bulbs are patiently waiting in hibernation until it's their time to poke their heads out of the ground for the first time and vibrantly come to life.

After yesterday, I feel like I've bloomed. It took a romance and an old lady to coax me out of hibernation, but it happened.

As I'm carefully driving home, I see Caleb at Paradise

Park at the basketball courts. I stop to let him know I'm not upset he betrayed me. I'll get over him. It might take a while, but I'm going to be just fine. I'll have other boyfriends and adventures in life, other times I'll be able to feel confident and carefree and happy. I'm a survivor. Even with my limp. Getting out of the car and gathering all my courage, I walk over to him.

He sees me, but doesn't stop dribbling the ball.

"Caleb," I call out.

"Why didn't you tell me about Mrs. Reynolds?"

"I didn't have a chance. I wanted to," I say, then step toward him.

"You better stay back or I might start harassing you."

Okay, I deserve that. I did slap him and refuse his help yesterday. But that was before I straightened everything out in my head. "I heard you got in trouble."

"You come here to rub it in or you want to challenge me to a one-on-one?" he says.

"You know I can't play."

He looks me up and down suggestively. "Oh, you play, Maggie. Maybe not basketball, your games are more complicated than that."

"What are you talking about?"

He takes the basketball and holds it at his side, then gives a short laugh. "I can't believe you're afraid of me."

I move forward, stepping closer to him and putting my chin in the air with confidence. "I'm not afraid of you."

He stands before me with as much confidence as I'm showing him. "Prove it."

"How?"

He tosses the basketball to the side of the court and steps toward me, closing the distance between us. "Figure it out."

My breath catches and I panic. "I . . . I don't know what you mean."

"I think you do," he says, coming so close I can almost feel his emotions as my own.

"You want me to kiss you?" I ask breathlessly.

"You've ruined me, you do know that don't you?" he says right before I stand on my tiptoes and touch my lips to his.

He grabs my waist and pulls me close so I can feel the full strength and length of his body against mine. My fingers wrap around his biceps at the same time. I'm lost in the protection of his embrace and the smell and taste that's uniquely Caleb Becker. Uniquely . . . us.

As our kiss turns more intense, I sense a change in him. He's kissing harder, fuller. Angry.

I stumble backwards and push him away from me. "What are you doing?"

He wipes his mouth with the back of his hand. "Making sure I scare you. It's what you want, isn't it? So you can claim being the victim."

We're standing here staring at each other. Controller and controlled. Perpetrator and victim. Boy and girl.

He picks up his basketball. "Go home, Maggie. You got what you came for."

Movement out of the corner of my eye catches my attention, breaking the connection. It's Leah.

"Caleb, Mom and Dad want you home. Now," she says.

I smooth down my hair, pat dirt off my pants, clear my throat, and do everything but look at the two of them.

Then I run back to the car as fast as I can.

FORTY-THREE
Caleb

"You didn't tell her that I hit her, did you?" Leah asks as she watches Maggie run away from the park.

I shake my head.

"But you and Maggie. I saw how you looked at her and I knew . . ."

"What?" I say quickly, then look my sister straight in the eye.

I start walking back home and my sister steps in beside me. "Getting mixed up with Maggie can ruin our family, Caleb."

"Lay off, Leah. I mean it." I turn to her. "I've just about had it."

When I get home, my parents are waiting for me by

the front door. My dad is standing rigid, a stern look on his face. My mom is beside him. I can tell she's totally out of it.

"Where were you last night?" Dad orders in such a stern voice you'd think I was out committing murder.

"Visiting an old friend. What's the big deal?"

My mom looks at my dad.

I hold my arms wide. "What?"

"I saw Maggie coming from the direction of the park," Dad says.

"So? It's a free country, Dad. People can walk where they want to."

My mom clutches her arms tight, grabbing on to her sweater. "We just don't want to see you get into trouble. People talk . . ."

"About what?"

"I don't want to discuss it," Mom says, then starts to walk woodenly back into the house, no doubt to numb herself again.

"Let's hash it out. Right here, right now."

"Caleb, please, not so loud." My mom glances nervously at the neighbors' houses, making sure they don't witness the scene I'm about to make. God, I wish she'd stop worrying about appearances and see that her family is falling apart.

"What are people saying?"

"Nothing, Caleb. Everything's fine. Now stop this nonsense."

I step into the middle of the front yard and say as loud as I can, "Are they saying I've been starting fights at school? Are they saying I'm harassing Maggie? Making my friends drink alcohol? You think it's true, don't you? Come on, hit me with the fucking gossip already!"

"Now you've crossed the line," Dad says, stepping between us. "Go inside the house and calm down. You can apologize to your mother before supper."

I snap, like a rubber band that'd been pulled so tight for so long it just breaks apart violently. Kissing Maggie, school suspension, Kendra's manipulations, my sister's warning, my parents' inability to face reality, my mom's addiction problem, the false gossip . . . all of it is driving me nuts.

"I'm not leaving this spot until we have it all out on the table," I say. I look at my sister.

"Caleb!" Leah cries. "Please stop."

My dad's posture stiffens even more, his lips purse and the expression in his eyes is hard. "This is my home," he says. "And as long as you live here you'll abide by my rules. Now go inside the house, leave your mother in peace, and . . . calm . . . down!"

I swallow, hard. It's not easy for me to say the next words coming from my mouth, but I can't hold it in any longer. My family is screwed up, each and every one of us. They want to stay ignorant, to forget reality and live in a made-up world they've created. It's fake, it's sick . . . and I can't do it. I think the only way they'll heal is if I'm not here. I'm the root of their problems. If I take the root away, I'll remove the problem.

"I'm leaving," I say.

My thoughts turn to Maggie, the one girl who I used to think wasn't worth a second glance. But when it comes right down to it, she's the strongest girl I know. She confronted me about Kendra before the accident, she goes to school even though people laugh at the way she moves, and she worked her ass off for Mrs. Reynolds in order to achieve her dream of going to Spain. The accident made her a stronger person. Hell, she made *me* a stronger person.

"Where do you think you're going?" Dad demands.

"Inside to pack, then I'm out of here. I can't live with shame and denial around me. And you shouldn't, either."

"This is who we are now, son. The accident changed us . . . all of us. We were fine until you messed it all up."

I shake my head. "Don't you want to go back to the way it was before? I would do anything to make this family normal again."

"Shouldn't you have thought of that before you hit Maggie? I would have never thought I'd say this to my own son, but you . . . Caleb Becker . . . are a selfish bastard."

I walk past my parents and Leah, heading to my room. Pulling a duffle bag out of my closet, I stuff it without really thinking. I'm ready in five minutes, then look back at my room one last time.

My lightsaber is still on my shelf, waiting for me until I return. But I'm not coming back. Hopefully, after I leave, my mom won't have to drug her life to make it bearable and Leah can live her life the way she wants—with or without the truth. And Dad . . . well, one day he'll have to face reality. When he's ready.

It's up to me now to pave the way for myself and to stop trying to make sure life is back to normal. Screw normal. Normal doesn't exist. Caleb Becker's family doesn't exist. I'm on my own now.

With a sigh of determination I step back in the room, snatch the lightsaber, shove it in the duffle, and head out. Leah is at the front door, blocking it. "Don't leave," she begs.

"Get out of my way."

"Mom and Dad need you, Caleb. I need you."

I give a short laugh. "Mom and Dad'll be just fine. They like living in denial. As for you . . ." I take in her black attire. "You've got to get past the accident. Face the facts before people like Kendra make you face them. I can't protect you anymore. It's time to protect yourself."

I move around her and walk outside. I have no clue where I'm going or what to do, but I feel free. Tossing my duffle over my shoulder, I start walking. When I reach Maggie's house, I don't see her but I know she's inside.

I give her a goodbye salute and keep walking.

Mrs. Reynolds' gazebo is where I spend the cold, lonely night. When a shooting star flies above me as I stare up at the sky, I wonder if it's the old lady giving me a sign.

FORTY-FOUR
Maggie

Caleb kissed me last night at the basketball courts. I kissed him back. I still can't believe either of those things happened. I thought I was okay without needing him so much. I should have wiped off my lips and washed them with soap before I'd gone to bed, but instead I kept looking in the mirror. My lips are still puffy, a reminder of how Caleb's own lips were hot and demanding.

For years I'd imagined what kissing Caleb would feel like and taste like. To be honest, I wanted to push him away, to make him want me like I wanted him and to reject him like he rejected me.

But I couldn't.

All those feelings from my childhood came back, from the time Caleb urged me down from the tree in front of my house to the time he took the blame for that broken statue. I can't even forget the times he patted my back while I was crying to Leah about my parents' divorce. For the past year, the accident ruled my life and molded me into who I've become.

I've taken back my life.

Sitting on my bed, I pull up my pant leg. I notice that my heart is racing a little less as I scan the scars with my eyes. I used to think of them as angry scars, but now I don't see them as angry. They aren't even scary. I trace the lines with my fingers, and I don't even wish they'd disappear. They're a part of me.

I close my eyes, remembering the accident. It's so strange to think about that night without massive emotions running rampant through my veins. Through the darkness behind my lids, the image of Caleb driving the car that hit me is outlined in my head. But something doesn't feel right.

Chills run up and down my spine.

Because, as I shut my eyes tight, the image of the driver becomes clearer and the foggy haze dissipates.

It's Leah. A look of horror and fear in her eyes as she loses control of the car.

Leah was the one who hit me that night.

Not Caleb.

Why would he . . . why would they . . . ?

The doorbell rings while I'm still trying to sort it all out. My stomach is queasy. I want to throw up. But I can't, because my mother is calling me downstairs. I almost fall down as I greet a man and a woman wearing matching dark navy suits.

"Maggie, we're from the Illinois Juvenile Department of Corrections. We're here to investigate your complaint about Caleb Becker."

"I didn't file a complaint," I tell them.

The woman opens her briefcase and pulls out a folder. "We have documentation you called the 1-800 juvenile justice number complaining to the operator that Caleb Becker was harassing you."

Oh my God. I shake my head and look to my mom. "I didn't call. Mom, I swear I didn't call."

"Are you sure?" the man asks. "You don't have to be afraid, Maggie. We're here to make sure you're protected."

I stand up. "I'm not afraid of Caleb. We're friends."

My mom says, "Please excuse my daughter. She doesn't know what she's talking about. She's been instructed not to have any contact with that boy. Right, Maggie?"

I bite down on my bottom lip. "Mom . . ."

"Maggie?"

Last night at the park makes sense now, why he was testing me. Oh, how he must hate me, thinking I'd call and complain when I would never do anything to hurt him. Kendra would hurt him. I wouldn't. "I have to go see him."

"Maggie, come back here!"

I hobble over to the Beckers' house before anyone can stop me. Mrs. Becker answers the door.

"Is Caleb home?" I ask frantically. "I really, really need to talk to him. I know you probably hate me for being the reason he went to jail, but I think it was all a mistake and—"

"Caleb is gone," she says, totally unfazed by the words coming from her mouth. She even has a strange smile on her face. "He left."

By now my mom has followed me over to the Beckers' house with the investigators in tow.

Mom regards Mrs. Becker strangely. "Penny, what's wrong with you?"

As soon as my mom says it, Mrs. Becker slips and falls right into my mom's arms. After Mom shrieks, the two investigators help her carry Mrs. Becker into the house. "She's passed out," one of them says.

As they're taking care of Mrs. Becker, I step back. What did Mrs. Becker mean when she said Caleb *has gone?* I rush home, grab my keys and drive to Mrs. Reynolds' house. I check the garage, gazebo . . . he's not here.

All along, I blamed Caleb for hitting me, without questioning his guilt. He pleaded guilty, but deep down I detected something strange in him. I thought it was a lack of remorse for hitting me, when all along it was a lack of guilt.

My heart sinks lower with each passing moment as I drive around Paradise. I'm looking for Caleb, or some sign he's still here. Before I know it, I'm at the place where my life changed.

The scene of the accident.

The skid marks from the car are still on the curb, a dark reminder of that day. I haven't come here since the accident. I wouldn't have had the strength before to relive it up close. I step out of the car and walk over to the fading skid marks, staring at them for what seems like forever. Will they eventually disappear altogether, so the only physical reminders of the accident will be the ones I carry with me?

I know the truth, though. That the visible scars aren't as deep as the emotional ones Leah and Caleb have been struggling with. I have a burning desire to help them, just as Caleb helped me. The most important thing I've learned the past few months is that friends are invaluable. People you love can get you through the toughest of times. They need me just as I need them. I miss Leah as my confidante, my best friend. And the love I have for Caleb is the forever kind that will never go away, no matter how hard I try to deny it.

"Maggie."

I turn around. Caleb is riding in a black Toyota, a guy I don't recognize at the wheel. Caleb tells the guy to stop the car, then he walks up to me. He looks sad and lonely and worried.

"How did we get here?" I ask.

"Here's where it all started."

"I didn't call and complain about you," I say hurriedly.

"You see, these investigators came to my house this morning and said they were following up on a complaint I made and I insisted I never made it and then I realized you must have thought I did and then—"

Caleb puts a finger to my lips, stopping my babble. "It doesn't matter."

"But it does. And I trust you. Isn't that what we're all about? Trust and honesty."

I need to prove it to him, a sign that I trust him without any reservations. I pull up my left pant leg with one hand, revealing all my scars up to my knee.

His brows knit together in pain, as if he was the one who put them on my leg. I take his hand in mine and together we trace the swollen lines with our fingers. "You see, there's nothing I want to hide from you anymore. Do you feel the same, Caleb? No secrets, no lies?" I need him to tell me the truth about what happened that night. I need to hear it from his own lips, his own words. *Tell me you didn't hit me*, I want to say. *Tell me the truth.*

"Yo, *amigo*, you ready to *vamónos?*" a guy yells from the car.

"Who is that?"

"Rio."

I'm worried. "I mean, who *is* he?"

"You don't want to know, Maggie," Caleb says. "Listen, I gotta go."

I look up into his beautiful, intense face. At the same time I know he's never going to give away the secret he's been holding inside. That fierce, protective spirit is a part of him, a bond he can't break.

"Where are you going? When will you be back?"

"I'm not coming back."

Looking into his serious, sad eyes, I know he means what he's saying. My eyes start to water and tears roll down my cheeks. "You can't leave me. Not now." I want to beg and plead and cry and grab him until he changes his mind. I want to play tennis with him today, and tomorrow, and the next day.

He gently swipes my tears with his fingers. "Then come with me."

The tables have cruelly turned. I tell him, "I realized you were right. It's a copout to leave. I'm going to stay in Paradise until I graduate, and save the money Mrs. Reynolds gave me for college."

"Becker, you comin' or not?" the guy in the car calls out.

Caleb nods and says, "Yeah, I'm coming."

I lean in and touch his forehead to mine. "Tell me what we had was real," I whisper. "Please."

Caleb's hands lightly clasp my head on both sides, enclosing us into our own private world. "As real as it gets. Don't ever question that, no matter what. Okay?"

"Right now I'm questioning everything. Why did I even come here?"

"Because you're ready to start a new life, Maggie. You're free of the past now. It can't hurt you. For me, being free means leaving Paradise." Leaning in, he kisses me. So soft and full of warmth and longing and remorse.

I want to grab him and keep him safe. "Does that mean we're both free?"

He nods, unable to put it into words.

I know he'll never write or call. He's going to cut all ties wit his family and this little town that's caused him so much grief. Including me. God, how I wish Caleb never pled guilty to hitting me. Although if the accident had never happened, if he'd never gone to jail and been stuck doing community service, Caleb and I might never have been together.

I wouldn't have changed that for anything.

He steps back and winks at me. "Bye."

"I'm not going to say it back to you, you know," I tell him.

He gives a short laugh and keeps retreating backwards. "Then tell me something I can remember as your last words to me. Tell me you love me. Tell me you'll think of me every night before you sleep. Tell me—"

"*The red hen has flown the coop*," I say.

He laughs. "I'll always remember Mrs. Reynolds, the gazebo, the daffodils, you and me in the gazebo . . ." Caleb winks at me one more time and turns around, his back to me as he walks to the Toyota. I want to scream at him for leaving me. I want to run up to him and forget being sane. Let us live in the streets together. As long as we're a team, nothing can bring us lower than we were apart.

But he never did tell me it was Leah who hit me. He's the one who, in the end, didn't trust me . . . or himself.

I'm sobbing now, more than I did after the accident. And my heart hurts, more pain oozing from it than my leg ever had.

"Caleb!" I yell right before he slides into the passenger seat and closes the car door. I hold my breath, waiting for him to come back to me. To turn around. But he doesn't.

The car screeches away, its red lights a blur through my watery eyes.

I head back home and some time during the ride I stop crying. There's strength within me that I didn't know existed before. It's as if Mrs. Reynolds is nudging me to stay strong. Life is too short, she'd once said. She was right. As I pull into my driveway and get out of my car, I notice Leah. She's standing in the front doorway of her house, her eyes puffy.

I walk over to her. "Is your mom okay?"

She shrugs. "I guess. Your mom's with her."

Well, it's a step in the right direction. It's about time we mended that invisible fence. I look up at my old best friend.

"You saw him, didn't you?" she asks me.

"Yeah."

She holds her arm over her eyes and starts to sob. "I need to tell you something really, really important. But I can't look at you while I do it."

I take her arm and lower it. "You don't have to tell me right now," I say. "When you're ready, we can talk."

"You're going to hate me, Maggie. For the rest of your life you're going to hate me."

"I'm not going to hate you. I know, Leah. I know what it is."

"You do?" she says, all glassy-eyed.

"Yeah. But it's okay."

"It is?"

"Let's just say our friendship means more to me than holding a grudge or living in the past. You know what always helps me forget?"

"What?"

"A pie run."

Leah gives me a small smile behind her tears. "You're kidding, right?"

"Nope. Come with me for a drive to Auntie Mae's. Let's get our moms . . . I think they need some pie, too."

Acknowledgments

First of all I want to thank my agent, Nadia Cornier, for always believing in my stories and my talent. I also want to thank my editor, Andrew Karre, for his insight and support while I wrote this book, along with Brian Farrey and Rhiannon Ross, two people who deserve medals for putting up with all my questions and changes. Lisa Novak gets special kudos for designing the beautiful cover!

Karen Harris's, Marilyn Weigel's, and Ruth Kaufman's advice has been invaluable while I wrote this book—you ladies ROCK! Other friends who have been incredibly supportive are Lisa Laing, Sara Daniel, Erika Danou-Hasan (hereby officially dubbed The Nice One), Martha Whitehead, Amy Kahn-Randi Sak-Liane Freed-Debbie Feiger-Marianne To-Stacy Leiter-Michelle Movitz (after my surgery you all went above and beyond the call of duty), Nanci Martinez (who has the Spaghetti Spectacular recipe), and the plethora of friends I have in Chicago-North RWA. A special thanks to Heather Davis and my www.booksboysbuzz.com blog friends.

And to Pat McCurdy, whose music always makes me laugh when I'm going through the toughest of days.

Thanks to Dylan Harris for his brilliant wrestling advice and to my cousin Rob Adelman for being such an inspiration.

Derrick Bankston spent hours with me at the Juvenile Justice Complex and his hospitality went beyond my highest expectations. If my kids ever get into trouble, I'm calling you for advice.

And finally to Samantha, Brett, Moshe, and Fran (a.k.a. Mom). We're on this journey together. Whee!

RETURN TO PARADISE

For
Erika Danou-Hasan,
Ruth Kaufman,
and Marilyn Brant—
three women who continue to remind me that
friendship is selfless and has no boundaries.

ONE
Caleb

Some people are damn lucky. Unfortunately I've never been one of those people. In fact, I think I'm one of those guys destined to always be caught in the crossfire. As I sit in the back of a squad car with handcuffs digging into my wrists, I think back to the first time I got arrested, almost two years ago.

I'd been drinking.

I was wasted.

And I was arrested for a crime I didn't commit.

Didn't matter, though. I got locked in juvie for a year anyway, mostly because I pled guilty to the hit-and-run drunk driving charges.

This time I'm getting arrested for drugs. Except I didn't

smoke, inhale, ingest, snort, shoot up, or buy the shit. Okay, I admit I was living in a drug house. It was either keep a roof over my head and ignore the illegal stuff going on around me, or live on the streets.

I chose the roof. Looking back, maybe it wasn't the wisest choice. Living on the streets sounds mighty tempting right now. Nothing is worse than being locked up like a caged animal and relinquishing control of your own life. Being told when to shit, shower, shave, eat, and sleep isn't my idea of paradise. But then again, Paradise, where I grew up, wasn't paradise either. I'm wondering if paradise is just some word in the dictionary with the definition: *this doesn't fucking exist.*

I lean my head against the back seat of the squad car, wondering how I'm gonna get out of this. I have no money, no real friends, and my family ... well, I haven't had any contact with them since I left Paradise eight months ago.

When we arrive at the police station, the cop escorts me to a lady who has the exciting job of taking my mug shot. Then the cop orders me to his desk and introduces himself as Lieutenant Ramsey.

"Don't try anything stupid," he tells me as he unlocks the handcuff on my right wrist and secures it to a metal hook on his desk so if I wanted to flee I'd have to lug a fifty-pound desk with me. Needless to say, I'm not going anywhere.

After asking me a bunch of questions, he leaves me alone. I look around for Rio, one of my five roommates.

We all got busted at the same time, when Rio and another one of our roommates were selling a crapload of meth to three guys who, if you ask me, looked like undercover cops who were just dressed up as badass gangsters. I think it was the gold tooth on one of the guys that gave it away. It looked like it'd been glued on and I could have sworn it became loose at one point and he swallowed it.

That was right before they pulled out their guns and yelled for us to kneel on the ground and put our hands on our heads. I'd been watching some reality show about a pawn shop, because the last thing I needed was to be involved in Rio's business.

Rio had asked me to help him make some runs a couple times, and I did. But I don't get off on selling drugs to guys who're so desperate to get high they'll give me their last dime to get it. The last time I was supposed to sell drugs for Rio, it was to a guy with three kids. He brought his three kids to our house, and when I saw their long, drawn faces and their ragged, torn clothes, I couldn't do it. I refused to sell him the stuff. Not that that makes me a good person or anything, especially because I know if I didn't sell it to him someone else would.

"Listen, Caleb," Ramsey says as he opens up a file folder with my name on the tab at the top. "You've got yourself in big trouble. Chicago judges aren't lenient on repeaters, especially when they're living in drug houses with over fifty thousand worth of meth and Z-tabs."

"I'm not a dealer," I tell him. "I work at Chicago Recycling."

"Just because you've got a job doesn't mean you don't deal." He picks up his phone and hands me the receiver. "You get one phone call. Tell me what number to dial."

I put the receiver down on his desk. "I waive my right to a call."

"Family? Friends?" he suggests.

I shake my head. "Don't got any."

Ramsey rests the handset back on the phone. "Don't you want someone to bail you out? The judge'll set bail later today or tomorrow. You should be prepared."

When I don't respond, he flips through my file. He looks up after a couple of minutes. "It says here Damon Manning was your transition counselor."

Damon Manning was supposed to make sure I stayed out of trouble back when I got released from juvie. He was a big black guy who scared my mom to death when he walked in our house during his scheduled visits. Damon assigned me my community service job and constantly drilled me on how to transition from being in jail to being back at home. He wouldn't take one-word responses or silence for an answer. The guy was a hardass who didn't take shit from anyone, and whenever I fucked up he let me know I better shape up or he would be personally responsible for telling the judge to lock me back up. I had no doubt that he'd do it, too.

Ramsey jots a number down and sets it in front of me.

"What's this?"

"Damon Manning's phone number."

"And why would I want it?" I ask him.

"If you don't have family or friends to bail you out, I suggest you call him."

I shake my head and say, "No way."

Ramsey pushes the phone toward me and leans back in his chair. "Call him. If you don't, I will."

"Why?"

"Because I read Damon's reports on you, and he's rarely wrong about his assessments."

"What did he write?" That I was a complete fuckup who deserved to be locked up permanently?

"Why don't you call him and ask him yourself? You're in big trouble, Caleb. You need someone on your side right now."

I look at the phone and shake my head in frustration. Ramsey doesn't look like he's giving me a choice. I pick up the phone and dial the number.

"This is Damon," a deep voice answers.

I clear my throat. "Umm ... this is Caleb. Caleb Becker."

"Why are you callin' me?"

"I kind of got in trouble," I say, then clear my throat. I take a deep breath and reluctantly blurt out, "I need your help."

"Help? I didn't know you knew that word."

I briefly explain the situation. He sighs heavily a bunch of times, but says he's on his way over to the station. After my call, I'm escorted to a holding cell and wait for him. An hour later I'm told I have a visitor and am led to what I assume is one of the interrogation rooms. Oh, man. If things weren't bad enough, I have a feeling they're about to get worse as a very pissed-off Damon walks through the metal bulletproof door.

"What the hell did you get yourself into, Becker?"

"A shitload of trouble," I tell him.

Damon crosses his arms on his chest. "I could have sworn you were a guy who made one mistake and was going to turn his life around." He gets a distant, almost sad look on his face, but it's quickly masked. "I got to admit you reminded me of myself when I was your age."

"Yeah, well, you were obviously wrong."

He narrows his eyes at me. "Was I?"

This isn't the way it was supposed to be. I left Paradise to make everything better, but all I've managed to do is fuck things up for myself. I look Damon straight in the eye. "I didn't do it," I tell him. "I'm not a dealer."

"Why should I believe you?"

"Because it's the truth." I let out a breath, knowing it's a lost cause to plead my case but doing it anyway. "I don't expect you to believe me."

"Have you lied to me in the past?"

I nod.

"About what?"

I close my eyes and shake my head. I can't tell Damon that I wasn't the one who hit Maggie. I told Leah I'd take that secret to the grave. I can't betray my own twin. Not now, and not ever. "Forget it."

"You're on the wrong path," Damon tells me.

"I didn't have a choice." I let out a long, slow breath and decide to level with him. About some stuff, anyway. "I found out my mom was addicted to meds. I think me being home made it worse. She kept expecting me to fake it that everything was okay. My entire family went along with the bullshit. I couldn't. Maggie was the only one keeping me sane, but I couldn't see her without getting shit from the cops, my parents, her mom, and even you. You once said I should get out of Paradise instead of getting close to Maggie. So now I'm here."

"Living with a drug dealer isn't a better option," Damon says, stating the obvious.

"It was a roof over my head."

"There are always options other than living with thugs," Damon tells me.

"Yeah, right." I look down at the red mark the handcuffs left on my skin. I seem to be all out of options right now.

"I'm really disappointed in you."

Disappointed is better than angry. I've seen Damon angry. He stiffens up like a bull with a thorn up his ass. Hell, when I got suspended from school for fighting, Damon looked ready to single-handedly kick my ass. The guy is huge and must weigh close to two-eighty. I'm not a lightweight, but he could sit on me and crush my bones.

"I'll be right back," Damon says, then leaves me alone in the room.

Ramsey comes back a half hour later, with Damon following in his wake. The officer sits on the edge of the small table in the room and looks down at me. "You're lucky, kid."

I'm about to be tossed in jail. I'm not feeling lucky right about now.

"I just talked to Judge Hanson," Damon says. "You'll have your arraignment this afternoon, and I'll pay any bail set. I'm friends with the district attorney who'll help you."

"Why would you do that for me?" I ask.

"Because someone did it for me a while back. There's one condition," he says.

Here it comes. The ax is about to fall. "What?"

My ex–transition counselor has a stern look on his face. "You join Re-START."

"What's that?"

"It's a group of kids whose lives have been affected by reckless teen driving. We're traveling for a month together, and each participant shares their story with various groups of kids in the Midwest. We'll be roughing it, so don't expect fancy hotels or the royal treatment. We'll be staying in dorms and campgrounds. This arrest isn't about drugs, Caleb. It's a direct result of your accident in Paradise. Join the program and help others. If you don't agree to come with me, I'm out of here. If I leave, I have no doubt they'll lock you up for good and throw away the key. You're eighteen now. If you thought juvie was awful, I guarantee that adult lockup will be one hundred times worse."

"So I really don't have a choice?"

"You do. Stay here and enjoy the fine hospitality of our state prisons, or get off your ass and follow me."

So there isn't a choice. One of the options is something I'd do practically anything to avoid. Even if it includes spending time with my old transition counselor.

We don't speak much the entire one-and-a-half-hour drive out to Redwood. He tries to ask me questions and I do my best to dodge them. When we pull up the driveway of a one-story duplex, he explains, "You'll sleep at my place tonight, and meet up with the rest of the group tomorrow afternoon."

Inside, I drop my duffle next to a faded plaid couch. On the mantle above the empty fireplace is a picture of Damon with a little boy, about eight years old, in a Little League uniform.

"Is he yours?" I ask him, wondering how this guy ended up living alone in a small town in the middle of the boon-docks of Illinois. Paradise isn't too far away from here.

"Yeah."

It's obvious from the look of the place he lives alone. There's no artwork on the bare white walls. The place isn't like my house back in Paradise — it's too plain and too unused, like he just comes here to sleep and that's it.

"You divorced?" I ask.

"You gonna stop asking questions? I think I liked you better on the ride here, when you didn't talk at all."

After Damon makes a surprisingly good dinner of chicken and rice that reminds me of my mom's cooking, he heads down a narrow hall to bed. It's quiet in the house. I'm not used to this much silence. At Rio's place, there were always people partying or coming in and out at all hours. I didn't mind, because I don't sleep much anyway.

I turn the light off although I know I'm not going to get much sleep tonight. It'll be like usual … every fifteen minutes I'll wake up and stare at the ceiling and pray for sleep to come. It does, but in such short spurts I wonder what it'd be like to get a full night's sleep with no interruptions. That hasn't happened for years … since before the accident.

In the morning I'm eating some healthy whole-grain type of cereal when Damon walks into the kitchen. I can't help but ask, "Why did you help me?"

"Because I think you're a good kid," he says, his back to me as he stands in front of the stove and fries some eggs. "You just have to make better choices."

In the late afternoon, we throw our bags in the car. Damon stops off at the Redwood community center, where a big white van is waiting for us. He gets summoned into the building and tells me to hang by the van and introduce myself to the rest of the group. There's two other guys and three girls standing there waiting with their baggage.

When one of the girls moves aside and I get a glimpse of the person she was shielding, my entire body goes numb.

Maggie.

TWO
Maggie

I watch my protein bar fall onto the blacktop in slow motion, and the bite in my mouth tastes like dust. *What is Caleb doing here?* Where has he been the past eight months? He left town without a trace after our brief and crazy relationship. Why didn't he try to reach me, or at least give me a sign that he's alive?

He's got those same blue eyes, that same chiseled face, and those same lean muscles peeking out of his T-shirt. He's real, and live, and walking right toward me.

I can't look away, even though I desperately want to.

He lets out a slow breath and says, "This is kinda awkward, huh." His voice sounds familiar but different. It's got an edge to it that wasn't there the last time we saw each other.

"Yeah," I manage to squeak out. Umm …

"How've you been?"

I can't answer that question. It's too fake. If he cared how I've been, he would have figured out a way to see me or talk to me. He left me before Christmas, before New Year's, before Valentine's Day, before my birthday, before prom and graduation. Before I got the news I'd have a permanent limp for the rest of my life without any hope of a full recovery. "What are you doing here?"

He shrugs. "I was asking myself that same question this morning."

One of the other guys standing with us, the one with long curly hair that falls in his face, farts. What's worse is that he makes a big show of moaning and pushing it out, like a little kid.

"Dude, do you mind?" Caleb asks.

"What?" the guy says, unfazed. "I had to let it rip."

"Let it rip when you're alone, man. Don't be a fuckin' prick."

"What are you, the fart police?" the guy says, stepping toward Caleb. Caleb stands tall, as if he's been in a lot of fights and isn't afraid of adding another one to his tally.

This is unreal. I can't feel my toes because I'm in shock, and Caleb and this guy are going to get into a fight over … farting?

"Cool it, guys," bellows a rough voice. A tall black guy

with a clipboard points to me. "Maggie, can I have a word with you for a minute? In private." He points to Caleb. "You too, Becker. *Now.*"

I follow the guy away from the van, painfully aware that Caleb is following close behind. I'm tempted to turn around and demand to know where he's been, but I don't even know if I could get the words out.

The guy stops at a picnic table and drops his clipboard on it. He introduces himself to me as Damon Manning, the senior leader and chaperone of our group, then looks pained as he says, "Obviously, you two can't be on this trip together. Maggie, I had no idea my assistant put you in as the replacement after Heather dropped out."

"I'll drop out," Caleb offers eagerly.

"The hell you will, Becker. You've got no choice but to do this."

That means Damon expects me to drop out. If I was the old Maggie, the one who was afraid of the least bit of conflict or confrontation, I'd drop out in a heartbeat. But I'm stronger now, and I don't back down from anything. Even Caleb.

I turn to Damon with determination. "I'm not dropping out."

"Maggie, I'm sorry but it's not going to work with both of you—"

"I'm not leaving," I interrupt.

Damon rubs a hand over his bald head and sighs. I can tell he's wavering ... at least a little bit. What can I say to convince him I don't have to quit the trip just because Caleb happens to be on it? Truth is, being with Caleb will be a challenge—a huge one I hadn't expected. But I decide I'm going to prove it to myself and to him that I've moved on. I don't let the past dictate my life anymore. We're both eighteen now, both considered adults in the eyes of the law.

"This is a bad idea," Damon chimes in. "A *really* bad idea."

"Can I talk to Caleb alone?" I ask him.

Damon looks from me to Caleb. "Okay. You've got five minutes."

When Damon walks away, I swallow hard and force myself to face Caleb. He looks worn out, but at the same time a fierce strength radiates from him.

I used to think he was everything I wanted and needed. If I had Caleb Becker at my side, my life would be okay. And it was, for a little while at least.

"It's been eight months," I say in a small voice. Thinking of how much I've missed him makes my eyes well up. I blink and pray my tears don't fall. Not now, when I have to stay strong. I say something, anything, so I don't lose it. "You missed graduation."

"I missed a lot of things," he says, then slowly starts to reach out his hand before he shoves both hands in his pockets.

I know I probably look pathetic. I *feel* pathetic. But I'm sick of feeling sorry for myself. I've had to move on.

I've gotten stronger every day. I can't get sucked back into the soap opera of Caleb's life. I won't let that happen.

I look at the big white van that's supposed to take us on a four-week trip together. We're going to share our stories publicly, hoping to prevent others from experiencing what happened to us. I bite my lip at the irony. How can we do that, when the truth of Caleb's and my accident is still buried?

I kick at some loose pebbles of tar on the blacktop. "He said you have no choice but to go on this trip. Why?"

Arms folded, Caleb leans against the picnic table and sighs. "Okay, here's the deal. Big surprise: I got myself in trouble again. It's either this program, or I go to jail. The ball's in your court, Maggie. You want me to quit, I will. I'll take the consequences."

The last thing I want is Caleb back in jail. I'm afraid to ask for details of how he got into trouble, so I don't. If he wants to tell me, he will. But I know he won't because he doesn't know how to trust anyone, least of all *me*. I might have been a part of his life once, but now I'm not. I'm a stranger to him, and he's a stranger to me.

"It's only four weeks," I tell him. "I think we can handle it."

"Four weeks stuck in a van together, and then you never have to see me again."

I close my eyes when he says that. He shouldn't disappear again. His sister needs him, and his mother struggles every day with her prescription drug addiction. "After the trip, you should go back to Paradise."

"Not gonna happen, so get that thought out of your head."

Forgetting my sadness and gathering courage, I stand up straight and look him in the eye. "You know what I think?"

"What?"

"I think the tough and stoic Caleb Becker takes the easy way out." There, I said it.

"My life is a lot of things, Maggie, but easy isn't one of them," he says. He clears his throat. "And if you think seeing you right now is a piece of cake for me, guess again..." His voice trails off.

"Maybe this was fate giving us a second chance at saying goodbye. You know, before we both go our separate ways again."

"That must be what it is," he says sarcastically. "So you're absolutely cool with going on this trip together?"

I clear my throat and look over at the van. "I'm cool with it as long as you are."

Pushing himself away from the table, he walks away from me and heads over to Damon. They talk for a second, then Caleb tosses his duffle in the back of the van and climbs inside.

"Caleb said you worked it out," Damon says to me when I limp over to the van.

"It's only four weeks. It'll be fine."

Damon looks about as convinced as I feel, but I assure him the past is behind us and we'll get beyond it. I really hope I'm not lying to myself.

In the van, the two girls who I met this morning are sitting in the front seat. The girl named Erin has a pierced nose and lip and has tattoos running up and down her bare arm. She's reading a book while leaning against the window. The other girl, Trish, has long, really shiny blonde hair and could definitely pass for one of the popular cheerleaders back in Paradise. She has dark makeup on her eyes and wears light pink lipstick. It looks good on her.

I purposely avoid even glancing at the rear bench—I'm not going to look where *he's* sitting—and slide next to Matt on the middle bench. I know Matt from physical therapy, since his appointments are usually after mine on Wednesday nights. Matt lost three quarters of his left arm, and his right arm is scarred, but I'm not sure exactly what happened. I'm sure I'll find out once we share our stories.

Matt gives me a friendly but reserved smile. "I didn't know you'd be here," he says.

"It was a last-minute thing," I tell him, eyeing Trish and Erin in the seat in front of us and wondering if Caleb will decide to ditch the trip at the very last second. Part of me wants him to leave, but the other part wants him to stay so I can prove to myself that I'm truly over him, that the pain that lingered after he left is gone.

My pulse quickens when I hear Caleb shifting in his seat behind us. It's not a good sign that I'm hyper-aware of his every movement. I'm probably in for four weeks of real torture—maybe even worse than the year of physical therapy after the accident.

Never mind how I felt when Caleb abandoned me. In the weeks and months after he left town, I prayed that he'd come back. I used to keep my light on at night, so if he came back he'd see it as a sign that I was waiting for him. He lived next door, so I would gaze out my window for hours on end, hoping to see the light on in his room. My fantasy was that he would tell me he made a huge mistake by leaving Paradise.

But he never did.

In the end, I realized I had relied on him too much.

Damon gets into the driver's seat and turns around. "Well, guys, this is it. Our first stop is a camp-based summer school for teens. We'll be sleeping in cabins at their campground tonight, and you'll be expected to share your stories with them. Tomorrow we'll leave and head to our second gig. But right now, take a second to introduce yourselves while we're waiting for Lenny. As y'all know, I'm Damon Manning and I'm your chaperone."

"I'm Trish," Trish says, with an edge to her voice that implies *don't talk to me unless I want you to*.

Erin doesn't look up from her book as she says in a small voice, "I'm Erin."

Matt clears his throat. "I'm Matt."

"I'm Maggie," I say, unable to resist a glance at Caleb.

He looks like he'd rather go diving in shark or piranha-infested waters than be in this van. He stares at the floor mat. "I'm Caleb."

"And I'm Lenny," the guy who passed gas says, practically bouncing into the van and slipping into the spot next to Caleb.

Caleb winces. "Dude, if you fart again I'm gonna kick your ass."

"Caleb, no threatening the other members of the group," Damon orders from the front seat. "Lenny, let's keep it flatulence-free for now. Cool?"

I stifle a nervous giggle.

"I'll try," Lenny says, giving Damon a thumbs-up. But as soon as we turn out of the parking lot, I hear Lenny say to Caleb, "Wanna pull my finger?"

I have to look. Instead of pushing Lenny's finger away from his face or, better yet, ignoring him, Caleb grabs Lenny's finger and bends it back.

"Stop it," I tell Caleb as Lenny winces and tries to wrest his hand free. "You're hurting him!"

What happened to Caleb to make him lash out so quickly?

Caleb releases Lenny's finger. Lenny shoots Caleb a look that says he'll retaliate later, then scoots to the other side of the bench.

"You asked for it," Caleb says smugly as Lenny examines his bruised finger.

"I'm gonna sue you if it's sprained," Lenny warns. "I play the guitar, man."

Caleb smirks, then looks at me shaking my head. "What?"

"Nothing," I say.

I turn back around. I won't look at Caleb again. Not until I have to, at least.

Next to me, Matt pulls out his cell phone and starts texting with his one hand. His palm cradles the phone while his thumb taps the keypad. I can't imagine it's easy for him, but he seems to be managing fine.

I lean forward, placing my hands on the seat in front of me. I'll make small talk with Trish and Erin. Anything is better than wondering about Caleb, and because we're going to be living in close quarters for the next month, I need to make friends with these girls. But I realize, pretty quick, that they don't want to chat. Trish puts headphones in her ears and lifts her hoodie to hide her face. Erin is so engrossed in her book I'm not sure she knows that real life is going on around her.

I slump back in my seat and stare out the window. The cornfields and farms outlining the Illinois landscape are a blur.

"Yo, Matt," Caleb says.

"Yeah?"

"Switch seats with me."

THREE
Caleb

I think Maggie still has her mouth open in shock when I climb over the seat and Matt changes places with me. I don't like seeing another guy sitting next to her. I know it's stupid that I feel possessive when I have no right.

Damon glances back. "Caleb, stay in your seat."

"I was getting carsick," I say. "It's either switch seats or puke all over Maggie and Matt."

I look over at Maggie, who doesn't look too happy. She scoots further away from me when our knees touch, but she meets my stare with her own.

"I was carsick," I say dumbly. "And Lenny smells like shit...literally. I can't take it."

"I heard that," Lenny says.

"Good," I say back.

Maggie flips her light brown hair back with a confidence I only got glimpses of when we were together. She tosses me a sideways glance. "Why are you trying to start a fight with Lenny?"

"I'm not. *He* started it." I sound like a little kid, but at this point I don't care. What does Maggie think, that I'm perfect? She should know by now that I'm far from it.

"You're being confrontational."

"What's wrong with being confrontational?" I ask.

Maggie puts her regal nose in the air. "I'm sure you can figure that one out on your own."

"Everything okay back there?" Damon pipes in.

"My finger hurts," Lenny blurts out. "I need an ice pack."

I roll my eyes as Damon asks Lenny what happened. After a slight pause and a warning glare from me, Lenny says it's nothing.

Maggie takes out a travel guide of Spain and puts on a pair of wire-rimmed glasses. They must be new, because I haven't seen her with glasses before. She turns away from me and focuses on her book while chewing on the middle of her pencil. I watch as she makes circles on some of the pages and dog-ears others.

"Planning a trip to Spain? Again?" I ask. Right before I left Paradise, she'd said something about changing her mind and not taking her spring semester abroad after all.

She closes the book and shoves it and the gnawed pencil in her backpack. "Yes."

That's it. No details, no explanations. Not that she owes me any. She obviously doesn't want to talk to me, or look at me for that matter.

After two hours, Damon parks the van at a rest stop. "Everyone out. Go to the bathroom and stretch your legs. We'll be eating a quick dinner here."

While we're waiting for everyone else to come back from the bathroom, I walk up to Maggie, who's standing over by the vending machines.

"What's up?" I ask, trying to act normal.

She gives me a look of both disgust and surprise. "*What's up?* Are you kidding me, Caleb? You disappeared for eight months. You've kind of passed the *what's up* stage by seven months."

Shit. I have a feeling nothing I say will be good enough, but I give it a try. "Sorry."

"I'm sorry too." Maggie turns and walks away, her limp a stark reminder of that fateful night two years ago. For a semi-crippled girl, she sure limps away fast. I jog to catch up to her, because I'm stupid and can't leave well enough alone.

"You telling me you haven't thought about us while I was gone?" I ask her.

She shrugs. "I've thought about you. And then I thought about how you left me."

"It wasn't about you, Maggie. You know that."

"I don't want to rehash it," she says as she nears the van. "I've moved on."

I step in front of her, stopping her before she gets too close to the rest of the group. They don't need to know our private business. "You can't ignore me forever."

She shakes her head and pushes me away. "No, I can't ignore you. I couldn't even if I wanted to. But don't try and make me talk about ... us."

She whispers the "us" as if it's a big secret and she doesn't want anyone to know we had a relationship that went beyond a simple friendship.

Back in the van after dinner, she puts her hands in her lap and stares straight ahead as Damon drives us to the campground. After a while, I notice her eyes starting to close.

"You can lean on me if you want to sleep," I offer. "I promise I won't, like, touch you or anything."

"No, thanks. I brought a travel pillow." She reaches into her backpack and pulls out a plastic blow-up fluores- cent green airplane pillow. She puffs air into it and wraps it around her neck, just like the Maggie I used to know. Emotional, self-aware Maggie.

She falls asleep almost instantly, and an hour later, everyone except Damon and I are asleep. The girl with the headphones is snoring so loud I wonder if Maggie and the tattooed girl will have to get earplugs before this trip is over.

"Take a nap, Caleb. We've still got a ways to go," Damon says.

"I stopped taking naps when I was two years old," I tell him, stealing another glance at the sleeping Maggie.

I blow out a frustrated breath, then stare at my knee. I'm bouncing it up and down to the rhythm of the van's engine. I'm anxious and don't even know why. I wish I could get up and walk off this nervous energy, or run until my body screams for me to stop. Instead, I'm stuck just sitting here, thinking.

When I was in juvie, I had too much time to think. Thinking too hard and too long is dangerous for anyone with demons they're trying to fight off.

While Maggie sleeps, I envy her. I'm glad she's moved on, but I'm not sure I have. I left Paradise, but I'm the same guy in the same predicament I was in then.

When we finally arrive at the campground, Damon hops out of the van to sign us in. He comes back five minutes later, frowning. "Bad news," he says.

"The campers decided they didn't want to listen to a bunch of sob stories?" I ask.

"No. They only have one unoccupied cabin. That means..."

"Guys and girls are sleeping in the same cabin?" Tattoo Girl asks.

Damon sighs. He's obviously thrown off by this deviation from his plan. "Yeah. I'll be sleeping in the next cabin, with the counselors. I'll check in on you guys every few hours. Everyone okay with that?"

"Umm, no!" the other girl announces. "I'm not changing in front of guys."

"There's a girls' bathroom just a few feet away from the cabin," Damon informs her. "You can change there, Trish."

"If that's the only option, then I'll live with it," Trish says. "But for the record, I'm not happy about it."

Everyone else is okay with the unexpected sleeping arrangements. Maggie looks a little nervous now that Damon has parked beside the super small cabin. We all pile out.

Inside the barely habitable cabin are three bunk beds, with sheets and pillows at the foot of each mattress but not much else. I worked construction a bunch of summers for my uncle and am pretty sure this place is put together with spit and glue ... and a few nails that popped years ago and nobody bothered to fix.

"I get the bottom bunk," Matt says as he plops himself down onto one of the thin mattresses and sinks almost to the floor. "Damn, Damon, this is roughing it to the max."

"I want a bottom one, too," Trish says.

"Me too," I say, then watch as Maggie limps into the cabin. "On second thought, I'll take a top bunk. Maggie needs a bottom bunk because of her, uh ..."

"Leg?" Maggie finishes for me. "You can say it, Caleb. It's not like it's a secret. Everyone can see I walk with a limp."

"Oh, and while we're talking about obvious imperfections," Matt says, "I might as well announce that I'm aware I have a stump for an arm. It's the obvious white elephant in the room, so I just want y'all to know it's okay to talk about it or ask me questions about it."

"Eww," Trish cries out. "Do you have to call it a stump?"

"Would you rather I call it my partial appendage?" Matt asks, pulling up his sleeve and showing off what remains of his left arm.

She takes a quick look at it. "No."

Damon claps his hands together, getting our attention. "Okay, everyone. Now that that's settled, get situated and then meet me outside in ten minutes."

"Outside?" Trish asks. "For what?"

This girl is definitely going to be in the race with Lenny for the most annoying person in our group. She hasn't smiled or said one remotely positive thing since this trip started. I have a feeling she's trying to make everyone have as miserable a time as she wants to have. Then again, I'm with her—I'd rather be back in Chicago than here.

"Just come outside in ten," Damon says, then pushes open the screen door and disappears.

Tattoo Girl, whose name is Erin, jumps onto the top bunk above Maggie's bed. I take the one above Matt, knowing it doesn't really matter what bed I take because I probably won't fall asleep until I'm so exhausted my body gives in.

After we've organized our stuff, we line up outside. It's starting to get dark, and the mosquitoes are definitely out. We take turns spraying ourselves with repellent while Damon explains how the event will go. "It's casual, so no pressure. Take a deep breath, and know that we're all here to support each other. Since it's late, not all of you will talk tonight, but that's okay. You'll all get a chance to share at some point."

Damon leads us into the woods. About twenty kids are sitting beside a campfire on tree stumps, waiting for us. They all look up when we approach.

The crackling of the wood makes me think back to the time when my dad and I used to go with Brian and his dad camping up in Wisconsin. Last time I talked to Brian, he was dating my ex-girlfriend Kendra and working at his dad's hardware store.

"Take a seat," Damon says to our group. "Pick an empty spot anywhere."

I sit next to this guy with a bunch of acne, who must be a freshman with out-of-control hormones. He smiles weakly at me.

A woman gets up and says the kids are from high schools in the Chicago area and are required to take summer school to move on to the next grade level.

After the woman talks, Damon stands. "I've brought some teens here to tell their stories about how reckless driving has affected their lives. I know some of you think you're invincible, but guess again. Listen to them. Hear their stories. You'll be smarter for it." He sits down.

Silence.

What does he expect us to do, jump up and tell our sob stories? Does he actually think these kids sitting around the fire will give a shit? This is a joke.

Someone coughs.

Someone sneezes.

"Hey, guys. I'm Matt." Matt's voice cuts through the silence. He clears his throat. A few kids look up, but most are picking at their nails or staring into the fire. A few are whispering to each other, totally uninterested in what Matt's about to say. "I guess I'll go first. A few months ago, I was coming home from a high school football game. I was an all-state wide receiver. We'd just beaten our rival team on their turf, and I was stoked. The entire time on the bus back to school, we were joking around. I was feeling good. Damn good." He looks up. "Invincible, even."

Some of the kids are still talking amongst themselves, not giving a shit that poor Matt is pouring his heart out to them. Matt doesn't seem to notice they're not paying attention, or maybe he doesn't care.

"After we got back to school and piled in our cars, I was at a stoplight. A friend of mine was next to me. I revved my engine. He revved his." He pauses. "When the light turned green, I pressed down on that pedal so hard my head jerked back. It was a rush, especially knowing I was leaving my friend in the dust. That's when I lost control of my car. I don't remember much before slamming into the tree, and when I woke up I found out they'd had to amputate my arm. The crushed metal mangled it beyond repair."

As if that isn't enough, Matt struggles out of his T-shirt. Now he's got their undivided attention. A few kids gasp, some cringe, and some stare. His chest is still scarred and he's got less than ten inches of his arm left.

He sits back down. "I'm not feeling so invincible now. Lost any chance of a football scholarship and … and … and …" He swipes at his eyes. "And I'll never be able to catch a football again." He looks up, his expression defiant. "Try putting your pants on using one hand. Just for one day, try doing that simple task with one hand. I can tell you right now, it isn't a piece of cake when you've got one arm. If you want the God's honest truth, it sucks. I wish I could turn back time, but I can't. I made a stupid decision because I thought I was invincible, and I'll pay for it the rest of my life."

He sighs and hangs his head.

Well, that was a downer. Damn. And all along I'd hoped we were gonna roast marshmallows and make s'mores. Some bonfire this turned out to be.

My gaze turns to Maggie. Our eyes meet for an intense moment, but then she breaks the connection quickly and focuses on the ground.

When she looks back up, she says though the strained silence, "I'm Maggie. Almost two years ago I was hit by a car …"

When she stands, she focuses her accusatory gaze on me. Is she going give it up that I was the one convicted of hitting her? I wasn't the one who did it, but she doesn't know I'm holding that secret. Or, even worse, does she expect me to stand up and say I ran into her while driving drunk? I'd choke on the lie. Dammit, I can't deal with this. Not now.

Before she says another word, I stand and head back to the cabin.

"Caleb, get back here," I hear Damon hiss.

I ignore him and keep walking.

FOUR
Maggie

I pause as Caleb retreats into the darkness, the light of the campfire flickering against his dark shirt. I want him to hear my story. The accident changed my life forever, and if anyone needs to hear my side of it, it's Caleb. He owes it to me to listen. The fact that he picked up and walked away was a slap in the face. It means he doesn't care... about me, about what happened to me, and about our relationship that he professed to be real.

Feelings of anger and betrayal settle inside me. I take a deep breath and look around at the faces of the teens watching me, waiting for me to explain how teen reckless driving affected my life.

"I still have scars..." I say, my voice trailing off. I let

out a slow breath as I think about the reality of it. "Inside and out. A boy I liked was convicted of hitting me, and he went to jail for it. The sad part is, the accident not only affected the two of us, it affected both our families ... and pretty much our small town as well. None of us have been the same since."

A small blonde girl with French braids raises her thin hand. "What about the boy?" she asks. "What happened to him?"

I look over at Damon, leaning against a tree in the back. He thinks Caleb was the one who hit me. "I don't know. I think he blames me for being the reason he went to jail."

"That's stupid," the girl mumbles.

"If you make a mistake, you pay the price," one of their counselors says.

The woman has no clue of the truth ... that Caleb didn't make a mistake but paid the price anyway.

Trish stands next. She talks about how she was at a high school party and someone at the party slipped cocaine into her purse. When she got pulled over for speeding and running a red light, she got arrested. The drug charge is on her permanent record, and now every time she applies for a job she has to check the box that she's a convicted felon.

With emotions running high, Damon and the rest of the leaders say it's time to head back to our cabins.

When we reach the cabin, Damon storms inside. "Yo, Becker!" he yells in a deep voice I swear could scare the toughest person. The girls are startled and the guys are practically standing at attention. "Get the hell up!"

Caleb is lying on his bunk, his arm resting behind his head. He's wearing loose sweatpants and no shirt. He sits up, seemingly unfazed. "What's your problem?"

Damon walks right up to the bunk. "Get down here, you smartass."

"Nice language, Damon." Caleb jumps down in one movement and faces Damon straight on. They're about the same height, but Caleb is lean and muscular compared to Damon's bulk.

"Yeah, well, I call it as I see it. Apologize to Maggie for walking off," Damon demands as he gestures in my direction. "It was totally disrespectful and rude."

"Sorry," Caleb mumbles insincerely.

Furious, I nudge Damon aside and stand toe-to-toe with Caleb. It's too bad I'm hyper-aware of the ripples in his bare chest just a few inches away. "Why are you so intent on acting like a jerk?"

Caleb gives a short laugh. "'Cause I am one."

"Why are you doing this?" This isn't the real Caleb, the Caleb I grew up with. This is a hardened, fake representation and I hate it.

"I'm not doing anything. This is me, sweetheart. Take it or leave it."

"What's going on between you two?" Trish asks.

"Nothing," I say to her. "Nothing's going on. Right, Caleb?"

I limp out of the cabin, the loose floorboards creaking beneath my sneakers as I get some needed distance between me and everyone else. When I step into the warm night air, I feel better. As I cling to the railing and awkwardly maneuver myself down the three stairs to the grass, I feel Caleb's presence behind me.

I ignore it, even if my stomach is twisting in knots. I have so much to say that I'm holding back.

"Maggie," Caleb's voice echoes through the night air.

I continue walking. When he catches up to me, I turn on my heel and limp away from him. "Leave me alone," I say over my shoulder.

"What'd you want me to do, listen to you talk about how I hit you with my car while I was drunk, then left you for dead lying in the street, then how I went to jail, then after I came out of jail we started … started …" He winces and presses his palms to his eyes, as if putting our story into words makes it unbearably real.

"A relationship?" I ask, unfazed.

"Whatever you want to call it. It would never have worked."

"You didn't even give us a chance."

"Your mom hates me. My parents would freak if they saw us together. Hell, Maggie, even Damon warned me away from you. You should have been thankful I left, but it's obvious you're still holding out for something to happen between us."

I walk up to Caleb so close I can almost feel the heat

and energy radiating off him. "You need to get over yourself. What we had was a short fling. I'm so over you it's not even funny."

"Come on, Maggie. Admit there's still a part of you that wants me, even though you keep acting like you've gotten me out of your system. You protest too much."

"I feel nothing for you."

Just when I'm about to step away and go back to the cabin, Caleb reaches out and wraps his fingers around my wrist. "Really?" he says.

I swallow, hard. Those fingers on my wrist are full of reckless energy ... I know about those fingers all too well. I get mad at myself for remembering how it felt to have that energy focused on me ... those fingers lightly caressed my skin once upon a time. All I should be thinking about is putting him in his place, instead of feeling a connection. But when I look up at him, I forget about everything else because those intense, ice blue eyes that are oh, so unique to Caleb Becker are sucking me in.

I twist my wrist out of his grasp, determined to break whatever spell he has on me once and for all.

I'm walking back to the cabin when I hear Caleb laughing behind me.

I stop and turn around. "What's so funny?" I demand. I hope I don't have toilet paper on my shoe or gum on the back of my jeans.

Caleb's laugh turns into a cocky grin. "I figured it out."

"Figured what out?"

"Why you're so adamant about letting me know it's over between us." He crosses his arms on his chest. "It's because you're trying to convince *yourself* it's over. But you and I both know there's something still going on between us."

"You're delusional. The only thing going on between us is hatred and resentment. And I'm not just talking about me here. You resent me just as much as I resent you."

When he steps forward, I take a step back. "You sure?" he asks, his expression even more cocky.

"Yeah. I'm sure," I tell him. "One hundred and *fifty* percent sure."

"Then prove it."

I narrow my eyes at him and wonder what he's up to. "How?"

"Kiss me, Maggie. Right here, right now."

FIVE

Caleb

"One kiss," I say, and step closer. "If you're so over me, then it won't be a big deal."

She puts her nose in the air. She has no clue how watching her act like she's a tough chick makes me want to get under her skin even more. I'm not sure of my motives... I don't want to think about it too hard for fear I might actually come up with answers.

"I don't kiss guys just to prove things," she declares with an attitude I've only seen her put on a few times. "And I especially don't have to prove anything to you."

She doesn't want to admit we've still got something between us. It's simmering beneath the surface of hatred and resentment, or whatever the hell she wants to label it.

As much as I want to keep my distance, at the same time I want to see how far I can take it. Testing her is a bad idea; I know that. It's good if she's over me. But I can't resist—I've got to know for sure. "What are you afraid of? If you're really done with me then our kiss won't mean anything and you can move on."

"I *have* moved on, Caleb. But if you really want me to prove it to you, I will."

I paste a mischievous smile on my face. "Bring it on."

The old Maggie would have blushed and stared at the ground in the face of being challenged. The old Maggie would have turned and run. She used to be predictable. Now she's not, and it's throwing me off my game.

The new Maggie, the Maggie who puts me in my place and gets under *my* skin, reaches out and steadies herself by putting her palm on my chest. She tilts her head back and gazes up at me, her chameleon eyes shining a dark gray in the moonlight. "You shouldn't challenge me," she says.

"I know," I say, careful to keep my voice even and cool.

Having her this close makes my body so aware and alive I have to fight to keep myself in check. My heart is racing and my senses are heightened so much that I can smell her flowery perfume from the short distance between us. I hope and pray she doesn't realize the powerful effect she still has on me. I haven't felt like this since, well, that night in Mrs. Reynolds' gazebo when I wanted her more than I've ever wanted any girl. It ended innocently, but man I wanted to take it to the next level ... or even further.

While I'm sure Maggie can feel my heart beating hard and fast against her palm right now, I try and forget it as she reaches up and weaves her hand in my hair.

"You ready?" I ask in a gravelly voice.

"Sure," she says tentatively as I bend my head down. I want to put my hand on her cheek and feel her soft skin beneath my fingers, or brush away the stray hair that's fallen in her eyes. But I don't. It would be too intimate and break what little control I have. My lips hover over hers, teasing. I want her to want this as much as I do.

"Just don't tell anyone, okay?" she warns, pulling back the slightest bit.

Those words deflate my libido as fast as it was fired up.

Don't tell anyone? Okay, to be honest I'm not surprised she doesn't want to let anyone know about our private little moment of truth or dare. But at the same time her words cut. She doesn't want anyone to know because she likes another guy? Or because she's suddenly embarrassed of being associated with an ex-con? Shit, maybe she really is over me. Reality, like a tidal wave, washes over me.

What the hell am I doing? I can't do this. When we got together back in Paradise, nothing was calculated. It just happened. But now, this entire scene is a challenge, a total setup. Being emotionally involved with any girl, *especially* Maggie, is the last thing I need. And that's where this is leading to.

Maybe I just need to get laid. Maybe I just need a one night stand with some ditz like Trish in an attempt to wipe

Maggie from my thoughts. A one night stand right now would probably restore my sanity.

I take my hands off Maggie and step back. I shrug and give her a cocky glare. "You're right," I say. "This is stupid. You don't have to prove anything to me."

I can't tell if she's relieved or disappointed. It doesn't matter, really. I don't want to wait around while she analyzes what just did, or didn't, happen. I don't want to analyze it, either.

I leave her standing alone and walk toward the fire pit. I hear her call my name but keep going, worried I'll lose my resolve, take back my words, and kiss her like no other guy would. Hurrying down the moonlit, wooded path to increase the distance between us, I finally reach the clearing. The fire is almost out, except for a few stubborn embers.

I sit on one of the benches, which is really just a wooden log tossed on the ground. Less than an hour ago, in this same exact spot, Maggie shared our story. She still doesn't have a clue about what really happened the night of the accident. The story she tells is truth to her, but a total fabrication that I've lived with for a long time now.

I sit by the fire until the last struggling ember dies. When I finally go back to the cabin, all the lights are out except for the few leading to the restrooms. Inside the cabin, everyone seems to be sleeping or, in Trish's case, snoring a barnyard symphony. Even Maggie is out, although her back is to me and I can't see her face. The sheet covering her is moving up and down, slowly and rhythmically, with each breath.

I rummage through my duffle. For a brief moment I wonder where Damon is, then remember he's crashed out in the air-conditioned counselors' cabin with real beds while we're stuck here roughing it "to the max," as Matt had pointed out earlier.

After washing up, I hop on my top bunk, careful not to wake Matt although the metal bunk and springs creak loudly as I settle into the mattress. When I hear Matt stir, I mumble, "Sorry, dude."

"No prob," he whispers. "I wasn't really sleeping anyway."

"Who can sleep when we've got Trish the fuckin' bulldozer in here with us?" Lenny cries out, then growls in frustration.

As if on cue, Trish's snoring increases in tone and volume. It's not one of those heavy breathing jobs, either. First she starts gurgling as if she's storing phlegm in the back of her throat. Then she lets out a symphony of snorting and gurgling noises I've never in my life heard before, even from a guy.

Lenny, who's sleeping above Trish, leans down to look at her. "Trish, shut the fuck up!" he practically yells.

Trish doesn't stir. She does stop snoring for half a second, but then starts up again, even louder than before.

"I can suffocate her with my pillow," Lenny offers as an option.

Matt sits up. "I hear if you put someone's hand in warm water while they're sleeping they stop snoring."

"That's to make someone pee in their bed," I tell him.

"Does it really work?" Lenny asks, obviously excited. "We should try it. Who's got a bucket?"

"You're kidding, right?" Maggie chimes in from below in a low whisper. "You can't do that."

A big snort comes out of Trish's open mouth. Lenny sits up, grabs both sides of the top bunk, and starts rocking the bed from side to side.

"Don't do that!" Maggie shrieks.

Hearing Maggie shrieking makes me jump off the bed just in time to see Lenny and Trish's bunk start to tip over. As the metal is about to crash on metal, I reach out and grab the bed frame before it collides with Maggie's bunk and Maggie. Her leg is damaged enough as it is. My leg stops Trish, but it's too late for Lenny, who falls with a huge thump.

Trish slowly slides down my leg and lands ass-first in a puddle of tangled sheets on the floor. She looks up, startled and scared. For a girl who I assume prides herself on looking tough as nails, startled and scared doesn't fit.

"What happened?" she asks, her eyes wide as I make sure her bed is upright and stable again. She stands, then rubs her butt a few times before scooping up her sheets and pillow.

It's obvious Lenny isn't gonna explain, so I offer a quick explanation. "Your bed fell over. Go back to sleep."

"How did it fall over?" she asks, dumping her armload back onto the bed.

"Holy shit, that was awesome!" Lenny cries out from

the floor. He's laughing, as if scaring the girls half to death was crazy fun. He's a moron.

"Dude, get a grip," I tell him.

Trish narrows her eyes at Lenny. "Did you tip the bunk on purpose?"

"You were snoring like a fuckin' pig, Trish. I tried to wake you, but you sleep like the dead. I was doin' us all a favor."

Like an attack dog, Trish lunges at Lenny. I catch her just in time and hold her back. "You're an asshole!" she yells at Lenny.

"Tell me what I don't know," Lenny responds, then snorts loudly like a pig to piss her off. If he didn't notice, the girl has some scary-ass fingernails. They're long, they're pointy, they're digging into my arms now, and I have no doubt Trish will use them as weapons the first chance she gets. The last thing I would do is set her off and have those claws come out slashing.

"Trish, don't let him get to you," Maggie says calmly as she gets between Trish and Lenny. Maggie is wearing a pink tank top and matching pajama bottoms that cover just about everything. I'm all too aware that if Trish lunges again, Maggie could easily fall and hurt her leg. "Caleb, let her go."

I release Trish slowly, ready to grab her again if I sense she's about to pounce. Maggie stays between her and Lenny, who finally stops laughing.

Everyone is awake now, all of us glaring at Lenny.

"You losers have no sense of humor," Lenny complains. He moons us with his hairy ass before stomping out of the cabin.

Erin shrieks, then pulls her sheet above her head.

"I'm not sleeping below that jerk," Trish declares.

"I'll sleep below him," I offer. "Take my bed." Trish seems too tired and pissed to be thankful as she climbs onto my mattress.

I sit on the rumpled pile of bedding on Trish's bed and realize now I'll be sleeping right next to Maggie. I look at her. I didn't notice before, but now it's plain to see that Maggie isn't wearing a bra. While I'm sitting on the bunk and she's standing next to me her breasts are at eye level. I hear her suck in a breath.

She points to my hand and whispers, "You're *bleeding*."

I look down. Sure enough, blood is dripping off the back of my hand. I guess when I stuck my hand between the metal bunks it got cut. I wipe the blood off on my shorts. "It's not a big deal."

Maggie furrows her eyebrows as she pulls a towel out of her suitcase and hands it to me. "Here."

"I'm not messing up your towel with my blood," I tell her, tossing it back.

She catches it with one hand, then rolls her eyes and sighs. "You can stop playing the hero at any time, you know."

"You think I'm a hero?"

"No comment," she says as she grabs my wrist and

pulls my hand toward her so she can examine the cut. Her face is tense and stern as she dabs her towel on my hand. Reaching into her backpack, she pulls out a water bottle. She pours water on the towel, then continues to clean the cut. It stings, but I don't make a sound. I can't even remember the last time someone actually took care of me, and it feels foreign. I shift on the bed, feeling uncomfortable. I'm used to being alone and taking care of myself. I've never played the needy guy before, and I'm not about to now. Especially in front of Maggie.

I pull my hand back. "I'm fine."

Maggie *tsks* and bends down so we're face to face. Her gaze meets mine. "No, you're not."

I need to turn the tables or lose whatever control I have when it comes to me and Maggie. My resolve to push her away is weak as it is. I better step up and be the guy she thinks I've become.

"Are you bending over like that on purpose?" I ask her as I gesture toward her chest. "'Cause I've got damn good view of your tits right about now."

SIX
Maggie

At Caleb's words, I straighten and cross my arms over my chest to prevent further ogling. "You're disgusting," I whisper, hoping nobody else heard his crass remark.

"Thanks," he responds.

I slide under my covers, unwilling to look in Caleb's direction. "Bleed to death for all I care."

"Want your towel back?" he asks, his cocky attitude out in full force. Why does he do that? One minute I feel like he's being his true self, the Caleb I once knew, and the next minute he acts like the guy he wants everyone to think he is.

"No."

"Will you two quit flirting already?" Trish chimes in.

"Either admit you guys have a thing for each other or go to bed. Or both."

"I don't have a thing for him," I declare.

"You used to," I hear Caleb mutter under his breath from his bed beside me.

"Ancient history. Didn't I tell you I moved on?" I mutter back.

"Go to sleep, Maggie," Caleb says roughly. "You're getting repetitive."

I turn my back to him. So what if I keep insisting it's over? It's true. If I'm completely honest, I guess a part of me still yearns for the way things were when we were together. But I know he's the last thing I need in my life, and it's obvious Caleb and I are on the same page in that respect. He's been trying to push me away by goading me, and he's doing a great job of it.

When my body finally relaxes and I feel like I'm drifting off, Trish starts snoring again.

I glance at Caleb. He's lying on his back, wrapped in a wadded-up sheet, with his arms folded behind his head. He's obviously not sleeping. As if feeling my gaze on him, he turns to look at me. The bunks aren't that far apart, and if I reached out I could touch his bare shoulder.

He sighs and slightly shakes his head, then looks away. I turn on my back and focus on the squeaking springs above me, wondering how I got here. When I got the call from my physical therapist asking if I wanted to be part of this program, I really felt like it was my chance to close this chapter of my life. I thought if I could share my experience with others instead of keeping all my feelings bottled up inside me, I could make the accident a part of my past and be able to look forward to the future.

I wish Caleb felt the same way and could put our ugly past behind us. To be honest, though, I don't think he'll get past it until he admits the truth.

The truth.

He has no clue that I know he didn't hit me with that car. I've been itching to tell him I know the truth.

But I can't. He's obviously keeping up the facade for a reason.

I force myself to fall asleep and forget that Caleb is sleeping next to me.

In the morning, when I'm walking back from the bathroom on the gravel path that leads to our cabin, I find Lenny sleeping soundly in a patch of grass. He's snoring so loud the sound echoes through the entire campground. I suppress a laugh. He could definitely give Trish a run for her money in the snoring department.

Damon is waiting inside the cabin. "Can someone tell me why Lenny is sleeping outside instead of in a bed?" he demands.

"Maybe he wanted to sleep with his relatives?" Trish says, shrugging.

Damon doesn't look happy. "Not funny. His face already looks like a tomato from the morning sun beating down on him and there are a crapload of mosquito bites on him. Someone wake him up. Now."

"I'll do it," Caleb says.

"I'll go with you," Matt offers and the two boys leave the cabin.

When the three boys walk back in the cabin a few minutes later, one good look at Lenny and my mouth drops open. I didn't realize it as I walked past him this morning, but Damon was right. Lenny's face is bright red and totally sunburned. Mosquito bites are scattered on his face and body.

Lenny points at each and every one of us and says in a warning tone, "Don't. Say. Anything."

"What the hell happened to you?" Damon asks Caleb as he gestures to the dried blood now caked on Caleb's hand. Damon is totally confused.

"One of the beds tipped over last night," Erin chimes in. "Caleb caught it before it crashed on Maggie and me."

I think the rest of us are shocked Erin actually spoke— she's been so quiet.

"*Lenny* tipped the bed," Trish says. "*On purpose.*"

Lenny sneers at Trish. "Do you know what they do in jail to people who snitch?"

"Lenny, I won't tolerate threats so knock it off. Follow me to the infirmary. Caleb, you too. I want your hand checked out. The rest of you, pack up the van and go to breakfast. The dining hall is the big building by the front office."

When we're all ready, Damon, Lenny and Caleb head for the infirmary while the rest do as instructed. The dining hall is a huge building with rows of picnic tables. At the end of the room, teens line up with trays and choose their food.

"So what's the real story with you and Caleb?" Matt asks me as we join the line.

I wonder how much I should reveal. "It's super-complicated." I grab a carton of milk and look at Matt. "Need help?" I ask when he picks up a tray and balances it on his arm.

"I got it," he says.

I really admire Matt for that.

I watch him balance his tray steadily on his functional arm while we pick our breakfasts and head to one of the tables to eat.

"Nice way to avoid the question about Caleb, Maggie."

"I'm not avoiding it," I tell him.

He raises an eyebrow, obviously not convinced.

Trish and Erin sit down opposite us. What should I say? How much should I tell Matt? This trip is supposed to be about not holding back and letting it all out. Caleb hasn't been truthful with me or anyone else … and I feel like it's eating away at him. I won't let it eat at me.

I turn to Matt. "Caleb and I were involved after he was released from juvie."

"Wow."

I watch Matt's reaction go from shocked to curious. The accident and the consequences connect me and Caleb forever, whether we want it to or not. But Matt doesn't know the entire story. Damon, the guy who's supposed to know everything about each Re-START participant, doesn't even know the entire story.

"What did he go to juvie for?" Matt asks.

"Umm..." I take a second to figure out what to say, how to put it into words.

"Tell him, Maggie," Caleb says, sticking his head between us. "Spill it." Before I can even answer, Caleb snaps, "For hitting Maggie while driving drunk."

Matt's mouth opens wide in shock. "Holy shit. For real?"

"For real. Right, Maggie?" Caleb narrows his eyes at me as if I betrayed him. "Why don't we announce it to the entire room?"

"No."

"Come on, Mags. Be adventurous."

"You're not serious," I say.

He clears his throat. "Watch me."

SEVEN
Caleb

I wasn't really gonna tell everyone in this damn place that I'd gone to juvie, but seeing Maggie on this let's-share-absolutely-everything kick pisses me off. This Re-START program is a bunch of crap. They think talking about the accident will miraculously fix everything. I have news for Damon and everyone else involved. *Nothing* will fix my shitty life. *Nothing* will erase the past two years. *Nothing* will change the fact that I've got no friends or family left. I'm just living… surviving, really.

Finding Maggie in an intense conversation with Matt made me want to grab the guy's shirt and pick a fight with him. The guy is cool, unlike that tool Lenny, but when I moved in closer and found Maggie confiding in him, my veins fired up.

I scan the room and eye a bullhorn by the front door.

"Caleb, don't," Maggie says.

I ignore her as I cross the room and pick up the bullhorn. I click the siren switch. An obnoxiously loud, piercing shriek echoes throughout the building—a good thing, because everyone immediately has their attention focused on me.

I bring the bullhorn to my lips. "I've got something to say," I bellow into the mouthpiece.

Damon is standing in line with a tray full of food. I expect him to run up to me and grab the bullhorn out of my hand, but he doesn't. Instead, he puts down his tray and nods for me to continue.

"I drove home drunk from a high school party," I say, my voice sounding foreign to me as the words flow out through the bullhorn. "I hit a girl, and left her lying in the street not knowing if she was dead or alive. I was a jock, a guy who'd probably get a wrestling scholarship to college and I didn't want to screw that up. So I ditched her. In the end, I was busted and went to jail for a year."

I unclick the sound button. The place is silent. I can imagine what I must look like...the cool high school jock boy who screwed up and is now whining about it. Nobody is gonna feel sorry for me, not that I want or expect them to.

When I look over at Maggie, she shakes her head and turns her back on me. She's shutting me out once again, but I don't care.

I press the talk button again. "When I came out of jail, I got involved with my victim."

More than a few teens in the room go wide-eyed at this new piece of information. They're whispering in shock and pointing at me.

"We kissed, we fooled around … she snuck me in her house and we *slept* together. People warned me not to get involved with her, but I did. Biggest mistake of my life."

Out of the corner of my eye, I watch as Maggie slides off the bench and heads for the swinging doors. Good ol' Matt follows her.

"Maggie!" I say through the bullhorn. She flinches and stops in her tracks. "You want to add something? I skipped the part when we were in Mrs. Reynolds' gazebo."

I follow Maggie, who thinks that talking is better than keeping your mouth shut. I hope I've changed her mind, and she realizes that living in La-La Land is better than facing reality.

"That's the girl I'm talking about," I say, pointing.

"Shut up, Caleb," she hisses at me.

I hand her the bullhorn. "Truth hurts, huh?"

EIGHT
Maggie

We're back in the van headed to our next destination, Freeman University. After the dining room incident, I hobbled far into the woods and cried. Matt followed me. He didn't ask whether Caleb's statements were true or not... he just stood there while tears rolled down my face and I wiped them with the back of my hand.

Caleb's little show this morning was beyond obnoxious.

He lied.

He twisted the truth.

He mocked me, and he mocked whatever relationship we'd had.

Taunting me to reveal what happened between us in Mrs. Reynolds' gazebo was too much for me. That night

Caleb and I shared precious private moments I'll remember for the rest of my life. It was perfect; from the twinkling lights he'd carefully wrapped around the entire gazebo to the romantic way he kissed me after I slow danced in his arms. He treated me like I was the only girl in the world who mattered, and the only girl he'd ever want to be with.

This morning, he tainted my memory of that night forever.

Thank goodness Damon ordered Caleb to sit in the passenger seat. I don't think he's too happy with Caleb right now. I'm not, either.

We park at Dixon Hall, one of the Freeman University dorms. It's across from a big brick library with floor-to-ceiling windows.

Damon leads us to a suite on the second floor of the dorm. It's got a kitchen with a table, and two couches in the common living room area. "Girls in that bedroom," Damon says as he points to a door. "Guys in the other." He smiles as he tosses his suitcase into the third room, closest to the couches. "I get this room for myself."

"How long are we staying here?" Matt asks.

"This will be our home base for a while," Damon tells him. "We'll be taking day trips from here."

"My face hurts," Lenny complains. "And it itches." He resembles a mime, with all the white cream the nurse put on him from his sunburn and bites. He walks up to Trish and sticks his face close to hers. "Scratch me."

Trish sneers at him, looking like she'd rather die than

touch his cream-covered face. "Get out of my face, you freak."

"Enough, you two," Damon says sternly. "Trish, I'm not fond of name-calling. Lenny, if you've got an itch, scratch it yourself please."

Erin looks like she's going to throw up just looking at Lenny's cream-colored face.

Lenny walks to the window overlooking the grassy courtyard below. "Check this out, Caleb! Hot college chicks laying out in bikinis."

Ignoring him, Caleb heads for the guys' bedroom with his duffle.

"Get settled, guys," Damon says as he walks into his own room. "I want to have a group meeting in a half hour."

"Great," Caleb mutters sarcastically from the doorway to the guys' room. "Just what I need."

Damon swings around. "You do need it. And before you ask to get out of it, you'll participate just like everyone else." His tone makes clear this is nonnegotiable.

Trish, Erin, and I pick our beds in the girls' room.

"Erin, how come you don't talk?" Trish demands.

Erin shrugs as she unpacks her suitcase and hangs her clothes in the small closet.

"You know this trip is supposed to be about sharing your experiences, right? What did you do, besides get too many tattoos on your arms?"

Erin doesn't answer. She fidgets with a shirt she's trying to fold and put in one of the drawers.

"Leave her alone, Trish," I say. "She'll talk when she wants to."

"Okay, if that's the way it's gonna be, that's fine," Trish says, giving up. "But just so you know, I'm not gonna pretend to be all buddy-buddy if you hold back on me."

I think Erin will stay silent like usual, until her hands still and she turns to us. Her eyes are glassy, as if she's holding back tears.

"My boyfriend is in jail for three years for killing someone in a drive-by. My parents kicked me out of the house. And . . ." She wipes at her eyes and says in a soft voice, "I'm pregnant."

"Holy crap," Trish says. "No wonder you don't talk."

I elbow Trish in the ribs, hoping she'll get the hint and not say anything that will upset Erin. She's pregnant? With a boy who'll be in jail for three years? Hearing her story makes my problem with Caleb seem about as important as a hangnail.

"If you need anything, we're here for you," I tell her. "Right, Trish?"

"Yeah," Trish is quick to say. I think Erin just earned Trish's loyalty by sharing her story. Maybe Trish practically forcing Erin to talk was a good thing.

"And what about you?" Trish says, turning to me.

I lift my head from my suitcase. I must look like a deer in headlights. "What about me? I told my story at the campfire last night."

"Not about the accident. Caleb said something today about you and him in a gazebo. Care to go into details?"

I quickly shake my head. "Maybe later. We don't want to be late for Damon's meeting." I shove a stack of my clothes into a drawer.

"I think you're stalling."

"You're right, Trish," I say. "I don't want to talk about it."

"Suit yourself." Trish opens the closet door and looks confused. "Wait, where's the bathroom?" she asks as she holds out a plastic bag with her toiletries.

"In the common area, I guess," Erin offers. "We're probably sharing one."

Trish shakes her head as if she heard wrong. "No way. All seven of us can't share one bathroom."

She hurries out to the common area to investigate. Erin and I follow her. Sure enough, there's a bathroom between the guys' room and Damon's room.

Damon comes out of his room. "What's going on?"

"Damon, did you know there's only one bathroom for *all seven* of us?" Trish asks.

Damon shakes his head. "That's not true."

You can feel the sigh of relief from Trish, Erin, and I . . . until Damon says, "*I* have my own bathroom. Only the six of you have to share one."

Trish puts her hands on her hips. "That's not fair."

Damon chuckles. "Didn't anyone tell you that nothing in life is fair, Trish?"

She peeks her head inside the common bathroom. "Eww!" She points to the toilet. "The seat is up. And there are little droplets of pee and stray pubes on the ring. That's *not* okay."

As if on cue, all three guys join us. "What's the problem?" Matt asks Trish.

"The *problem* is that six of us have to share a bathroom." She glares in the direction of our leader. "And Prince Damon gets his own throne to sit on."

"This isn't a luxury hotel," Lenny informs Trish. "Anyway, what's wrong with the bathroom? It looked fine to me."

Trish gets in Lenny's face. "So you're the culprit. You were in the bathroom."

Lenny shrugs. "So what if I was?"

"Haven't you ever heard the phrase, *If you sprinkle when you tinkle please be neat and wipe the seat*? That goes for stray pubes, as well."

"Haven't you ever heard the phrase, *Shut the fuck up, bitch*?" Lenny fires back.

"I think it's time we have our meeting," Damon says. "Right now."

I avoid eye contact with Caleb as I pick a seat on one of the couches. Trish and Erin sit on either side of me. The guys sit on the opposite couch from the girls.

Damon pulls over a chair from the kitchen table. He takes a deep breath and claps his hands. "Okay, kids, here's the deal. Some rules have to be set, 'cause you guys are drivin' me nuts. First of all, let's try to eliminate the profanity flying out of your mouths. Second, there's to be no consumption of drugs or alcohol. We're on a college campus and I've no doubt they're easy to find. Third, I'm tired of the bickering. It's giving me a headache."

"But—" Trish starts to say, but Damon holds a hand up and stops her from talking.

"About the bathroom situation. You all have to share the one bathroom. Deal with it. There's another bathroom at the end of the hall right next to the elevators if you need it. Guys, put the seat down after you do your thing. Girls, make sure there are no feminine products lying around. Are all we all cool about that?"

We all nod.

"Where are the air-conditioning controls?" Lenny asks. "I'm sweating my butt off in this sauna."

"There is no air conditioning, Lenny. Like you pointed out, this isn't a luxury hotel. Any more questions?"

When nobody answers, Damon says, "Great." He sighs as if a weight has been lifted off him. "Now that that's settled, I've got one more thing. We had some drama this morning thanks to Caleb, and I want to talk about it."

"How 'bout we don't talk about it," Caleb mumbles. "Hell, I'd rather talk about Lenny's pubes."

I'd rather talk about Lenny's pubic hair loss issues, too. It's better than having Caleb and me actually talk about our past ... or talk to one another. I'm not going to do it. Not now, when his insults are so raw.

A wave of numbness washes over me. I stand. "I'm sorry, Damon. I just can't. I don't mean to disrespect this group, or this process. I just ... need time."

I intentionally look away from Caleb and I'm all too aware of my limp and his nearness as I head to my room and close the door. I don't lock it, though, since I'm sharing it with two other girls.

When I hear a knock as I sit on my bed, I flinch.

"It's Matt. Can I come in?"

"Sure."

Matt opens the door. "Wanna talk?"

"Not really. Is Damon mad?"

"No. He wanted to see if you were okay, but I volunteered to come instead."

"Thanks," I mumble. "I feel bad I just left in the middle of the meeting."

"Don't feel bad," he tells me. "I think everyone understands. Well, except Caleb."

"Why? What did he say?"

Matt comes in the room and stands beside my bed. "He didn't say anything. He just got up and walked out."

NINE
Caleb

I wish Damon hadn't followed me out of the suite. I hear his thundering footsteps behind me before he grabs my shoulder and pulls me around to face him.

"Leave me alone," I tell him, my fists tight and ready to lash out.

"You can't just leave every time the going gets tough, Caleb."

"Watch me," I say roughly as a couple of college guys pass us.

"You want out of the program? You want to go to jail?"

"Is that a threat?"

"Don't test me, Caleb. And give me a damn break. I've got to deal with Trish and Lenny. That alone could give a guy a coronary."

I let out a breath and look away from him. "Give me a damn break, man. I just want to be alone."

"Being alone isn't good."

"It is for me." It's better than watching Matt and Maggie start a relationship right in front of my eyes. The way he ran after her when she fled from the lounge made me sick. I don't blame the guy ... but I sure as hell don't need to see it. "I'm stuck here, I get it. I don't have a choice. But can you give me a night off from being around everyone? One night, Damon. It won't kill you ... or me." I let out a breath and say quietly, "*Please.*"

My transition counselor, the guy who's always been a hardass and whose job was to force me on the straight and narrow, steps back. "Fine."

I'm shocked. Maybe I didn't hear right. "What does that mean?"

"It means I'll give you a pass ... for tonight; a pass to be alone and figure things out. I'm taking the rest of the group to dinner with a local youth group and then to a movie."

A night without having to be stoic and pretend I'm a rock is a fucking miracle. A night without having to share my secrets makes me feel like a free man. "Thanks," I say.

"No problem. But tomorrow I expect you to put a damn smile on that mug of yours and suck it up. Got it?"

"Yeah. Yeah, I got it."

Feeling like the noose is loosened, I follow Damon back to the suite. Maybe I should apologize to Maggie for this morning. I knew I'd hurt her with the gazebo comment. We'd made out like crazy that night. Nobody knew about our secret time together except maybe old Mrs. Reynolds, who'd gone to bed after dinner. I think she knew Maggie and I were getting it on, and I've got a feeling she didn't care. Hell, maybe in a way it helped us get over all the shit we'd been going through.

Problem is, the night in the gazebo ended with me trying to ease Maggie's skirt up so I could see her scars. Maggie pushed my hand away. She didn't trust me. The night kind of went downhill from there.

In the suite, Erin and Trish are in the lounge area. I peek into the girls' room. Having Maggie mad at me isn't my intention.

Maggie is lying on one of the beds. Matt is sitting on the bed next to her. They're obviously in an intimate conversation, because they're alone and whispering. Oh, hell.

I retreat and head back to the guys' room, glad they didn't catch me watching them. Lenny is sitting on his bed, wearing nothing but his skimpy briefs. He's holding a personal mini-fan up to his chest.

"You do know the girls can walk in here at any second, don't you?"

The door wasn't closed or locked. Trish and Erin are sitting right outside the door, and if they crane their necks they'd probably have a good view of Lenny practically naked.

"I don't give a shit, Caleb. I'm fucking hot as hell."

He proceeds to lift up the band of his briefs and faces the mini-fan toward his dick. "My poor ball sacks are sweatin' so bad I swear I won't be able to have kids. My boys are being cooked to death in there."

"Might be a good thing. I'm not sure you should be allowed to procreate anyway," I murmur as I turn away. I'm glad Damon isn't making me go to dinner with the group, 'cause getting a glimpse of Lenny fanning his sweaty nuts made me lose my appetite.

Seeing Maggie and Matt talking on her bed hasn't helped my appetite or mood, either.

"Just an FYI," Lenny says, his face still red from the nasty sunburn. "I've got a shitload of condoms in my duffle. Front pocket."

"For what?"

"Listen, if you don't know what condoms are for I'm not gonna teach you."

"I know what they're for, shithead. I just highly doubt you're getting any ass on this trip."

"Watch me," Lenny says. "My boy gets action all the time."

"Yeah, I bet your right hand is tired from all that action," I mumble as I walk to the bathroom.

"I'm a leftie!" Lenny calls after me. I try not to wince from thinking about it.

I take a quick shower to cool off, then change into jeans and a T-shirt. I don't have a chance to explain or apologize to Maggie, because she's too busy talking with Matt.

Thing is, they deserve each other. Matt's a decent guy. I can't blame him for going for her. Maggie might not be the girl who stands out in a crowd or the one with a model's body, but once you get to know her, I mean really know her, you just see her . . . a girl who wears her heart on her sleeve and is so genuine you're afraid every word out of your mouth will come out wrong. She's someone you don't have to worry will cheat on you, like my ex Kendra did. Maggie is—

I've got to stop thinking about her. It's like I'm torturing myself for no reason except to piss myself off.

After the group leaves for dinner and whatever additional festivities Damon has planned, I need some air. The suite is too hot even with the windows wide open.

I walk through the tree-lined Freeman University campus, trying not to think about how I got here and what I'll be doing after this program is finished. I've got nothing to look forward to.

I walk past a bunch of guys playing football on the quad. The quarterback has no aim and the ball flies right in my direction.

I catch it.

"Nice catch," one guy says. "We could use another receiver. Wanna play?"

"Sure," I say, shrugging.

I join one of the teams and play with them until it's too dark to see the ball and one of the guys tells the others they're late for their own frat party.

"What's your name?" the quarterback asks me as we walk off their makeshift field.

"Caleb."

"I'm David. Listen, Caleb. My buddies and I are having a little get-together at our frat house. Come with us."

"Yeah. Come on," one of the other guys says as he tosses the football in the air. "It's the least we could do for having you help us kick Garrett's ass on the field today."

"That was suh-weet!" the quarterback agrees, and they give each other an enthusiastic high-five.

I follow the guys two blocks until we reach their fraternity house. It's impressive—a massive three-story house with four white columns in front. It looks like a damn mansion. A bunch of girls and guys are hanging on the front porch. Music blares from inside.

As soon as I walk in with David and the other guys, I realize their little party isn't a little party. It's a big one, and it's in full swing.

Before I know it, David shoves a red plastic cup in my hand. "So, Caleb, you a freshman? Haven't seen you around FU before."

"I'm not really a student," I say, then take a sip of whatever's in the cup. Beer. Cold beer. I'm sure Damon had some rule about drinking, but the alcohol tastes so good going down my throat that I'm not about to toss it. The fact that I know the more I drink the more I'll stop thinking about Maggie and Matt sitting on her bed this afternoon deep in conversation is a bonus. "I'm staying in the dorms for a stupid program I got stuck on."

"I hate stupid programs," David says.

"Hey, Davie," says a blonde girl with a short skirt and low-cut top. She finishes off the beer in her plastic cup, and I get the distinct feeling she started partying way before us. "Who's your hot friend?"

David drapes his arm on the girl's shoulders. "Caleb, this is Brandi. She's one of our frat house neighbors and our resident babe. Brandi, show my man Caleb here a good time." He excuses himself with a wink to me.

The girl looks me up and down, then flashes me a wide smile with a peek of tongue showing.

"Wanna dance?" she asks.

I finish what's left in my cup. "Sure."

She takes my hand and leads me to a crowded room off to the side. There's a keg and we both fill up our cups. Cup in hand, she starts moving her sexy body to the music. I hastily gulp my beer down and walk toward her. Our bodies grind together with the beat of the music, and one thought goes through my mind: tonight I need this girl.

TEN

Maggie

"Where's Caleb?" I ask Damon as we walk to the pizza place a few blocks away from the campus. He said a high school youth group is meeting us there, so their members can talk to us and hear our stories.

"He's gonna stay in tonight," Damon says. "I think he needs time to cool off and think about why he's here."

I sigh, knowing the truth of it all. "He doesn't want to be a part of this group."

"Yeah, well, he needs to be here nonetheless," Damon says as his cell rings. "He just needs to get a grip on his emotions."

As Damon takes the call, Matt is at my side. "You okay?" he asks.

I nod. "I'm kind of glad Caleb isn't coming with us."

"Me too."

I flash Matt a questioning look. "Why?"

"'Cause you seem upset when he's around." He shrugs sheepishly. "I don't like seeing you upset."

I put my arm around Matt and smile up at him. "Thanks for being a good friend," I say, leaning into his chest as we follow the others.

He puts his arm around me. "No prob."

It's nice knowing I have Matt here. During physical therapy we'd talk a bit, and complain about Robert, our physical therapist. Robert loves to push his patients to the limit whether they like it or not.

"Caleb's not such a bad guy," I tell him.

"I know," Matt says. "Caleb's cool. All of us have screwed-up shit we have to work out. Caleb just seems to have sunk deeper than we have."

"You seem to be handling your problems better than most of us on this trip," I tell him.

"I fake it. Truth is, I'm glad I'm here, but I've got to admit that some of those kids last night looked at me like I was a complete moron." He pauses, then adds, "Then again, I *was* a complete moron, but it's like going through it all over again. I wonder if I'll ever get used to the looks and the stares."

"I won't," I admit to him. "At first I was super self-conscious whenever I'd walk into a room … I noticed all eyes on me. I still get the pity stares, which might be worse than your moron stares."

"Come on, Maggie. We both have obvious disabilities, unlike the rest on this trip. And we're both trying to get over our past relationships."

Matt stops and lets the others go ahead of us. "Can you imagine *us* as a couple?" he asks me.

I'm not sure if he's wondering how people would react to seeing a limping girl and one-armed boy together, or if he really is wondering if I could imagine dating him.

I've never thought about it before.

Matt's sweet.

He's cute.

He's a good guy.

But...

"That was rhetorical question, wasn't it?" I ask.

He brushes a stray hair from my face and tucks it behind my ear. "Maybe. Then again, maybe not."

He leans down and I know he's going to kiss me. I should do it, if for no other reason than to give Matt a chance and prove to myself that I'm open to being with someone besides Caleb.

His lips meet mine and he wraps his arm around me. It's not passionate and hot like Caleb's kisses, but it's nice and safe and warm and...

I pull away. "I can't."

Matt looks sad. "Maybe we're not ready to move on after all."

My cell phone in my purse starts ringing. I don't know if Matt is right or wrong. I like Matt...I've always liked Matt. He's a great guy that any girl should be proud to date.

So why couldn't I kiss Matt without thinking about Caleb?

My phone rings again and I fish it out of my purse. It's probably my mom, since I'd left a message for her after I charged my phone in the suite. But when I look at the Caller ID, I feel a jolt of surprise. It's Leah Becker, Caleb's sister. We stopped being friends after the accident, but after Caleb left Paradise, we started talking again. Leah's emotions run high, and they're right on the surface. She's emotionally fragile and no longer the best friend I once knew. I hope she'll snap out of it at some point.

"Hey, Leah. I'm glad you called." I watch as Matt joins the rest of the group, giving me privacy.

"Hey, Maggie," Leah says softly. She's still got a lot of issues regarding the accident, and even though I've forgiven her, she hasn't actually forgiven herself. "How's the trip?"

"Good. We've only talked to one group so far, but it was okay. Right now we're staying at the dorms at Freeman University, right by the Wisconsin border. What have you been doing?"

Silence. Leah doesn't talk as much as she used to, so I pretty much hold up our conversations now. It's okay. I know it's part of her own healing process.

"Not much," she finally says. "Just hanging around, mostly."

That's pretty much all there is to do in Paradise in the summer. Some people take vacations, but most people stay in Paradise and never leave. I know two people who left Paradise—my father and Caleb.

That thought freezes me in my tracks, and I just stand on the sidewalk as the rest of the groups walks ahead of me. I stare blindly after them while the reality hits me: I get left behind by the men in my life who are supposed to love me.

I blink, and focus on the restaurant a half a block away. Everyone is out front, gesturing for me to get off the phone. I can't hang up with Leah without telling her, "Caleb's here."

"W-w-what do you mean?" she asks nervously.

"He's on the trip."

"With you?"

"Yeah."

"Why? How? Where has he been? Is he okay?" she asks, panic laced in her voice. "Okay, that's so weird. I really called you because I wanted to talk about Caleb and I didn't know who else to call besides you. How did you end up on the same trip as my brother?

"I don't know how it happened, exactly. I think he's been living in Chicago since he left town. He's changed, though. He's not the same." I don't tell her my goal is to get Caleb back to Paradise to work things out. Leah needs him. His family needs him. I thought I needed him, but now we're too different. I can't be emotionally involved with someone who resents the world and wants to push everyone away.

I hear hesitation in Leah's voice as she says, "I always used to think an ESP thing between twins was something people made up. But I couldn't sleep the past few nights, Maggie. I swear Caleb is in trouble, or *really* unhappy. I feel his pain as if it's my own. That's stupid, isn't it?"

"No, it's not stupid," I tell her. I believe anything is possible. It's probably because I'm an over-emotional person. It's one of my flaws.

"Do me a favor, will you?"

"What is it?" I ask.

"Take care of him, Maggie. Promise me you'll watch out for my brother," she says almost desperately.

Watch out for him? Caleb is strong enough, if not emotionally than definitely physically, to take care of himself.

"Don't worry, Leah," I tell her. I swallow a lump in my throat and temporarily push away my newfound resolve to let go of Caleb once and for all. "I'll make sure he stays out of trouble."

ELEVEN
Caleb

"You're a great dancer," Brandi says as we walk outside after we unload a beer bong in the kitchen. This girl is no stranger to beer bongs, I'll tell you that much. She's a damn pro.

I mumble, "Thanks."

She holds on to my elbow to steady herself and looks up at me with big brown eyes. "You know what they say about good dancers, don't you?"

Sure I know, but I want to hear the explanation come through Brandi's little lips ... so I've got to ask. "What do they say?"

She gives me a wicked smile and giggles. "Good dancers are good in bed."

Brandi's words make me feel like a rock star. She definitely feeds my bruised ego.

"Wanna test that theory?" I ask. Okay, I'm officially drunk.

She bites her bottom lip, assessing me like a car. I wonder if she thinks I'm a Chevy or a Rolls Royce. She leans in and whispers in my ear, "I'm a good dancer, too."

I pull this sexy girl close. Her arms wrap around my neck and she presses against me. It's a hint of more to come. I'm gonna let myself enjoy Brandi. She's a surefire solution to this pity party I've been throwing myself for way too long. No doubt she's gonna make me forget about Maggie and everything else.

I don't know how much alcohol I have in my system, but it's enough to make my head swim and make me believe the only girl I'm interested in is the one pressing her hot body against mine, which is good. Very good.

"Let's go to your place," I tell her. I don't think Maggie or Damon would be too appreciative if they came back and caught me gettin' it on with a girl. And if Lenny found us ... hell, the guy might be demented enough to ask to join in the fun.

She leads me down the quad, tripping a couple of times. I steady her and she calls me her hero. Yeah, right. We stagger past the place I played football earlier, but she stops when we get to Dixon Hall.

"You live *here*?" I ask her as I fight the sobering thought that we might get caught by the Re-START posse.

"Yeah. Don't worry, though. My roommate is out for the night."

She leads me up the stairs to the second floor. Damn. Her room is just down the hall from ours. Brandi doesn't have a suite like the one I'm in—hers is just a small dorm room with two single beds.

I watch with lazy eyes as she stumbles over to the bed and unbuttons her shirt. She watches me with raised eyebrows as she pushes the material aside like curtains being opened to let in the daylight sun, revealing a lacy black bra that doesn't hide much. I like easy girls who don't expect me to be one of the good guys. If they wear lacy black bras, all the better. I whip my shirt off and walk toward her.

"Your tattoo is so sexy," she purrs as we lie on the bed together. "It's like black fire." I got my tattoo in Chicago as a symbol of my rebellion.

Being here with Brandi is a symbol of my rebellion, too.

We haven't kissed yet. I'm not sure I even want to kiss her. And while that thought should be alarming me, I don't think about it too hard because (1) it's damn difficult to think straight when you're drunk, and (2) she maneuvers around to straddle me and my mind goes blank.

She traces the tattoo on my biceps with her fingers. "Wanna see mine?"

"Sure."

She kneels above me, turns around, and pulls down the back of her pants. Sure enough, she's got a tattoo of a red unicorn with rainbow wings right above her ass crack.

"Nice," I say, but I'm starting to feel anxious so I add, "Show me what else you've got." We'd better get this party started because I should go back to my own room soon. I better not be missing when Damon and the rest of the crew comes back.

Brandi licks her heart-shaped lips as she twists back around and unbuttons her low-slung pants. "I like a guy who knows what he wants. What do you want, Caleb?"

"I'm up for anything and everything."

"Me too," she says, raking her nails down my chest and moving lower. And lower. It hurts, and I think she's scratching off a layer or two of my skin. She slithers down my body, and I decide I don't care.

I lie back, welcoming what I know will come next. As her expert hands unsnap and unzip my jeans, then free me from confinement, I watch, my head spinning. She's having no problem focusing, even though she's as wasted as me. Everything she does is so well orchestrated; this girl is a total pro at more than just beer bongs. I close my eyes and tell my lower region to enjoy the attention.

I am definitely into this.

Way into this.

To say I'm turned on right now is an understatement of mega proportions. I'm just not sure if it's a problem that behind my eyelids I'm imagining a girl who limps and hates me...

Maggie.

"What did you just say?"

Huh? "What?" I open my eyes and look down at Brandi, poised above my unzipped pants.

"Did you just call me Maggie?" she asks accusingly.

"No." Whether I did or didn't, Brandi is *definitely* not Maggie. "Sorry," I add lamely.

She shrugs. "That's okay."

Without hesitation, she reaches into her side table drawer and pulls out a little plastic bag. She picks out a yellow pill with a smiley face on it, pops it in her mouth, and breathes in slowly as she savors the taste. "Here, take an Adam," she says, holding another one out to me.

I look at the pill. "What's an Adam?"

"You know, Ecstasy. Take it and put it under your tongue. I promise you won't think about anything else but having a good time with me."

Sounds great. I sit up and take the pill from her. If taking this little thing can make me forget everything except having a good time, I'm all for it.

But as I'm about to pop it into my mouth, I think about my mom. My mom is a prescription drug addict. Getting shitfaced drunk is bad enough, but taking pills…

Fuck.

Ingesting pills takes this thing to an entirely different level. I hand the pill back to her. "I can't do this."

"Do what?" she asks hesitantly.

I move out from under her and pull up my jeans. "I don't know. I need a minute."

"For what?" she asks, now completely confused.

Good question. I look Brandi up and down. She's totally got it goin' on. She's beautiful and has a rockin' bod...but she's not Maggie. And while I don't want Maggie, or can't have Maggie, or whatever the hell it is that I can't put into a coherent thought because I'm drunk, this isn't gonna work unless I can pull it together.

"Where's the bathroom?" I ask.

"Down the hall. You okay? If you're thinking about buying protection out of the bathroom dispensers, you don't have to worry. I've got some."

I head out the door and mumble, "I'll be right back."

I stumble over to the guys' bathroom and lean over one of the sinks. This sucks. I should be enjoying my night off. Instead, I'm a moody drunk. I look into the mirror in front of me, and it makes me feel worse. I run my hand through my messed-up hair and wonder if I should shave it all off like they did in juvie, 'cause right now I'm not just a moody drunk...I'm a moody drunk who looks like shit.

What's worse is I feel as bad as I look.

I splash water on my face to help bring me out of this mood, but it's no use. Brandi was turning me on, but it wasn't Brandi making me hard. It was thoughts of Maggie. Twisted, I know. There's no way I can go through with this thing with a girl who's just a stand-in.

I head back toward her room. She's probably tripping by now and ready for some serious action. I hope she's not too pissed I'm skipping out on her XTC party early.

In the hallway, just as I've got my hand on Brandi's

doorknob, I hear Maggie's voice from behind me say, "That's not our suite, Caleb."

I look toward the girl who's been haunting my nights ever since I was locked up in jail. The girl who just ruined my sexual escapade with Brandi without even knowing it. She's got hazel eyes that change with her mood, so different from the girl I was lying in bed with a few minutes ago. And while Maggie looks damn hot to me, I doubt she has any unicorn tats above her ass or wears lacy black bras. I'd like to find out, though.

"I know," I say.

Maggie limps over to me, her eyebrows furrowed in confusion. "Then what are you doing out in the hall without a shirt on?" She looks me up and down. "And why are your, um, pants unbuttoned ... and unzipped?"

The door to Brandi's room opens and Brandi appears. Her hair is mussed, her pants are undone and hanging loosely on her hips, and she's got her shirt clenched against the front of her bra. I'm screwed.

"Oh," Maggie mumbles, obviously getting her answer without me having to say a word.

"There you are," Brandi says with a smile, then looks over at Maggie. "Who are you?"

"His *girlfriend*," Maggie answers with a stern, straight face.

Brandi looks from Maggie to me, then back to Maggie. "You're kidding, right?"

TWELVE
Maggie

The girl with her barely there shirt clutched in front of her is waiting for an answer. Obviously she doesn't believe that a girl who looks like me could be dating a boy who looks like Caleb.

My insides clench in disgust. Caleb isn't my boyfriend and technically never was, but it still hurts to see him standing here in the hallway, his shirt off and pants unzipped, obviously ready to get it on with this girl.

I don't wait for him to tell the girl that the last person on earth he'd call his girlfriend would be me. Whether it hurts or not, I promised Leah that I would look after Caleb. She senses he's in trouble. Leah's twin-ESP senses were right on.

I skipped the movie tonight after the youth group dinner because I was tired and my leg started to ache. Little did I know I'd find Caleb here, like this, with another girl.

Looking at them together is a slap in the face. The girl he'd obviously already spent time with tonight is really pretty. She's got big brown eyes, perfect blonde hair, and a waist so small it's a wonder all her internal organs can fit inside her body. Maybe they're all stuffed into her huge boobs instead.

"No, I'm *not* kidding," I tell her, finding my voice again. "Caleb, come back to our suite."

He looks confused.

"Your shirt is still in my room," the girl says with a big grin. She probably expects him to blow me off, and she's probably right.

To my surprise, Caleb slings an arm over my shoulder. He smells like beer. "I gotta go with her."

I can detect a slight slur in his speech, confirming that he's not completely sober.

The girl ducks back in her room, but reappears a second later. She whips his shirt at him. "You're a loser," she says, and then looks at me. "You can have him."

When she slams the door, it's just Caleb and me standing in the hall. I shrug off his arm. He hasn't put his shirt back on and his zipper is still undone.

"Are you coming?" I ask impatiently.

I'm kind of surprised that he follows me back to our suite. I unlock the door.

"I need help," Caleb slurs as he drapes his arm across my shoulders again. I can feel the heat of his bare skin through my clothes. In the past I would have done anything for Caleb to put his arm around me. But not now.

"You have beer breath," I tell him, pushing him off me. "And if you want help zipping up your fly, you've asked the wrong girl."

He stumbles into the suite behind me and collapses on the couch. "So you're the wrong girl for me but the right girl for Matt?" he asks.

"Shut up, Caleb. Matt's just a friend."

"I don't think so. I think you've moved on to him."

"My relationships are none of your business. And just because I talk to a guy doesn't mean I've moved on to him."

"Right. I knew that." He looks around, confused. "Wait, where's the rest of our little dysfunctional group?"

"At a movie."

"Why aren't you with 'em?"

As if on cue, a sharp pain starts at my ankle and shoots up my calf. I would suck in a breath, but I don't want Caleb feeling sorry for me. "I need to rest my leg."

He pats the cushion next to him. "Take a load off and sit next to me."

Caleb's hair is sticking up in all different directions and that damn zipper is still open as a reminder of what he was doing with that girl tonight. Problem is, he still looks good. My top lip curls, thinking about him and that other girl. "No."

"Come on, just for a second."

His eyes are at half-mast and he's attempting to act all vulnerable and innocent, but I know better.

"You should probably go to bed before Damon catches you drunk or on drugs or whatever you ingested tonight," I tell him.

"Sit with me for a minute, then I'll disappear into my room and you won't have to see me for the rest of the night. I promise." He fumbles with his fly and finally zips and buttons his pants, then leans his head against the back of the couch. "And just so you know, I didn't do drugs. Could've, but didn't. Don't want to end up like my mom," he mumbles.

That's the first time I've heard him talk about his family since this trip started. I hear a distinct sadness in his voice when he mentions his mom, which makes him seem even more vulnerable.

I stand right in front of him, determined to be the rational one. "You were drinking tonight. Don't deny it."

His lips curve into a small smile. "Yeah, I drank. Feels good to not have to think about … everything."

I hesitate. Being close to Caleb isn't a good idea. "I should report you to Damon."

"Yeah, you should."

I sigh. "But I won't."

"Why not, Mags? Could it be that deep down in that frozen heart of yours you still like me?"

He reaches out and pulls me toward him. Not being very steady in the first place, I stumble forward, but he cradles my body with his arm and gently lowers me to the couch until I'm lying down. Under him.

"Don't answer that question," he says.

My brain tells me to scramble away and keep my distance, but my body isn't listening to my brain. My body has a mind of its own. I look up into Caleb's intense, sea blue eyes. Those depths are totally focused on my lips, reminding me of the first time we kissed back in Paradise. It was at Paradise Park, right after he held me while I cried in his arms.

I swear the air grows thicker around us, closing in like a dark cloud. All I hear is the sound of our breathing. I forget everything else and let myself enjoy being this close to him again.

He brushes my hair away from my face with unexpected gentleness, the pads of his fingers a soft caress brushing across my cheek. I bunch my hands at my sides, afraid that if I actually move I'll slip back into reality.

Caleb shifts and moves closer. "Maggie, do you want this as much as I do?" he asks, his face poised right above mine.

"I ... I can't answer that."

He leans back just the slightest bit, but he's still close enough I can smell the alcohol he drank tonight.

"Why not?" he asks.

I move my hand to his bare chest to stop him before

I lose all common sense. Having him this close makes me breathe harder and my pulse race, which just makes me even angrier with myself than with him.

"Do you really have to ask? You were obviously with another girl tonight, Caleb. I'm not degrading myself by being sloppy seconds."

"I didn't kiss her. I swear."

When I give him an I-don't-believe-you look, his expression turns gravely serious. "I'm not gonna say we didn't fool around, but I couldn't go through with it 'cause I was..." He squeezes his eyes shut. After a second he opens his eyes and stares right into mine with that serious look again. "Forget it."

"Just go to bed," I tell him, trying to push him off of me. "It's obvious you're drunk and aren't thinking straight."

"Kiss me, then I'll go to bed."

"You're crazy," I choke.

"Yeah, I know." His lips are twisted into a half smile. "But humor me just this once." His head slowly dips toward mine. I watch and hold my breath as his beautiful, full lips get closer and closer. "Oh Maggie," he murmurs softly when I instinctively wrap my arms around his neck. "I need this."

I must not be thinking clearly, because I say against his lips, "Me too."

His hands are braced on either side of my head as he brushes his lips over mine. We kiss tentatively, as if we're both not sure it's okay. My heart is slowly melting. My entire body tingles with excitement and anticipation as one of his hands grabs my waist and pulls me closer.

I close my eyes and pretend we're back in Mrs. Reynolds' gazebo when it was just the two of us. It felt so good; it couldn't have been wrong. Back then he held me and made me believe that as long as we were together, everything else would fall into place.

I sigh into Caleb's open mouth; it comes out as a little whimper. He leans away from me. I open my eyes and find him smiling—a one-hundred-percent-satisfied male smile.

As if my response is his cue to take this further, Caleb gives a guttural growl right before he lowers his head again. His mouth is on mine, open, his tongue searching. I think my brain is trying to send off warning signals, but my body and my own tongue are enjoying the attention too much to listen. The sounds of our tongues and lips and moans spur me on, and I find myself raking my hands through his hair, pulling him closer.

"Touch me," Caleb urges as he reaches out and traces my lips with the soft tip of his finger and dips it into my mouth.

I convince myself to think of the gazebo. As long as I keep my eyes closed, we're there—we're in the past and not the present. He's going to tell me how much he cares about me any minute now. He's going to tell me that I'm the only girl he wants and needs.

He traces a wet path down my neck and dips his finger into my the V of my T-shirt. His mouth follows with little kisses before he moves up and kisses me again. I start to sweat with passion. I'm on fire.

It's all slow and erotic, our tongues reaching out and gliding and searching as if we're both savoring the taste of each other. The bitter taste of beer has been replaced by this sweet scent that reminds me solely of Caleb. I'm lost in the present, but my mind and body are stuck in the past. It feels good and oh, so right to be finally kissing him like this. And touching him.

He said he needs this.

I wasn't lying when I admitted I needed it, too.

When he reaches under my shirt and rubs his thumb across the top of my bra, the rest of his hand cradling my breast, I feel like the world has stopped and it's just the two of us left. I feel a warm sensation running from my breast to the tips of my toes and back again. My insides are slowly melting into little puddles.

Until my cell phone rings. It's in my purse, ringing loudly and interrupting my fantasy.

"Don't answer it," Caleb rasps. "Ignore it."

He kisses me again, but the gazebo is gone. The moment is lost.

My cell phone keeps ringing. I turn my head, breaking the kiss, and blink a sudden tear of frustration away as I send my arm flailing for my purse.

"I can't." My hand finds the side pocket and I grab my cell. The number glowing on the Caller ID makes me suck in a breath. "It's my dad," I say slowly as I nudge Caleb's hand away from under my shirt. I let the phone ring and ring until the call gets transferred to voicemail.

My dad, the guy who calls me once or twice a year. My dad, who left me and barely looks back.

I look up at Caleb, still poised above me. He's the boy who left and didn't look back until we were forced together on this trip. He betrayed me just like my dad did. He lied to me just like my dad did.

He fooled around with another girl tonight, then moved on to me like it didn't matter. Different face, different body, same interchangeable good time.

I'm pathetic and the only one I can blame is me. I could have said no. I could have acted like I didn't want this. I could have walked into my bedroom and shut the door.

But I didn't.

Instead, I stepped closer to him ... almost testing him to see if he'd make a move. Sure enough, he took the bait. I'm no better than that girl he was with tonight.

"Caleb, what are we doing?" I ask.

He leans away from me to sit up again and sighs. "Oh, no, here it comes. Your introspective, emotional, and philosophical self is coming out."

"Why shouldn't I be introspective? *We* don't make sense."

"Neither does chocolate and peanut butter, but somehow it works," he says. "Somehow the mixture of those two things is genius."

"You're drunk. I'm not talking about food. I'm talking about two people with a really screwed-up past—"

"Stop thinking so much," he says, finishing my sentence. "No matter how much time has passed, it doesn't seem to matter." He rubs my arm gently, tickling my sensitive skin. "I don't know why we're both fighting it so much. Hell, I couldn't do it with Brandi tonight because all I could think about was you. I even called her your name," he says, rambling. "Yeah, it's screwed up, we're screwed up, but why hide the fact that we still want each other?"

I push him away. "You, Caleb Becker, are one big jerk."

"I don't get you," he says, his hands in the air and his eyebrows furrowed in confusion. "I admitted I couldn't be with another girl because I was thinking of you. I want you, Maggie. Is that so wrong?"

"Yes."

"What, admitting you turn me on? Why are you treating it as if it's an insult?"

"I don't want us to just 'want' each other." I take a deep breath. "I want a real relationship with a guy. Love. And you, you don't even know what love is. Love is *honesty*. Love is a *mutual respect* for one another, something you and I don't have."

"Oh, really?" My words obviously make him pissed, because he stands up and fires back, "So you're saying you have no respect for me?"

"Yeah, that's what I'm saying."

"Fine," he says.

"Fine," I say.

"I guess I pegged this thing going on between us all wrong, then."

This time the sharp pain strikes my heart, but I stay strong. "It's all about honesty, Caleb."

"Yeah, well, *honestly* you're being ridiculous."

THIRTEEN
Caleb

I'm lying in bed staring at the ceiling. Lenny and Matt are asleep. I haven't talked to or heard from Maggie since we both stormed to our rooms four hours ago.

I told her I still want her. Admitted that I never stopped wanting her. And she goes and starts talking about love. Fucking love. And honesty.

Love isn't about honesty. It's about protecting the people you love from things that will hurt them. That's love.

Oh, hell. I told Maggie I still want her and we should give in to our lust for each other. Stupid, I know. I didn't mean to blurt it out then and there—it just happened. Maybe it was the beer. Yeah, right. I'm still buzzed, but I knew what I was doing. Doesn't make it any less stupid, though.

For the next week, Maggie practically ignores me. We travel each day to some event where Damon introduces us and urges us to share our sob stories. All of us share. My story is the shortest. "I drove drunk and hit a girl. Went to jail for it. I was practically kicked out of my parents' house and lost my girlfriend. I got my license suspended for three years and I'm pretty much living on the streets now. So, um, don't drink and drive."

Yep, that's my story and I'm sticking to it.

It's not until we're on a panel at some random high school auditorium sitting behind a table when I get asked a question I'm not sure how to answer.

It comes out of the mouth of a fifteen-year-old kid in a summer school driver's ed class. "This question is for the guy in the blue T-shirt on the end," he says.

I look at everyone else. Unfortunately nobody but me is wearing a blue shirt. Erin passes the microphone to me. "What's your question?" I ask lazily, my voice echoing through the auditorium.

"Why did your parents kick you out?"

Shit, do I really have to answer that? My sister refused to tell the truth about the accident, my mom is addicted to prescription drugs, and my dad is in denial. "That's a good question," I say, stalling. I don't know what to say. The truth and the lies are starting to melt together as I clear my throat and think of how to answer. "My parents were embarrassed to have an ex-con as a kid. On top of that, they weren't too keen on the fact that I was fooling around with the girl I went to jail for hitting with my car."

"Why'd you do that?" the kid asks. "I mean, why fool around with the girl you hit? Wasn't that a bad idea?"

"Yeah. It was a really bad idea. One of the stupidest ideas I've ever had. Next question?"

The next question is for Lenny. They want to know why he drove a car into the lake.

"It seemed like a good idea at the time," Lenny says. "Of course I was drunk, but that's no excuse. I paid a big price and I wish I could do it over."

That seems to be the theme of our lives...wishing we could turn back time and make different choices.

During the van drive back to Freeman, Maggie won't even look in my direction. She sits next to Matt and chats with him about tennis. When we're back at our dorm, she heads straight for her room. Damon heads for his room, too. When his door closes and the rest of the group is in the lounge area, I step into Maggie's room.

"What's your problem?" I ask softly so the rest of the group can't hear.

"I don't want to talk about it," she says, then starts to move away from me.

I grab her wrist and tug gently, urging her to face me.

"Get your hand off her," Matt says from behind me.

I glare at the guy who obviously wants Maggie to be more than a friend. "What are you, her bodyguard?"

"Maybe." Matt steps between me and Maggie.

"Don't get in the middle of this, man." I'm all tense because, well, once I was Maggie's protector against this asshole Vic Medonia, and now Matt's making me feel like I'm no better than Vic.

"She obviously doesn't want to talk to you right now."

When I look over at Maggie, she's pointing toward the door for me to get out.

"I'm done," I tell her.

In the morning, when Damon shakes me awake, I tell him I'm taking the day off.

"Caleb, get your butt up. You're not getting out of today's activities, so don't even think about it," Damon says.

"I'm sick," I say.

"With what?"

"Annoyance. Seriously, Damon, Lenny's cell phone went off every couple of hours last night."

"He's telling the truth," Matt says as he pulls a tank over his head. "We kept telling him to turn the damn thing off, but he wouldn't."

"I turned it to vibrate!" Lenny calls out from the lounge.

Matt walks to the door and yells out, "Having it vibrate on the desk is as bad as having it ring, dude."

Damon leans down and pulls the covers off me. "I'll confiscate Lenny's phone tonight, but you're still joining us today, Caleb. I have a special activity planned. No excuses."

I drag myself out of bed, shower, and get dressed. I think Maggie has the girls on her side, because they're all ignoring me today. Even during breakfast, Trish offers everyone a blueberry muffin except for me and Lenny. How I got to be lumped in the same category as a fucking tool like Lenny is beyond me. On the other hand, Saint Matt is treated like a damn king. Not only does he get a muffin, but Maggie actually pours him a glass of orange juice from the small fridge. And smiles at him as she places the glass in front of him.

I'm even more annoyed now.

After breakfast, we all pile into the van. I'm stuck sitting in the very back with Lenny, who doesn't seem to mind or care that the girls are ignoring him. Or maybe the guy is just used to people ignoring him, or is too stupid to realize it.

Damon pulls up to a wooded property with a big sign that reads *VICTORY BOUND—BUILDING STRONG FOUNDATIONS IS THE KEY TO SUCCESS.*

"Is this a Habitat for Humanity project?" I ask. To be honest, I wouldn't mind getting a hammer and nails in my hands. I used to work construction for my uncle during the summers. Getting my frustration out on a nail and a two-by-four sounds like a sweet idea right about now.

"No, it's nothing like that," Damon says, to my disappointment.

We pile out of the van and Damon tells us we're having a meeting. "This is a skill-building camp. I've noticed that many of you have issues with asking people for help and trusting others."

"Maybe we like it that way," I murmur.

"Not a good way to live, Caleb. It's human nature to need people and to live in harmony with others. You need this ... and I'm not just talking about Caleb." He points to everyone else in the group. "You *all* need this."

A guy comes out of the door marked *Office*. He looks like a mountain man or Bigfoot come to life, complete with a long beard and unruly hair. "You must be the Re-START group." He holds out his hand to Damon and they shake. "I'm Dex, the owner of Victory Bound."

The first thing Dex does is have us stand in a circle under some trees. He instructs us to say one word that describes ourselves.

Matt says, "Loyal."

Lenny says, "Funny."

Erin says, "Sad."

Trish says, "Angry."

Maggie says, "Confused."

I don't miss the fact that she's looking directly at me when she says it. Is she confused about *us*? That's news to me. Maggie pretty much shuts me down every time we get close. She doesn't seem confused at all.

When it's my turn, I say, "Screwed up" because that pretty much sums up who and what I am.

"That doesn't count," Lenny says. "Dex said to say *one*

word that describes you. 'Screwed up' is technically two words."

"And 'shut up before I kick the shit out of you' is ten words," I say in a warning tone.

Dex/Bigfoot holds his hand up. "No threatening your teammates, Caleb. Victory Bound rules. Apologize," he orders.

Apologize? Is this guy serious? I'd rather eat broken glass then apologize to Lenny.

Damon the Enforcer gives me a level stare. "Come on, Caleb. Spit it out so we can move on."

"Yeah," Trish says, then snorts. "Don't be such a jerk."

I look over at Maggie. "Just do it," she mouths silently.

"Nope." I used to play by the rules, but I haven't done it for so long I've forgotten how.

"Channel your energy into positive actions," Dex says to me.

I stick my hands in my pockets and face Dex. "What if I don't feel positive?"

"*Doing* something positive will help turn your mood around. When you smile, your body relaxes. When you experience positive human touch and interaction, it eases tension in your body."

The last time I had positive human touch was with Maggie when she kissed me and touched me on the couch in our suite. It felt amazing until she pushed me away.

"I want to see you two hug," Dex says.

"You're kiddin' me, right?"

"I'm not kidding. I think you should hug Lenny."

I don't move my hands out of my pockets. "Yeah, umm, I don't think so." I want to say *no fucking way* to Bigfoot, but hold back.

Lenny opens his arms out wide and smiles at me. "Come to Papa."

"Come on, Caleb," Damon urges. "Just try it."

"I'd rather hug one of the girls, Damon. Or Matt, for that matter."

Nobody seems to care about listening to the list of things I'd rather do than hug Lenny. They're all just waiting for me to cave.

Lenny steps forward, his arms still open.

I step out of the circle, an obvious outsider. Bigfoot doesn't seem pleased. "It's not about the hug…it's about your character. Doing something you don't want to do to please someone else is an act of kindness."

I give a short laugh. "Listen, Dex, I'm being kind by warning Lenny before I kick his ass. Give me some credit. Shit, man. I hung out with gang members in Chicago who thought kindness was asking what limb you wanted cut off before they chopped you into pieces and fed you to dogs."

"Do you want to be a part of this group, or not?" Bigfoot asks, ignoring my gang scenario.

"Not."

"He has no choice," Damon bellows loudly. "He's part of this group whether he likes it or not. Right, Caleb?"

"Right," I say. Unless I ditch them all and take my chances. But I won't, because if juvie sucked, I've got a feeling the big-time jail will put me over the edge. I step back into the circle.

"We can hug later," Lenny says to me.

I shake my head. "Don't count on it."

I'm definitely on Dex's shit list, that's for sure. He shoots me these looks probably designed to make me feel bad, but they don't. After what happened with Maggie, I'm done with feeling remorse.

Dex tells us we'll be expected to complete a bunch of Victory Bound tasks that have us working together as a team. The first task is a puzzle we have to complete while three of us instruct three blindfolded members of our group on how to organize the pieces. The next task is a maze we have to wind through while attached to each other with rope. Then we have to build a race car using items found in nature. Maggie doesn't look my way the entire time.

After lunch, Dex leads our group into the woods behind the main office. He stops when we get to a thick oak tree with a small platform nailed to the trunk about a foot off the ground.

"This is a trust exercise," Dex explains. "I'll split you up into pairs. Each of you will turn your back to your partner while standing up on the platform, then fall into your partner's arms. Then we'll switch who falls and who catches."

He pairs Lenny and Trish, then Matt and Erin, then

me and Maggie. I stand next to my frowning partner. "Don't look so depressed," I tell her.

"I'm not depressed. Didn't you hear him say this was a trust exercise?"

"Yeah, so?"

She shakes her head. "Forget it."

Before I can respond, Trish cries out, "Lenny will flatten me! I hope you have medical insurance, Dex."

Lenny laughs. "You're not a lightweight yourself, Trish. If I drop you, will your boobs burst when they hit the ground?"

Dex holds up his hand, which we've all learned by now is his special signal for "shut up." "You can all do this, I assure you. You'll be attached by a bungee cord secured to the tree, which will lessen the weight load. Lenny and Trish, you two go first."

"No, way, Dex," Trish says. "What if he drops me?"

"He won't."

"How can you be so sure?"

"Because the entire group is counting on him, and he won't let us down. Right, Lenny?"

Lenny's eyebrows are furrowed in confusion. "Is that some psychobabble bullshit you're using on me?"

"Yes. Now stand on the platform and attach the bungee around your waist. Show Trish how easy it is."

Lenny does as Dex instructs. With the bungee taking the brunt of the weight, Trish has no problem catching him. They switch places, and to our relief Lenny catches Trish and doesn't test his theory about her boobs.

"Okay," Dex says, moving on. "Caleb and Maggie, you're up."

FOURTEEN

Maggie

I step to the edge of the platform, hook the bungee cord attached to the tree around my waist, and look down. Caleb is standing there with his arms out, ready to catch me.

Suddenly, somehow, this exercise goes beyond whether I believe he'll catch me or not.

That's why I've been so angry with him since that night last week ... the thought brings me up short. I haven't been mad at him since just that night. I've been mad at him for eight months. Since I found out he lied. Since he left without telling me the truth.

I think of all the things left unsaid ... all the things I should have said. There's so much dishonesty between us.

I back myself against the tree and wrap my arms around myself. "I can't."

"Why not?" Caleb asks.

Everyone is staring at me, waiting for an explanation. And while I don't want to talk about this in front of the group, I'm so tired of the secrets. I desperately want to say what I'm feeling right here and now because I might just lose the nerve to say it later.

I unhook the bungee cord and step off. "I just don't want to do it."

"I'm not gonna let you fall," Caleb says. "I promise."

I look into his piercing blue eyes, which get darker when he's upset.

"It's not about whether you're going to catch me or not," I tell him. "It's about the accident."

Caleb looks wary and confused, and I'm pretty sure his mood is about to get even worse when I tell him, "This whole exercise is about trust. The truth is, I don't trust you."

"This is gettin' good," Lenny says, rubbing his hands together. "And all along I thought you two were gettin' it on while nobody was watchin'."

Caleb shoots the guy a glare. "Shut your mouth for once, Lenny, or I'll shut it for you." His hands are now in tight fists at his side and the muscle in his jaw is twitching. I think he's ready to take Lenny on, but this isn't about Lenny. It's about us.

Dex holds a hand up, but I don't think Caleb cares.

"After all we've been through, I think you owe me trust," Caleb says to me.

He doesn't get it. Oh, how I want him to tell me the truth about the accident on his own. It's the only way we can move past this. I *need* to move past the lies and deceit.

Thinking about the accident and all that's happened since makes my body shiver. I'll never be the same physically. I'll always be looked at as a cripple. I wanted to believe Caleb wanted me despite my injuries, but maybe it was just a tactic to encourage me to keep my mouth shut.

The only person who can bring the truth out in the open is standing here with me now.

"Face the cold, hard facts, Caleb. You don't trust me, either." I can't stop now. Tears roll down my face as I walk right up to Caleb and jab my finger at his chest. "You lied to me! You deceived me! The least you could do after we started getting close was be honest."

He stares at me, his eyebrows drawn tight over his confused eyes.

"Tell me the truth about the accident, Caleb. I *dare* you."

I see the moment he gets it and stiffens, shocked.

Caleb shakes his head and steps away from me. "Don't do this."

"Tell everyone here what really happened that night." I open my arms wide and look up at the sky. "Scream it out loud and set us all free from the lies!"

Lenny holds his hands up as if he's in church. "Hallelujah!"

Caleb rushes Lenny, and tackles him. And punches him. Lenny punches back. I'm scared, and I'm screaming for them to stop wrestling, especially because Caleb is a trained wrestler and Lenny doesn't stand a chance against him. In an instant, Damon pulls Caleb off Lenny and starts yelling for Caleb to calm down. Caleb is in a rage now, and I'm not sure he can hear anything though his anger.

"Caleb, get a hold of yourself," Damon orders.

Caleb breaks free of Damon's hold. His hands are in fists, ready to fight. "No!"

"This isn't about Lenny!" I yell, trying to get his attention. "It's about you and me."

Caleb looks at me. His breathing is ragged and his eyes look intense and fierce. He's not ready to back down, not by a long shot.

"I'm the one who got hit by that car, not you," I tell him. "Don't act like you're the victim here. You made choices I didn't ask you to make. I'm not sure anyone asked you to make them." I'm screaming the words, not caring that the entire world can probably hear me. "You think I like limping everywhere I go? I don't. I'm the victim! Be honest with me! You didn't care about me enough to trust me. I gave you my heart, but it wasn't enough." I start to walk away, the leaves crunching hard beneath my shoes.

"Let's get one thing straight, sweetheart," he says from behind me. "I *never* asked you to be my girlfriend."

I stop and turn back to him. "No, you didn't ask. But you sure did everything in your power to make us a couple. You kissed me by the tree in Paradise Park. You were the one who told me at Mrs. Reynolds' house that you wanted to be where I was. You were the one who..." My throat feels like there's a lump the size of a baseball inside. "You said what we had was real, but it was all a lie. Admit it."

"What do you want me to say, Maggie?"

"The truth! That's all I've ever wanted."

"I can't."

"*Can't* or *won't?*"

"What's the difference at this point?"

I swipe my eyes with the back of my hand because tears are blurring my vision. I don't care at all about our stunned audience. "You're nothing but a coward! Every guy in my life has disappointed me. First my dad, now you."

He looks at me like I'm the enemy. "I'm nothing like your dad. Don't insult me by putting us in the same sentence."

I give a short laugh. "He left me. You left me. He betrayed me by leaving and never turning back to see if I was okay. You betrayed me by leaving and never turning back to see if I was okay. He lies to me. You lie to me. You're *exactly* like him."

"You have no fucking clue, Maggie."

I continue limping away, heading for the office, or the van, or ... I don't know where I'm headed except that I know I need to get away. Maybe if I put some space between Caleb and me this crushing pain in my heart will subside.

"Lies are easier to swallow than the truth, Maggie," Caleb yells. He doesn't follow me this time.

I stop but I don't turn around. "You're wrong."

"The *truth* is that I didn't want to have anything to do with you when I got released from jail and came back to Paradise. I *blamed* you for being the reason I went to jail. I *blamed* you for ruining my life. And even through all the blame and all the resentment, I fell for you. Your damn humming, your damn insecurity, your damn vulnerability... and that time you cried in my arms and held onto me like I was your pillar of strength, I was lost because I knew whatever was brewing between us was real. I hated myself for falling for you."

"So you left."

"What did you want me to do? We had to hide our relationship from your mother, my mom was on drugs, my dad was a damn doormat, and my sister... well, you saw her. She looked like death warmed over."

"If you just told the truth—"

"The truth sucks!" Caleb yells, anger and frustration dripping off his words.

"So you've decided to hide behind the lies, right?" Now I turn to face him across little patches of grass and dirt and leaves. I look him right in the eye. I'm not backing down.

Tense seconds tick by.

Caleb pounds his fist hard into the tree trunk. His knuckles are bleeding from the force, but he doesn't seem to notice as he storms up to me.

"The truth is that I didn't hit you with that car! I went to *fucking* jail for a whole *fucking* year for something I didn't *fucking* do! And you know what? It sucked. I resented every moment in juvie because I wasn't supposed to be there in the first place!"

His eyes go wide, his breathing is fast and furious. He turns around and focuses his attention on an outwardly shocked Damon, then scans the other members of our group, all of whom are equally shocked.

Caleb squeezes his eyes shut and winces, as if he wants to take back every truthful word he just spouted. When he opens his eyes, there's no emotion in them anymore. He's masked it.

"Happy now?" he growls.

FIFTEEN
Caleb

If my life wasn't complete shit before, it's definitely shit now. I just gave away the secret I promised to take to the grave. I betrayed my twin sister, and myself, all because I couldn't stand the way Maggie looked at me as she peered down from that damn platform. Her eyes were like glass, and the disappointed furrowing of her eyebrows made me want to scoop her up and take her to a place where nobody would deceive her or hurt her. A place where even I couldn't hurt her.

I fucked up. With Maggie, with Leah, with my parents … with everything.

At this point I can't even trust myself *not* to fuck up. What's the use in trying to stay out of jail when, maybe, that's the best place for me? At least in jail I know where I stand and don't have to see disappointment on the faces of the people I care about.

Problem is, I don't want to be locked up again. I felt like a restless, caged animal in juvie, especially because I knew I didn't deserve to be there in the first place. Or maybe I did. Maybe I deserved to be locked up for lying to the judge and everyone else. I was piss drunk the night Maggie got hit with the car, and maybe my judgment was off when I told my sister I would cover for her.

By then it was too late.

All I wanted to do was protect Leah, since I knew she wouldn't be able to handle the stress of being arrested and stuck in a cell. I don't even know what's right and wrong anymore.

How did Maggie know I'd lied to her? A second ago, I thought the only way I could take that betrayed look off her face was to tell her the truth. Another bad move. She already knew the truth.

I want to escape, but I'm stuck here. I might not be in a cage, but it feels like I'm in one.

"No, I'm not happy," Maggie finally says, her voice low and sad.

I glare at her. "Great, 'cause that makes two of us."

"Three of us," Lenny says, still on the ground. "I think I'm gonna have a bruise on my sensitive ass cheek from you tackling me."

Tears are falling down Maggie's cheeks. She blinks a

couple of times and swipes them away with her fingertips. "Do you hate me, Caleb?"

I should. I should hate her with all my soul, but I don't.

"You knew all along I didn't run into you, didn't you?" I say.

She nods. "I remembered bits and pieces like it was a puzzle, but it wasn't pieced together until—"

"Did you realize I wasn't the one who hit you before I left Paradise eight months ago?" I ask, needing to know the answer even though I'm dreading hearing it.

"Yes," she says softly.

I remember the times we spent together working at Mrs. Reynolds' house, when we fooled around in the gazebo and I ran my hands over her smooth, milky soft skin. "You knew I didn't hurt you, but you let me go along with thinking that you did. How could you?"

"By the time I realized who was really driving the car, I'd already forgiven you. It didn't matter."

"The hell it didn't matter!"

"Umm, time out. I think this activity is over," Damon says. "The three of us need to talk, like right now."

Now. That's Damon's favorite word.

The three of us leave the rest of the group at the platform with Dex and head for a picnic table by the parking lot.

Damon sighs as he looks at Maggie and me sitting opposite him. "Caleb, let me get this straight. You pled guilty to a crime you didn't commit?"

I look the guy straight in the eye. "I plead the fifth."

"You can't plead the fifth, Caleb," Damon says. "You're not in court."

Yeah, and I don't want to end up there again. "I'm still not answering the question."

Damon turns to Maggie for answers, since I'm obviously no help at all. "Maggie, what do you know about all this?"

Maggie shrugs.

Damon shakes his finger at both of us. "You give me no choice. If you won't explain, I'll have to reopen your file and investigate on my own."

"I went to jail, Damon," I blurt out. "I paid for the crime. Case closed."

"If you really went to jail for a crime you didn't commit, the case is far from over. Ever hear of taking responsibility for your actions? You think you did someone a favor? Guess again. If it wasn't you who hit Maggie, who was it?"

I stay silent while Damon looks to Maggie for answers. She stares at the ground.

"I warned you. This isn't over," he tells us.

We trudge through the rest of the exercises. I'm sure as hell not saying a word, and I'm freaking out wondering exactly how much Maggie knows.

After dinner, Damon pulls Maggie and me aside. "Tomorrow morning the rest of the group is going to another school for a panel talk, and the two of you are coming with me."

At the dorm, I overhear Damon talking a bunch of times on his cell, and I get the distinct feeling that he's about to have me arrested and interrogated.

I can't do this. The rest of the night is a big blur to me. All I can think about is that I have to get away. I have to ditch the group and head out on my own again.

In the middle of the night, when everyone is asleep, I toss everything I own in my duffle. Getting away from Damon and his ties to the Illinois justice system is the only solution. If they can't find me, Damon might not have a case against Leah. I looked at some legal books in the juvie library. The statute of limitations on a felony is three years. In a year, Leah can no longer be charged with the crime.

I leave our dorm suite and trot down the stairs. As I start across the dark campus, I hear a familiar voice behind me.

"Caleb, wait."

"Maggie, what are you doing?"

She's wearing silky pants and a T-shirt. Her hair is back in a ponytail, and she looks so vulnerable right now. And sexy, but she doesn't know it. Before I went to jail, I never gave her a second glance. She was just our neighbor and my twin sister's best friend. I was only interested in Kendra Greene, with her big hair and layers of makeup. Maggie's beauty is more subtle … it can be missed if you're blinded by other girls, or compare her to them.

She bites her bottom lip. "You're leaving, aren't you?"

"I can't stay here." I toss my duffle over my shoulder and start walking again.

"I'm going with you," she calls out.

"No, you're not." I glance back at her. She's limping behind me with a backpack on her shoulders. "Go back to the dorm."

"No."

"Don't be stupid, Maggie. Go back to the group and move on with your life. Forget I ever existed."

"I can't do that," she says. "I wish the accident never happened, and that you hadn't gone to jail, and that you hadn't left Paradise, and that you didn't think getting involved with me was the biggest mistake of your life."

Shit. I hate having those words thrown back at me, especially when they were lies. I hurt her, even if I swore I'd never do it again. "Being with you wasn't a mistake."

She gazes up at me with those innocent, expressive eyes. "But you said—"

"Yeah, I know what I said. I lied. But you still can't come with me."

"You asked me to go with you the last time you left Paradise. Remember?"

I nod slowly.

"I'm not making that same mistake again. This time I'm coming with you."

SIXTEEN
Maggie

I can't let Caleb go. Not now. Not until I can convince him to go home again and make everything right. If I let him leave, I may never see him again. He disappeared without a trace eight months ago and I won't let that happen again. Not when everything is out in the open and there are no more lies between us.

"You don't have a choice," I tell him, putting my foot down.

He shakes his head. "Don't piss me off more than I already am."

He walks down the sidewalk that leads off campus. I follow. If he starts to jog, there's no way I can keep up with him.

"I didn't intend to piss you off," I tell him, matching his stride.

"Just ruin my life?"

"Me? I didn't ruin your life, Caleb. You've done that just fine on your own."

"Do me a favor. If you're so intent on joining me, keep the blabber to a minimum."

"You're crabby."

"Damn straight." He stops and turns to me. "Do you know what you did to me today? You made me give up information I promised to take to my grave. I feel like shit."

"If it makes you feel better, I feel like shit too. I don't want you to be pissed or sad, Caleb."

"If you want me to be happy, go back to the dorm."

I think he actually expects me to stop following him. But I don't. I can't.

For the next ten minutes, I follow him in silence. His pace is slow enough that I can keep up.

"What's the plan?" I ask when we reach the center of town. Every store is closed for the night and the streets are completely dark except for the occasional streetlight. "I hope you have one."

"I don't." He looks defeated.

"We're in this together, at least," I say, in a weak attempt to cheer him up.

"Then let me hold your backpack."

Our footsteps on the sidewalk make a rhythmic sound that echoes through the night. We walk through a residential neighborhood on the edge of town. Every fifteen minutes or so, when Caleb spots a big rock or a bench, he orders me to sit and rest my leg.

"We should stop here," he says when we reach a toddler park. In the middle of the playground is a big wooden castle with jungle gyms, wobbly bridges, and slides attached to every side of the structure. I nod.

Caleb leads me to the castle. We have to crouch down to get through the small entrance. It's hard, but he braces my back and supports me while I maneuver inside the cramped space designed for little kids.

Caleb sits in the corner on wood chips. He pulls a jacket from his duffle and places it on the ground next to him. "Sit next to me," he says. "You can use my leg as a pillow."

I'm glad we stopped. I have no clue what time it is, but the sun isn't up yet and I'm running on fumes.

I see a blue plastic tube sticking out from his duffle. "What's that?" I ask, pointing to it.

He pulls it out and pushes a button. The blue plastic lights up. "It's my lightsaber."

"I remember you used to chase me and Leah around your house with that thing."

"Those were the good ol' days." Caleb waves the lightsaber around, lighting up the inside of the castle.

I reach out and take the lightsaber from him. "You think I'd be a good warrior?" I ask.

"No. You follow the enemy too closely."

"You're not the enemy," I tell him, then bring the lightsaber down to strike his leg.

He catches the lightsaber in his hand before it reaches its intended destination. Our eyes meet, and the bright blue light illuminates both our faces. "I am the enemy, Maggie. You just haven't realized it yet."

"You're wrong." When he turns the lightsaber off and stashes it back in his duffle, I lean into him and get into as comfortable a position as I can. "Wouldn't it be cool if this was a real castle?"

"Only if I was the king of it." He looks up at the sky. "But I'd prefer a castle with a roof over it."

"We can pretend, can't we?"

"Yeah, we can pretend."

Pretending is nice, especially when it takes you away from your problems and worries. "Do you ever think of Mrs. Reynolds?"

"She was hilarious." His mouth quirks up, remembering. "I loved the look on your face when she made you wear that dress to plant flowers in."

"It was a muumuu."

"It was ugly as sin."

"I know. I think of her every day. If it wasn't for her…"

"If it wasn't for her, you probably wouldn't be here lying in wood chips with an ex-con running from the law. You'd be in a warm bed back in the dorm."

"I like it here with you better."

He shakes his head. "You're crazy, you know that?"

"Yep."

He puts his arm around me. "Go to sleep. I know you're tired."

"What about you?"

"My mind is racing and I won't be able to sleep tonight, so you should."

I nestle into his lap and try to forget why and how we got into this situation. I just keep telling myself that it'll be okay. We'll figure a way to work it out. In the end, I'll make sure Caleb reunites with his family in Paradise. I don't know exactly how I'm going to orchestrate it, but I will.

I have to.

"Are you still mad at me?" I murmur against his thigh.

"Definitely."

"What can I do to make you less mad?"

"Stay the hell away from me, Maggie."

"Is that really and truly what you want?" I ask.

"Don't make me answer that question," he says, chuckling cynically.

"Why not?"

"Maggie, I gotta tell you something." I notice that the frown lines on his face are pronounced.

"What?"

"Being with you was never a mistake." He gives a short laugh. "Hell, being with you kept me sane while I was home. You and Mrs. Reynolds made being in Paradise bearable."

I reach up and stroke his stubble with the tips of my fingers. "Thanks, Caleb. I needed to hear that. I know I'm not ideal, and I'll never be normal—"

"Maggie, don't ever say that, okay?"

"But—"

"There are no buts. You're here with me, and I don't fucking deserve your time, let alone your support. I lied to you, I deceived you, and I left you. Why you're here with me is beyond my comprehension."

"You know why I'm here," I tell him. "I believe in you."

"Yeah, well that makes one of us." Without another word, he wraps his arms around me and holds me tight. "I'm sorry I lied to you," he whispers.

"I know you are."

Feeling safe with Caleb's arm around me, I let myself relax and get really sleepy.

He brushes stray hairs out of my face. The last thing I remember is Caleb lightly tracing random patterns on my arm, leg, and back. It feels so good I let myself drift to sleep.

He hasn't changed. He's the same boy I fell in love with back in Paradise.

I love you.

The words hover on the tip of my tongue, and I feel my lips frame the syllables, but no sound comes out as my eyelids droop and Caleb gently strokes my hair over and over again.

In the morning, I wake to find him watching me.

"Morning," I say as I stretch. My leg is retaliating from sleeping on the rough wood chips, but I try and hide the pain from him. "Do we have a plan yet?"

"Yeah, I've got a plan," he says. "But you're not gonna like it."

SEVENTEEN
Caleb

Maggie sits up and bites her bottom lip. She's got wood chips stuck in her hair and her eyes are all bloodshot. "Don't you think we should discuss the plan together?"

"No," I say stoically.

"Why not?"

"Because you're not rational."

"*I beg your pardon*," she says, wood chips falling from her hair with each word. "But I'm the one who actually slept last night. You've had no sleep. I vote that I'm the rational one, and I vote that we discuss this *together*."

I stand and hold out my hand to her. "You've never been rational. And before you go begging my pardon again, you were the one who ran off with me in the middle of the night with just a backpack full of stuff."

She takes my hand and lets me help her up. I can tell she's not steady, so I hold her by the waist and support her while her body adjusts.

When she's steady, I let her go. She folds her arms on her chest and puts that straight, aristocratic nose of hers in the air. There isn't a lot of space in this castle, so our bodies brush against each other. "That wasn't irrational. Leaving with you was a calculated risk."

"Calculated?" I ask, skepticism lacing my voice.

"Just forget it." She picks up her backpack and grabs my hand for support as she maneuvers out of the castle. It's early but there are already a few moms with their kids on the playground. They give us dirty looks, as though we were caught fooling around inside the castle's walls.

"So what's this plan you have that I'm not going to like?"

"I'll tell you later," I say.

"You're just stalling the inevitable."

"I know. I'm good at that."

I can tell Maggie's leg is stiff by the way she's walking slowly and tentatively stepping on her left foot. Man, I wish I could take the pain myself. It sucks knowing she'll always have that limp.

Anger at what my sister did to Maggie rushes through me. If it weren't for Leah's irresponsible choice of getting into that car when she'd been drinking, maybe she wouldn't have swerved so much when that squirrel jumped in front of her and Maggie wouldn't have been hit.

I can play the "what if" game forever, but it won't change the fact that Maggie is the one who'll always have the physical repercussions of that night. Nothing I do or say will ever change that.

"Do you need to sit down?" I ask, silently kicking myself because I've put her in this situation.

"I'm okay. Walking usually helps lessen the cramping."

I take her backpack and sling my own duffle over my shoulder. I shake my head as I watch her struggle.

She stops and puts her hand on her hip. "Don't look at me like that."

"Like what?"

"Like you blame yourself. We both know ... well, actually, now *everyone* at Re-START knows, that it's not your fault at all even though you've been paying for it for almost two years." Her eyes take on this look of pity, which doesn't sit well in my gut. "Just point me to the nearest place I can go to the bathroom and get some breakfast. I'm starving. I've got about two hundred dollars to spend before we have to beg for money."

Her words slice right through me. "You're not begging for money. *Ever*. Got it? I've got about twenty bucks. After that, I'll figure something out." Just the picture in my head of her having to beg for anything makes my skin crawl.

"I was kidding," she says, surprising me with a grin. "I'm not the begging type."

"Sorry," I say. Sorry for overreacting. Sorry for putting her in this situation. Sorry for every fucking thing.

We walk a couple of blocks until we get to Pete's Place, a little diner which should probably be condemned by the look of the grease-and-mildew-stained ceiling tiles, but they've got a free bathroom and dirt cheap food, and that's what we need. After we get seated in a booth and Maggie heads for the bathroom, I sit back and think about how I'm going to break the news of my plan to her.

I look around at the two other occupied tables. A guy with a ripped flannel shirt is sipping a cup of coffee by the counter. An old guy is eating alone in another booth, looking out the window as he takes one slow bite of his bread after another. I wonder what he's looking at or waiting for … or if staring out the window is better than remembering that he's alone at a diner eating by himself. Or maybe he's not really looking out the window. Maybe he's daydreaming about some girl he loved and lost.

I don't want to end up like either of those guys—alone and pathetic.

When Maggie comes back, her ponytail is gone. She doesn't look like she slept on a bed of wood chips anymore. She slides into the booth opposite me. I reach across the table and take both her hands in mine. The fact that she was willing to walk away with me last night with just a backpack humbles me.

"Maggie…" I get a lump in my throat the size of a grapefruit. I don't want to say it, but dammit, it has to be said. "I'm taking you back." Her eyes grow big and she opens her mouth I'm sure to protest, but I add, "Do you know what it does to me every time I see you wince in pain?"

She pulls her hands away and lays them in her lap. "I'm fine."

"Stop pretending. I thought we weren't gonna lie to each other anymore."

I watch as she bites her bottom lip. "Okay, I'm lying. But I don't care if I've got a little discomfort or pain." She looks up at me and tilts her head. I can tell the wheels are turning and she's thinking too much. She hesitates at first, but then blurts out, "Have you ever told a girl you loved her? Not like your mom, but like—"

"You mean Kendra."

"Yeah. I mean Kendra."

That's a loaded question. Kendra told me on our first date that she was in love with me. It didn't take long before we were a couple and were making out … and not long after that we had sex. Lots of it. She spouted the word "love" as if it was water. I don't think I've heard or said the word "love" since I was arrested.

I did tell Kendra I loved her, but I'm not even sure I knew what it meant at the time.

"Why do you want to know?"

She shrugs. "I just do. You've never said it …"

She doesn't finish her sentence, but I know what she was going to say. I don't want to go there. Not now … but after what she's done for me, I can't totally avoid the sub-ject. She deserves that much.

"I don't say it to anyone, which is why you're going back to Re-START. I can't let you come with me. It's not safe and you don't deserve this. You're going to Spain, like you've always wanted. If I said the L-word, it would change everything. I know you, Maggie. You'd feel obli-gated to stay here and ditch your plans. I'd feel like shit for making you change your life for me... it's not worth it."

I'm not worth it.

The waitress brings the eggs and toast we ordered then disappears just as quickly as she appeared.

Maggie smiles sheepishly from across the table as she picks up her fork. "So come to Spain with me. I'm regis-tered to be an exchange student for my freshman year. It's only for nine months."

"You know I can't. What am I gonna do there, sit and watch you study? I didn't even graduate high school and I hardly know a lick of Spanish."

"You could get a GED and apply."

I shake my head. As if that's even an option at this point. I'm a lost cause with a pathetically bleak future, and hardly a penny to my name. "Oh, sure, then we could get married and live happily ever after if you'll hop on my fly-ing carpet and rub the genie lamp I have in my duffle. Maybe we could buy a Spanish castle while we're at it."

When my dad married my mom, he was going to school to be a dentist and she was president of the ladies' auxiliary. Everything in their lives was strategically planned, up until the day I got arrested and went to jail. "My mom would shit if she heard this conversation."

"I was going to tell you this earlier, but I didn't know how. Caleb, your mom was in rehab when I left Paradise."

My entire body tenses. "I don't want to talk about her. I don't want to talk about my family *at all*."

A bell over the diner door makes me look to see what other misfit is about to patronize Pete's Place. A big black guy comes walking toward us.

Damon.

I'm busted.

I shake my head in frustration and look over at her. "You didn't."

"I did." She holds up her cell phone. "I suspected you were about to run off and ditch me."

I can't *fucking* believe this. "You sold me out. What happened to your desperate plea to make decisions together?"

"You weren't being rational, Caleb," she tries to tell me, her tone too calm, like she's talking to a little kid. Or a crazy person.

"Maybe you heard me wrong. I said *you* weren't rational."

As I watch Damon walk toward us, I contemplate how I'm going to get out of here.

Damon slides in the booth beside me, blocking my escape. "How are my two Re-START runaways doing?" He looks down at my plate of half-eaten food. "Come on,

Mr. Becker, eat up. You'll need your strength for the busy day ahead of us."

I don't touch my plate or look at Damon. I just stare right at Maggie.

"You were going to bring me back to the dorms and leave again." She looks unsure and worried. Good. I want her to suffer. She betrayed me. "I couldn't let you run away again," she says.

"So better to have me locked up, right?"

"That's not what I meant. You can't just run away from people who care about you."

"If you *cared*," I say through clenched teeth, "my damn transition counselor wouldn't be sitting next to me right now."

The waitress comes by to take Damon's order. "I'll have coffee and, uh, just give me another plate of whatever these kids ordered," he tells her.

I stare out the window like the old man in the other booth. Now I know how he feels, wanting to forget the here and now. Why can't Maggie understand my situation? Doesn't she get that I lost what little honor I had by blurting out I wasn't the one who hit her?

Shit.

I need to get away from the truth, away from my past. I need a fresh start.

Except there's no such thing as a fresh start, not when people from your past keep popping up and hounding you, driving home all your mistakes even further. I thought

I'd done a good thing for Leah when I took the fall for her, but what did I really get? No hero's welcome when I came back home, that's for damn sure. The lies are starting to blur with the truth, and Maggie's stuck smack dab in the middle of it.

"All right, kids. Let's have it all out on the table right here and right now. Who was driving the car that hit Maggie?" Damon fishes his cell phone out of his pocket and puts it on the table in front of him. "If you both don't start talking, I'm calling the prosecutor's office. We can handle this my way or their way. Which is it?"

EIGHTEEN
Maggie

Caleb is really mad at me. He turns away and looks out the window. I know he wants to escape right now, which is why I'm so thankful that Damon is here. Physically I can't stop Caleb from leaving, but Damon can.

"Let Damon help you," I say.

Caleb tenses. "Nobody can help, Maggie. Get it through that thick skull of yours, okay?"

"She's not the enemy," Damon says in a terse voice. "Man, kid, you are one master of displaced anger."

"Be careful," Caleb says. "She's a wolf in sheep's clothing. This is your party, Maggie. Why don't you tell Damon everything he wants to know?"

"It's not my story to tell. It's yours."

While Damon eats, Caleb and I are silent.

"I'm waiting," Damon says as he reaches for the salt shaker.

"I can't tell you," Caleb says.

Damon takes a long sip of coffee before very deliberately setting his mug back on the table. "Why not?"

Caleb looks at me, his eyes bleak.

Damon drums his fingers on the tabletop. "I read the file, Caleb. You gave a detailed story about how you swerved to avoid a squirrel, hit Maggie, and panicked."

"I'm a good storyteller," Caleb mumbles.

The drumming stops. "Why did you take the blame for someone else?"

"I don't know."

"That's not an answer."

"Well, that's the only one you're gonna get out of me," Caleb says defiantly.

A squad car drives by the diner, making my heart beat in overtime. Did Damon call the police before he came? Caleb was right, I shouldn't have called Damon.

"Please don't have him arrested," I tell Damon. "Caleb has been punished enough."

"Tell you what," Damon says. "I'll forget I heard about your little secret for now and you finish my Re-START program. If you do, and promise to go back to Paradise and straighten everything out, I'll make sure you stay out of jail for the drug charges. Sound like a deal?"

"Why would you do that?" Caleb asks.

"Let's just say I think you're a good kid. That doesn't mean I think you make stellar choices in life. I think you've made some damn stupid ones, not to mention the little disappearing act you and Maggie pulled last night. But I made some crappy choices as a teen and I'm willing to give you one last chance. You with me?"

"I'm with you," I say, trying to sound cheery.

"What kind of crappy choices?" Caleb asks, challenging Damon. "You sit back and watch all of the Re-START crew tell our fucked-up stories, but you never say a damn word."

Damon picks up his mug and grips it tightly. "I was a coke addict, and I lost everything. I lost my girlfriend, my kid, and my money. One day I didn't pay my supplier for the coke I used and they beat me up real bad. Luckily, I got out, but not a day goes by when I don't regret treating my girl and my kid like they were garbage. I'd do anything to get them back, but it's too late now. She moved to Arizona and lets me see my kid once a year."

"Can't you get them back?" Caleb asks. "Tell them you got your life on track and want to be a family?"

"It's not that simple. I did horrible things—I stole money and property from family and friends. Some things can't be forgiven, and I've come to terms with it. She's moved on. I have to, also. So now that you know my story, are you coming with me?"

Caleb gives me a look that tells me he doesn't trust me anymore, but he's resigned to his fate. "I guess I'm with you, too."

Back at the dorm, we find the rest of the group in the lounge area waiting for us.

"Where did you two sneak off to?" Lenny asks. "A secret rendezvous to do the nasty?"

Caleb and I ignore him. Damon walks up to Lenny and smacks the back of his head while the girls follow me to my room.

"I'm glad you're back," Erin says.

"Me too."

Trish sits on the edge of my bed while I unpack the stuff from my backpack. "Where'd you guys go?"

"Nowhere special. Caleb needed to get away, and I couldn't let him go alone."

When we first walked off campus, I thought that was it for us and Re-START. But even before I knew Caleb was going to make me come back, I realized I couldn't run away. One night in that playground castle proved I couldn't physically do it ... I can't leave even if I want to.

"Caleb needs you," Trish says.

I smile weakly. "I don't think he'd agree with you right now. He's pissed that I called Damon to come get us."

"He'll get over it if he knows what's good for him. He probably just needs some time to realize he has to rely on other people. Guys are control freaks and hate when other people know what's best for them."

Damon calls us out in the living room after we're all showered and dressed. He's got a clipboard tucked under one arm and claps his hands together kinda ... excited. "We're going to juvie," he announces.

"Been there, done that," Caleb mumbles under his breath.

"It's time to share your stories with troubled teens who are locked up." Damon eyes us over the clipboard in his hands. "Maybe when they get out they'll think twice before getting drunk, or doing drugs, or showing off to their buddies before getting behind the wheel of a car."

Damon walks over to Caleb and gets into his personal space. He doesn't touch him; he just stands there. "You'll be okay, Caleb."

Caleb turns his face away, but as if he can't help the words from coming out against his will he says, "I don't want to go back there, Damon. Cut me some slack, will ya?"

I know how hard it is for Caleb to ask anyone for a favor. I know how much that request cost him.

Damon shakes his head slowly and pats him on the back. "It's important, Caleb. And we'll all be there for you."

In the van, I purposely sit next to Caleb in the back row. The muscles in his jaw are twitching and he's got his hands folded on his chest. He's tense.

"Want to talk about it?" I ask him quietly so nobody else can hear.

"No comment." He looks out the window, shutting me out.

It takes us almost two hours to reach the juvenile detention center, or DOC—Department of Corrections— as Caleb calls it. Our van is cleared and ushered through the tall barbed-wire gate. I can feel the tension and stress radiating off Caleb. He doesn't want to be here. I don't know everything that happened to him here, but a while back he gave me a few glimpses into what he went through.

I'm having second thoughts about calling Damon and telling him we were at the diner. Maybe I should have let things stay as they were. At least then I wouldn't have Caleb mad at me.

"I'm sorry I made you come back to Re-START," I mumble.

"Whatever," he says as he stares out the window at the barbed-wire fence surrounding the compound. "It's over and done."

"What's over and done? Ditching Re-START, or us as a couple?"

A man and woman in dark suits are in the parking lot, waiting for us. We all step out of the van, but Caleb stops me when everyone else is out but us.

"Listen," he says. "I'm not gonna say I haven't thought about what it would be like if you and I, well, you know. But I think we should cool it for a while. At least until after this Re-START bullshit is over."

"And after it's over, what then?"

Damon pounds on the side of the van, startling me. "Come on, slowpokes, get a move on!" Damon yells. "You're holding everyone else up!"

I step out into the hot summer air and stare at the guards with guns in their holsters. It makes me feel safe and scared at the same time.

The guy with the suit walks right up to Caleb. "We haven't seen your mug here since you got released. I trust you're staying out of trouble."

Caleb almost stands at attention, his face as grave as I've ever seen it. He barks out an "I'm trying to, sir," which makes the guy in the suit narrow his eyes at Caleb.

"Try? I'm sure you can do better than try, Becker."

"Yes, sir."

After staring Caleb down, the guy paces in front of all of us. "I'm Mr. Yates and this is Ms. Bushnell," he says loudly, so that we can all hear him. He points to the woman standing next to him, her hair pulled back into a tight bun. "The girls will be visiting our female population with Ms. Bushnell and the boys will be visiting our male population with me. You ready?"

We all nod, except Caleb. I watch as he pulls Damon aside and says quietly, "I can't do this."

NINETEEN
Caleb

"I can't do this," I tell Damon again. Shit, my knee has been shaking nonstop since he started driving.

Damon pats me on the back again, as if he's a friend of mine and will stand by me no matter what. "Yes, you can. Trust me."

Trust him? When was the last time I actually trusted anyone without getting screwed? "Whatever, dude."

"Listen, you're stronger than you think, Caleb. These kids are looking for role models."

I swipe sweat off my forehead. "Get a clue, Damon. I'm not a role model, and I don't want to be one. What am I gonna tell these guys, that I went to jail for something I didn't do?"

"It's your choice what you tell them."

I look up at the brick building that I lived in for almost a year. I had to get up at six thirty and shower in front of others, I had to eat when they said eat, and when I needed to use the facilities during juvie school, I was escorted into the bathroom so I could crap. It was pathetic.

Just like back then, it doesn't seem like I have any choice in the matter. I follow Yates and the other Re-START guys towards the male sector, but look back and watch Ms. Bushnell escort the girls to the other sector. Maggie is limping behind her. Very soon she's going to see the reality of how I lived for a year. I wish I could stop her from going in there.

When I was in the DOC, the girls and guys never saw each other. We had school a few hours a day, went to group therapy, were assigned chores, went outside for an hour, ate three meals, and had the rest of the day to chill in our cells. We were encouraged to read a lot or study to pass the time, but a lot of the guys hated reading or couldn't read worth shit.

In the intake center waiting room, my hands are shaking a little, so I shove them into my pockets as I stand and scan the security guards and security cameras and securely locked doors. I glance at the waiting cells, where you get locked up before they register you. Bad memories come flooding back.

After registering as an offender here, they confiscate every single piece of clothing and personal item and keep them locked up until you're released. The strip search is next, and let me tell you, the guard who does it makes sure you're not hiding any contraband in any crevice of your body.

Yates holds out a clear plastic bin. "Empty all your pockets. I mean *everything*, including pens, pencils, money, wallets, and paper."

We all do as instructed, then we're escorted through a bunch of locked doors and corridors. We come to a room where inmates meet their families and friends on visitors' day.

"We've decided to pair you off," Yates says. "You'll each be meeting with our residents one-on-one. That way, we can have shifts and you guys can share your stories in a small setting. No cussing or lewd comments are allowed. No touching the residents."

Damon, Matt, and I all look over at Lenny, who puts his hand on his chest. "You guys think I'm lewd?"

Is he kidding me? The kid urged me to pull his finger so he could fart, he fans his sweaty ball sacks in front of us, and doesn't clean his wayward pubes off the toilet seat. If *he's* not lewd, God help us all.

I roll my eyes.

"No comment," Matt says and laughs.

Damon gives Lenny a sharp stare. "Keep it appropriate, Lenny, or you'll find yourself on bathroom cleaning duty for the rest of the day."

Lenny mocks Damon by saluting him. "Yes, sir."

Damon shakes his head. He's probably counting down the days until this program is over and he can kick us to the curb.

Yates sits on the edge of one of the tables in the room and points to me. "Caleb will attest to the fact that some of our residents come from broken homes and/or gangs and don't have a grounded filter when it comes to making good choices. A lot of these kids will trust you if you've also gone through tough times like they have. They think hardships are a badge of honor."

My hardships are a pain in my ass, not a badge of honor. And make no mistake about it, the guys locked in the DOC are far from *residents*. Yates makes it sound like these guys are paying rent for their living quarters. What a fucking joke. In reality, they're locked up like animals.

We're each assigned a table. It's eerily quiet as the first round of inmates join us. They walk in the room with their hands behind their backs as required by the guards, their expressions blank. The familiar dark blue polyester jumpsuits take me back to the first day I was here. That suit was a constant reminder my life was not my own any-more ... while I was locked up, it was owned by the Illinois Juvenile Justice Department and the Department of Corrections.

Their heads are all buzz-cut or shaved, a requirement for all new inmates. When the final person walks in the room, it's like a ghost appears right in front of me.

It's Julio, my old cellmate. He's wearing an orange jumpsuit instead of the regular blue one, meaning he's under harsh restrictions for getting into trouble in the DOC.

I haven't heard from or talked to Julio since I left this place. He was a complete ass when we were first assigned as cellmates, but after he realized I wasn't afraid of him and saw me stand toe-to-toe with gang member Dino Alvarez in the exercise yard when he cornered me, we got along just fine.

Julio, tattoos on his neck peeking out of his suit, sits opposite me. "Long time no see, *amigo*."

"How you been?" I ask.

"Chillin' in the DOC. I get released in two weeks, if not sooner," he says with a grin. "Hoo-rah. Just got to stay out of trouble."

Not easy for a guy like Julio.

Julio was the one who hooked me up with his cousin Rio. I lived with Rio until... "Rio got busted."

Julio shakes his head. "I heard. Fuckin' shame. My cuz ain't gettin' out anytime soon 'cause he's a repeater. I'm screwed too, 'cause I was gonna live with him. My ma moved back to Mexico with her boyfriend."

"I got busted too," I tell him. "That's why I'm on this program. It was either this, or get locked up again."

I watch Julio lean back in his chair as the news sinks in. "What you gonna do after you're done?"

I shrug. "Don't know."

Damon walks over to us. "Sounds like a reunion, guys."

"Julio was my cellmate," I explain. "Julio, this is Damon. He was my transition counselor."

147

Julio nods to Damon and shuts up immediately. There's no way Julio is gonna be friendly or chat with anyone who works for the DOC in any way, shape, or form. Julio is a gang member with connections inside and outside this place, and he doesn't trust anyone outside of his circle. I'm surprised he still trusts me, but then again we spent almost a year as cellmates and slept, ate, and shit in close quarters.

Damon walks over to Matt's table. Matt is talking to a kid who looks like the typical newbie. He's scared as hell to be here but is putting on a tough front.

A guard stands right by the solid metal door, a stun gun on one side of his belt and a shoot-to-kill gun on the other. I notice that one of the guards has his eyes trained on Julio. This isn't the typical juvie. This place holds big-time offenders who just happen to be underage. Yates is on the opposite side of the room, his arms folded on his chest as he narrows his eyes at us. They're watching us like hawks like they did when I was an inmate here.

Julio leans in and whispers, "Yates thinks this shithole is the Club Med, but it sucks. I can't wait to get out of here, man. Hell, maybe I'll come visit you in Paradise. I've always wanted to know how the hicks in the boondocks live. I hear the chicks in Paradise are easy."

"Some are," I say, thinking about my ex, Kendra, "and some aren't," I add, thinking about Maggie.

My thoughts turn to Maggie. She's probably freaking out meeting tough girls who eat innocent girls like her for breakfast.

Yates passes our table and gives us the evil eye.

What does the guy expect, that I'll slip Julio some drugs or a shovel so he can dig his way out of here?

I clear my throat and lean toward Julio. "So I'm supposed to share how reckless driving has changed my life and caused pain to others. It's part of the program."

Julio rolls his eyes and snorts. "All right, hit me with it."

"Reckless driving changed my life and caused pain to others," I say, as if I'm reading off a cue card.

Julio grins. I'm making a joke of this visit and Julio gets it. But the truth is, it's not a joke. It's reality. Suddenly, I get serious.

I take a deep breath and let it out slowly. "I guess I, um, never told you what really happened the night I was arrested."

"You never talked much about it."

"Yeah, 'cause I didn't do it." I shrug and look at my former cellmate. "I pled guilty even though I wasn't guilty."

Julio chuckles. "You're shittin' me, right?" He says it low so nobody can hear him cuss. Yates doesn't take cussing lightly, not in his jail. Luckily Warden Miller isn't here, or Julio would probably get some sort of punishment for cussing. Warden Miller takes his rules seriously and expects everyone else to. If not, you better be prepared for extra chores, early bedtime, or even solitary.

I shake my head. "Nope."

"Why'd you plead guilty? To protect someone?"

"Yeah," I whisper. "Something like that."

"Wow. Can't say I'd do the same thing." Julio looks at me sideways. "Unless it was family. I'd die for my family."

I nod slowly. "Me too."

Julio nods back in complete understanding, because even though we come from totally different backgrounds, we're cut from the same cloth. He knows just by my nod that I sacrificed myself and went to jail for a family member.

"You regret it?" he asks.

I pause to think about what my life would have been like if I hadn't been arrested. "Yeah, I do. Fucked-up thing is, I can't say I wouldn't do it again."

"Loyalty and honor and all that shit really screws with your head, doesn't it?"

"Yeah." I wince, because images of Maggie aren't far from my thoughts. I don't want to think about her now. "And girls really screw with your head, too."

Julio raises an excited eyebrow. "My boy Caleb's got a girl? Nice goin', dude. Who is she? Last I heard, you and your skanky ex broke up 'cause she was gettin' it on with your best friend."

"One more minute guys," Yates bellows. "Wrap it up!"

"I don't have a girl," I say, chuckling at the thought. "Besides, the only chick I might want hates me. I never say the right thing around her. Hell, I try and push her away so I don't have to deal with the drama. And she pisses me off most of the time."

"Sounds like a match made in Heaven to me." Julio

leans across the table. "Take advice from a guy who hasn't seen a girl under twenty in over a year—the only female I've talked to lately is the cafeteria worker, and she's so fugly I'm not even sure she's female. You only live once, so take advantage of what you got when you have it."

"You too."

"I hear you loud and clear. No regrets anymore, okay? Live every day like it's your last. *¿Comprende?*"

Yates orders the inmates to line up at the door.

I crack a smile. Julio is right. I've been living every day with regret, when it should be the other way around. "Yeah, I understand."

"See you on the outside, Caleb." He holds up two fingers. "Peace." With those words, he shuffles out of the room.

I'm ready to live my life without regrets. I've just got to figure out a strategy to make that happen.

TWENTY

Maggie

I'm sitting across from a girl with dyed-blonde hair and dark roots. She's wearing blue sweatpants and a blue T-shirt like the other girls in jail. Ms. Bushnell assigned her to my table. The girl is staring at me as if she doesn't want to be here.

"I'm Maggie," I tell her.

"So, Maggie, what's your story?" she asks impatiently, totally uninterested.

I tell her how I was hit by a car in a hit-and-run accident and spent a year in hospitals and rehab. Her eyes glaze over and at one point I think she might be falling asleep.

When I explain how I didn't fit in when I came back to start my senior year of high school, she asks, "Is that supposed to make me feel sorry for you? Listen, I've got more to deal with than a busted-up leg. My dad's a drunk, and my mom walked out on us five years ago. I'm not really crying over your limp, so you might as well save your breath and the rest of your story for someone who actually gives a shit."

I didn't get much sleep last night. Caleb's not talking to me. I'm crabby and my nerves are on edge. If this girl doesn't want to have sympathy, fine. But that doesn't mean I have to sit here while she patronizes me.

"*You* listen," I say, then lean across the table so I've got her undivided attention and to make sure she hears me loud and clear. "Just because you've got a bad home life doesn't give you the right to sit there and be rude."

"Sure it does," she fires back. "I bet you've got parents with money—"

"My mom works as a waitress in a diner."

"Well I bet your dad ain't a drunk—"

"I wouldn't know," I tell her. "My dad walked out on my mom. I haven't seen him in years. Oh, and I forgot to mention that I fell for the guy who went to jail for hitting me with his car. I wasn't supposed to be talking to him in the first place. Then he came on this trip, but now he's not talking to me again, and I'm supposed to pretend like we're just friends and I'm afraid of losing him although I know that's stupid because I feel like I've already lost him ... and none of it would have happened if it weren't for a reckless driving incident. So when you get out of this place, please don't drive recklessly or you might end up with a permanent disability, boyfriendless, and an outcast at school."

Instead of the girl falling asleep or giving me attitude, she's now staring at me wide-eyed. "All right. You made your point. I get it."

"Thanks," I tell her, and mean it.

"Does it suck when people stare at you when you walk?" she asks.

At first when I got out of the hospital I didn't even want to get out of my wheelchair and walk, because I knew I drew more stares from my ridiculously pronounced limp than being confined to a wheelchair. I hated the stares.

"I hate being stared at, but I try and block it out," I tell her. "I admit it makes me feel like I'm the main event at a freak show." I look down and say what I don't like to put into words but it's the honest truth. "There's not a day goes by that I wish the accident hadn't happened and that I could be normal. It's on my mind every day."

"Not a day goes by where I don't regret doin' what I done to get myself locked up in here," she says.

"I don't know if I can ask you questions about why you're here."

"Let's just say I hurt someone *real bad*," she tells me, then focuses at a spot on the wall. Maybe she doesn't want to see my reaction.

I look at the female guard blocking the door and Ms. Bushnell on the opposite end of the room. They're eyeing the inmates. I wonder if there's ever a time they're not being watched or evaluated. I think of Caleb, who told me he hated being watched by guards every second of the day. I wonder how he's holding up now, being here again.

"It must be horrible being in here," I mumble.

The girl shrugs. "Actually it ain't that bad. Beats bein' home. I guess I hate bein' here 'cause it reminds me of what I done. I hurt this girl. The memories of that night give me nightmares most nights. I was thinkin' about writin' her a letter, but she'd prob'ly throw it out and never read it."

"You could try. If anything it'll probably make you feel better to write it down."

"I don't think so."

"Just think about it."

"You have one more minute, ladies!" Ms. Bushnell announces loudly. "Say your good-byes and line up at the door."

"Yeah, well, I guess it was cool meeting you," the girl says. "The girls who don't got no visitors got to come to talk to you guys. It sucks when it's visiting day and nobody calls out your name that you got a visitor, so, uh, thanks for bein' here." She clears her throat. "I'm Vanessa. My friends back home called me V, but to be honest I don't got no friends anymore."

I raise my hand. Ms. Bushnell walks over to our table. "Is there a problem?" she asks.

"No," I'm quick to tell her. "I just wanted to know if I could have Vanessa's address ... so we can be pen pals."

Ms. Bushnell's stern face softens. "That would be fine. I'll give you the information before you leave the building."

"You didn't have to go an' do that," Vanessa says when Ms. Bushnell walks away.

"I know."

Vanessa smiles, the first smile I've seen from her since she walked in the room. "You're okay, Maggie. And if you do ever write me, I promise to write back. Just don't expect no fancy writin'."

"It's a deal."

"And just so you know, I don't think you're a freak at all. In fact, I think you're one of the coolest girls I've ever met."

I smile. "I'm a geek," I tell her.

"No you're not." She points her finger at me. "You, Maggie, are one cool chick. Don't forget it."

A cool chick? "Nobody has ever called me cool before."

"That's 'cause you don't act it. If you think you're cool and act like you're the shit, everyone'll start treating you like you've got it goin' on. You get what I'm sayin'?"

"I think so."

"Don't waste a single day thinkin' you're a geek, or you might as well be locked in here like me."

Vanessa and the other girls get in a single file line by the locked metal door with their hands held behind their backs. Some of the girls look really young ... like they're barely in high school or even younger than that. The guard leads them out. Before Vanessa leaves, she looks back and gives me a small good-bye nod.

According to Vanessa, my limp and scars don't matter. I'm a cool chick. I just have to start believing it.

Our whole Re-START group is quiet as we leave the DOC. I head for the back of the van where Caleb usually sits, but when he sees me, he slides into the front row next to Trish.

I'm stuck in the back with Lenny.

When we get back to Dixon Hall, Damon tells us we have two days off to rest and have fun. Matt suggests we go to Independence Grove tomorrow to rent canoes and fish in the lake.

Caleb seems really distant since we left the detention center. I wonder what happened with him on the guys' side of the jail. I don't find out, though, because Caleb spends the rest of the evening alone in his room. Damon calls him to the lounge area for dinner.

"I'll just grab something from the fridge later," he says. When we're about to watch a movie in the lounge, I peek in and see him lying on his bed, staring at the ceiling.

"Caleb, we're watching a movie."

"Watch without me."

"Are you okay?" I ask tentatively. "Want to talk?"

He gives a short laugh and shakes his head.

"Are you going to be mad at me forever?"

He doesn't answer.

The next morning, as we're all rubbing on sunscreen, Caleb is the last to get ready. He slaps on a baseball cap, long shorts, and a tank top. Caleb's tattoo reminds me of black flames licking his skin. It makes him look tough and untouchable, which I'm sure was the look he was going for when he got it.

At the park, Damon buys us worms. He rents fishing gear and three boats, and tells us we're on our own and he'll be back before noon with lunch.

"Hey Trish," Lenny says as he watches her lay out a towel on the sandy beachfront. "Do you know you can see your nipple outline through your bikini top?"

"You're a pig," Trish says, then pushes Lenny away.

Lenny holds his hands up. "What? I was gonna say you have nice nips. Geez, Trish. Get a grip and learn how to take a compliment."

We're all looking at Lenny as if he's out of his mind.

Trish crosses her arms over her chest and makes a big deal of checking out Lenny's lower regions. "Do you know you *can't* see your dick outline through your bathing suit?" She tosses her hair and says, "Just so you know, Lenny, that *wasn't* a compliment."

Without warning, Lenny picks up Trish and carries her into the lake, kicking and screaming.

"You better not throw me in!" she screams, still kicking, as she grabs onto Lenny's neck for dear life.

"Oh, yeah, baby, you're bein' tossed." Lenny says, seemingly oblivious to the kicks and pleas of the girl he's been at odds with since this trip started.

I look over at Caleb, who's watching Lenny and Trish. He turns to me and an evil look crosses his face. He nods, as if Lenny is carrying out the most brilliant punishment to a girl who pissed him off.

"You're not thinking of tossing *me* in the lake," I tell him.

"Yeah," he says. "I am."

TWENTY-ONE

Caleb

This is the first time since I met Lenny that I get a glimpse his brain is capable of making a smart decision.

My mind does the mental gymnastics to justify what I'm thinking: Maggie's leg hinders her on land, but in the water she's just like the rest of us. She really screwed everything up for me by calling Damon. I need to take control of the situation and have no regrets. Which means...

Maggie needs to get wet. And, to use a Damonism: right now.

"Come here," I tell her. I strip off my tank in one swift movement.

She steps back, her bare feet sinking into the sand.

"Promise me you won't toss me in the lake." She glances quickly at the water, then looks back at me. "There's *fish* swimming around in there."

"They won't hurt you."

"I can't swim," she says quickly as she takes another step away from me.

"Caleb, not a good idea," Matt chimes in from beside her.

I give Matt a *you're an idiot* look. "I've known Maggie all my life. Don't let her fool you—she's an excellent swimmer." So much for her being honest with me.

A big splash brings our attention back to Lenny and a now very wet Trish. I take this break in Maggie's concentration to catch her. I lift her and carry her to the water's edge.

"I'm wearing pants!" she screams, wiggling violently. "Let me down! Seriously, Caleb. I'm the shit, so back off!"

I suppress a laugh, 'cause I never expected those words to come out of Maggie. "You're the shit, huh? And all along I thought I was the shit."

I walk further into the water. Her hands are wrapped tight around my neck, locking behind me like a vice.

"Okay, joke's over Caleb. Let me down."

Her head nestles into the crook of my neck, and her wild hair is flying in my face. If I wasn't so angry with her I might be tempted to like the way she's clinging to me.

"Don't throw me in. Promise me."

I go deeper. The sand on the bottom of the lake is

soft, making my feet sink in. The water is up to my knees now. I pass Lenny and Trish, who are splashing each other. They're both soaked.

Maggie and I are about to get soaked too.

"I'm not gonna toss you in," I tell Maggie as I turn into a little bend in the lake for some privacy. Nobody on shore can see us now. "I promise."

She loosens her hold on my neck and leans her head back to look into my eyes. "You're not?" she asks, letting out a sigh of relief.

"No." I hold in my amusement as the next words fly out of my mouth. "But hold your breath or you'll get a mouthful of lake water."

Before she can ask why, I dunk us both. She tries pushing away from me as soon as we come up completely drenched a second later, but I hold onto her tight. I may be pissed at her, but I don't want her drowning from shock, or weighted down because she's wearing long pants.

Maggie comes up sputtering, but not from lake water getting in her mouth. The girl is mad as hell. "How ... could ... you!"

"It was pretty easy, actually," I tell her, still holding her tight while she tries to push me away.

She splashes my face.

"Don't do that," I tell her.

She does it again, so I let her go. She maneuvers to stand a few feet in front of me, her hands already underneath the water. She's definitely ready for a splash war. I play dirty, though, and splashing is a kids' game. We're not kids anymore.

Maggie is about to get a dose of what it's like to play in the big leagues.

I wade closer to her. She starts splashing, but I don't reciprocate. I'm soaking wet, but I ignore the water hitting in my face and stinging my eyes. I just keep moving closer until I'm close enough to reach out and grab her wrists so she can't splash me anymore.

I hold her hands behind her back and pull her snugly against my body. She's so close I feel her breasts pressed against my bare chest. When she looks up at me, our lips are inches apart. Her hair is dripping wet, her face has droplets of water glistening from the sun reflecting on them, and her lips are shiny and wet.

I don't know how I ever could have thought of this girl as plain.

"What are you gonna do now that I'm helpless?" she asks.

I lean down and whisper in her ear, "You've got it all wrong, Maggie. I'm the helpless one here."

"Oh," she says, eyes wide.

I loosen my hold on her wrists while I slide my lips across her cheek. The sensation of her soft skin against my lips combined with her body still pressed against mine is driving me insane. Oh, hell. I don't want to want her. It would be so much easier to hate Maggie and ban her from my thoughts and my life. But Julio's words echo in my head: no regrets.

When my lips reach the corner of her mouth, I let go of her arms and move my hands to her waist. At the same time, I lightly glide my lips across hers. She sighs and breathes faster as our wet lips slide ever so slowly back and forth, back and forth.

It's erotic. Painfully erotic.

I'm not gonna deepen the kiss, that's her move. I'm gonna make her want it so damn bad she'd rather die than not feel my tongue sliding against hers. She's gotta want this even more than me.

There's one problem here. My body is betraying me, big time. I'm glad we're under water so the evidence of my arousal is hidden from view.

When her hands reach up and sneak around my neck, I know I've got the upper hand. She wants this. I'm gonna make her beg for it and make out with her like there's no tomorrow. Then I'll walk away as if I don't give a shit.

Cruel, yes. But I've got to prove to her once and for all that I'm a badass ex-con. Yesterday at the DOC, seeing Julio and the other inmates reminded me where I came from. Who I really am. Doesn't matter if I didn't hit Maggie and went to jail for my sister.

I'll always be an ex-con. It's branded on me like an invisible tattoo. But I need to live each day like it's my last … with no regrets.

I hold back a groan as Maggie opens her lips and tilts her head. Her lips slant, slightly open, against mine. This is it. Finally. I'm waiting impatiently for her tongue to snake out and reach mine. It's gonna happen any second. It's *gotta* happen, 'cause this is fucking torture. I know she's no stranger to French kissing. Hell, we did it back at the dorm and it was earth-shattering.

I'm ready. *Damn, I'm more than ready.* My entire body is screaming of readiness. She's got to be ready for this, too.

She opens her mouth wider and moans, a moan that makes me fantasize about what it would be like to witness her having an orgasm. I'm so turned on I know I'm gonna pay for it later.

But that doesn't matter.

I swallow a triumphant smile. Here it comes. That moan of hers was a clue that she's dying to take this to the next level. I wish my body wasn't ready to take this to the next *three* levels.

She moans against my lips again, and my tongue is twitching in my mouth ready to be unleashed like a fucking caged animal. I'm usually a patient kisser, but…

Still nothing.

What the—

I lean back. "What the hell are you doing?"

"What do you mean?" she asks, innocently batting her eyelashes against the hot sun beaming down on us.

Is she *kidding* me?

"Where's your tongue?" I ask stupidly.

Her wet little eyebrows furrow. "In my mouth. Why, where's it supposed to be?"

I let go of her, step back and rub my hands through

my soaked hair to get a handle on reality. "You're fucking with me, right?"

She shrugs. The movement creates ripples around her body that move across the water. "Maybe."

Oh. No. She. Didn't.

My tongue is unleashed now, but it's to argue not to kiss. "You were trying to get me all hot and bothered to get back at me for dumping you in the water, weren't you? *Admit it*. You're not the innocent little Maggie you want everyone to think you are. You're a damn tease, that's what you are."

"And what were you doing, Caleb? Weren't you trying to get me all hot and bothered on purpose? *You're* the tease."

"You have no clue," I bark back. This lying bit can go both ways, sweetheart.

Maggie starts wading toward shore.

I'm left here, all alone. Not how I thought this scenario would go down. "So you're just gonna walk away?"

"Yes," she calls out, her back to me. "You were the one who said we needed to break things off until this trip was over. I'm just following your rules."

I wish I could follow her, but I need to stay waist-deep for at least another minute until my body cools down.

"I said we needed to cool it."

"I'm cool," she says over her shoulder.

"I'm not." I'm all hot and bothered. Being in the cool lake should help, but doesn't.

Maggie one-upped me. My ego is busted, big time. But I manage to forget it for the time being and get out of the water. I lie on the beach and wonder if I need to try a different tactic.

A half hour later, we all head into our little canoes with our fishing gear. None of the girls know how to put a worm on a hook, so each guy has to go with one of the girls.

"I'm going with Matt," Maggie declares up front. Matt is all too eager to accommodate her.

In the end, I'm stuck with Trish, because she says she's afraid Lenny will tip the boat on purpose.

Lenny and poor Erin are paired up, and she looks like she's about to puke. She looks that way most of the time lately. I'm starting to think she's either got a case of the flu or a case of pregnancy.

"So what's the real story with you and Maggie?" Trish asks as we row out to the middle of the lake. "It looks like you two are a couple again."

"We're not."

Trish rolls her eyes. "Oh, puh-lease. It's obvious you guys having something hot and heavy going on. Just spill the beans already so the rest of us don't have to speculate about it anymore."

I laugh. "What've you speculated?"

"That you're still in love with her." She hands me the worm container and her fishing pole. "You want to know what I think?"

"Not really. Why don't we talk about you and Lenny?"

"What about me and Lenny?" she asks, her face scrunched up like I'm nuts.

"Admit you've got a thing for him."

"Eww. Don't make me throw up, Caleb." I put the worm on the hook and Trish winces. "How can you do that? It's inhumane."

"Think of it as feeding the fish."

Trish folds her arms across her chest. "Yeah, right. Feeding them, then sticking a hole in their face as punishment for wanting a little food."

I hand the pole back to her, all ready to go. "You want to fish, or not?" I ask her as I notice Matt and Maggie across the way with their poles in the water. They're talking. I wonder if she's complaining about me.

"She's scared, you know," Trish says. "She thinks you'll leave her again."

"She's probably right."

"Then let her go, Caleb. Stop confusing her and giving her mixed signals. She deserves a guy who'll stick around and be there when she needs him."

"Like Matt?" I say harshly.

Trish holds her hands up. "Don't get all pissed off. I'm just saying what I think."

"I think you should keep your opinions to yourself."

Trish puts her fishing pole into the water and says with certainty, "And I think you know I'm right."

TWENTY-TWO

Maggie

For the rest of the Re-START trip, Caleb keeps his distance. He acts like we're mere acquaintances. He only interacts with me when he has to. When we talk to groups around Illinois, Indiana, and Wisconsin, Caleb shares how he was arrested and how he'd do anything to avoid jail in the future.

He doesn't talk about going to jail for Leah. I think he wants to forget that part of the story, although in my opinion the reality of what he did for his sister looms over him every day. I wish I could get him to talk about it, but at this point he doesn't trust me at all.

I'm not sure he trusts anyone.

It's the day before the end of the trip, and we're staying in a big rented cabin in Lake Geneva, Wisconsin. The cabin has nine bedrooms, so we each get our own. But I can't sleep with the thought of losing Caleb again pressing on me. I peek into his room at two in the morning, but his bed is empty. My heart is panicking, thinking he's skipped out early.

Relief washes over me as I spot Caleb from my window. He's skipping rocks by the lake.

My brain tells me it will be better to just let him go.

My heart ... not so much.

I still want to convince him to go back to Paradise. I haven't done a great job of doing what I set out to do. Tonight is my last chance. Thinking about what Vanessa said, I brace myself to confront Caleb once and for all.

I slip through the sliding glass door. The melodic sound of the crickets chirping follows in my wake as I walk down the gravel path to the lake.

"I guess this is good-bye ... again."

He doesn't look at me. Instead, he skips another rock. "I guess so. Have fun in Spain."

I haven't thought about my impending year abroad for a few weeks now. This Re-START trip has been exhausting both physically and mentally. I've learned a lot about myself this past month. I've also become good friends with Trish and Erin, who are now like sisters. Trish thinks she's Erin's protector, and the three of us have spent most nights talking until the early morning hours.

I sit on a big boulder and watch him. "Where are you headed?"

He shrugs. "Arizona, I think."

Arizona? That's too far. There are so many loose ends he needs to tie up before he goes away. "Come back to Paradise, Caleb."

"This conversation is over."

I stand and step right in front of him. He's about to skip another rock, but I take his hand and open it up so the rock falls to the ground. "Go back to Paradise," I say again.

He lowers his gaze to the ground, and I feel his defeat as if it's my own. "I can't. When I came back home, my entire family wanted me to pretend the Beckers were this picture-perfect family. In reality, each one of us was fucked up. I couldn't fake it before. I still can't, so don't even ask me to. I'm living with so many regrets, I can't add another one to the roster."

"Give them the benefit of the doubt. They need you."

He shakes his head. "I have nothing to go back to. Hell, even Mrs. Reynolds is dead. The only person I'd go back for is you, and we were doomed from the start." He steps away from me and runs his fingers through his hair. He does that when he's frustrated. "Forget I just said I'd go back for you. That was stupid of me."

I'm waiting for him to say our cooling-off period will be over, that he's ready to try again. But he doesn't. Maybe he realized that what we have isn't worth the hassle, especially because I'm leaving for Spain and he's leaving for Arizona.

I think of the times we kissed and held each other. I thought nothing could feel as amazing as I felt then, so powerful and explosive.

"Are you really leaving?" I ask, my voice coming out as a whisper.

"Yeah. No regrets."

"What?" No regrets? "Why do you keep saying that? What does it mean?"

He cups my chin tenderly and urges me to look up at him. "It means I can't leave until I do this..."

He bends his head. I wait for his warm, full lips to meet mine as my heart pounds like crazy in my chest. His lips hover over mine, and we both smile because it brings us back to the lake where we were testing and teasing each other. It was playful and dangerous. We're playing a playful and dangerous game right now, but I tell myself to enjoy it and ignore the warnings in the back of my head.

At least that's what I keep trying to tell myself as I close my eyes and he presses his lips to mine. I savor every moment of our kiss. It's not hot and heavy and hungry. It's slow and sexy and sensual. He takes hold of my waist and pulls me closer.

Oh, God, I want to melt in his arms right here and now. I wrap my arms around his neck as we keep kissing and holding and touching. He lifts me off the ground. I can't imagine anyone else being able to make me feel invincible and beautiful and worthy like Caleb does. I want to scream *I love you, Caleb! Don't you feel what I feel when I'm with you?*

His lips slowly pull away from mine and he unwraps my arms from around his neck. "I won't regret that ... ever. Good-bye, Maggie."

"Bye, Caleb. I'll ... miss you."

"I'll miss you, too."

I take a deep breath, holding back the flood of emotions. I push past him and hurry toward the cabin so he doesn't see the tears streaming down my cheeks. I quickly get into bed and bury my head into my pillow so he can't hear my heartache as I cry.

Why do I do this? Why do I let him go without a fight? Because I'm a coward, that's why.

I hear the sliding door creak open a few minutes later. Caleb must be back in the cabin. I think of Vanessa, who is stuck in jail and can't fight for what she wants.

I can.

I realize what Caleb's motives were for kissing me tonight. That sweet kiss was an attempt at closure.

It wasn't enough, at least for me. I want more. I need more. But do I have the nerve to show him what kind of closure I want in order to finally let go?

I take a deep breath as I sit on the edge of my bed. I can do this. I'm careful to take soft steps and pray the wooden floor of the cabin doesn't creak as I make my way down to the basement.

To Caleb's room.

His door is open. Lenny is sleeping soundly in the room across the hall. Lenny's snores echo through the walls, but Caleb's room is quiet. I don't even hear him breathing as I step in.

There are no windows, so it's almost completely dark. A green glow is coming from a permanent night-light in the hallway.

"Caleb?" I whisper. "You awake?"

"Yeah." I hear his sheets rustle as he sits up. "Is something wrong?"

"Kind of."

I close the door, then feel my way slowly around the room, hoping I don't trip and fall. I bump into something warm and hard and distinctly male. Caleb. He's not wearing a shirt, because I feel his hot skin and muscular chest against my fingertips.

I look up into the darkness. "Hi."

"Hey," he says, his familiar voice comforting to me somehow. I'm going to miss that voice. "I don't suppose you got lost."

"No. I, uh, couldn't sleep. And I thought ... I just ... well ..."

"What is it, Maggie? Just say it."

Okay. I might as well gather up the nerve. It's now or never. "I thought we could spend our last night together. I know we might not see each other again after tomorrow, but I can't help but want to be in your arms tonight. Just one last time. Is that okay?"

Caleb takes my hand in his and leads me back to his bed. "It's more than okay."

I slip under the covers and wait for him to join me, but he doesn't.

"Where are you going?" I ask.

"To lock the door. You don't want Lenny to suddenly barge in on us, do you?"

I laugh nervously. "No."

It's cool in the basement, so I pull the blanket up to my chest. Caleb slides in beside me, and I feel his bare legs against mine. "You're shivering," he says, his voice a low whisper.

"I'm a little cold ... and a little nervous."

"Don't be nervous, Maggie. It's just me."

It's the real Caleb, without the tough facade. I'm glad it's completely dark now and he can't see my trembling fingers as they move up to his beautiful face. "I know."

He pulls me closer. I rest my head in the crook of his arm and am more content than ever.

"Maggie?"

"Yeah?"

"Thanks."

"For what?"

"For making me feel alive again."

I drape my arm across his chest, the warmth of his skin melting into mine. I want to remember this night forever, because we'll probably never get another chance to hold each other like this again. It makes me want to do more than just sleep in his arms. I try and relax, to slow my own erratic heartbeat as I wrap my right leg, the one that wasn't severely damaged in the accident, around him. It's a definite hint that I'm ready to do more than just lie in his arms.

He moans in response. "Maggie, you're treading into dangerous territory. I'm trying to be a good, honorable guy here."

"I know. But I'm not asking you to be one."

"You sure you know what you're getting into?"

"Nope. I've got no clue." I start kissing and feeling my way across his broad chest.

"You're killing me," he says, his hands slowly reaching for me and urging me up so we're face to face. "We can't do this. Don't get me wrong, I'm ready and willing. But we're going in completely different directions tomorrow. You and I both know fooling around or having sex will complicate everything."

"I have a great idea," I say matter-of-factly. "Let's just make out all night until we're exhausted. That's okay, isn't it?"

"Make out, huh?" He pulls me on top of him. "We can definitely do that," he murmurs against my lips.

Afterward, when we're both coming down from a high I've never felt before, I lay my head on his chest while he wraps his arms around me. "That was a great make-out session."

"Mmm," he agrees sleepily. "The best." A few minutes later, I feel Caleb's body relax. His slow, even breathing lulls me to sleep.

TWENTY-THREE
Caleb

I slept like the dead last night. Maggie's soft, warm body snuggled up to me was just the sleeping pill I needed after our little (okay, not so little) make-out fest. I knew the second she snuck out of my room this morning, because I was immediately awake when the cool morning air reached my skin.

I pretended not to wake up, even when she lightly kissed me on the lips.

Breakfast was practically torture, because Maggie and I were both trying to avoid eye contact. Damon called us into the main area of the cabin, where he gave an entire half hour speech about how much he respected all of us for finishing the program, even though he knew how hard it was to share our stories.

During the ride back to the Redwood community center, where this whole trip started, we're all pretty silent. Even Lenny. His solemn attitude is unnerving because it's so out of character. At this point I'm tempted to ask if I could pull his finger.

At the community center, Damon pulls me aside.

"You're going back home, right?" he asks. "You promised."

"Yep," I lie. "I'm gonna come clean to my parents. Thanks, Damon. For everything. I know it's your job to try and reform kids like me, but—"

"Just so you know," he interrupts. "It's not *just* a job to me. Remember that. Call me if you need anything. I mean it."

"I'm out," Lenny calls out once he collects his stuff from the van. "My bus'll be here soon."

"If you need a ride—" Damon begins.

"I'm cool." Lenny waves bye to everyone as he heads over to the bus stop to wait.

"That's it?" Trish calls out to him. "You spend four weeks with us and all you can give us is a backwards wave?"

Lenny, still walking, flips her the finger. "Sit on this and spin, Trish," he yells back.

Trish is yelling something snarky back at Lenny while Damon is trying to defuse the situation so it doesn't escalate into a huge profanity/yelling match in front of the community center. As we're all saying our good-byes, Damon gets an emergency call from one of the kids in the juvenile probation program. He leaves after making us promise that we'll all make sure to call him if we ever need him.

Maggie's mom pulls into the parking lot next and heads toward us. The look on her face when she realizes I've been on the Re-START trip with Maggie makes me wince. If I had any doubts about whether or not Maggie and I could ever see each other again, even casually, her mom's horrified expression says it all.

I'm not welcome near her daughter. Ever.

"Mom, I want to say good-bye to everyone. I'll be there in a minute," I hear Maggie say. Her mom throws me a warning glare.

Maggie hugs everyone in the group. Tears come to her eyes as the girls all promise to call and see each other before Maggie leaves for her year abroad.

She hugs Matt next. "Take care of yourself," she says. "And don't give up on Becca."

"Who's Becca?" I ask them.

"My ex." Matt shrugs. "We broke up before the trip, but I kinda, well, you know… Maggie's been giving me advice."

So he's not into Maggie? I just wish I'd figured that out sooner.

Maggie kisses me on the cheek. "Well, I guess this is good-bye…again."

I nod. "Don't forget to show those Spaniards that Maggie Armstrong is a force to be reckoned with."

"Right," she says, amused. When she steps back, I

shove my hands in my pockets for fear I'll reach out for her. From the look of us, you'd never know we slept in the same bed last night and made out like the world was going to end if we stopped.

"Just so you know," she says, "I'm okay with saying good-bye this time. Really, I feel like we both have closure. I think you should go back to Paradise, but I can't force you to go home if you don't want to."

Her mom beeps the horn, reminding us that reality is always just around the corner ready to slap us in the face.

I gesture to her mom's car and give her a small smile. "You better go."

She takes another step away, but doesn't turn her back to me. "Stay out of trouble, Caleb. I mean it."

I don't take my eyes off her as she gets into her mom's car and they drive away.

Regret tugs at me, but I ignore it. There are some things we can't change even if we want to.

Trish gets picked up by her parents, sister, and brother. After hearing Erin's story, Trish's mom had to take a tissue from her purse so her own makeup wouldn't run. After that, the entire family packed Erin up in their van. I think they might just adopt the silent, tattooed girl. Matt left right afterwards, when his big brother came to give him a lift.

Re-START is officially over. I guess it's time for me to figure out where to go next.

One thing is for sure—I need to get far away. This time

Chicago is too close. I wasn't joking when I told Maggie I was going to Arizona. Problem is, I have exactly twelve dollars and sixty-three cents to my name. I can work odd jobs, construction day jobs if I can find them, until I can save up enough money to get me out of Illinois.

I swing my duffle over my shoulder, glad I have at least a few bucks to my name. I know of a cheap campground a few miles from here where I can stay a couple of nights while I figure out if there are any temporary jobs I can take to make some quick cash. I'll need at least a few hundred to get me a one-way bus ticket to Arizona.

"Hey, Caleb, wait up!"

I turn to find Lenny jogging to catch up with me. "Miss your bus?" I ask.

"Nah." He shrugs. "I didn't really have a bus to catch. I was thinking of, you know ... going with you," he says, as if it was something we'd already discussed and agreed to.

Umm ... I don't think so.

"No, you're not. Go find out where Trish lives and follow her to her house."

"Are you kidding? The girl hates me."

"Maybe that's because you didn't wipe your pubes off the toilet."

I keep walking.

Lenny doesn't get the hint, and I'm starting to think he's serious about coming with because he continues to follow me.

"Come on, Caleb. Have a heart. Think of us as Fred

and Barney, Ben and Jerry, Thelma and Louise. You know you want to."

I stop walking and look right at Lenny. "Thelma and Louise died at the end of that chick flick."

"They died holding hands. Didn't it bring you to tears?"

"No."

"You still owe me a hug, remember?"

"No, I don't."

"So you're gonna leave me stranded here? What, afraid I'm gonna cramp your style?"

"I don't have a style, Lenny. Go home. You do have a home, don't you?" He doesn't answer. "You told Damon you were going home."

"I lied."

Shit. "If you haven't figured it out yet, I don't have a house to go to either. I'm going to a campground so I can at least have a place to do the four S's—shit, shower, shave, and sleep."

"Cool."

"There's nothing *cool* about it." I can tell Lenny's not letting up. He's like a damn stray dog that's following me. I glance at him. Normally he sports a cocky-ass expression, but not now. Now he looks worried, as if he's afraid I'm gonna ditch him and leave him alone.

I keep walking, feeling déjà vu. Maggie followed me off campus and look where that got me.

Lenny walks beside me. I don't tell him to back off, because I think the guy is scared to be left alone.

"Thanks, Caleb," he says after a while.

"Just ... don't piss me off," I tell him.

"I won't. I promise."

It takes us almost an hour to walk to the Happy Camper Campground. I register and pay the lady in the office for a camping spot that costs me seven dollars a day. It would've cost me twenty-two if I required a water spout, but I can just go to the community bathroom for that.

No matter how cheap this place is, I've got to find some quick cash. Once the Illinois summer is over, winter creeps in fast and furious. I'll freeze my ass off and die if I don't head for Arizona by then.

When it's dark and we've bought a couple of hot dogs at the little on-site store, the family at the site next to us gives us a few pieces of their wood and fire starters. Gotta love the generosity of campers.

After I've washed up in the Happy Camper Campgrounds community bathroom/shower area, I pull out a light blanket I bought when I was living at Rio's place.

"Here," I say, handing it to Lenny. "We can switch off days we use it."

"I'm fine," he responds.

I watch as Lenny rolls one of his shirts up to make a pillow, then pulls out a pair of sweats from his duffle and puts it over his face, making a circle in the middle where his mouth is.

"Why the hell are you wearing pants on your head?" I ask. "You look ridiculous."

"I'm not risking getting sunburned or mosquito bites on my face again. I've got an extra pair of boxers if you want to cover your face. They're not washed, but—"

"No thanks." Just the thought makes me want to puke.

Thank God we got assigned a grassy campsite. I spread the blanket on the ground. A sleeping bag would be great, but I'm happy to have my little spot of land for the night without having to worry about getting busted by the cops or bothered by other homeless people.

"Really, Lenny, why are you here?" I ask. "I mean seriously, man, what's your story?"

"I don't got a story," Lenny says, lifting his pants off his face. "You heard me the past four weeks tell all the sordid details. I got drunk, stole a car, and drove it into a lake. End of story."

He turns his back to me and faces the opposite direction.

I stare up at the sky, the stars and moon lighting up the endless universe. Wherever Maggie is, whether she's in Paradise or in Spain, she'll be looking up at the same moon and same stars.

Will she ever think about me? Will she remember the night we spent in the castle or last night when we slept in each other's arms? Or will she only remember the times we argued and tried to push each other away, because it was easier than admitting or accepting what was really happening between us?

Damn. I better get a grip and forget about Maggie Armstrong. *This* is my life—here on this little seven-dollar rented piece of land … I look over at Lenny … *and it doesn't seem like my lot in life is gonna get better anytime soon.*

The biggest torture right now is knowing I won't sleep much. When it's all quiet and I'm just lying down at night, that's when my mind wanders to things I have no right thinking about.

"It was my mom's boyfriend's car," Lenny says, his voice cutting through the silence. He'd been so quiet the past hour I thought he was sleeping. I guess I should've known better, since he wasn't snoring. "He packed up and left her five years ago and I thought he was gone for good. I can't *believe* she took him back. Want to know what he did?"

"You don't have to tell me." I'm not one to pry into other people's business, 'cause I don't want them prying into mine.

I look over at Lenny, who's got his palms pressed to his eyes. I've never seen him so serious.

"When my mom wasn't home he used to touch me."

"Damn, Lenny. That's some serious shit."

"Tell me about it." Silence fills the air, and he doesn't say anything else for a while. "At first I didn't really get what was goin' on, as if my brain couldn't wrap around the reality of what was happening. I was only twelve when it started. By the time the asshole split, I just wanted to erase it from my mind and forget it ever happened. I didn't tell anyone. But when he showed up in March and my mom said she invited him to live with us, I freaked."

"Did you tell your mom about what he did to you?"

"Yeah, but she pretty much got pissed off and called me a liar. The first night the guy moved back in, I got drunk, stole his car, and drove it in the lake. My mom didn't even come to court. I hear she married the douche. Damon said I could join the Re-START program instead of serving probation time. I promised him I'd go back home and work things out with my mom, but that's never gonna happen. She chose to trust a boyfriend over her son."

"I don't even know what to say." Somehow Lenny's story makes me feel like all the stuff I've gone through is nothing.

"You don't need to say anything. I didn't tell you to get your pity."

"Does Damon know what the guy did to you?"

"Nah."

"You should've told him."

"Yeah, well you should've told your parents the truth about the night you *didn't* hit Maggie with your car, but you didn't have the guts."

A flash of regret makes me tense up. "You're right," I admit. "But I promised I'd keep quiet."

"Yeah, well, I made a promise to that scumbag that I'd never tell my mom what he did to me, but I didn't keep that promise. I don't have choices anymore, Caleb. I *can't* go back home. It'll be different for you."

"What are you saying?"

Lenny sits up. "I'm sayin' that you've got choices I don't have. Hell, just because your mom's got some prescription drug addiction and wants you to act all perfect and your old man's a pussy doesn't mean you have to give up on them." Lenny turns his back to me again. "If I were you—"

"Yeah, well you're not me," I cut in harshly.

I get up and walk around the campground, angry at myself and at Lenny and at Leah and at the world in general. I'm glad most people are sleeping and the place is quiet except for the crackling of fires and low whispers of the few campers still awake.

I circle the campground five times, thinking the entire time about what Lenny said. Indecision replaces my anger. As I start walking faster and faster, crazy thoughts run through my head. Soon I start running. The faster I run, the more my mind races with thoughts of what was and what could be. *No, I can't,* I tell myself. *But what if I did?*

I get back to my little piece of rented land and see Lenny lying there by himself, sleeping on the ground. It's like looking at myself from far away, and it's pathetic—*I'm* pathetic. I have tons of regrets, stemming from my fear of being rejected by people I care about.

I don't want to be alone. I don't want my family to think I gave up on them. I also don't want Maggie to think

I gave up on us. My mouth goes dry and my heart is racing as I realize what I'm going to go.

I'm going back to Paradise.

I'm going home.

TWENTY-FOUR
Maggie

"Mom, it was no big deal."

"How can you say that, Maggie? It's the biggest deal."

I've been sitting at our kitchen table for the past twenty minutes not being able to eat any of the lunch set in front of us because I'm too busy getting lectured by my mother about the dangers of being on the Re-START trip with Caleb. Last night she hardly talked to me. Now she's giving me a lecture.

"I'm appalled that the program coordinator allowed it to happen."

"Mom—"

"He could have hurt you."

"Mom—"

"If you think the Caleb Becker you saw on that trip is the same boy who lived next door to us when you were growing up, guess again."

"Mom—"

"How can I trust you to make the right choices when you're over four thousand miles away in Spain, Maggie? If you think it was okay to travel around the Midwest with *that boy*, what other irresponsible decisions are you going to make?" She picks up her fork and pokes her chicken breast. "To be honest, I hoped when he left, he was gone for good."

"He *is* gone for good, Mom," I tell her. "He didn't think he'd be welcome back in Paradise, and I told him he was wrong. I told him people would give him a chance and not judge him." I take my napkin off my lap and put it on the table. "I guess I was wrong."

"Why are you so rebellious all of a sudden?" she asks when I get up and grab my purse.

I sigh. "I'm not, Mom. I'm just frustrated. I love you, but sometimes you have to trust me."

"I can't. Not when it comes to Caleb. His family is still struggling to bounce back from the pain and suffering he caused *all* of us. You were the one physically hurt by his reckless stupidity. How can you protect him? Because he's a good-looking boy? There are plenty of them out there, honey. Trust me."

I can't listen anymore.

"I'll be back later," I say as I walk out of the kitchen. I

turn around before I leave and say, "I love you, Mom. You know that, right?"

"I do. I love you, too."

"Then trust me. I don't stick up for Caleb because he's good-looking. I stick up for him because he doesn't deserve all the bad things that have happened to him." I hold my hand up when I think she's going to cut me off. "He made a mistake. Mom, we all make mistakes. Don't we all deserve a second chance?"

I head for Mrs. Reynolds' house in the Cadillac she gave me in her will. I miss her so much. She was the person who urged me to forgive Caleb, and she was right. I didn't want to at first. Just looking at Caleb when he came back from jail made my pulse race and my body shiver with anxiety.

But then we talked. A lot. Before I realized he wasn't the one who hit me, I forgave him. And fell for him.

I pull up to the house, expecting it to be vacant. Lou, Mrs. Reynolds' son and my mom's boyfriend, is standing out front watering the grass. There's a *For Sale* sign out front.

When he sees me pull up, he smiles. "Hiya, Maggie," he says. "What brings you to this side of town?"

"I just wanted to check the daffodils out back," I tell him.

"Some are still blooming. I've been trying to sell this place for months now, without a bite. Market is dead out here, so I'm probably not going to be able to sell it anytime soon." He sighs. I know he grew up in this house and it has sentimental value. His mom, Mrs. Reynolds, is gone, but her spirit is still here. "Where's your mom?" he asks.

"At home." I guess I should let him know about the drama back home. "She got mad because I never told her Caleb had joined the Re-START trip."

"She called me about that a few hours ago," he tells me. "Care to talk about it?"

"I guess." We walk to the backyard, side by side. My dad never walked with me anywhere. He was too busy going out of town for work or watching television. He didn't have an interest in me, or my mom. I used to pray he'd come back. The last time we talked was months ago. He said he'd come see me graduate from high school, but he never did.

I didn't even get a congratulatory call on graduation day.

I stop thinking about my dad when I catch sight of the gardens in the backyard. I'm surprised to see the daffodils are still thriving, the bright rainbow of colors immediately raising my spirits. It's breathtaking.

If Mrs. Reynolds were alive, she'd love them. She gave me meticulous directions on how to plant each bulb even though she knew she was dying and would never see them come up to display themselves with such radiance and, strangely enough, pride. Each variety seems to have an attitude all its own.

I wish Caleb were here to see them. He made the gazebo while I planted the daffodil bulbs, both of us slaving away to please Mrs. Reynolds.

"My mom's mad that I didn't quit the trip when I found out Caleb was on it," I tell Lou.

"You have to admit she has reason to distrust him."

"I get it, but..." I don't know how much to tell him. If he finds out Caleb didn't hit me with the car, he'll have to tell my mom. If *she* knows, she'll try and find out who really did hit me. And the vicious cycle would repeat.

I don't want that to happen. Since Caleb won't be coming back to Paradise, it's not worth the havoc it would cause.

"It's not like he's coming back to Paradise. He's not."

Lou sits one of the rocking chairs his mother used to sit in. "How do you feel about that?"

"I don't know." I look over at Lou, rocking away. He reminds me of his mom. "We kinda got close on the trip. It was nice."

"Should I ask how close?"

"Probably not."

I sit in the rocking chair beside him. We rock for a while, neither of us talking. The fresh summer air is warm even as the sun moves lower in the sky.

Lou chuckles. "You know, my mother would be giving us a piece of her mind right now. She'd call us lazy, then she'd give us chores and wouldn't be satisfied until we were working and sweating our butts off."

"I loved her," I tell him. I try not to think about losing her too much, or I'll break down and cry. Mrs. Reynolds was a strong lady and wouldn't want me to cry for her. "Even when she made me work my butt off, I appreciated it. She was the first person after I got home from the hospital who didn't treat me as if I had a disability."

"She loved you, too. And I figure she liked Caleb," he says, gesturing toward the gazebo he knows Caleb built all by himself. He was assigned to work here to finish out his community service obligations. "My mom always said I shouldn't hold grudges. Said they'd ruin your life."

"I wish my mom felt the same way."

"Want me to talk to her about it?" he asks. "Maybe I can smooth the waters some."

I look at the guy who has not only been my mom's boss and the owner of Auntie Mae's diner, but also the only man who's made my mom smile again.

"That would be great."

"Your mom's a sweet woman. She's just protective of you."

"I know." I wipe away an invisible piece of lint as I look down at my jeans. I used to hate that Lou was dating my mom. But now I can't help but be thankful he's in her life. And mine. "I don't know if I've ever told you, but my mom's a new person since she started dating you. She needs you."

That makes him smile. He clears his throat and says, "I've been meaning to ask you this for a while now, but I didn't gather up enough nerve before you left for the Re-START program and now that you're here…"

He clears his throat again.

"I'd like to ask your mother to marry me. Would that be okay with you, Maggie?"

TWENTY-FIVE
Caleb

I walk toward my house, the biggest one on the entire block. Maggie's house, next door, is practically dwarfed by ours.

I follow the brick sidewalk that my dad and I laid three years ago up to the front door. My house looks familiar and yet... in some ways totally foreign to me. I notice the paint peeling off of the wood trim. One of the gutters is falling off, and no flowers have been planted out front. My mom used to plant them every summer. She said it made our house look like a home.

She was right.

I take a deep breath and focus on the front door.

How do you come back home after running away? If I

open the door and just walk in like I used to, they'll think I'm an intruder. A stranger.

Will they treat me like one once they take a look at me?

I look back down the street, wondering if I should retreat and forget coming home. I can just retrace my steps and disappear again. Nobody would know, and it would be easier than dealing with the drama about to unfold. But disappearing would be the coward's way out.

I'm not a coward.

Not anymore, at least.

I put my duffle down and ring the doorbell. My pulse is racing a billion times a second, like I just ran a marathon. Different scenarios about how my parents and sister will react are flying through my head.

I hear footsteps. Is it my mom, dad, or Leah? I don't have time to think about it too long because the door opens and my sister is standing in front of me.

My twin sister.

The one I went to jail for. She's still got dyed-black hair, light brown at the roots, but her clothes aren't as freaky as when I left. Instead of chains dripping off her jeans, she's wearing normal jeans. Her shirt is black to match her hair.

The last time I saw her she looked like death. Her hair was black, her nails were black, and her mood matched her black clothes. It freaked me out at first, but then it pissed me off. I was the one who went to jail so she'd live an easy life at home. How dare she become a recluse and change her appearance and attitude and live like the dead? She had no right...

At least her nails aren't black, and she's not wearing black eyeliner and black lipstick. It's a big improvement.

My throat goes dry at the same time tears flood her eyes.

"Caleb," she squeaks out. "You came back."

"For a little while, at least," I manage to say.

When I came home from jail, Leah had catapulted herself into my arms and hugged me tight. Not this time. She's definitely keeping her distance. Does she think I'm a ghost or that I'll suddenly disappear if she gets close?

"Maggie said she was going to urge you to come home, but I didn't believe her." Her hands are stiff at her sides. "I can't believe you're here."

"Well, believe it." I crane my head to see if there's anyone else home. "Yeah, so, uh...can I come in?"

She opens the door wider and steps back. "Yeah," she says slowly. "Umm, Dad's not home."

"Where is he?" I ask as I step into the foyer.

Leah starts biting on one of her fingernails nervously. "He went to visit Mom."

"*Visit* Mom? She's in rehab right now?" Oh, hell. Maybe it's worse than I thought.

"She's been there awhile. It's not her first time."

I let out a slow breath. "All right." I can deal with this, but... "Anything else I need to know about?"

"Like what?"

"I don't know, Leah." I'm on edge and want answers. Will she give them to me? "Is Dad coping with things okay? What's *your* story these days?" Man, why did I say that? I don't want to confront her when I haven't even been back for five minutes. "Forget I asked that last part."

Leah opens her mouth to say something, then closes it.

"I invited a friend to stay over," I say.

"Who?"

"His name's Lenny. If a guy who needs a haircut and wears a green T-shirt that says *I'm Your Daddy* rings the doorbell, assume it's him." I couldn't leave Lenny out on the streets. When he isn't trying his best to be a complete asshole, he's not so repulsive. He even insisted on giving me a couple hours to get reacquainted with my family before he came in.

I take my duffle and head up the stairs.

"Where are you going?" Leah asks, her voice clearly in a panic.

"To my room."

"Wait!" Leah yells, but it's too late.

I open the door to my room. Or what used to be my room. It's been turned into an office. No bed, no curtains, no closet full of clothes. Wow, they even got rid of my trophies. No sign of me anywhere.

In eight months all evidence of my life has been erased.

I have a feeling coming back here was the biggest mistake of my life.

TWENTY-SIX
Maggie

My mom is getting married. Well, she will be getting married after Lou proposes to her sometime this weekend.

I pull out some stationery and head over to Paradise Park. I want to write a letter to Vanessa. I don't want her to think I forgot about my promise to write her.

I sit leaning against the big tree at the park where Caleb and I first kissed. I feel at peace right here, and wonder if Caleb is doing okay in Arizona or wherever he is.

I write about the Re-START trip, and I tell Vanessa about Lou asking my permission to marry my mom. I thought I'd write a small note, but I end up getting carried away. I tell her about Caleb and Trish and Lenny... by the time I'm done I've filled out the front and back of three pages.

When I get back home, Matt calls. He's really nervous about seeing his girlfriend again.

"I need you as a buffer," Matt says. "Becca agreed to go out with me tomorrow night. I need you there."

"I'm not gonna be a third wheel, Matt." That's the last thing I want.

"Things with Becca have been strained since the accident. I know you two will get along. Just ... come on, Maggie. You need to help me break the ice. Pleeease. I know you're not leaving for Spain for another couple of weeks. What else are you doing besides sulking about Caleb?"

"I'm not sulking."

He laughs. "Okay, what have you done since coming back home from Re-START?"

"I unpacked."

"And ...? You've been home almost a week."

"And went to see Mrs. Reynolds' daffodils."

"Sounds like a blast so far. And?"

"And I just wrote a letter."

Matt laughs again. "Yeah, I see you have the most exciting life. I'm surprised you have time to talk to me on the phone."

Okay, so maybe Matt's right. I should go out with him and Becca tomorrow, and prove to myself that I'm not living in the past.

"Okay, fine," I tell Matt. "But who am I going to find to go out with me?"

"I've got an idea."

"Oh, no. I feel a headache coming on."

"Be adventurous," Matt says, now totally excited. "I'll find you a date. Just give me your address and be ready to go out tomorrow night at six."

After I hang up, I go to my room. There's a note on my bed. It's from my mom, telling me that my dad called and wants to talk to me.

I crumple up the piece of paper, toss it in the trash, and sit on my bed staring at the garbage can. What's so important that he wants to talk to me now?

I used to call and practically beg for five minutes of his time. I begged him to come back home, but he said he'd moved on. Why should I give him the time of day now? He doesn't deserve it.

If he plans to tell me his new wife is pregnant, does he expect me to jump up and down? Am I a bad person for resenting his new wife and his new life without me? He never once invited me to Texas to visit him. He shut me and my mom out in the same breath.

But what if he's sick? What if it's not that he's having a kid, but that he's got cancer or some other incurable condition? I hate my dad, but I still love him. I know that doesn't make sense, but then again, nothing in my life makes sense lately.

I feel like a hypocrite telling my mom to give Caleb

another chance when I'm unwilling to give my father another chance.

I pick up my phone and dial my father's number. I hold my breath each time the phone rings.

"Sweetheart, is that you?"

I feel numb when I hear his voice. Not excited, not angry, not anxiety-ridden. Just numb. "Yeah, it's me. Mom said you called."

I wait for the big news he needs to tell me.

"I've been trying to reach you for weeks. I have news," he says, then pauses.

I brace myself for it. Here it comes…

"I'm getting divorced," he blurts out.

Whoa, I didn't expect to hear that. "Sorry."

"Don't be. Sometimes these things work out, and sometimes they don't. You want to know the best part?"

I'm taken aback by his nonchalant attitude. "The best part?" I echo.

"I'm moving back in with you and Mom."

What?

No.

It's a mistake.

I must have heard him wrong. "You're moving back here? In our house?"

"I knew you'd be excited."

"Does Mom know?"

He gives a nervous laugh. "Of course she knows, silly. Isn't it great news, Maggie? We'll be a family again."

"Yeah," I say without emotion. I'm stunned, and I feel like my entire world has just tilted on its axis. "That's, umm … great."

"I'll be flying in on Thursday, and the movers are coming on Friday to move my stuff back in. I've got to get packing and wrapping things up here, so I'll see you next week. Bye, sweetheart."

As usual, he hangs up before I say bye back.

I wait impatiently until my mom gets home at six. Before she can take her waitress uniform off, I corner her in the hall.

"Why are you letting Dad come live here?"

"You called him," she says, stating the obvious. She slowly takes off her apron and drapes it over her arm. "Because he's getting divorced and wants to try again."

"So you're letting him? He left us, Mom. He left us and didn't look back."

"He's looking back now."

I want to give my dad a second chance, but then realize he's had many chances to come back and hasn't. I get a sinking feeling he'll only stay here until something better comes along.

"What about Lou?"

She starts up the stairs. "Lou is great, but he's not your dad. You always said you wanted to be a family again, Maggie. Your dad is the man I married."

"He's the man who divorced you. And replaced you."

She turns around and waves a finger at me. "Don't disrespect me. Your father made a mistake. He wants to make things right."

Tears well in my eyes. "Lou has been more of a dad than my own flesh and blood. He makes you happy. He makes us happy. I don't understand, Mom. It just doesn't make sense."

She stops when she reaches the top of the stairs. "I broke up with Lou tonight. I told him about your father coming back. It's over."

This can't be happening. Just when things were going right, they're all going wrong. I press my hands to my eyes, trying to shut out the world. But it's not about me. It's about my mom.

I hobble as fast as I can up the stairs and envelop her in a big hug. I start to cry. "I just want you to be happy, Mom."

She hugs me back and squeezes me tight. She's crying, too. "I want you to be happy, too."

We stand here, crying and holding each other for what seems like forever. We're two women who've been left to fend for ourselves for a long time now. When the doorbell rings, it startles both of us.

My mom wipes her eyes with the skirt of her uniform and heads back downstairs to open the door.

"Lou!" she says, startled.

Lou is holding a huge bouquet of red roses in one hand and a ring box in the other. He kneels on the porch, and I notice his eyes are bloodshot and puffy as if he's been crying.

"Marry me, Linda." He opens the ring box and takes my mom's hand gently in his. "Please tell me I'm not too late."

Caleb

Leah, Lenny, and I are sitting in my parents' living room, waiting for my dad to come home. Leah's got her fingers folded neatly in her lap and Lenny is looking at her with one cocked eyebrow. I drilled him endlessly before we came here, making sure I had his word that he wouldn't talk about the accident or the fact that he knows I wasn't the one who really hit Maggie.

"So, Leah," Lenny says as he looks across the room at Leah with one eyebrow cocked. "You got a boyfriend?"

I whack Lenny on the chest with the back of my hand. "What're you doing?"

He looks at me as if *I'm* the crazy one. "Makin' conversation, Caleb. Someone around here has got to fill the dead air. Neither of you is doin' such a bang-up job at it."

"You don't have to fill the air with bullshit," I tell him.

Lenny rolls his eyes. "Okay, Mr. Crabbypants."

"Didn't anyone ever tell you to talk only if you have something to—"

"No," Leah interrupts, her voice almost a whisper.

Lenny and I both look at my sister.

She looks down at the carpeting. "I meant no, I, uh, don't have a boyfriend."

Lenny leans forward. "Why not?"

She shrugs.

"Maybe if you smiled it would help."

What is this, the Lenny Self-Help Show? "Seriously, man, shut the fuck up. What do you know about girls, anyway? You're in love with Trish and all you can do is piss her off and dump her in a lake. You don't know shit about girls."

"And you do?" Lenny laughs. His stupid long hair falls in his eyes and he flicks it back. "I got one word for you, Mr. Crabbypants—Maggie."

At the mention of Maggie, my sister's eyes meet mine. I bet we're both thinking about our little deception that messed up both our lives.

"I'm going to get some water," Leah mumbles, then scurries away.

As soon as she disappears, the door opens. I stand, stiff at attention, as my dad walks through the front door.

He's wearing a suit, carrying the briefcase he's had for the past ten years, and sporting the same mustache he's had for the past twenty years.

When he sees me, his expression goes from blank to shocked. He freezes in his tracks.

"Hey, Dad," I manage to say.

"Caleb."

I walk toward him, not knowing if I should hug him or shake his hand or pat him on the back or ... do nothing. It's sad when your own father has become a stranger.

I stop in front of him. He's still holding his briefcase and staring at me. What do I say to him now?

I blurt out, "I know I should have probably called and told you I was coming, but—"

"We haven't heard from you in months, Caleb."

"I know. I couldn't stay here anymore, Dad. Not like the way things were."

"Your mother is sick," he tells me. "She's been in the hospital on and off for months now."

He says it as if she has a terminal disease. I bet calling her "sick" is the standard excuse he's decided to use instead of saying "she's in rehab" or "she's a drug addict."

"I know."

I step back, realizing this isn't going to be a joyous reunion where my father welcomes me back with open arms. I should have had a clue that's the way it was going to be when I saw my room had been converted to an office and all signs I'd ever existed had vanished.

He's holding his briefcase in front of him, almost like a barrier between us. "We didn't know if you were dead or alive. Your mother had to make up a story."

I shouldn't be surprised. My mom is the queen of making up stories to make our family look good. "What did she say?"

"She said we sent you to an exclusive boarding school in Connecticut."

A hearty, snorting laugh comes from the couch. Or, to be exact, it comes from Lenny who's sitting on the couch.

"Who's that?" my dad asks.

"Lenny."

Lenny springs off the couch and envelops my dad in a huge bear hug. My dad steps back, totally caught off guard, but keeps his balance. I bet he's silently thanking his high school football coach for those balance drills in high school.

"Nice to meet you, Dad," Lenny says. "Or should I call you Dr. Becker? Or Dr. B., or just Doc?"

I push Lenny off my dad. "Lenny's kind of a friend of mine," I tell my dad. "More like a sidekick."

I figure that's better than explaining that Lenny is a delinquent who thinks he's funny and doesn't have a filter when it comes to his mouth.

My dad puts his briefcase in the hall closet and says to Lenny, "You can call me Dennis."

"Cool. Give me a fist bump, Dennis." Lenny holds out his fist mid-air and waits for my dad to do the same.

My dad doesn't. I'm not sure he's ever given anyone

a fist bump. It's not that my dad is stupid or old fashioned. He's just … proper. He doesn't stray from the norm, because he likes his life neat and tidy.

Me being home is messing up his tidy life.

I'm sure it's killing him that my mom is in rehab. He probably doesn't know what to do about it, and there's no rule book or game plan when it comes to the grim realities of our lives.

"Are you guys, uh, in town for a while?" Dad asks me. "Or are you just passing through?"

It's a question you'd ask an acquaintance, not your son.

Leah is leaning against the stairs, waiting intently for my answer.

I'm tempted to say I'm just passing through. It would be easier than telling the truth, that Lenny's story made me realize I need to come back and make peace with my family.

"I was thinking of staying for a few weeks," I mumble.

"At a hotel, or …" Dad's voice trails off.

"I was hoping to stay here, Dad."

Lenny sticks his chin on my shoulder. "Me too, Dennis."

My dad scratches his head. "Umm … I guess, umm … we don't really have beds to spare. We turned your room into an office."

"I'll sleep on the couch," I tell him, feeling like I'm begging for a place to stay in my own house. It doesn't sit well in my gut.

"I'll sleep on the floor," Lenny chimes in, apparently having no problems begging. "Unless you want me to sleep in bed with Leah." Lenny holds his hands up when all of our heads snap up at his last comment. "Just kidding."

My sister steps forward and says, "I'll go get some sheets and blankets from the hall closet."

"Okay," my dad says. "But you boys better keep the house clean. My wife hates a messy house."

"Got it," I tell him, wondering if I need to remind him that "his wife" is my mom. And that she's in rehab, not here.

The loud sound of Lenny clapping his hands together makes us all turn to him. "Now that that's settled, what's for dinner?"

"Maybe we should order in some pizza," Dad says as he walks upstairs. He always changes into jeans and a T-shirt after work. It's his ritual.

When my sister and dad are out of hearing range, I let out a slow breath.

I'm home.

It doesn't feel like home, though. I wonder if I'd get a better reception if I showed up at Maggie's house. Who am I kidding? Her mom would toss me out or call the cops to have me thrown back in jail.

"Your dad is one weird dude," Lenny says. "But I like him."

At dinner, when Lenny excuses himself to go to the bathroom, I ask, "So, can I go see Mom?"

My dad puts down his pizza. "I don't think so, Caleb."

"Why not?"

"Because she's fragile. I'm not sure she could handle it right now."

"I'm her *son*," I say through clenched teeth.

"After you left, she said you were dead to her."

I look to my sister for confirmation, but she's staring at her plate. Anger starts to fire up in my veins. "Leah!"

She looks up. "What?"

What? All she can say is *what*?

I stand, my chair scraping the floor. "Thanks a lot, Leah," I grind out. "Thanks a lot for *nothing*."

TWENTY-EIGHT
Maggie

I peek into my mom's room as I'm getting ready for the double date. She's sitting on her bed, staring at the open box with the ring Lou gave her still inside. She didn't say yes to him when he came over last night and proposed, but she didn't say no.

She said she needed time to think.

She's definitely thinking.

"Did you tell Dad about Lou?" I ask her.

"I called him today," she says, her voice sad and wistful.

"And?"

"And... I don't know," she says, then shrugs. "I'm confused. I thought I knew what I wanted, but when Lou came by last night he got me thinking, and now … now I'm just confused."

I sit on the bed next to her and smile. She brushes the hair out of my face and sighs. "I thought for so long that if your dad came back, it would make our lives whole again."

"I know. I did, too. Until Lou came along."

"But he's not your dad. I fell in love with your dad first, and I don't know if I can give Lou as much of myself as I gave your father."

"He loves you, Mom."

"I know. But is it enough?"

"That's for you to decide. I'll support you, no matter what you choose."

"I just thought … well, forget it. Don't think about anything except having fun. I'm glad you're going out."

"Me too." I hadn't been looking forward to tonight, but when I took a shower and started getting ready, I got excited. Well, not excited for my mystery date, but excited to be doing what I said I was doing—moving on with my life.

Sometimes moving on takes effort.

Sometimes moving on is harder than it looks.

Going out is the first step to Maggie Armstrong moving on in life. I may have a limp, but that doesn't mean my social life or dating life has to be dead.

I take a deep breath and tell myself, *it is what it is*. I can't turn back the clock and undo the accident. It happened. This is who I am now, take it or leave it.

But when I look at my clock and notice it's five forty-five, I have second thoughts. I don't know if I'm ready to move on. I can't imagine myself kissing anyone besides Caleb. I know that's ridiculous, but right now it's true.

At five after six, as I'm ready to bite my fingernails to the core with anticipation and anxiety, the doorbell rings.

I plaster a smile on my face and open the front door. Standing in front of me is Matt, a girl with short spiky blonde hair, and...

"No way!" I say with a smile.

My physical therapist, Robert, opens his arms wide. "You didn't think I'd let you leave for Spain without one last goodbye, did you?"

I narrow my eyes at Matt. "Did you have this planned all along?" I ask him, as Robert hugs me like a brother.

"Yeah. So shoot me if we wanted to surprise you. Becca, this is Maggie. Maggie, Becca." While I greet Matt's girlfriend, Matt nudges Robert. "Maggie even put on makeup for you. I've never even seen her with makeup on."

My mom comes in the foyer, pretending she was just passing through on her way upstairs instead of having it all timed so that she could meet my "date."

"Robert?" she says, confused.

Robert, wearing a fashionable brown sports jacket to match his fashionable glasses says, "I couldn't let Maggie leave for an entire year without a goodbye celebration. She's my date tonight."

My mom has known Robert for almost two years now,

ever since he came to the hospital after my surgery and was assigned to be my personal torture instructor ... I mean physical therapist. I used to fantasize about pulling his perfectly spiked hair right out of his head when he wouldn't give up on me and I desperately wanted him to.

More times than not, I cried in front of him. I hated when Robert expected me to push myself to the limit. When I thought I couldn't bend my leg any more, Robert would make me go one step further.

I didn't appreciate him at the time, that's for sure. It took us a while to become friends. I was actually entertained by all of his stories about dating girls. Robert is a self-proclaimed bachelor and says he'll never settle down because he gets bored easily when it comes to girls. He says just like he can't eat Chinese food every day, he can't date the same girl without getting the itch to find someone different.

I once told him he'd die a very lonely man, and his good looks would one day fade, but he didn't seem worried. The guy has way too much confidence, but I wouldn't trade him for anything.

After my mom hugs Robert and meets Matt and Becca, she says, "You kids stay out at long as you want. Just have fun."

We decide to go to Dusty's Sports Bar & Grill. They serve food in the restaurant, so as long as you don't drink, you can be there if you're under twenty-one. Robert is already twenty-four, and he orders a beer while the rest of us order sodas.

It's nice that my first real date is a nondate, so I don't have to obsess over whether or not my disability is going to be an issue.

"Maggie, have you been doing the stretching exercises we'd discussed before you went on your trip this summer?" Robert asks.

I take a fry from the basket we'd ordered and dip it in some ketchup. "Can I lie?"

Matt, Becca, and I all laugh while Robert shakes his head. It feels good to go out and get my mind off of Caleb. I feel like every minute my mind isn't occupied, it wanders to thoughts of him.

Like now. While I'm having a good time, way better than I expected, I wonder if Caleb would have his arm around me like Matt has his arm draped around Becca, if we were on a date. And the way she looks up at him reminds me of—

"I bet you've been stiff," Robert says.

Right. Back to the here and now. *Stop thinking about Caleb.*

I roll my eyes. "You're off duty. Remember, you're supposed to be my date tonight, not my therapist." My fingers make quotation marks in the air when I say the word "date."

"She did complain of stiffness on the trip," Matt chimes in. He holds his hands up when I mumble *traitor.* "I'm just sayin'."

Robert moves his chair back and says, "Give me your leg, Maggie."

I blow out a frustrated breath and rest my leg on his knee. "It's fine. I'm fine."

"Flex for me."

I look over at Matt and Becca across the table as I flex. "Better you than me," Matt says, chuckling.

"Do you give a physical exam to all your dates?" I ask Robert as he cradles my jean-covered calf in his hand and watches how far I flex.

"No." He winks at me. "It's a first for me."

If it were any other guy, that wink would be cheesy, but I bet Robert practiced it in front of the mirror until it looked cool.

I cock an eyebrow and say, "I don't fall for your charms."

"Really? Wait, let me try it again." He winks a second time.

"Nope, doesn't do it for me. Besides, it's *really* inappropriate," I tell him, totally joking and he knows it. He's given me such a hard time in the past, I feel it's only fair for me to return the favor. "I'm your patient."

"Not anymore, you're not. You quit physical therapy. You're fair game."

"Ugh, you're too old."

"I'm twenty-four. How can that be too old?"

"I think you have some gray hair, Robert."

Robert's mouth goes wide and his hand cups his perfect head of hair. "I. Do. Not."

"Umm, Maggie," Matt says, then coughs a bunch of times. "I think the guy you really want just walked through the door."

TWENTY-NINE
Caleb

I'm trying to act like seeing Maggie with another guy is no big deal. I've wanted to call her since I came back. I should have called her. I didn't, and now she's out with a guy. She's got her leg resting on his knee, her calf cradled in his slimy hand.

What the fuck?

Does the dude know that a week ago she was lying in bed with me?

When Maggie looks my way, she whisks her leg off the guy's lap.

"Maggie! Matt!" Lenny practically yells across the bar. He's standing next to me, waving his arms as if he's on a desert island attempting to flag down a passing ship. Nobody's missing his presence, that's for damn sure.

Matt motions us over.

He shakes my hand when I reach their table. "Caleb and Lenny, this is my girlfriend Becca and that's Robert, our physical therapist."

Robert holds out his hand and shakes mine, then Lenny's. I give him a strong, hard shake so he knows I'm not a dead fish. The guy is drinking beer, and he looks like he came out of a damn *GQ* magazine spread. Is that the kind of guy she's looking for, an older one who wears fancy clothes?

"What are you doing here?" Maggie asks, totally confused.

"I came back."

"Have you seen Leah and your dad?"

"I'm staying with them." I pause. "For now. Lenny had some issues with his mom, so he's staying at my house too."

I'm trying to read her, but I can't. The guy she's with seems amused that I'm here. Has she told him about me? Does she even give a shit that I'm back, or was all that talk about coming back to Paradise solely for my parents' and sister's sake?

"Why don't you guys join us?" Robert asks.

Nice way to shove it in my face, dude. He has no clue if he attempts to stick his tongue down Maggie's throat in my presence, I'll be on him like a pit bull. "No, thanks."

Lenny spots an empty booth across the way and heads over to it.

"We'll talk later," I tell Maggie. I follow Lenny and slide into the booth.

As if the night couldn't get worse, my old high school friends walk through the door. I spot my old best friend Brian Newcomb right away, the guy who was dating Kendra while I was still dating her. She was sleeping with both of us and I had no clue. Brian knew, but he was too chickenshit to tell me about it.

He's with Tristan and Drew. The four of us were on the wrestling team together. We'd hung out since grade school. After I was released from jail, Drew was a cocky asshole and Tristan's mom ordered me to stay away from him. Tristan didn't argue.

I try not to make eye contact with the guys, and instead attempt to concentrate on whatever nonsense is flying out of Lenny's mouth. I think he's reminiscing about tossing Trish in the lake, but I'm hardly listening, because out of the corner of my eye I see Brian walking toward us.

"Holy shit, it really is you," Brian says, leaning into the booth and slapping me on the back. "Where you been, man?"

I try to fight off the feeling of camaraderie with Brian, but I can't. We were best friends for too damn long for me to turn my back and pretend he doesn't exist.

"I was in Chicago for a while," I tell him. Brian nods as if he understands. I gesture to Lenny. "This is Lenny. Lenny, these are my old friends."

"Cool." Lenny nods at each of them.

"Hey, Caleb," Tristan says, shaking my hand. "You're back, huh?"

"Just for a little while," I tell him.

Drew has a sly grin on his face as he sits on the bench beside me. "Brian, give Caleb the good news."

If Brian tells me he got a wrestling scholarship to Notre Dame, I won't be surprised. He always wanted to be one of the Fighting Irish, even though he's German. It was one of our running jokes. Brian is a smart guy, and worked hard to get the grades so he could get in.

Brian shoves his hands in his pockets. "Yeah, umm, I'm getting married."

"To *Kendra*," Drew chimes in, as if he can't keep the salacious info off his tongue. Drew hates Kendra, but he loves gossip that's sure to ignite sparks between Brian and me.

He's not going to get those sparks, at least from me.

I reach past Drew and hold out my hand to Brian. "Congrats, man," I say. And I mean it. I thought he'd go the college route, but if this is what he wants, more power to him.

Brian shakes my hand. "Thanks, Caleb. That's really cool of you."

I nod, and I'm glad that's over. The ice is broken. Tristan slides in next to Lenny, and Brian pulls up a chair to sit on the end.

This is one cozy little group.

Speaking of cozy little groups...I peer over at Maggie. She's having all sorts of fun with Matt, that guy Robert, and Becca. Okay, well not exactly *fun*. They're all just talking. I shouldn't give a shit. I don't give a shit.

How old is that dude, anyway? He's got a sports coat on as if he's about to broadcast the five o'clock news, and he's drinking his beer out of a glass instead of a bottle. The dude is a diva.

"So when's the wedding?" Lenny asks Brian.

"In two weeks," Brian mumbles as the waitress comes over.

After we order, Brian pulls out his cell phone and starts texting. For a guy who's getting married in two weeks, he doesn't look happy. In fact, he looks downright depressed.

I wouldn't put it past Kendra to manipulate him into marrying her, except for the fact that ever since sophomore year, Kendra has been obsessed with leaving Paradise and moving to California. She always wanted to be an actress or model and used to make fun of the people who graduated from Paradise High and stayed here their entire lives. She called them white trash losers.

Tristan tries to grab Brian's phone, but he pulls it out of his reach. "Stop it," he orders.

Our food comes, and I have to say thank God for Lenny. I don't feel like talking much, and Lenny can carry on a conversation about anything. When Lenny finds out Drew is into sports cars, he pulls all this random sports car knowledge out of his ass. Funny thing is, he sounds like he really knows what he's talking about.

When Tristan mentions the new Frisbee course that went up at the south end of Paradise Park, Lenny says he "loves frolfing" and that "technically it's called disc golfing because Frisbee is a brand name, yadda yadda."

Who knew Lenny was an encyclopedia of useless information? I'm just glad I don't have to carry the conversation, especially because I keep looking over at Maggie.

Oh, shit. I catch her looking back. Our eyes lock on one another.

"I've got to go," Brian says.

"Sit down, Bri," Drew says. "I drove you, remember? I'm not goin' anywhere until I finish my food."

Brian reaches into his wallet and tosses a ten dollar bill on the table. "You don't have to interrupt your meal, Drew. Kendra is picking me up."

Brian keeps looking at the door and holding his cell phone in his palm, as if he's expecting to be summoned by text any minute. Something's not right.

Apparently Kendra decides to come in rather than just text him, because she walks through the door and heads toward us. Her big blue eyes are focused on me and her long blonde hair is perfectly styled. Her makeup makes her look hard, not like the pretty girl I started dating when we were sophomores. She was my first serious girlfriend, and the one who I lost my virginity to. I used to think she was the sexiest thing alive.

"I thought you were going to text me when you got here," Brian says.

Kendra doesn't break her eye contact with me. "I had to see if it was true." She wets her top lip and throws me one of her all-too-familiar sexy looks. "So … Caleb Becker is back. Again."

"Hey, Kend," I say. "I hear congratulations are in order."

She looks down at her ring finger and the small diamond. "Thanks."

"You ready?" Brian asks, taking her hand.

Kendra removes her hand from Brian's grasp. "Can I talk to CB outside for a minute?"

I haven't heard that nickname in a long time. CB, my initials. She always called me that.

Brian looks at me, then back at her. "Yeah, I guess so. But I thought you said we were late for the cake tasting."

"It's fine," is her response. "I need to talk to Caleb first."

Drew rolls his eyes, but slides out of the booth to let me out.

"We'll be right back," Kendra tells Brian. "Wait here."

She heads for the exit, and doesn't stop until we're next to the gravel parking lot.

"I can't believe you came back," she says.

I tell her the truth. "I needed to tie up some loose ends."

"Am I a loose end, CB? 'Cause I swear, all I've done since you left is think about you and me. Do you think about me?"

I'm confused. Why is she bringing us up when she was the one who cheated on me? "Why are you marrying Brian? 'Cause neither one of you look happy about it. I know for a fact that after graduation you were dying to leave this town and go out to California, and Brian was dead set on going to Notre Dame."

Kendra crosses her arms around her stomach. "I'm pregnant, Caleb."

Shit. Pregnant? Didn't see that coming, although I guess the evidence is right in front of my face. Kendra isn't wearing one of her signature tight shirts that hug her body. She's wearing a loose shirt with a light jacket.

Tears start welling in her eyes, making her eyelashes sparkle. When she blinks and black mascara falls down her cheek along with her tear, I don't know what to say.

"Sorry," I say dumbly.

"Brian doesn't even want to apply for college, Caleb. He wants to take over his dad's butcher shop. Can you imagine me staying in Paradise and being the wife of a butcher?"

She wraps her arms around my waist. I keep my hands off her, because damn it, I don't want Brian coming out here and thinking we're about to get it on. And I don't want Maggie seeing me with Kendra, either.

It was a bad idea coming out here with her. I take her wrists and unwrap her arms from around my waist.

"Kend...shit, why didn't you just use a condom or something? We were always careful."

"Yeah, well the next time a guy says he'll promise to pull out I'll remember that's not effective birth control."

She wraps her arms around me again. We dated for over two years, but she doesn't have a hold on me now.

I also know that Kendra can turn the damsel-in-distress act into the diva-with-an-agenda act in a matter of seconds.

She buries her head into my chest. "Take me with you," I think I hear her say.

"What?"

She looks up with wide blue eyes and blinks her long lashes.

"Take me back, CB," she says. "I never stopped loving you."

THIRTY
Maggie

I saw Kendra and Caleb leave the restaurant together, but I didn't expect to find them in an intimate embrace in the parking lot. As we walk out of Dusty's, I can't help but stare.

Kendra is looking up at Caleb. He's looking down at her.

Suddenly, I don't feel good.

If he bends his head further, they're going to kiss. I look down at the gravel. If he kisses her, I might have to hurl a rock at them.

Stop it, Maggie.

Okay, I need to get a grip. Caleb and I parted amicably. We're friends, above all else. And I'm glad he's finally back in Paradise, because I know his family needs him.

We get back to my house and hang out for a while, until Robert starts yawning and Matt drives him and Becca home. While I'm saying good-bye to them, Kendra drives up in her little sports car and parks in front of Caleb's house. She tosses her blonde hair back with a flick of her wrist. The pieces fall in perfect waves down the side of her face and land in little curls at the bottom.

She doesn't even look my way when she walks up to Caleb's door and rings his bell in all her sexy glory. I try not to pay attention as he opens the door and lets her in, but I can't help it. Old habits die hard.

After Matt drives off with Robert and Becca, I have the urge to ring Caleb's doorbell and fight for him like Lou is fighting for my mom.

Instead, I sit on our front steps and think. And wait. And wait.

What are you waiting for, Maggie? I ask myself.

I stand and go inside, feeling defiant. I get ready for bed, then peek outside. Kendra's car is still parked out front. Damn. I talk to my mom about my night, then peek outside again.

Sure enough, that sports car is still out front.

I toss and turn all night, resisting the urge to look out my window and check whether Kendra is staying the entire night.

Right now, I wish Caleb and I didn't live next door to each other.

In the morning, her car is gone. Caleb is sitting on his porch as I leave to go to the grocery store.

"Hi," I say curtly when he sees me.

"Hi," he says back.

I head toward my car. "Have a good night last night?"

"Yep. You?"

"The best. Robert's amazing."

"You trying to make me jealous?"

"Why? Are you jealous?"

"I didn't like his hands on you."

"He's my physical therapist," I say. "He just touched my leg."

Caleb jumps off his porch and heads my way. "Regardless, I still didn't like it."

I can't help but ask. "What *really* made you come back to Paradise? Was it Kendra?"

"No, it was Lenny, my parents, my sister." He shrugs. "You."

"Can we go for a walk?" I ask, putting my keys back in my purse. Without talking, we fall into step next to each other. Instinctively, we head for Paradise Park. "I was ready to let you go. I moved on."

"I know."

"And then I saw you hugging Kendra last night. When I saw her go into your house ... I've never felt more possessive in my life."

"Don't," he says. "She's marrying Brian in two weeks. They're engaged."

"I think she still wants to be with you."

"Well, that's not gonna happen. Nothing happened last night. We talked. That's it."

We stop when we get to the big oak tree. Caleb and I kissed here for the first time. I'll never forget how lonely and lost I felt until that kiss. It changed me.

He changed me.

Caleb looks up at the thick branches and green leaves waving at us from above. "This is our tree, you know."

"You used to climb it until you broke your arm when you fell off it. I watched you from afar back then." I give a short laugh. "I used to always watch you. I liked you for so long."

"Why?"

"Because you were popular and smart and cute and weren't afraid of anything or anyone. When Leah and I made you watch our dance shows, you pretended to be interested. You were selfless. When you took the blame for me breaking your mom's ceramic owl statue, you were my hero. I loved watching you, even if you didn't notice me then."

"And what about now?"

I sit on the ground with my back resting against the tree. "I still can't keep my eyes off of you. God, if my mom knew I was here with you admitting that fact, she'd freak out."

"You want to know what I realized last night?"

"That you miss having Kendra in your life?"

"No." He crouches on the ground, facing me. "I miss having *you* in my life. You're my best friend, Maggie. Call me crazy, but I want you to be my girlfriend—"

Oh, God, how I dreamed this day would come. But

it's too late, isn't it? I reach out and cup his beautiful face in my palm. "Caleb, I'm leaving in two weeks. I'll be gone for almost a year."

"I know. But we're here now, right?" He looks determined, as if he knows we can do this. "Why don't we test drive being a couple the next two weeks? Let's not think about what's gonna happen after that. What do you say, Maggie?"

THIRTY-ONE
Caleb

After I ask Maggie to be my girlfriend, she looks nervous. "What about your parents, my mom ... and Leah?" Her eyebrows are furrowed in worry.

Maggie and I are nothing like Kendra and Brian. I think my old best friend and my ex-girlfriend make each other weaker. Maggie and I, together, are one strong team.

"We're going to tell them about us."

Her eyes go wide. "Remember how upset they were last time? I can't."

"Maybe *you* can't, but together we can." I lean and kiss her on the lips. "Don't be afraid."

When I pull away, our eyes meet.

This is the girl I draw strength from. She's got more

power than she thinks, and she taught me the definition of resilience.

A slow smile crosses her lips. "You really think we can do this?"

"Yeah, I do." For the time being, I do.

In the evening, we decide to meet at the park after dark. Maggie's still nervous about telling people about us.

The moonlight glows on her beautiful face as she comes up to me. I sling my arm around her and we walk quietly. "What happens after I leave for Spain?" she finally asks.

Her trip does kind of throw a monkey wrench into the girlfriend plan. But can't we just live for today and not worry about the future? "I don't know. I guess we'll figure it out as we go along."

Maggie smacks her sweet lips together and holds her chin high. She looks ready for a challenge.

For the first time in forever, I feel like I can handle being in Paradise. I stroke her shoulder and slowly trail my fingers down her arm until our fingers touch. I love it when I touch her and hear her breathe harder and faster. It's a total turn-on. It makes me want to see just how much I can please her. "I wish we were back at the cabin right now."

"Me too," she whispers. "I'd make out with you all night."

I chuckle. "I got to be honest with you, Mags. I'd try to do a lot more than make out."

I like just being with Maggie, talking to Maggie, doing stuff with Maggie ... but I also like fooling around with Maggie. It drives me nuts that she doesn't realize how much sex appeal she's got.

That brings a shy smile to her face. "I like what we did at the cabin. It was hard to leave you in the morning."

"Tell me what you liked. You know, so I know for next time."

"I'm too embarrassed." I watch as she nibbles her lip, then cocks her head to the side, thinking. She turns to face me. "Um ... how about if I show you?"

This girl never ceases to amaze me. The more comfortable she is in our relationship, the more her feisty spirit comes out.

"Bring it on."

Without hesitation, she leans forward and brings her face right up to mine. Hoping nobody can see us, I grab her butt and back her up against the tree. "You okay?" I murmur.

"Mmm." Her legs instinctively go around me, and I press into her as she moans against my lips.

Damn, her kisses are hot and sexy. I feel her energy and eagerness as if it's my own.

I definitely don't have to wait long this time for her tongue to come out and play with mine.

When her soft hands reach under my shirt and toy with the waistband of my jeans, it feels so different than it has with any other girl. Sure, I lust after Maggie. But she makes me nervous, because I also love her. I love her for everything she is and wants to be. She challenges me to forgive others.

She's my best friend. That thought is humbling.

"Get a room," I hear a voice say from behind me.

Damn. One day Maggie and I are going to get some alone time even if I have to save up money to take her to Lake Geneva or Rockford for a weekend like my parents used to do.

I give a frustrated moan as I look over at the spawn of Satan, who can only be named Lenny. What I wasn't expecting was my old cellmate Julio to be standing beside him.

I gently release Maggie and stand in front of her. It's a sorry attempt at protecting her from Lenny's ridicule, but we're kind of caught in a compromising position.

"Hey, what're you doing here?" I ask Julio.

"Thought I'd pay you a little visit."

I assumed he'd go back to Chicago when he got released, to see his family and hang with old friends. I never really believed he'd come to see me.

Oh, man, what is Maggie going to think of Julio? I'm kind of glad it's dark, so she doesn't see all his tattoos. His shaved head makes him look like a badass, but his crazy tats are even more intimidating.

"Maggie, this is Julio. We shared a cell when I was in the DOC."

"Nice to meet you," Maggie says, holding out her hand and smiling.

Julio slaps her hand and shakes it like she's one of his homegirls. I'm amused that she doesn't seem fazed in the least. Julio nods at our obvious disheveled appearance. Maggie's hair is a mess from my fingers running through it, and I think she somehow managed to get my jeans unzipped without me even knowing. "Sorry to interrupt whatever you two were doin' … or about to do."

As long as I've got an entourage, I might as well lay down the line. "Next time, if either of you catch me making out with my girlfriend, just pretend we don't exist and walk away."

"Girlfriend?" Lenny asks. "Since when did that become official?"

"Since just now," Maggie says.

"I can't imagine you came here just for a visit," I tell Julio.

Julio, as always, looks and acts cool. In his neighborhood, guys are afraid to screw around with guys who have swagger. You play the game and you don't get messed with.

"You know I don't like taking nothin' from nobody, but I need a place to stay."

If it was only up to me, no problem. Julio's not as crazy as he looks, and his being here is a sign he's breaking away from his gang ties. "I need to ask my dad. We'll work something out."

We walk to my house. The entire time I'm thinking about how I'm going to break the news to my dad that there's another friend of mine who needs a roof over his head.

Hell, I was just getting revved up to break the news

that Maggie and I are a couple. Now I have to deal with Julio needing a place to stay. I feel like an intruder or guest in my own house as it is. Bringing a second random guy to stay might cause my dad to freak out.

Maggie squeezes my hand. It's a silent message that everything will be okay. Somehow I believe her. In the end everything will be okay. But hurdles have to be jumped through first.

When we get to my house, I find my sister watching television in the living room. She looks surprised when all four of us walk in.

"Hi," she says as she clicks the television off. Her focus immediately goes to Julio.

"'Sup?" he says, nodding to her.

"Leah, this is Julio. Julio, Leah."

"Hi," she says.

"Where's Dad?" I ask her.

"He's either watching TV in his room, or sleeping."

I should have known. "Be right back," I tell everyone, then take the stairs two at a time and knock on my parent's bedroom door.

"Come in."

I open the door and find my dad lying on his big king-sized bed watching television. He turns it off when he sees me come into the room.

"Hey, Dad."

"Did you have a good time tonight?" he asks.

I think of Maggie and me. I don't know what the future

holds with us, but I feel good about it. I feel the best I've ever felt about us, actually. "Yeah. I had a great time, thanks. Listen, I've got to ask you a favor. This guy who I roomed with at juvie stopped by." I clear my throat, because I don't know how to proceed with asking for yet another favor from my dad. "He needs a place to crash."

"For how long?" Dad asks. I can't read his reaction, so I tread carefully. I'm at his mercy here. It's his house. Just before I left Paradise he'd said to follow his rules or leave. I left, because I couldn't pretend to be a perfect son when I clearly wasn't one.

"I don't know. A few days, maybe."

"We have valuables. Your mother wouldn't like it, Caleb."

"Mom isn't here," I tell him.

"What about Leah?" Dad says. "She's almost as fragile as your mother."

The floor creaks, alerting us there's someone else in the room. It's Leah.

"Let him stay, Dad."

"Why?"

"Because it's the right thing to do. He needs a roof over his head, and we have one." She looks at me and gives me a small smile, as if we're in this together.

"Fine. He can stay," he tells me. "Caleb, I'm holding you responsible if anything is stolen. And he can only stay a few nights and that's all. While your mother might not be here now, this is our home and I have to respect the way she'd want it to be."

"Thanks, Dad." I'm about to head back downstairs, but I need to get something off my chest first. I look at Leah, then my dad. "I just want both of you to know that Maggie and I are going to be spending a lot of time together the next two weeks."

"I don't think that's a great idea," my dad chimes in. "She's the reason you went to jail, Caleb."

I look right at my sister and say, "Maggie's not the reason I went to jail, Dad. Right, Leah?"

"I don't know what you're talking about," Leah mumbles. She retreats quickly and disappears down the hall.

"What are you thinking, Caleb?" my dad asks. "You're setting yourself up for trouble by messing around with Maggie. You're screwing up your life."

"You got it all wrong, Dad. I'm trying to fix it."

THIRTY-TWO
Maggie

I'm doing laundry in the morning when the doorbell rings. When I open the door, Caleb is standing on my porch with a steaming mug in his hands. "I made you coffee," he says, holding it out to me. "I forgot how you liked it, so I put in a little milk and sugar. If I had the money, I'd have gone out and gotten you gourmet stuff—"

"I don't need gourmet. You know that." I feel like everything is falling into place so perfectly, and it scares me. I take the cup and invite him in. "You didn't have to make me coffee at all."

"I wanted to. Besides, I figure we can talk to your mom and, you know, kind of break the news about us to her together."

"She's already at work," I tell him as I lead him to the laundry basket in the living room. "Sunday mornings tend to be busy at the diner."

I'm still not sure how my mom will react when she not only realizes that Caleb is back in Paradise, but that we're a couple now.

A couple.

I'm still trying to get used to the fact that we decided to make things official. It's so weird having him here, in my house, bringing me coffee just because he thought I'd want some.

"Did everything go okay last night after I left?" I ask as I pull out some T-shirts to fold.

He leans against the edge of the sofa, watching me. "I told my dad and Leah about us."

I stop folding and brace myself for the aftermath. "What did they say?"

He shrugs. "It doesn't matter."

Yeah, it does. But I know dealing with his family is a raw subject, so I don't press him further. The last thing I want to do is cause him more stress. He's dealing with enough just being back in Paradise.

"What are your plans today?" I pick up the mug and sip the warm, smooth coffee. It has just a hint of vanilla. I look at Caleb over the rim and wish I didn't feel like the clock is ticking when it comes to the amount of time we can spend together. The more we're together, the more I want to be with him.

"I was wondering if you want to hang out," he says.

"Sure. What do you want to do? I know Lenny and Julio are staying with you, so I'm sure you can't ditch them all day."

"We're all going frolfing. You know, disc golf."

"Frolfing?" I've never been frolfing before. I'm not even sure I can play with my limp. "Why don't you and the guys go play, and we can meet up after."

Caleb shakes his head. "Mags, you're going. It's kind of a date thing. We're playing in pairs."

"A date thing?"

"Yeah. Get ready, 'cause we're meeting on the course at eleven."

"I've never played. We're going to lose."

"I figured as much."

I instinctively throw what I'm folding. Oops. A pair of panties, which he catches in one hand and holds up. It's a neutral-colored pair, without any designs.

"Please tell me these are your mom's."

"They're mine."

One of his eyebrows go up. "Maggie, panties are supposed to be sexy. These aren't. I hope you have one of these in every color to bring to Spain."

I snatch them back and shove them to the bottom of the basket. "What's wrong with my underwear?"

"They're not sexy."

"They're comfy."

That makes Caleb laugh. "Just be ready at eleven. Enjoy the rest of the coffee before it gets cold."

An hour later, he's back to pick me up. He's got a bunch of discs in a backpack. I swallow my insecurity about playing because Caleb is so dead set on me joining them.

To my surprise, Trish and Leah are coming with us as well as Lenny and Julio. It's great to see Trish, but … are she and Lenny a couple? They're arguing about something, and Leah and Julio are walking ahead of us, obviously having a serious, private conversation.

I guess we're all a bunch of mismatched couples—that actually fit.

"Where's Erin?" I ask Trish.

"My mom was taking her to the doctor today for a sonogram," Trish explains. "Hopefully she's having a girl. Boys are gross." She gestures to Lenny. "My case in point."

"You haven't even seen me be gross, girl," Lenny says.

I don't want to, either.

"Explain how to play," I say to Lenny, diverting the argument. Lenny seems to be the frolfing expert in our group.

"It's simple. It's playing golf, but with discs instead of golf balls. Instead of eighteen holes of golf, there are eighteen metal baskets. The goal is to make the least amount of tries for each basket. Get it?"

"I think so."

Caleb takes my hand in his as we walk to the park. Not once do I feel like he's frustrated that I can't move faster. In fact, everyone slows their pace to match mine.

Only Leah seems uneasy. Every time she glances back

at me as I walk along, she quickly looks away. She knows I'm aware she was the one who hit me, but we don't talk about it. I know talking about it will bring out raw emotions for both of us, so I avoid the subject.

Am I mad that Leah ran into me? Yes, but I can't change it, and I know she didn't do it on purpose. It took me a long time to come to terms with what happened to me. It used to eat at me every single day. I was mad and upset and felt so sorry for myself I pretty much stopped remembering what life was all about.

Then Caleb got out of jail, and I learned that life was worth living. He made me realize I should stop living in the past and enjoy the present, no matter what. For example, I can still play tennis, the sport I've always loved with a passion—I just have to play differently now. I can't run, but I can still hit the ball with the racquet.

I've come to terms with the accident and the result of it. The biggest problem is that Leah still struggles with her role in what happened that night.

I do wish she'd come clean and tell the world that she was the one who hit me, but doing that has major consequences. I'm not sure she's ready for those consequences. She may never be.

At the frolf course, Caleb hands me three discs. "One is for long range, one is for mid range, and this is a putter disc—only use it when you're close to the basket."

"Got it."

"Just so you know, Lenny, this isn't a date," Trish says.

"Then what is it?"

"It's me feeling sorry for you, because you're such a loser."

Lenny tosses his disc up in the air and catches it. "Okay, Trish, so if I'm such a loser you won't mind making a bet with me. If I beat you, you agree this is a date and you have to promise to scream at the top of your lungs that I'm a fucking stud and you've had a crush on me since you met me."

"And what if I beat you?" Trish asks, rubbing her hands together. There's fire in her eyes.

"Name your price."

I wince. I'm afraid of Lenny and Trish challenging each other, because whenever they're involved there is sure to be drama and craziness.

"If I win," Trish says, "you have to come to my house and clean my room … and all of our toilets. For a week." She crosses her arms on her chest, looking pretty pleased with herself.

"Fine," Lenny says.

"Fine," Trish says. "Let's shake on it."

"Oh, no. We're gonna kiss on it."

He puts his arm around her waist and pulls her forward. I thought for sure Trish would slap him or knee him in the groin, but she doesn't. She kisses him back. I turn away, because it's sloppy and they make noises that should only be made in private.

"Ugh, I just lost my appetite," Julio chimes in as he

watches Trish and Lenny go at it. "Break it up before Leah and I ditch you guys and go somewhere else."

As he says that, Kendra comes walking up to the frolf course.

"Hey," she says. "Sorry I'm late."

I step away from Caleb. "Did you invite her?"

"Yeah," he says. "I did."

THIRTY-THREE
Caleb

Maggie's shoulders are slumped. She stopped smiling as soon as Kendra showed up. I know things are tense with Kendra and Maggie right now, but as long as I'm in Paradise, I can't ignore Brian. And where Brian is, Kendra is.

I just didn't expect Kendra to come alone.

"Where's Brian?" I ask her.

"We broke up last night. The wedding is off."

"The hell it is," Brian says, appearing off in the distance. He's walking in a crooked line, as if he's on something.

"Go away," Kendra tells him.

"No," Brian slurs. He reaches for her. "You're my partner."

Kendra pushes Brian out of arms reach. "Not anymore."

"Can we start the game already and stop bickering, everyone?" Julio says.

When Julio talks, people listen. Even Kendra and Brian, who ignore each other even though they're partners in this game.

We start tossing our discs toward the baskets. At first Maggie is horrible. Her disc flies about ten feet in front of her, and she's not even using the putter disc.

"Flick your wrist," I tell her.

She tries, but the disc flies backwards and almost hits Kendra in the head.

Maggie's hand flies over her mouth as the disc whizzes past Kendra. "Oops, sorry."

"I bet," Kendra mutters.

Brian tells Kendra to be nice. She sneers at him and I think *oh, buddy, you are going to pay for that remark later.*

Moving from one fairway to another isn't easy for Maggie, who has to tread lightly on the uneven ground. At one point when she stumbles and falls, I almost offer to take her home.

"Hop on my back," I tell her instead, as we head to the next fairway.

She looks at me as if I'm crazy.

"Come on, Mags. It'll be fun."

"No, it won't," she says. When I take her discs and bend down so she can easily maneuver onto my back, she asks, "You sure about this?"

Yeah, I'm sure. "Just hop on." She grabs my shoulders

and I carry her to the next hole. "You suck at this game. The last one was a par three, and how you managed to get an eight on it is embarrassing. I think I need to give you private lessons, so next time we can kick a little frolf ass."

"Private lessons sound good," she says, then kisses the back of my neck.

"You guys are dorks," Kendra says when we finally arrive at the next hole. I kneel so Maggie can slide off my back without too much stress on her leg.

"Don't call my best friend a dork, Kendra," Brian says.

Kendra puts her hand on her hip and flips her hair back. Oh, no. That's not a good sign. "Don't defend him. And he's not just your friend, Brian. He's my ex."

"He was my best friend before either of us dated you."

"We slept together behind his back," Kendra spits back with venom. "Some best friend you turned out to be."

With those words, Brian takes something out of the waistband of his jeans. It's a flask.

"Man, what're you doing?" I ask.

"None of your business."

Oh, shit. This is not happening. Not in front of Lenny and Julio and my sister. And not in front of Maggie, who hates Kendra drama more than anything. I want her to forget my past, not be reminded of it.

Kendra tosses one of the discs, aiming directly at Brian's nuts. Brian barely dodges the disc, takes another swig of whatever he's got in the flask, and looks his fiancé right in the eye. "Let's have a contest."

Lenny's eyes light up. The dude loves challenges more than anything.

Julio leans into me and says so nobody else can hear, "*These* are your friends? They're all fuckin' lunatics."

And this is coming from a guy who's been in jail for robbery and money laundering.

"Tell you what," Brian says, getting really pissed at Kendra now. I can tell because his face is getting all red and splotchy. That only happens right after he works out or when he's really pissed. "If I win the next hole, the wedding's back on. If you win, you're free to call it off and be with Caleb."

Um, not happening. "Brian, don't be an idiot," I tell him, but he's not listening. I don't know if he's high on top of being drunk. He's definitely not himself.

"Agreed," Kendra says, ignoring me. "But it's not a fair matchup."

"Fine. You pick who throws for me, and I pick who throws for you."

Maggie attempts to hide behind me.

"I pick Maggie. She'll throw for you," Kendra says through clenched teeth.

"Then *I* pick Leah," Brian says.

"Can I opt out?" Maggie asks them.

A red-faced Brian and a raging Kendra both say "no" at the same time.

"Guys, just kiss and make up already," I tell them. "You're pregnant, Kendra. And it's not happening between us, so get over it."

"Shut up, Caleb," Kendra says, venom in her voice.

"I got this," Maggie says, a fierce and determined look on her face.

I get it.

Maggie's fighting for me. She wants to win me, fair and square. Doesn't she realize she already has me, and doesn't have to fight?

I watch in awe as my girl takes a disc in her hand and goes to the tee.

"Maggie..." I say. "Umm...You grabbed a putter. That won't go too far."

I hold out another disc for her, which she takes with a murmured thanks.

Maggie takes a deep breath, then lets it rip with an impressive grunt. She winces when it veers to the right and almost lands in some bushes.

Her hand flies to her mouth in horror.

"Good goin', babe," I joke.

"It's not funny," she says, taking this competition way too seriously.

My sister is next. Julio tries to give her some pointers, but I'm not sure my twin sis wants Kendra to win. My sister whips the disc, but it also veers and lands in the bushes.

Oh, man, this is torture.

In the end, it's neck and neck. My sister holds her putter while Maggie holds hers.

"Wait," Maggie says before Leah aims for the metal basket.

Leah stills.

Maggie holds her disc at her side. "I can't do this."

"Me neither," Leah adds.

Maggie limps up to Kendra. "I don't play games with people's lives like you do."

'Atta girl!

Maggie drops the disc at Kendra's feet. "If you let him go and he doesn't come back to you, he wasn't yours to begin with. It's a lesson I learned in first grade."

Man, my girl is one tough chick when she wants to be. I wonder if it has something to do with those big, comfy granny panties she's got on.

Maggie limps away, my sister at her side. It reminds me of when we were kids and they were inseparable. I like that they're figuring out how to be friends again.

I watch until Maggie and Leah are out of sight.

"I'm out of here," Kendra says, storming off to her car.

"Me too," Brian says, turning to storm off to his.

I step in front of him. "I can't let you do that."

"Why not?"

"Because you're drunk. I can't let you drive while you're fucked up."

"Move out of my way, Caleb, and don't be such a dork."

"I'm a dork, too," Lenny says. "'Cause I won't let you drive, either."

"Give Caleb your keys," Trish orders Brian. "Now!"

Damon the Enforcer would be proud of us Re-START misfits. Too bad he's not here to see us all in action.

THIRTY-FOUR
Maggie

I head toward home with Leah.

"Thanks for that," Leah says. "I was gonna miss on purpose. I never liked Kendra."

I stop and turn to her. "What would you think about Caleb and me as a couple?"

She doesn't answer. Her non-answer is my answer.

"I'm leaving for Spain in less than two weeks, so you won't have to see us together for much longer." My words come out quick and I know she can tell I'm upset. "Leah, something's gotta give."

I limp away from her now, but I hear Caleb calling after me.

"Where's everyone else?" I ask.

"Lenny ended up driving Brian home—he was pretty wasted—and Julio and Trish went with them," Caleb says. "Listen Maggie. About the game ... I'm sorry." He moves in front of me. "I shouldn't have forced that situation on you. I just thought we could be a normal couple and—"

"We'll never be a normal couple, Caleb. We have so much baggage it's ridiculous." I hold a hand up when I see he's about to protest. "I'm living in reality. Reality is that Kendra still wants you in her life and your sister still wants me out of your life—it's easier on her that way."

Just thinking about Kendra and Leah is overwhelming right now. "I need to get away from here," I tell him.

"Where are you going?"

I take out the keys to my car. "Where I always go to think."

"If it's any consolation," he says, "I don't give a shit what anyone else thinks about us being together."

"I know. I wish I didn't care, but I do."

When I get to my car, I immediately head over to Mrs. Reynolds' house. Lou isn't there, and neither is the *For Sale* sign. A sinking feeling forms the pit of my stomach when I think about someone else living in this house.

As I finger the white-painted wood of the gazebo, I think about what I said to Caleb. I know he's still struggling being at home where he doesn't feel like he belongs. I saw where he's been sleeping—on the couch in his living room.

Lenny can't stay in the Beckers' house forever. I don't

know why he doesn't have a home or family to go back to after our Re-START trip, but he's obviously sleeping at the Beckers' because he has nowhere else to go.

And Julio was practically begging for a place to stay.

Even though I don't want to, I need to brace myself for the inevitable. Caleb is in my life temporarily. When I leave for Spain, we'll be going our separate ways. Should I make the most out of what we have now? Reality is, Caleb will soon be out of my life for good.

THIRTY-FIVE

Caleb

Two days after the frolf game, I'm standing in front of my sister's bedroom door. Lenny and Julio went out, and my dad is at work. It's the perfect time to have it out with Leah.

I knock on the door and wait. She cracks it, but doesn't let me in.

"Do you need something?"

"Yeah," I say. "We need to talk."

She opens her door wide and sits on the edge of her bed. Her room used to have posters of guys in boy bands, but now she's got pictures of skulls and crossbones and posters that remind me of death.

It's too fucked up for words.

"You've got to come clean to Mom and Dad." There, I said it. "I'm done taking the fall. It wasn't just telling the cops I was the one driving. It wasn't just pleading guilty and being locked up in jail for almost a year. Our lie is like a fucking cancer that's spread to every single area of our lives." I point to the posters on her wall. "You do realize this is your cry for help. It's sick shit, Leah."

The more I look at those skull pictures staring at me with their empty-holed eyes, the more I want to rebel against it. I'm not dead. I don't want to be dead. I don't want my sister to be dead. And I sure as hell don't want to be haunted by the past anymore.

"You promised," she says in an eerily calm voice. "When I told you about the accident, you said you'd take care of it."

"I was *drunk*, Leah. I hardly knew what I was doing, and by the time I realized I shouldn't have lied to the police, it was too late."

"I was scared."

"And I wasn't?" I snap. But maybe she didn't know how I was feeling, because I masked every emotion I had after I got arrested. I take a deep breath and try again. "It's time to tell Mom and Dad."

I look up and see a picture of a skeleton with its teeth sunk into a heart and I can't take it anymore ... I rake my fingers across the wall and rip them all down. "I'm done with you looking like death warmed over. I hate what you did to Maggie. I hate it, and I hate you for making me promise to take our secret to the grave and then paying me back by being a fucking recluse."

"Caleb, lay off her."

I turn to see Julio standing in the doorway.

"Stay out of this, Julio," I growl.

Instead of listening to me, Julio walks into the room and stands next to my sister. "I said *lay off*."

Is he kidding me? "This doesn't have anything to do with you."

"Yes, it does," Leah murmurs. She looks up at me with tear-filled eyes. "Because last night Julio and I stayed up all night and talked. He convinced me to turn myself in."

Huh?

I didn't expect that. I expected a lot of things to come out of my sister's mouth, but not that.

Relief floods all my senses, followed by worry and fear. What will happen when she turns herself in? Will she have to serve time? Those questions have been running through my head every time I thought about what would happen if Leah confessed.

How was it Julio who convinced her to come clean?

"Leah's tougher than she thinks," Julio says as he puts his arm around her shoulder. "She can do this." He squeezes her shoulders and looks into her eyes. "You can do this."

"You've known my sister all of three days, Julio."

"Yeah, and I bet I know her better than you."

Just when I'm about to laugh at that ridiculous comment, Leah says, "Julio's right. For the longest time I wanted to tell you how I felt, but I couldn't. You were sad or angry or pissed off... and I was afraid of hurting you again."

My sister chokes back tears and runs into my arms. "I'm so sorry about what I did to you. Julio told me how it was in jail for the two of you, and I'm just ... so sorry." She swipes at her eyes and says, "I think we need to call Dad and have him meet us at the rehab center. Whether Mom realizes it or not, she needs her son back."

An hour later I'm sitting in the waiting room of New Horizons Recovery Center. My dad didn't really want us to have this meeting because he thinks my mom's emotional status is too fragile, but when Leah and I said we were coming to see her with or without him, he agreed to meet us.

A woman with the name *Rachel* on her nametag greets us, then has us go into what's called a group therapy room to wait for my mom. It makes me feel stiff and uncomfortable, because we had mandatory group therapy sessions when I was in jail. I have to remind myself that this isn't jail. My mom wants to be here. She could leave on her own, but has chosen to stay because she doesn't trust herself not to use prescription drugs as a crutch when things get tough.

"You can have a seat, Caleb," Rachel says in a soft voice probably meant to calm me.

I try not to pace back and forth in the room like a caged animal, but I can't sit because I've got a bunch of pent-up nervous energy. "No, thanks."

The chairs are situated in a circle. My dad is sitting in one chair in his three-piece suit and tie. My sister, surprisingly, isn't slumped in her chair. She's sitting straight up and has a determined look on her face. If Julio was the one who talked her into facing all this crap head-on, he's a fucking genius.

My sister doesn't know it yet, but I'm not abandoning her. She's not the only one who made mistakes the night of the accident.

As soon as my mom walks in the room in grey sweats with the New Horizons logo on the front, I realize she's different. Her face is drawn and her spirit seems somehow …lost.

My first instinct is to go up and hug her but I figure out, by the way she has her hands folded on her chest, that she doesn't want any affection from me or anyone else in the room.

Mom stops in her tracks when she sees me step toward her. "Why are you here?"

My veins are pumping hard and I'm so damn tense my arms are stiff at my sides. This is already a billion times harder than I imagined. "I came back. Maggie told me you guys needed me. At first I didn't want to believe her…"

"You left me. A good son doesn't leave his mother."

Her words cut deep. Oh, man, I should never have left. I thought it would be best, that everything would be okay if the "Caleb Quotient" was out of the equation. I was wrong. I've managed to screw up so much in such a short amount of time.

"I'm sorry, Mom."

Deflated, I sit in the chair next to Leah.

"I'm sorry, too," Leah says. "I need to apologize to everyone in this family."

My sister turns to me and puts her hand on my knee. I put my hand on top of hers.

I feel her hesitation and fear as if it's my own. But I also feel her determination to set the wrongs of the past right.

"Mom, Dad," Leah says after I nod to her, giving her silent support. "I was the one who hit Maggie the night of the accident."

Watching the expression change on my parents' faces is pure torture. At first they cock their heads to the side as if they've heard the words wrong. When Leah doesn't say anything else, the reality of what she said starts to sink in.

"No," my mom whispers, shaking her head. "No. No."

"What are you saying, Leah?" my dad asks, his voice about to crack. "*What. Are. You. Saying?*"

A stream of tears start flowing down Leah's face. "I was at the party. I'd had maybe two beers. When I was driving home, I swerved to hit a squirrel. I didn't mean to hit Maggie." She's choking on her tears now, and I look up at the ceiling in an attempt to hold myself in check.

It's not working.

Dammit.

Tears start forming in my eyes. I try to blink them back, but it's no use. Seeing my sister so upset, seeing my dad and mom frozen in shock, and knowing that one fateful night destroyed my family and permanently damaged Maggie's leg is just too much for me.

I dab at my own tears and attempt an explanation.

"When Leah came back to the party all freaked out, I told her I'd take care of it," I tell them. "I was so wasted that night, I wasn't thinking straight. When the cops asked who was driving, I said it was me."

"Oh, God, Caleb, I'm so sorry," Leah cries out. "I don't know how you could ever forgive me. I don't deserve forgiveness for the hell I put you through."

She buries her head in her hands.

"I can't believe this is happening," my dad says. "This *can't* be happening."

"No," my mom says again.

I look over at Rachel. I think she was expecting a regular family therapy session, and from her deer-in-headlights look I think we've shocked her into silence.

I nod. "It's true." Man, I feel a sort of freedom I haven't felt in a long time. I want to share this with Maggie. I guess now is as good a time as any to say the other piece of news I've been holding back.

"I know this is another bomb I'm dropping, but Maggie Armstrong and I are dating. I didn't mean for it to happen. I denied it for a long time, then hid it for a while … and I'm not gonna do that anymore."

"Does she know …" my dad says, his voice trailing off. I know he's on the brink of breaking down. I can see it in his trembling lip and shaking hands.

"Yeah, she knows." I look over at Leah. "Maggie knows everything."

My mom looks at me. It's the first time she's looked at me without contempt or scorn since I was arrested. She keeps shaking her head, as if she's trying to wrap her brain around this new, totally unexpected information. "Leah, how could you?" Mom asks, her words coming out slow. "How could you stand by and let your brother go to jail for something you did?"

"I don't know, Mom. I don't know. But I'm going to make it right." Her puffy, bloodshot eyes meet mine. "I'm turning myself in tomorrow."

THIRTY-SIX

Maggie

"Maggie, can I come over?" Caleb's voice comes through the phone. He doesn't sound happy.

"Sure. What's wrong?"

"I'll tell you when I get there."

My mom and Lou are right downstairs. I haven't told her about Caleb. I wanted to. To be honest, I've been stalling because the last thing I want to do is upset her when she's still trying to figure things out with my dad and Lou.

It's time I confess to my mom the truth about me and Caleb.

Lou and my mom are in the kitchen. They're both chopping vegetables for some sort of soup concoction they're making. She's still not wearing his ring, but he's come over every day and is really fighting for the right to be with her forever. She made my dad postpone his move here…indefinitely.

"Mom, can I talk to you?"

My mom, complete with flour in her hair and a carrot in her hand, looks up from the cutting board. "Is anything wrong?"

"No. It's just that…if it weren't for Caleb, I might have given up on life."

My mom stops chopping. "What?"

"After the accident, it was Caleb who made me realize life was worth living."

"Maggie, that's a bunch of nonsense."

"No, Mom, it's not. You want to know why?"

"I'm sure you're going to tell me no matter what I say."

I don't know how she's going to react. She's not exactly happy, but at least she's listening. "Because he pulled me out of my depression. You didn't even see it because you were so happy I was home and not living in hospitals anymore. But I wasn't happy. I was miserable until Caleb came back from jail and helped me realize I was worth something even though I had a disability."

"Why are you telling me this now?" my mom asks.

"Because he's coming over, and I want you to be prepared…" The doorbell rings. "That's him, Mom. Just, be nice and don't judge him until I tell you everything."

I rush to open the door. Caleb's bloodshot eyes greet me. He doesn't say anything; he just pulls me close and hugs me tight right on the front steps of my house.

"I saw my mom today," he mumbles into my hair. "Oh, God, Maggie, it was so awful. Leah told our parents she was the one who hit you."

I know that was probably the hardest thing Leah has ever done. "How is she?"

"She was crying. A lot." He pulls away, but holds on to my hands. "She's determined to turn herself in. I don't know what's going to happen. I just called Damon. He's coming over tomorrow to advise us on what to do."

I touch Caleb's forehead to mine. I can see in his face how much this is tearing him apart. "I'm sorry. I'll go with you. Whatever I can do to help, I will."

"What's going on?" my mom asks, confused. "I don't know why you're here," she says to Caleb. "And pray tell, why are you two holding hands?"

I take a deep breath and squeeze Caleb's hand. We're going to do this together. I lead him inside my house and stand before my mom and Lou. "Caleb and I have something to tell you both." I look at Caleb through watery eyes. "I know this is going to be a shock, but try and understand…"

This has got to be one of the toughest days of Caleb's life. While he's freeing himself from blame, the reality is that he's incriminating his sister at the same time. "I wasn't the one who hit Maggie," he says. He clears his throat. "Umm…" He holds my hand tight. "It was Leah."

"You're lying."

"He's not, Mom," I tell her.

"Why?" my mom asks, tears now streaming down her face. I'm crying, too.

Caleb gives a half-shrug. "I thought I could handle it better than Leah. I thought I was sparing her from going through something that would ruin her. I could handle going to jail, but my sister couldn't. The whole thing just kind of spiraled out of control, and I realized I was wrong, but it was too late." He looks at me. "And Maggie was caught in the middle of it all."

Lou walks out of the room for a minute, then reappears with a box of tissues. He hands a few to my mom. She dabs her eyes with the tissue. "This is a lot to take in. Maggie, did you know about this?"

I nod.

"How could you not say anything? I'm your mother."

"I didn't figure it out until right before Caleb left. I didn't say anything because I wanted Caleb to be the one to reveal it. Somehow I felt it was his secret to tell. Besides, I was desperate to stop reliving the accident. I wanted it over. I needed to move on for my own sanity." I look up at the boy who filled the void in my life. "Caleb helped me realize I couldn't stop living my life because of my disability."

My mom shakes her head. "I need time to digest this. This is just … too much for me. I need to be alone right now."

She hurries up the stairs. A minute later, I hear her door shut, and I wince. I never wanted to hurt her or make her feel betrayed by either of us.

The Re-START program really brought home the fact that accidents affect so many people ... they're like avalanches, affecting everyone and everything in their wake.

I look over at Lou. "I'm sorry. I didn't mean to upset her."

"I know. I think it'll take a while to sink in. Give her some time and she'll come around." Lou turns to Caleb. "You were brave to come back here."

"I don't feel brave right now. My home life is kind of a mess, and I have two guys staying at my parents' with me 'cause they're dealing with the same kind of fallout I'm dealing with."

Lou pauses for a moment, then smiles. "I have a proposition for you," he says to Caleb. "My mother's house is vacant. If you and your friends want to stay there for a while, and pay enough rent to cover the utilities and taxes on the property, it's yours."

"Are you serious, sir?" Caleb asks, totally shocked.

Lou nods. "I know my mother thought you were a good kid and wanted to help you. I figure this is fate; it's the way my mom would want it. What do you say?"

Caleb shakes Lou's hand vigorously. "I'd say you've got yourself a deal."

When I'm walking with Caleb back to his house so we can spend time with Leah and give the good news to Lenny and Julio, Caleb says, "Lou's a good guy."

"I know. I hope my mom gets over her fear of loving someone other than my dad."

"What are your fears?" he asks. "About us, I mean."

"After today I have none, because"—I give him the honest answer, which I've held in for way too long—"because I love you."

THIRTY-SEVEN

Caleb

It felt incredible hearing Maggie tell me she loved me yesterday. But now I feel as helpless as the day Judge Farkus handed down his sentence to me. I'm sitting at the police station in a remote lobby with my sister, my dad, my mom, Maggie, Julio, and even Lenny, who said he wanted to come because he already feels like part of our family. (Of course that was before he met my mom, who told him to sit straight and cut his hair or he wouldn't be invited to Thanksgiving dinner, which is over three months away.)

My cousin Heath is a lawyer, and he's here too. He'll be in the room with Leah when she confesses to hitting Maggie.

"You ready, Leah?" Damon asks as he kneels in front of my sister. He came to our house this morning and very calmly explained that the easiest way would be to make a sworn statement at the police station. Then Leah will be processed into the system. Damon stressed that it's all up to the state prosecutor to decide whether or not to go ahead and formally charge Leah, since the accident is still within the three-year statute of limitations. My record will be wiped clean, regardless.

My knee is shaking.

I look over at Maggie, who looks equally nervous. She didn't have to come, but she did. Hell, if I were her I'd probably be demanding that Leah be locked up for at least as long as I was, if not more.

But Maggie's not me. She's got a good, forgiving spirit. Just being around her makes me strive to be a better person.

Damon told my parents and me to write letters in support of Leah, vouching for her character. He said he'll attach it to the confession, so the state prosecutor or the judge assigned to the case will take it into consideration when deciding her sentence.

"I'm ready," Leah says with a weak smile. This can't be easy for her, that's for sure. But she's stronger than I ever gave her credit for. This morning when she walked down the stairs, she didn't have anything black on. She's wearing white pants and a yellow shirt. She looks so different, so ... bright.

"Good morning, sunshine," my dad had said after taking one look at her.

I thought we'd all be somber and crying, but we've held it together so far. When my mom called last night and said she wanted to leave rehab and come with us to the police station, I felt like the Beckers were starting to heal.

We just have to get over this one last hurdle.

Heath and Damon gesture to my sister to follow them.

"Wait," Damon says, stopping. "Do you have those letters I can attach to her statement?"

After we hand them over, Maggie pulls a piece of paper out of her purse and hands it to him. "Leah, I know you're not doing this for me, but … thanks."

It's a hugfest now, all of us hoping to transfer our strength to Leah before her confession. Even Lenny gets up to hug my sister, then turns and hugs me.

"I owed you one," he says to me. "I owe you more than one, actually. You gave me a family, something I haven't had in a long time."

I nod. Believe it or not, Lenny's grown on me.

Leah is still hugging Maggie. "I never meant to hurt you, you know that, right?"

"You've apologized about a million times," Maggie says, with tears in her eyes. "You *never* have to say it again, okay? I forgive you. It happened, it was a mistake."

They hug again, and then my sister heads for the heavy metal door. On the other side of that door she'll confess. Then she'll be booked, complete with fingerprints and a mug shot.

"Hey, Leah," Julio barks out.

Leah turns around.

"Remember what I said," he says, then winks at her.

She holds her head up high and smiles at him. Then she nods to Heath and Damon. "Let's do this."

When she's gone, it's eerily quiet. Until Lenny turns to my dad and says, "Pull my finger."

THIRTY-EIGHT
Maggie

Five exhausting hours later we're back at home. They released Leah on a five thousand dollar bond, so we're all together. I was so worried about Leah today, but she seemed okay about everything. She actually said finally telling the truth made her feel free, which is weird because she might have to serve jail time. Damon said he was going to talk to the prosecutor, and try to convince him not to charge Leah.

Caleb's mom decided to come back home, so everyone is happy but definitely on edge.

Caleb, Lenny, and Julio are moving into Mrs. Reynolds' house at the end of the week. Caleb and the guys are going to work for Caleb's uncle, who owns a construction company. He said he'll get his GED and get his life back on track.

The night before I leave for Spain, Caleb and I walk to the park and stand under the big oak tree. Our time together is ticking down by the minute, and I'm nervous.

"I wish you could come with me."

He gives a short laugh. "Me too."

"Before you leave, I gotta get something off my chest." He steps back, brushes a hand through his hair, and starts pacing. "Listen, I'm really fucking scared about you leaving. I'm sorry for cussing, but it's true. While I know I can go on without you, dammit, I don't want to. I've gotten used to having you in my life, and it just won't be the same without you."

My heart is beating fast and I reach out to hold his hand. "What are you saying?"

"I'm saying that I love you, Maggie." He looks at me through crystal clear eyes. "I was holding back and didn't want to say it, because I didn't want you to think I said it as some ploy to make you not date other guys while you're in Spain."

"I don't want to date other guys."

"That's what they all say, until some good-looking Spanish dude comes up to you and whispers some romantic Spanish shit in your ear and asks you out."

I laugh. "I don't see that happening."

"What if it does? What if you meet some guy and decide to stay in Spain forever?"

"I can say the same thing, Caleb. Not the staying in Spain thing, but what if you meet some girl while I'm gone?"

"Not gonna happen," he says, repeating my words.

I know he doesn't want to force me to make a commitment to him. The truth is, I want him to be free this next year. If we can make it through this, I know we'll be strong enough to last forever if we want. "I propose this," I say. "We promise not to go looking for someone else, but if it happens it happens and we have to be honest with each other about it."

"Deal. Now let's stop talking about it before I decide to convince you to stay in Paradise."

"What do you want to do?" I ask. "Kiss?"

"Oh, yeah. I want to kiss."

He pulls me toward him and I feel his warm body against mine. Caleb makes me feel happy and protected and loved all at the same time. He kisses me, his full soft lips making my body shudder with excitement. I can't imagine anything feeling this good. "This is perfect," I tell him.

He gently swipes his lips across mine. "It's pretty damn close."

Nine Months Later

"Welcome to Chicago's O'Hare International Airport. Please wait until the aircraft has come to a complete stop before deplaning."

My heart is beating so furiously in my chest I'm surprised the other passengers can't hear it. I gather my backpack when the plane stops and quickly limp toward the baggage claim, ignoring the pain in my stiff leg.

Caleb's not here. My mom is, though. She rushes up to me and hugs me tight. Lou is with her, so I hope that's a good sign. She's not wearing his ring, but the last time I talked to her she asked me what I thought of winter weddings. My dad visited me in Spain for New Year's, and we hashed out a lot of issues. I think we're on the mend, and even though he'll never be a doting father, I'm glad we've started to work things out.

"Did you have a nice flight?" Lou asks. "I bet you're hungry for some good ol' American food."

"I'm definitely hungry for one of Irina's pies from the diner," I tell him, and get a smile in response. Everyone loves Irina's pies, and I've been her taste tester ever since my mom started working there.

When we have my luggage and are driving back to Paradise, my mom drills me on how my leg is holding up. I answer her, but the entire time all I can think is, *where is Caleb?*

The last email I got from him said he'd meet me right when I got home. That was almost three weeks ago, though. A lot could have changed in three weeks.

I tell myself I'm over-thinking things. Ugh, I can't take the suspense.

"Have you heard from Caleb?" I ask, trying not to sound like I'm desperate to hear the answer.

"He came by this afternoon and left you a note in your room," my mom says.

A note. Notes are bad. Notes can't be good.

"Did he say anything when he left the note?"

My mom shakes her head. "No. He just asked if he could leave a note and I said it was okay. He was in the house less than two minutes."

I wish the ride home didn't take over an hour. The entire plane ride, I'd imagined hundreds of different scenarios of our reunion. None of them included a note.

At my house, I get out of the car and head inside after Lou insists on bringing my luggage up.

Upstairs, my bedroom is the same as I left it. My bed is made and on top of my big comforter is an envelope. On the front, one word is written in Caleb's handwriting: *Maggie*.

I pick up the envelope with trembling fingers and rip open the seal. I unfold the note slowly. I close my eyes and take a deep breath, then I open them and read what it says:

Do you remember the old oak tree? Go there, and wait for me.

Huh? The old oak at Paradise Park?

I tell my mom I'll be back later. She doesn't argue, probably because I'm practically out the door before I even finish my sentence.

It's dusk now, but the park isn't far away. I head for the oak tree. Nobody is here, except for a little squirrel running across the grass.

I wait ten minutes, staring up at the tree and wondering why he wanted me to wait here and how long he wants me to wait. Just as I'm starting to feel insecure, I see a silhouette running toward me.

I'd recognize Caleb anywhere. My heart soars.

"Maggie!"

He stands in front of me, toe-to-toe, totally out of breath. He's wearing ripped jeans and a stained white T-shirt. He looks like he hasn't shaved in a week, and his hair is disheveled.

"I'm so sorry I'm late." He reaches out and fingers my hair, which is long now since I haven't cut it in almost a year. "You look great, Maggie. Different."

"Thanks," I say. "You do, too."

I reach up and put my arms around his neck, not caring that I'm being bold. I don't want to hold back. "I missed you," I tell him.

His hands go around my waist and he pulls me close. "I have so many questions to ask you. But first…"

I think we're going to kiss, but instead he pulls something out of his pocket and holds it up. It's a bandanna.

"What's that for?" I ask.

"Turn around."

I cock an eyebrow.

"Trust me, Maggie."

I do as he says. "I was going to kiss you," I tell him.

He gently positions the bandanna over my eyes and ties it in the back. "You will. I promise. Just… be patient."

I'm not patient.

While I was in Spain, my feelings for Caleb grew infinitely stronger. I had guy friends my roommate and I would go out with, but none of them made me shiver with excitement. I get excited just thinking about being in Caleb's arms again.

"I can't see anything," I announce as I'm led across the park and into a car.

"That's pretty much the point, sweetheart."

I feel us winding through streets until we come to a

stop. He opens the door and leads me out of the car. He chuckles as he puts his hands on my waist and urges me forward to who knows where.

"Where are we?" I ask, wondering how long it will be before the suspense is over.

"You'll know soon enough. Okay, stop."

"Can I take the blindfold off?"

"Nope. Not yet." In one swift movement, Caleb picks me up and cradles me in his arms.

I wrap my arms around his neck for support. "The last time you held me like this you dunked me in water."

He walks forward. "Trust me, Maggie."

"I do. But I've got to be honest and say you smell like a sweaty guy from the gym."

"I've been working. I promise to take a shower after I show you something."

He walks a little more, then suddenly stops. "Okay, pull off the blindfold."

When I do, I realize where we are immediately. In Mrs. Reynolds' gazebo. The entire floor is covered in cushions and little twinkling lights outline the perimeter. On top of the cushions are thousands of little white and red rose petals.

"It's perfect," I say breathlessly as I slide my sandals off and walk onto the cushions. "Where are Lenny and Julio?" I ask. I know Lou took the house off the market and pretty much considers it a haven for Caleb and his friends. As long as they're employed and don't get in trouble, they've got a roof over their head.

"I told them to sleep out tonight. Tonight I wanted to be alone with you."

I swallow, hard. "Alone?" Racy thoughts a girl shouldn't have clutter my mind. I smile. "Really?"

"Yeah. It's been so damn long I was afraid you were gonna return to Paradise and tell me you never wanted to see me again."

"I was afraid of the same thing about you," I admit.

We both laugh, and for some reason it makes me feel better that we're both cautious and nervous.

"Have you seen Kendra and Brian's new baby recently?" I ask. He told me he's been going out with Brian and his high school buddies on occasion.

"Yeah. Cute kid, although I've got a feeling Kendra's gonna raise her as a little diva."

"How's their relationship?" I ask.

"Rocky, but they're trying. Last time I saw Kendra, she hardly spoke to me. I suspect she realizes I'm not looking at her like she's the goddess she wants everyone to think she is."

"Good."

"Maggie, I want to tell you something," he says in a serious tone, as we settle down into the plush cushions.

I shake my head. "No. Let me say what I have to say first." This is not going to be easy. I take a deep breath, gathering the courage to put everything on the line. There are things that I've held back because I was scared, but I learned something in Spain this year. One of my professors said if you tiptoe into cold water, you're missing out on the rush of plunging in headfirst.

I'm going to plunge in, without worrying about the consequences. I look at Caleb, at the twinkling lights, and at the beautiful petals surrounding us.

"I've been holding back because I've been scared. You can crush my heart like my dad did with my mom. You have power over me." A tear escapes my eye. "I still love you, Caleb. I fell in love with you right here in this backyard, and I never stopped. Being apart this year hasn't changed anything."

Caleb looks around, as if he's thinking of something to say but doesn't know how to put it into words. "Ever since we got locked in Mrs. Reynolds' attic, I knew I'd been missing out on a girl who really cared about me and wasn't self-absorbed. I was so blind for so long."

"What happens when I leave for college in the fall?"

"I'll come visit you whenever I can. U of I isn't far away." He touches my nose. "I want to kiss you, but I need to take a quick shower first." Hopping up off the cushions, Caleb starts walking toward the house. "Just ... wait here and don't move until I get back. I have a surprise for you," he says with a nervous edge to his voice.

I'm confused, but I promise not to move until he comes back. I lean back on the cushions. It's just right, being back in Paradise with Caleb again. I know he's working construction and trying to save up for college. He can do it. I'm sure of it.

He comes back ten minutes later, all cleaned up. His shirt outlines his arm muscles, which are bigger since the last time I saw him. I'm sure it's from working construction all day.

He looks at me with an intense expression. In the past, every time I caught him looking at me like that, I wanted to pinch myself. I thought the only way Caleb Becker would ever look at me like that was if I was dreaming or if he had an agenda.

I don't know when the switch happened. I think it was after Kendra stayed late at his house, talking. Afterward, he told me to trust him and asked me to be his girlfriend.

That was the moment.

The side of his mouth quirks up. "What're you thinking about?"

"You."

"I hope it's good."

I smile. "It is." I pat the cushions. We still haven't kissed, and I'm not interested in being patient right now. In fact, at this point I'd have no problem kissing a sweaty, rugged, smelly Caleb. "Come sit with me."

Instead of sitting with me, he holds out his hand. "I have a surprise for you."

He helps me up and hands me what looks like a remote control switch.

"You're not going to blindfold me again, are you?" I ask.

"No." He leads me behind the garage. I can barely see the outline of some kind of big structure. I can't make out what it is. Standing behind me, his arms holding me tight, Caleb whispers, "Push the button."

When I do, the entire structure lights up with twinkling lights … in the outline of … "A castle?"

A castle. A bigger version of that castle on the playground.

"I was finishing up the last-minute touches when your plane landed and lost track of time," Caleb says.

I can't believe I didn't notice it before. I don't know what to say … "It's a castle. I can't believe you made me a castle."

He takes my hand and leads me inside the structure. There are more petals strewn all over the wooden floor, surrounding a bunch of pillows and blankets in the middle.

"This is like heaven," I murmur as I look up into the open sky above us. It's just like it was at the park, but this is better. This time we aren't running away from anything or anyone.

Caleb sits down on the pillows. "Heaven, huh?"

"Definitely." I'm in shock as I sink down next to him. "This is amazing, Caleb. Did you build it yourself?"

"Lenny and Julio helped, but I designed it."

I look at the boy-turned-man who's the love of my life. I fish out a little box from my purse and hand it to him. "Here. It's a gift I brought back for you."

As he takes the top off and peers inside, I add, "I took a jewelry-making class." He pulls out the leather string and attached pendant. "It's a sword," I tell him.

He laughs. "I can tell what it is. It's really cool. I like it." He hangs it around his neck. I like that he's wearing something I made for him.

"It symbolizes strength," I say. "It reminds me of you."

In a surprise move, Caleb kneels in front of me. My heart just about leaps out of my chest.

He clears his throat.

He takes a deep breath and straightens his shoulders. "Okay, here's the deal. It was hell being apart from you this past year. Every day there was something that I did that reminded me of you."

I hold his face in my hands. When my lips are a whisper away from his, I ask, "Do you think we'll make it, Caleb? Do you think we'll last?"

"We've been to hell and back again. We're gonna make it. I love you, Maggie Armstrong, and always will."

"You promise?"

We lie back on the pillows together, and he places small, slow kisses across my neck. "Trust me," he whispers against my lips. "Maggie, you're my paradise."

Acknowledgments

I want to thank Brian Farrey, Steven Pomije, Sandy Sullivan, Marissa Pederson, and all the Flux staff for helping me work on this book and for letting me continue Maggie and Caleb's story. You've made my fans beyond happy.

My agent Kristin Nelson has been a rock, and her support overwhelms me. Thanks for being my champion. It means the world to me!

My extreme thanks, as always, to Karen Harris for her support and friendship ... without you my books wouldn't make sense to anyone but myself. I wouldn't have been sane this year without my amazing assistant Melissa Hermann—thank you for your hard work and dedication a million times over! And to Rob Adelman, the guy who brings the word *amazing* to the next level.

I can't thank Samantha, Brett, Fran, and Moshe enough for letting me write my books and neglect the laundry and dishes. I'll make up for it ... one day. Or not (don't tell them my little secret ... I hate doing laundry and dishes!).

Last but not least, thank you to my passionate and incredible fans ... they are my inspiration for writing books and mean more to me than I can put into words.

SIMONE ELKELES was born and raised in the Chicago area. The author of *Leaving Paradise, How to Ruin a Summer Vacation,* and *How to Ruin My Teenage Life,* she was honored to be named Illinois Author of the Year by the Illinois Association of Teachers of English. Fairfield, the town featured in *Perfect Chemistry,* is loosely based on a suburb near Simone's home—where two very different communities come together in one high school. Simone lives in Illinois with her family.

www.simoneelkeles.net

Read all about Alex and Brittany's love story in . . .

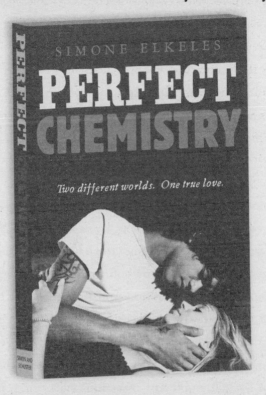

Brittany Ellis and Alex Fuentes couldn't be more different; she's the "perfect" cheerleader living a life of luxury and he's a gang member from the wrong side of town. But when they are forced together by a school project, sparks begin to fly and both Alex and Brittany realise that sometimes appearances can be deceptive.

Will their emerging feelings be enough to keep them together when the world is determined to tear them apart?

1

Brittany

Everyone knows I'm perfect. My life is perfect. My clothes are perfect. Even my family is perfect. And although it's a complete lie, I've worked my butt off to keep up the appearance that I have it all. The truth, if it were to come out, would destroy my entire picture-perfect image.

Standing in front of my bathroom mirror while music blares from my speakers, I wipe away the third crooked line I've drawn beneath my eye. My hands are shaking, damn it. Starting senior year of high school and seeing my boyfriend after a summer apart shouldn't be so nerve-racking, but I've gotten off to a disastrous start. First, my curling iron sent up smoke signals and died. Then the button on my favorite shirt popped off. Now, my eyeliner decides it has a mind of its own. If I had any choice in the matter, I'd stay in my comfy bed and eat warm chocolate chip cookies all day.

"Brit, come down," I faintly hear my mom yelling from the foyer.

My first instinct is to ignore her, but that never gets me anything but arguments, headaches, and more yelling.

"I'll be there in a sec," I call down, hoping I can get this eyeliner to go on straight and be done with it.

Finally getting it right, I toss the eyeliner tube on the counter, double and triple check myself in the mirror, turn off my stereo, and hurry down the hallway.

My mom is standing at the bottom of our grand staircase, scanning my outfit. I straighten. I know, I know. I'm eighteen and shouldn't care what my mom thinks. But you haven't lived in the Ellis house. My mom has anxiety. Not the kind easily controlled with little blue pills. And when my mom is stressed, everyone living with her suffers. I think that's why my dad goes to work before she gets up in the morning, so he doesn't have to deal with, well, her.

"Hate the pants, love the belt," Mom says, pointing her index finger at each item. "And that noise you call music was giving me a headache. Thank goodness it's off."

"Good morning to you, too, Mother," I say before walking down the stairs and giving her a peck on the cheek. The smell of my mom's strong perfume stings my nostrils the closer I get. She already looks like a million bucks in her Ralph Lauren Blue Label tennis dress. No one can point a finger and criticize her outfit, that's for sure.

"I bought your favorite muffin for the first day of school," Mom says, pulling out a bag from behind her back.

"No, thanks," I say, looking around for my sister. "Where's Shelley?"

"In the kitchen."

"Is her new caretaker here yet?"

"Her name is Baghda, and no. She's coming in an hour."

"Did you tell her wool irritates Shelley's skin? And that she pulls hair?" She's always let it be known in her nonverbal cues she gets irritated by the feeling of wool on her skin. Pulling hair is her new thing, and it has caused a few disasters. Disasters in my house are about as pretty as a car wreck, so avoiding them is crucial.

"Yes. And yes. I gave your sister an earful this morning, Brittany. If she keeps acting up, we'll find ourselves out of another caretaker."

I walk into the kitchen, not wanting to hear my mother go on and on about her theories of why Shelley lashes out. Shelley is sitting at the table in her wheelchair, busily eating her specially blended food because, even at the age of twenty, my sister doesn't have the ability to chew and swallow like people without her physical limitations. As usual, the food has found its way onto her chin, lips, and cheeks.

"Hey, Shell-bell," I say, leaning over her and wiping her face with a napkin. "It's the first day of school. Wish me luck."

Shelley holds jerky arms out and gives me a lopsided smile. I love that smile.

"You want to give me a hug?" I ask her, knowing she does. The doctors always tell us the more interaction Shelley gets, the better off she'll be.

Shelley nods. I fold myself in her arms, careful to keep her hands away from my hair. When I straighten, my mom gasps. It sounds to me like a referee's whistle, halting my life. "Brit, you can't go to school like that."

"Like what?"

She shakes her head and sighs in frustration. "Look at your shirt."

Glancing down, I see a large wet spot on the front of my white Calvin Klein shirt. Oops. Shelley's drool. One look at my sister's drawn face tells me what she can't easily put into words. *Shelley is sorry. Shelley didn't mean to mess up my outfit.*

"It's no biggie," I tell her, although in the back of my mind I know it screws up my "perfect" look.

Frowning, my mom wets a paper towel at the sink and dabs at the spot. It makes me feel like a two-year-old.

"Go upstairs and change."

"Mom, it was just peaches," I say, treading carefully so this doesn't turn into a full-blown yelling match. The last thing I want to do is make my sister feel bad.

"Peaches stain. You don't want people thinking you don't care about your appearance."

"Fine." I wish this was one of my mom's good days, the days she doesn't bug me about stuff.

I give my sister a kiss on the top of her head, making sure she doesn't think her drool bothers me in the least. "I'll see ya after school," I say, attempting to keep the morning cheerful. "To finish our checker tournament."

I run back up the stairs, taking two steps at a time. When I get to my bedroom, I check my watch. Oh, no. It's ten after seven. My best friend, Sierra, is gonna freak out if I'm late picking her up. Grabbing a light blue scarf out of my closet, I pray it'll work. Maybe nobody will notice the drool spot if I tie it just right.

When I come back down the stairs, my mother is standing in the foyer, scanning my appearance again. "Love the scarf."

Phew.

As I pass her, she shoves the muffin into my hand. "Eat it on the way."

I take the muffin. Walking to my car, I absently bite into it. Unfortunately it isn't blueberry, my favorite. It's banana nut, and the bananas are overdone. It reminds me of myself—seemingly perfect on the outside, but the inside is all mush.

2

Alex

"Get up, Alex."

I scowl at my little brother and bury my head under my pillow. Since I share a room with my eleven- and fifteen-year-old brothers, there's no escape except the little privacy a lone pillow can give.

"Leave me alone, Luis," I say roughly through the pillow. *"No estés chingando."*

"I'm not fuckin' with you. *Mamá* told me to wake you so you won't be late for school."

Senior year. I should be proud I'll be the first family member in the Fuentes household to graduate high school. But after graduation, real life will start. College is just a dream. Senior year for me is like a retirement party for a sixty-five-year-old. You know you can do more, but everyone expects you to quit.

"I'm all dressed in my new clothes," Luis's proud but muffled voice comes through the pillow. "The *nenas* won't be able to resist this Latino stud."

"Good for you," I mumble.

"*Mamá* said I should pour this pitcher of water on you if you don't get up."

Was privacy too much to ask for? I take my pillow and chuck it across the room. It's a direct hit. The water splashes all over him.

"*Culero!*" he screams at me. "These are the only new clothes I got."

A fit of laughter is coming through the bedroom door. Carlos, my other brother, is laughing like a frickin' hyena. That is, until Luis jumps him. I watch the fight spiral out of control as my younger brothers punch and kick each other.

They're good fighters, I think proudly as I watch them duke it out. But as the oldest male in the house, it's my duty to break it up. I grab the collar of Carlos's shirt but trip on Luis's leg and land on the floor with them.

Before I can regain my balance, icy cold water is poured on my back. Turning quickly, I catch *mi'amá* dousing us all, a bucket poised in her fist above us while she's wearing her work uniform. She works as a checker for the local grocery store a couple blocks from our house. It doesn't pay a whole heck of a lot, but we don't need much.

"Get up," she orders, her fiery attitude out in full force.

"Shit, Ma," Carlos says, standing.

Mi'amá takes what's left in her bucket, sticks her fingers in the icy water, and flicks the liquid in Carlos's face.

Luis laughs and before he knows it, he gets flicked with water as well. Will they ever learn?

"Any more attitude, Luis?" she asks.

"No, ma'am," Luis says, standing as straight as a soldier.

"You have any more filthy words to come out of that *boca* of yours, Carlos?" She dips her hand in the water as a warning.

"No, ma'am," echoes soldier number two.

"And what about you, Alejandro?" Her eyes narrow into slits as she focuses on me.

"What? I was tryin' to break it up," I say innocently, giving her my you-can't-resist-me smile.

She flicks water in my face. "That's for not breaking it up sooner. Now get dressed, all of you, and come eat breakfast before school."

So much for my you-can't-resist-me smile. "You know you love us," I call after her as she leaves our room.

After a quick shower, I walk back to my bedroom with a towel wrapped around my waist. I catch sight of Luis with one of my bandannas on his head and my gut tightens. I yank it off him. "Don't ever touch this, Luis."

"Why not?" he asks, his deep brown eyes all innocent.

To Luis, it's a bandanna. To me, it's a symbol of what is and will never be. How the hell am I supposed to explain it to an eleven-year-old kid? He knows what I am. It's no secret the bandanna has the Latino Blood colors on it. Payback and revenge got me in and now there's no way out. But I'll die before I let one of my brothers get sucked in.

I ball the bandanna in my fist. "Luis, don't touch my shit. Especially my Blood stuff."

"I like red and black."

That's the last thing I need to hear. "If I ever catch you wearin' it again, you'll be sportin' *black and blue*," I tell him. "Got it, little brother?"

He shrugs. "Yeah. I got it."

As he leaves the room with a spring in his step, I wonder if he really does get it. I stop myself from thinking too hard about it as I grab a black T-shirt from my dresser and pull on worn, faded jeans. When I tie my bandanna around my head, I hear *mi'amá's* voice bellowing from the kitchen.

"Alejandro, come eat before the food gets cold. *De prisa*, hurry up."

"I'm comin'," I call back. I'll never understand why food is such an important part of her life.

My brothers are already busy chowing down on their breakfast when I enter the kitchen. I open the refrigerator and scan its contents.

"Sit down."

"Ma, I'll just grab—"

"You'll grab nothing, Alejandro. Sit. We're a family and we're going to eat like one."

I sigh, close the refrigerator door, and sit beside Carlos. Sometimes being a member of a close family has its disadvantages. *Mi'amá* places a heaping plate of *huevos* and *tortillas* in front of me.

"Why can't you call me Alex?" I ask, my head down while I stare at the food in front of me.

"If I wanted to call you Alex, I wouldn't have bothered to name you Alejandro. Don't you like your given name?"

My muscles tense. I was named after a father who is no longer alive, leaving me the responsibility of being the designated man of the house. Alejandro, Alejandro Jr., Junior . . . it's all the same to me.

"Would it matter?" I mumble as I pick up a tortilla. I look up, trying to gauge her reaction.

Her back is to me as she cleans dishes in the sink. "No."

"Alex wants to pretend he's white," Carlos chimes in. "You can change your name, bro, but nobody'd mistake you for anythin' other than *Mexicano*."

"Carlos, *cállate la boca*," I warn. I don't want to be white. I just don't want to be associated with my father.

"*Por favor*, you two," our mother pleads. "Enough fighting for one day."

"*Mojado*," Carlos sings, egging me on by calling me a wetback.

I've had enough of Carlos's mouth; he's gone too far. I stand, my chair scraping the floor. Carlos follows and steps in front of me, closing the space between us. He knows I could kick his ass. His overblown ego is gonna get him in trouble with the wrong person one of these days.

"Carlos, sit down," *mi'amá* orders.

"Dirty beaner," Carlos drawls at me in a fake deep accent. "Better yet, *es un Ganguero.*"

"Carlos!" *mi'amá* reprimands sharply as she comes forward, but I get in between them and grab my brother's collar.

"Yeah, that's all anyone will ever think of me," I tell him. "But you keep talkin' trash and they'll think that of you, too."

"Brother, they'll think that of me anyway. Whether I want them to or not."

I release him. "You're wrong, Carlos. You can do better, be better."

"Than you?"

"Yeah, better than me and you know it," I say. "Now apologize to *mi'amá* for talkin' smack in front of her."

One look in my eyes and Carlos knows I'm not kidding around. "Sorry, Ma," he says, then sits back down. I don't miss his glare, though, as his ego got knocked down a peg.

Mi'amá turns and opens the fridge, trying to hide her tears. Damn it, she's worried about Carlos. He's a sophomore and the next two years are either going to make him or break him.

I pull on my black leather jacket, needing to get out of here. I give *mi'amá* a peck on the cheek with an apology for ruining her breakfast, then walk outside wondering how I'm going to keep Carlos and Luis away from my path while steering them toward a better one. Oh, the fucking irony of it all.

On the street, guys in the same color bandannas flag the Latino Blood signal: right hand tapping twice on their left arm while their ring finger is bent. My veins fire up as I flag right back before straddling my motorcycle. They want a tough-as-nails gang member, they got one. I put on a hell of a show to the outside world; sometimes I even surprise myself.

"Alex, wait up," a familiar female voice calls out.

Carmen Sanchez, my neighbor and ex-girlfriend, runs up to me.

"Hey, Carmen," I mutter.

"How about giving me a ride to school?"

Her short black skirt shows off her incredible legs, and her shirt is tight, accentuating her small but perky *chichis*. Once I would have done anything for her, but that was before I caught her in another guy's bed over the summer. Or car, as it was.

"Come on, Alex. I promise not to bite . . . unless you want me to."

Carmen is my Latino Blood homegirl. Whether we're a couple or not, we still have each other's backs. It's the code we live by. "Get on," I say.

Carmen hops on my motorcycle and deliberately places her hands on my thighs while pressing against my backside. It doesn't have the effect she was probably hoping for. What does she think, that I'll forget the past? No way. My history defines who I am.

I try to focus on starting my senior year at Fairfield, the here and now. It's damn difficult because, unfortunately, after graduation my future will likely be as screwed up as my past.